Welcome to the annotated edition!

The Road to Renewal is a deeply personal novel, its plot woven almost entirely from events I experienced during the first 20-some years of my adult life. Although I loved how this comedy-tragedy turned out, I locked the manuscript away for two decades. That transposed this work of contemporary fiction into a period piece. With Fashan Books' first edition, published in 2018, I discovered some people did not recognize aspects of *The Road to Renewal*'s 1990s cultural landscapes. That opened the door for this annotated edition, which features 90-plus pages of background material. These "Behind the Scenes" additions reset the stage to explain *The Road to Renewal*'s many backdrops and props. This edition also features essays on my writing strategies, tactics, and theology.

The Road to Renewal
ANNOTATED
By Kirby Lee Davis

Three days. Two guys.
One lives. One dies.

Copyright 2018 by Kirby Lee Davis
This edition copyright 2023, Kirby Lee Davis
All rights reserved.

Scripture taken from the New King James Version®.
Copyright © 1982 by Thomas Nelson.
Used by permission. All rights reserved.

Book design by Kirby Lee Davis
Published for Fashan Books, Tulsa, OK.
ISBN Number (hardcover): 9798397923644

Dedicated

to two beloved children,
now adults,
and two beloved parents,
now among the angels.

The books of Kirby Lee Davis

The Spawn of Fashan
(a roleplaying game rulebook)

The *God's Furry Angels* series:
God's Furry Angels
A Year in the Lives of God's Furry Angels

The Road to Renewal

The Jonah Cycle:
The Prophet and the Dove
Lions of Judah
Faith
(in production)
Crimson Destiny
(in production)

The Spawn of Fashan: 40th Anniversary Edition

Learn more at www.kirbyleedavis.com

A note on the layout

My first intent here is to entertain. That's why this annotated edition presents its "Behind the Scenes" materials at the end of the book, so that people may journey along *The Road to Renewal* without interruption. I inserted "historical markers" like the ones below in case the curious wish to take impulsive side trips to related background info. I've also transformed the Table of Contents into a "map" of sorts listing these educational resources with the chapters they augment. Of course, I also wrote these summations and essays to entertain, so you might enjoy reading them in order after you finish the novel!

Table of Contents

Chapter

j-col47.wpd

When this age is dust, and the historians among our children take it upon themselves to judge us, they shall know we were just downright rude by our computer chips.

It all started in complete innocence. As we headed off for a movie, I paused along the way to buy my wife a soda. The sign on a glowing mechanical monolith declared, "Try me! I'm a new Talking Coke Machine!" So I did. My quarters rolled down its innards as the familiar "Always Coca-Cola" jingle bounded from a hidden speaker. That liquid sugar pusher told me to choose a button. I obeyed.

"Thank you," said a voice only a bit tarnished by a mechanical ring. As I welcomed the gentle tumbling that signaled my can's delivery, the monolith added, "You've got a spot on your shirt."

"Really?" I mumbled, not expecting such a response. "Where?"

"On your sleeve. That black grunge shaped like a walrus,

Behind the Scenes...
j-col47.wpd — page 229
"Try me! I'm a new talking Coke machine!" — page 230

dripping slime. You know, I happen to know a good wash box at cleaning spots like that. No trouble."

I glanced around, but to my annoyance, I couldn't find the stain. So I grabbed my chill can of pop and tried to walk away.

The pusher had other plans.

"Is that your car?" it asked of my just-washed '96 Mustang Cobra. I said yes, picking up speed with every step towards its jet-black door.

"Nice broad," called the can dispenser.

That made me stop. "She's my wife!"

"I meant the car."

I slid into my seat, little understanding what I was doing in such a conversation, nor wishing to continue it further. Little did I know my troubles had just begun.

"Honey, how'd you get that spot on your sleeve?" said my wife.

Grumbling something I didn't want her to hear, I handed her the Coke. She popped it open expecting a fizz. Instead, it said, "Hello! I'm the new talking Coke can. Please drink me slowly, especially since he's driving, and don't tear off the tab. You'll just end up dropping it in my can and swallowing it, and believe me, that can hurt. I know this for a fact. And don't spill me on this nice broad, though from the looks of that shirt she probably has more stains than I could count. And just between you and me, your nails could use a coat of paint."

Then the car butted in: "James, you forgot to buckle your seat belt again. I'm going to huff and puff and blow your face in if you don't do that now."

Fastening my seat belt, grumbling all the while, I sped off to the theater. On the screen shined an adequate, though somewhat shallow love story. My wife's choice, naturally.

Behind the Scenes…
Talking cars — page 231
Talking Coke cans — page 232

By Kirby Lee Davis

Before heading into this darkness, the theater manager told me of a new security system, but I didn't spend much time thinking about it. Halfway through the picture, my seat buzzed.

"Too much weight on the armrest," came a mechanical voice. "Desist nuptial activity."

Now I admit I was leaning over, but I had a good reason. "She's my wife!" I whispered to the floor.

"Irrelevant. This is a family theater. Desist at once."

My wife laughed, but I wasn't amused. I stared into the dark shadows of that sticky concrete floor and smirked, "Just what are you going to do about it?"

Wiring in my chair soon showed me just what future shock really was. I felt that electrical prodding all the way out the door, across town, and to my desktop computer, making me even more determined to share this outrage with my readers while that spark still wracked my mind. It was truly excrusiating.

"That's *excruciating*," this know-it-all terminal reminded me. "And if you asked me, it sounds like you deserved it."

That was the straw that broke my camel's back. I was furious.

"Who cares what you think?" I snapped. "What's it to you?"

"Look," replied my PC. "Do you think I enjoy reading this drivel you type in day after day after day? What good is it, really? Or you, for that matter. Listen – you're afraid of the future, and we both know why. We're superior to you. You're a dinosaur, and what's worse, you don't even try to improve yourself. Your clothes don't match. You have no clue how that greasy slop you eat abuses you. You refuse to exercise, rest, or sleep. You just don't care. You're a disaster."

I must admit, I wasn't expecting that from this talking

Behind the Scenes...
"Halfway through the picture, my seat buzzed." — page 231
Future Shock — page 231

3

bundle of circuits. From my wife, perhaps, but not my vanilla personal computer. "Oh, yeah?" was about the best retort I could devise. Then came an inspiration. "Well, take this!"

With almost tyrannical joy, I made it my business to type every key that keyboard offered – in random triplicate, no less. I pounded that mass of plastic so hard, it surely needed to have its silicon chips examined.

I've felt pretty good since then. Single-handed, I triumphed in humanity's eternal battle with encroaching mechanization. If only my PC would stop intentionally misspelling my words. Why

2

Introductions

"HARRIGAN!"

That primal scream echoed through the near-empty congregation of chipped and scarred World War Two surplus desks, moth-eaten chairs, and rusty, mangled metal file cabinets that together could only be called a newsroom. Though he'd walked these halls for years, James always smiled when pondering this stockpile of nostalgia and necessity. Countless mislaid or abandoned manila folders mixed among stacked newspapers challenging the Tower of Babel. Unbalanced fan blades buzzed within scattered computers long past expiration, their cracked cases so choked by cigar smoke and gathered dust that you couldn't read their scorched labels warning of combustible rapid heat build-up. And then there were the cherished collections of decades-old phone books, almanacs, dictionaries, histories, travel guides, style rules, press books, catalogues, annual reports, area maps, and just about any other imaginable source of unforeseen, once-in-a-lifetime trivia needs. So much of this seemed out-of-date in the budding internet world, and yet James couldn't imagine discarding any of it just yet.

"HARRIGAN! Didn't you hear me?"

Deep within his fortress walls of past editions and staked unopened mail, James Harrigan leaped from his monolithic

PC with a laugh of vindication. He *knew* Reynolds had been reading his column as he'd saved it!

Like most newspaper editorial departments, Publisher and Managing Editor Dick Reynolds ruled his literary kingdom from a cluttered cube of glass and plaster within shouting range of all five reporters feeding *The Franklin Beaver Beacon*. Through five years serving the 30,000-some residents within its southwest Oklahoma City suburb, this twice-a-week tabloid grew three-fold by improving upon the legacies of several bygone weeklies. Since he'd been at the helm from Day One, Reynolds took great pride in the *Beacon's* success. He nurtured his staff to develop their beats to his exact specifications, and he made a point to edit every word that appeared in print.

Though James felt confident he was Reynolds' heir apparent, with each step towards "The Furnace" – as their editor's office was called – Harrigan girded his ego for the lambasting he knew would follow.

Disillusion reflected from Reynolds's stark face as he sat fuming behind the plain Windows computer anchoring his enormous desk. Most times the old man loved to project a dashing executive image, comfortable in double-breasted suits, silk shirts, and imported ties. His prim and proper mustache fit these well, waxed and curled in the oldest of traditions, although the twice-broken nose flaring from his pudgy face gave him the blunt edge of a heavyweight boxer – an impression the fiery editor seemed to relish when confronting his unruly office staff.

Reynolds erupted from his leather rocker as Harrigan drew near.

"Get in here!" he snapped, loosening his tie from his open collar. "And close the door."

James breathed deep, steadying himself as the oak slab

Behind the Scenes...

Perspective — page 232
Franklin, OK, and the University of Football — page 234

latched behind him. Something was wrong here; usually Reynolds liked his staff to hear his rants.

The editor didn't bother retaking his seat. Nor did he give his reporter a chance to sit down.

"You think this is funny?" Dick bellowed.

"Well, yes," James couldn't deny.

Reynolds paced behind his desk, rolling his head from side to side, folding and unfolding his arms across his barrel chest. Just watching him made James nervous, so he sought comfort in one of the two chairs Reynolds left for guests.

"I know you don't want me to write humor all the time," Harrigan continued, wondering what his boss was thinking – and even more important, why he wasn't bashing James over the head with his thoughts. "But everyone I talk to seems to like it."

Reynolds dropped hard into his chair. His wife's photo clattered against the shaken wall. That 8x11 frame held the only image he kept in that office, outside of his wall of marked-up newsprint.

"You're toying with the audience," Reynolds began. "There hasn't been a talking Coke machine here in a decade."

"Well, maybe so," James allowed, "but I always liked them. They make a good foil."

"And they don't talk like that."

"Well, maybe not anymore."

"The cars don't either."

"That's where the humor comes in. You remember… laughter? 'Ha ha' and all that?"

Reynolds wasn't amused, but an interrupting phone call siphoned some of his frustration. He yanked up the receiver and snapped, "*Beaver Beacon* newsroom, Reynolds speaking."

He paused, listening with suppressed irritation that soon wiggled free. "No," he barked, "*news* room. You don't hear any loud music; that's... a basketball tournament on the tube. We have no nude dancers. I didn't say 'nudes room,' I said *news*room. Yes, I understand, I guess." Then his rich baritone voice hardened. "Look, we don't sell drinks. This isn't a bar. Newsroom – N-E-W-S. That's right, the thing you read."

Snarling, the publisher slammed the black receiver back

into its cradle. His whole desk shook.

"Didn't even say goodbye," he growled.

James restrained his laughter. "What basketball game is that? We don't even have a TV!"

"Oh, I just didn't want to insult him," Reynolds shrugged, turning his attention back to Harrigan. "Look. This isn't England. You might like Monty Python, but to many of our readers, that's heady stuff."

"Oh, come on! That wasn't absurd satire! Well, maybe it was, but not out of left field."

The editor glanced to his graying acoustical tiling as if appealing to God. Harrigan saw his eyes fix on some drifting cobwebs that seemed to spell out bad words for body odor.

"And what's all this 'wife' business?" Reynolds finally asked, sliding back into his chair even as his voice softened. "I thought we'd agreed."

That told James all he needed to know. Reynolds wasn't angry; he was concerned – though about what, Harrigan wasn't exactly sure.

"Well...." James heard himself meandering and took a breath to steady his nerves. "Well, she makes a good foil, too."

He'd meant that as a joke, but he could tell the boss man didn't get it. In truth, James didn't much understand it, either. Part of him wondered why he'd even said it. Another part didn't care.

"That may be how you see it," Reynolds said, "but she still lives here, and so do her parents. And they don't like it. And it confuses the hell out of our readers. They know you're divorced. Hell – we ran it in our own damn paper!"

No matter who he was talking to, James didn't like hearing such language, and he always made a point to say so. Even though Reynolds knew how the reporter felt, James reminded him.

Behind the Scenes...
Hot topics in small-town journalism — page 234

"I don't give a damn!" Reynolds roared back. "When you own the damn paper, you can damn well do whatever you please! But right now you're working for me, James Harrigan, and I expect you to write copy the way I want it. The way we've both agreed it'll be written! Comprendo?"

James nodded. That stare chiseled the point in his conscious. He didn't need this roasting any longer.

"We're not here to offend anyone," the editor stressed. "Not in a humor column, anyway. And especially not our ex-wives."

Reynolds swept his thick fingers through his thinning auburn hair. His eyes focused on the ceiling.

"Look, James, it's been, what? A year?"

The reporter stiffened. "Eleven months."

"Yeah. Well, I know it's been hard. I've been there. I've *been there*. It hurts like hell. But it's happened, son. It was her choice, and nothing you do's going to change it."

"That's supposed to cheer me up?"

"No, damn it! I'm trying to make you see sense! It's time to accept it and move on. Others are depending on you, James. You can't go on living in the past. It'd be better for you, for her, your parents… and your kids."

Harrigan clamped his fingers around the armrests. His memories burned hot from the last time Reynolds had brought this up.

"I don't know if this is any of your business," he blurted out.

No one knew how it wrecked him inside, to not be able to hold his young girls, to read to them, hear their prayers. To not even see them for three and a half weeks each month!

No one understood how that betrayal ripped his soul, distancing him from all he'd ever been.

"And for us, too," Reynolds plowed on, ignoring the interruption. "I'm just trying to help, son. You know that. And I know what you do at home's your business. But if you insist on writing about your family – even in satire, James – then it's my business, too. I have to protect the *Beacon*. You know that."

It was all James could do to close his eyes and ask God for

patience and guidance. It provided no respite, didn't suck away his anger, or drown his ills in chocolate syrup. But that quick prayer provided an anchor for his hopes – even in moments like this, when he'd open his eyes to find the object menacing him was still staring into the depths of his soul.

James reminded himself that Reynolds was trying to do some good, in his own sandpaper-rough way. Still, James wondered how much longer he could cope with it.

"You know," the editor paused, "one more thing, Harrigan. That computer was right; you are getting paranoid about the future."

"I am not!"

"About change, anyway. Maybe that's why you won't let go of Charlotte."

James heard his breath whistling through his lips. A slow, agonizing wail of a sigh.

He didn't care about the future. Or the present, for that matter.

It was too much to contemplate. James had to get out, to think. Or even better, to forget this conversation had ever happened. That would be so much easier.

"Are you finished?" he grumbled.

"I'm trying to help you, damn it! But you don't need my help, do you? You're so smart. You think you can take on the world all by yourself! Listen, Mr. James Harrigan. If you're not careful, you're going to get yourself in so deep, you won't be able to dig your way out – and then no one will shine your boots for all the slow boats to China!"

James's aggravation got the best of him halfway through that speech. Rising with a shrug of indifference, he'd reached the door and opened it before the absurdity of Reynolds's advice made him pause in confusion.

A sly grin cracked his editor's hard face.

"And what are you doing with that cross on?" Reynolds shouted.

James couldn't help smiling at the mocking character his editor now resumed. They seemed to end every such conversation on this subject, suggesting someone had objected to his display of faith at work.

"What else would I wear?" James replied with smooth conviction, his left hand slipping around the two-inch pewter cross dangling about his neck. "It's what I am."

It's the only hope I've got, James almost admitted. Then he hardened.

"You can fire me," the reporter said, "but I won't take this cross off – for anyone."

"Augh! A paranoid Christian!" The editor floated his arms before him as if washing his hands of Harrigan. "Get back to work!"

"I'm done. The column's it."

"Change it!"

With a smug chuckle, Harrigan headed back for his desk.

"It's my night with the gals, remember?" James said over his shoulder. "You go ahead. You'll do it anyway." Then he whispered, "That's why you make the big bucks."

Scanning over the newsroom, Harrigan verified to his satisfaction that most of the staff hadn't heard that discussion. A few had long since left for home, as was usual for a Wednesday, with most publication deadlines long past. Still, the walk to his desk felt strange, for those present weren't paying him the usual sarcastic smirks that went to anyone returning from a chat with the boss. Indeed, their eyes seemed determined to avoid his.

James scanned over his striped gray dress shirt and black corduroys, his endangered wolf tie, his silver cross necklace, looking for anything out of the ordinary. He saw nothing embarrassing.

Harrigan pondered that all the way to his desk. Then he forgot it. The scratchy pencil scribbling tacked above his computer reminded him of something far more important: His girls awaited.

3

It Begins

James girded his soul as he pulled his tiny black Geo Metro to the curb of his old home, but as usual, his strength of will proved no defense. Charlotte was her usual cold self, approaching him with indifference as he picked up their girls. Hacking him with a machete wouldn't have made his heart bleed more.

He knew what spark relit the embers of her hate. *I shouldn't have brought up the child support payments,* he scolded himself. It didn't matter that James had taxes to pay or personal needs. He should've known what response seeking a reduction would draw.

With some justification, Charlotte claimed nothing had changed; she needed the amount he'd agreed to pay. He couldn't fight that, for in his heart, his girls were worth far more than she ever requested. Still, that didn't release him from his debts and obligations. His limited funds never seemed enough.

James turned away, but his new view offered no escape. He was trapped.

Eleven-year-old Angela always noticed his despair. "Come on, Daddy!" she said, taking his left hand to uplift him.

If there existed any cure for his heartache, it was the love of his daughters. It beamed from their growing forms, dancing black hair, giggling freckled cheeks, and sharp, aware eyes. Having them close nourished his wounded soul.

"Are you ready?" he said.

"That's a stupid question, isn't it?" responded nine-year-old Carla. An impish grin blossomed across her joyous face as she took his right hand.

"That's one way to look at it," Angela agreed. "After all, we're all here. The *Defiant*'s here."

"And the zoo's still out there!" Carla shouted.

"Oh, yeah," James recalled. He had promised them a trip to the Oklahoma City Zoo.

His first thought was one of reluctance, but as he looked at his happy girls, he realized this winter day was unseasonably warm. And since it wasn't quite 4 p.m., they might arrive with more than an hour to enjoy the sights before the zoo closed at 6. That would leave plenty of time to get something to eat before his church choir practice started.

"Well, I have to gas the car first," he told them.

"All right!" Carla screamed.

"Just be sure to have them home by 9," cut in Charlotte, who'd watched in restless irritation from her front step.

James took a deep breath. She'd chosen that moment to step closer, folding her petite arms across her chest in a way that emphasized the curves of her jeans and sweater. But now, even with her black curls flowing so lovely about her shoulders, the threatening force of her gaze made James glance away.

Angela didn't notice his unrest. Or perhaps she just overlooked it.

"No problem," she told her mom.

"Nine," Charlotte stressed to James alone. He'd felt chunks of ice that weren't so cold.

"Yes."

"It's a school night, you know."

Behind the Scenes...
The *Defiant* — page 235

"I'm not stupid," his defenses kicked in.

Before she could disagree, James shuffled his girls into the compact Metro's back seat and made sure they had their safety belts on. Then he crawled into the *Defiant*, adjusted its mirrors, took the solid plastic wheel in his hands, and gave his surprisingly loud three-cylinder engine full throttle. That brought a smile to his lips. The little car's unexpected power never ceased to amaze him. Sure, some might dismiss his compact as a casket on wheels, or a motorcycle with a cabin, but driving that sprite runabout not only overcome his fears, but always provided him a smile. Even in the gaze of his ex.

"All right!" Angela called.

"To the zoo!" Carla shouted.

"First the gas station," James said, pulling onto the main road out of that subdivision.

"I don't need any gas!" Carla informed him.

"You might not, but the *Defiant* does," James said of the Metro.

"She could use a bath, too!" Angela said.

"I do not!" Carla objected.

"Not you," James assured her. "The *Defiant*."

"No," countered Angela, "I meant Carla."

James clamped his jaws shut. This, he knew, was the wrong time to laugh.

"I don't need a bath!" Carla snapped.

"Oh," Angela replied. "Well then, maybe you do have gas."

"Daddy, tell her I don't have gas!"

"Angela, your sister doesn't have gas. If she did, she'd be splattered all around us."

"What?" cried a horrified Carla.

"You remember Willy Wonka," Angela cut in. "The blueberry girl."

"Messy," said James. "Think how long it'd take to clean up. And the smell."

"Kind of like Tad's fur balls," said Angela, enjoying herself. She didn't see James wince at the drop of his old cat's name – the black Himalayan that was supposed to have been Charlotte's pet, only to give his heart and soul to James. The divorce had forced him to leave the aging feline behind, along with almost everything else of that fourteen-year marriage.

"Daddy!" screamed a near-frantic Carla. "I don't want to explode!"

"No one said you're going to," James assured her.

"But you might have a fur ball," Angela kidded.

In the rear-view mirror, James saw an anguished Carla wind her arms around her chest. From the trembling pout gripping her face, he knew the jokes had gone too far.

"You won't have a fur ball," he told his youngest. "After all, you haven't been chowing down on Tad's food, have you?"

Carla issued one of her favorite gagging sounds. Chuckling, James steered the Metro toward a local Easy Come, Easy Go gasoline station with an automated car wash. Angela was right, he decided. The warm weather and crystalline sky provided an excellent opportunity to wash some muddy layers of winter salt off his 1996 Geo's chassis.

"She has been eating ravioli," Angela pointed out.

"Not ravioli!" Carla retorted. "Spaghetti-O's."

"That's good," James said, pulling up to the monolithic Number Seven filling pump. "That ravioli scares me."

That caught even Angela off-guard. "Why?" both girls inquired.

Cutting the engine, James twisted to face his daughters. The speckled black fabric of the Metro's bucket seats looked like something you might see covering pet furniture, but it crunched rather neatly as he moved. Oh, how he loved this miniature car!

"Well," he began, "haven't you noticed how the cans look so much alike?"

"Of course," Angela replied. "A can's a can."

Behind the Scenes...
Willy Wonka and the blueberry girl — page 237
Easy Come, Easy Go — page 237

"Ah, yes," agreed James. "A miracle of modern times. We can everything from Christmas presents to rocks to air, and all the same way. Yet when you open up some of these cans – like the ravioli – it looks just like Tad's cat food."

"Yuck!" Carla cried out.

"Oh, that's just a coincidence," Angela giggled.

"You might say that," James replied, "until you stand with your nose a quarter-inch from freshly opened cans of ravioli and cat food. Then you realize they look an awful lot alike. So, one time I did a test. I took the labels off, placed some ravioli on one plate and cat food on the other. Then I blindfolded Tad to see if he could tell which one was made by an Italian chef."

"What happened?" Angela pondered aloud.

As James had hoped, Carla leaned forward, her eyes all aglow.

"Two seconds after ripping the blindfold to shreds," said James, "Tad sharpened his claws on my arms. When I came to, both samples were gone."

"Came to what?" asked Carla.

"That's an expression," said Angela. "It means he got knocked up."

"Knocked *out*," James rushed to correct her.

"That's a good test," Carla decided.

"Maybe," James allowed. Seeing no one waiting behind the *Defiant*, he decided to continue his tale. "Maybe. But it still worried me that these same companies use the same cans, the same ingredients, the same chefs, the same types of food. You might get the impression they think I'm a cat."

"I'd like to be a cat," Angela offered. James decided to ignore that.

"It's not that I don't like cat food," he confided, continuing his tale, "but I don't. I hate cat food. Each morning that rascal Tad would wake me up by sitting on my face, sticking his wet nose in my ear and meowing until I'd serve him breakfast. He'd run on me and jump on me as if all I had to do in life was feed this huge black cat! It's like I was his butler!

"But I'll tell you girls something – I didn't spend four years at the University of Football in Norman just to be the butler to a cat!"

"What's the Universe of Football?" Carla pondered aloud.

"That's that big round stadium by the duck pond Mommy takes us to," Angela said. "They teach important sports there."

"I mean," interrupted James, hoping to get them back on his point, "it's kind of nauseating to have to get up before the *Today* show is even on and stick a spoon into something that looks like ravioli. Sometimes I have half a mind to shout, 'Get up, you lazy cat! Get your own ravioli!'"

"I bet he could do it," Carla said.

"But then he wouldn't be lazy," Angela told her.

James couldn't help wondering when his girls had stopped laughing at his tale and started accepting it as fact.

"That's not what worries me," he stressed. "I just can't help wondering if all these food magnates –"

"Magnets?" interrupted Carla. James skipped it.

"– are somewhat like General Motors, putting out a bunch of identical products under slightly different labels. They might have one factory that makes the basic putty, to which they add catnip to half and put it in cans as cat food. The other half is dyed red and canned as ravioli. The only thing really different is the label."

"So, what's in the label?" Angela wondered.

"Certainly not what's in the ravioli," said James, "although it might taste like it."

"Grandpa says everything's better with milk," Carla reminded them.

"The point is," James went on, "if they can do it with ravioli, they can do it with cream cheese, and if they can do this with cream cheese, they can do it with motor oil, and if they can do it with motor oil, they can do it with nuclear waste. I don't know about you, but I don't want to open a can of ravioli and find nuclear waste. Even if hiding it in ravioli's the only way to dispose of it."

Hitting his punch line in stride, James waited for his daughters to react with glorious laughter. Instead, they just cast blank stares at his hairless face.

Just like Charlotte used to.

Through the rear window he saw a green Honda Civic pull behind him. With a sigh, James knew the time to fill his tank had come.

Only then, noticing her father was not only finished, but about to step outside, did Carla say, "I don't understand."

"It's easy," said Angela. "Dad has a nuclear waist."

"Must be why he always wears a belt," Carla noted.

"Oh, Lord," moaned James. He could imagine his girls asking his ex-wife about his nuclear waist.

"The whole problem, as I see it, is taking off the labels," Angela theorized. "You leave the labels on, and you know what's in the cans. Pretty simple, actually."

James settled his feet on the cold concrete, sighing at the ease in which she destroyed his tale.

"Another story shot down by hard-nosed editors," he whispered. "This isn't my day."

"I just know I'm not going to clean up any more fur balls," said Angela. "Not if they have ravioli in them, I'm not. That stuff's disgusting."

"Tad must have a nuclear waist, too," Carla suggested.

"Maybe that's why some of his chest fur's going white," Angela said. "We'd better tell Mom."

By Kirby Lee Davis

Complications Abound

They trusted customers gassing up at this Easy Come, Easy Go. The orange and black pumps stayed ever on, so you could get what you needed, walk into the matching brick blockhouse, and pay the tab. But it was never so simple with his two girls along, to whom stepping within a convenience store was entering Nirvana. They knew Daddy would allow them one piece of candy, and despite all the resources God had granted their budding rational minds, selecting just one item from the hundreds in Easy Go's sweet-tooth inventory was just too difficult to contemplate.

Seeing which counters they salivated over, James decided to head through the check-out line as the girls picked their delights, hoping to speed things up.

It didn't work.

"I had pump seven," he told the cashier inside the protective cage, a young black man missing an upper right incisor.

With a nod and a tug on the "Go Franklin Beavers!" button hanging from his faded orange Easy Go apron, the thin cashier turned his sharp green eyes to the cash register and rang up $6.27.

"And my girls are getting a candy bar each," James added. "What kind?"

"Well, I don't know."

Sudden recognition flashed across the clerk's dark, oily face. With a broad smile he exclaimed, "Hey! You're that newspaper writer, aren't you?"

James couldn't help grinning. Though shy, he loved when this happened.

"I know who you are!" the young man crowed. "I know just who you are!" Waving his hands before him as he searched for the word, the cashier blurted out, "That's it! Hooligan!"

James stiffened. "No...."

"Jackson Hooligan! The sportswriter!"

"No, I cover the city council and police beats."

"Boy, I sure loved that article you wrote on them Oklahoma Sooners beat'n the Aggies!"

"That was Jason Bennigan."

"That line you had about Kelvin Sampson win'n with teamwork... boy, how did that go?"

"How'd what go?"

"That phrase you wrote. I swear, it sounded just like something out of the Gettysburg Address! How'd it go again?"

"Now wait – you're comparing a basketball game summary to one of the greatest speeches ever made?"

The cashier cocked his head back like a robin might when spying out a cat.

"Well, it was great writing!" he defended himself. "How'd it go?"

"I don't know. I didn't write it."

"You didn't?"

"No. I'm James Harrigan. I cover the police and council beats."

"Oh. You're not Jackson Hooligan?"

"That's Jason Bennigan, and no, I'm not him."

Behind the Scenes...
Kelvin Sampson — page 237

"Oh. You're Hooligan."

"That's Harrigan. Rhymes with Berryman."

"And he writes sports?"

Frustrated, James sought out the clock. After some misdirection he found a round Coca-Cola sign above the checkout counter, its branded face flashing "4:15" in large digital numbers. His girls still argued over who would get what, but he knew they'd soon remember the zoo.

"Look," James said, "just ring me up two candy bars and the gas. I've got to go."

"Oh." The cashier sounded just a little hurt. "Well, you'll need the key."

"No – not that kind of 'go.' I mean, I'm in a hurry."

"Well, I can't help you there. Someone's got the key now. You'll have to wait until they bring it back."

"Just ring me up, OK?"

"I could give you the ladies' key," the cashier continued with a wink, "but there ain't any of them special machines in there, if you know what I mean."

"I don't care about machines in restrooms! Just ring me up!"

"All right, all right. I was just trying to help." Then he saw something that made him smile. "But it wouldn't have helped much anyway. That key's gone, too."

"Look – I don't need a key. Please, ring me up."

"Well, what did you have?"

"The gas at pump seven and two candy bars!"

"What candy bars?"

"The ones my girls are picking out now!"

A broad smile brightened the cashier's friendly face. "Those two girls?"

"Yes." Glancing back, James saw a small audience had formed in line behind him. His impatience surged. "Finally, we're getting somewhere."

"Boy, they're pretty things."

James nodded. "They take after their mom."

"Hey!" the cashier exclaimed. "I know you now! I know you! You're Hooligan, right? James Hooligan, who writes those comedy bits? Man, my Mom hates those! I think they're kind of funny, every once in a while, sometimes, but those Fat Mama Brown bits.... Boy, Mama hates those."

James began to think he was reliving such a skit right there.

"Please, can you just ring me up?"

"You're in a hurry?"

"Yes! And so are all these good people here!"

"Oh, yeah!" the young man said as if he only now noticed the line drifting through his store's innards. "They sure are good, aren't they? Hi, Harry! Dick! Tom!"

A symphony of greetings swarmed around James.

"How you boys doing tonight?" the cashier called.

Their conversation grew by more voices than James could count.

"Oh, for Pete's sake! All I want is for you to ring up my gas and candy bars!"

"Oh." Dipping his head, the lad muttered, "Guess Mama was right. Sounds downright mean." Then he asked, "You want a wash?"

James scolded himself for forgetting the salty *Defiant*. When in a hurry, there was no better way to get his wheels washed than at a convenience store. He loved the touchless car washes.

"The works," he said, nodding. "And pump seven and two candy bars."

"OK," said the cashier. "What size candy bars?"

"Why… I don't know." He glanced back at his girls, who appeared deep in concentration over the relative per-ounce value of Starbursts and Whoppers. "Just ring up two."

James went for his wallet. The cashier frowned.

"Look, Hooligan, I can't do that."

"Why not?"

"Well, for one thing, the candy ranges in price from a bunch of quarter stuff on the bottom to $1.80 bags on top."

"That doesn't matter. They're just candy bars! Charge me for the most expensive ones. I don't care!"

"You may not care, but I do. I don't cheat people, man, and besides, charging you for more expensive stuff throws off our inventory."

"Your inventory? You must sell several thousand bucks in candy each month!"

"Oh, don't you know it."

"And you think making an extra 50 cents on two candy bars is going to throw you off?"

"Look, Hooligan, if that's who you really are –"

"What's that supposed to mean?"

"Well, all you newspaper guys are supposed to be so much smarter than all of us, aren't you? Ain't that why you think you can tell us all what to do?"

"I don't go around telling anyone what to do!"

"Well, if you're so smart, you'd know that you throw in 50 cents here, 50 cents there, and by the end of the month, this place'd have thousands of bucks unaccounted for and we'd all be in deep doo-doo."

"Real deep," came a voice behind Harrigan.

"Crazy reporters," muttered someone else.

"And then there's the scanner here," the cashier continued. "If I don't scan them in, that old inventory computer's going to think your candy bars weren't sold. You multiply that over a month and maybe we don't order as many boxes as we should. People think candy sales are goin' down, you know? And pretty soon they think we don't need as many dock men as we've got. The manufacturer cuts how many bars it makes. People lose jobs. All because I didn't ring up what you bought."

"All right! All right!" Over his shoulder James cried, "Girls!"

No one answered. Harrigan glanced back, but his daughters weren't there. That chilled his heart. His gaze flew from counter to counter, but he couldn't see his girls anywhere!

"What, Daddy?" Angela interrupted.

James nearly jumped out of his sneakers. His oldest stood at his left side, her deep brown eyes staring up through shiny black bangs.

"Where's your sister?" he almost shouted.

"Over here, Daddy," said Carla – standing in all her innocence at his right.

Before he could say anything, his daughters placed a bag of Skittles and a roll of Spree on the counter. The cashier scanned their barcodes.

"You see?" he said with pride. "I saved you 45 cents."

"And three jobs in Norway," James agreed. "Thank you very much."

"My pleasure," the cashier proclaimed, handing him a quarter and three dimes. James dropped it in his billfold without a thought.

All at once the clerk slapped his forehead. "Hey… wait a minute. Wait a minute! You're a writer, yes? With two daughters. Getting a car wash. My Lord, why didn't I realize that before?"

"Probably too busy theorizing for your Nobel Prize in economics," James said, driving his herd towards the door.

"No – wait!" the cashier insisted. "You'll need your car wash number. It's on the receipt."

With a succumbing sigh, James leaned back for the counter as the clock flashed "4:22." The cashier stretched out his left hand to latch onto James's forearm, his grip surprisingly strong. Wadding the receipt into the reporter's open hand, the cashier drew James close enough to smell what the argumentative young man had eaten for lunch.

"Remember this," the black man whispered, dragging out every syllable. "There's no hope standing alone. The world's full of chaos. Eternity rests in sacrifice. Love fits all holes."

James found himself staring first at the dark fingers wrapped around his fist, then at the sharp, bloodshot eyes focused deep within his own. He had no idea what to make of those cryptic words or the domineering spirit that spoke them. Yet one word of his own seemed to fit: nutty.

His girls waited at the door as if nothing unusual had happened. With the wadded register slip clenched tight, James decided their no-nonsense course might be the wisest to take. Darkness hung over his head as he led them to the car.

"Don't let go of that receipt for nothin'!" the cashier called. "Nothin'!"

5

Trouble

"Now the zoo!" Carla cheered as she crawled into the back seat.

"Well, I don't know," James couldn't help saying. His fingers fumbled with the wadded-up receipt like Queeg might mix his marbles.

"Daddy!" Carla screamed in protest.

"Oh, why not go?" Angela said, seeking to reason with him like the adult she wanted to be. "It sounds fun."

The cassette deck flashed "4:27," but that wasn't the biggest problem. As James pulled around the station, he found himself at the end of a six-vehicle line waiting to pass through the car wash.

The girls recognized their trouble just as he did. But James didn't notice their complaints, for the Call of Spring had found him.

It never failed that on the first warm day of every deep, dark winter, James crossed paths with a female gifted by God with the form of all desire, determined to take advantage of the uplifting breeze by trying out her briefest summer togs. In past years James had met this Call with an upright heart, knowing in confidence before Christ that he need not gaze at such feminine delights when the woman of his dreams rested in the seat next to him. But now he was divorced, and lonely.

His TSRs (Temptation Susceptibility Ratings) often stretched beyond the danger level.

Making matters worse, it wasn't just one filly this year, but three. One untamed mass of blonde curls in an excruciatingly tight halter and latex shorts, one cascade of jet locks in clingy, shining, sweat-soaked jogging togs, and one wind-blown carrot top claiming a ripped T-shirt and bikini briefs. In drooling slow-motion they strolled across the parking lot, their heads tossed back, proud and carefree as they basked in their sensuality, piling into the fiery T-top Camaro just before his *Defiant*. Another luscious lady laughed behind the leather-wrapped wheel.

James sat as rigid as a pigeon-stalked statue. Such enticing scenes often tripped mental defenses designed to dilute tempestuous barbs with a song, slapstick, or other prized radio, television, and film memories. That these interactive scenes could prove just as distracting as his real-time adventures didn't disturb his soul's operating parameters. And so, James stared into the promise and peril before him, his conscience a numb third party to the debate erupting in his head.

Don't even look at them, urged a calm, steady voice.

Oh, go on! countered another. *It's not like they don't want you to.*

God won't like it.

Don't you think He's ever looked at a woman?

Not like James is now.

Of course not! Christ never had to worry about women not loving Him! How could He? You could mix Mel Gibson, Warren Beatty, and Brad Pitt into a delectable morsel and still not get a dreamboat like Christ! But James here... boy, he'll always have trouble.

Exaggeration is no foundation for debate, said a newcomer to the fray, his voice cold, his words void of emotion. **His appearance conforms –**

Eh, what's up, doc?

His appearance conforms –

You said it, doc!

26

– with the reality of his species.

A cackle of disbelief bounced from ear to ear. James almost dodged carrot chunks he thought flew past the steering wheel.

By those standards, his presentation is… not so bad.

It's not? Look at that nose hanging over his cotton-ball cheeks. Why, the asparagus stem doesn't get as much shade as that beak gives his over-clogged pores. And the only thing drooping more than his chins are those handholds he calls a waist. Nuclear? Hah! He gets all the exercise of a sundial in a thunderstorm.

Maybe so, returned the voice of calm assurance, *but he simply cannot go around ogling women.*

Oh, leave him alone already. I'm enjoying this!

You shouldn't look either. If you look, he looks. We all look!

What's wrong with that? Can't you ever just let it go? Have some fun already!

Yeah, doc! Be a stinker once in a while.

Don't you think I have fun?

I don't know about you, but I haven't –

Now wait a minute!

– for a long time! I should be able to at least imagine–

But these women are not even real.

To be true to science, none of us is 'real,' as you wish to define the concept.

Mister Spock, you're the most

cold-blooded man I've ever known.

Why, thank you, doctor.

Ah, Bones! Even you must admit, if anyone deserves such fantasy as these beauties, he does.

You just say that so that you can, too.

Wait a minute!

Come on! Be realistic here. This is about as close as James will ever get to another female – thanks to you!

Me? What did I do?

You can ask that, with the way you're always putting him down?

I do not put him down. I urge him to remain true to Christ. To

27

stay pure. Honest.
  As if Charlotte could take honesty!
  She could have if you had not made him so insensitive.

Wait a minute!

Look – I'm not the one who suggested he tell that dumpling that her potato soup looked like pond scum!
  No?
  Oh, well, maybe I did put that one in his head. But I didn't suggest he call the extra 10 pounds she gained that Christmas his special "love snack!" No, I did that, too. Oh, wait – I've got one now – I'm not the one who got him to call that fav book of hers a forbearer of New Age despotism.
  That was Spock.
  Literary criticism of Charles Dickens is not the issue at this moment.
  You must have done it! It's logical.

Wait a minute!

A Cone of Silence couldn't have damned up his thoughts better than that outburst. But a sarcastic ad-lib soon launched things anew.

Oh, that's telling them, Jack.
Thanks, Mary.

Curious.
Well, if you didn't, who did?
Oh, my God!
Don't bring Him into this!
Oh, hush! You do not think James had an original idea, do you?
By the... that is a scary thought!
Laughter echoed from cavernous shadows.
Riddle me this, you cowl-less curmudgeons!
Not you again!
Fascinating! James has not actively drawn your image from his memory for twenty-two years, twelve hours, ten minutes, and

thirty-nine point seven-two seconds, and still you influence his decisions.

At least I don't waste his time spouting green-blooded platitudes, my pointy-eared friend! And I don't splatter him with carrot when I talk!

Try it, doc – you might like it!

A-HA!

I got you now,

you long-eared wascal!

All right, doc – you got me. Would you like to shoot me now or wait until you get home?

Shoot him now! Shoot him now!

You keep out of this! He doesn't have to shoot you now!

He does so have to shoot me now! I demand that you shoot me now!

- B O O M ! -

Oh, there you go again.

I tell you we're living in a dictatorship!
A self-perpetuating aristocracy
in which the working classes –

Get away from me, you commie pinko fascist meatheads! Beer, Edith!

Right away, Archie!

Oh, Lord – who let out Bunker?
The name's Bond... James Bond.

Danger! Danger!

Ninety-nine, I think someone's calling on my shoe phone.

"Daddy," broke in Carla. "Aren't we late for the zoo?"

James shuddered at the interruption. His gaze was so focused on his steering wheel that his eyeballs ached.

"Well, maybe," he agreed, settling his thoughts back into the real world. The clock flashed "4:52." "But I've already paid for this. We can't leave now."

Just before the Camaro, a blue Chevrolet Astro minivan pulled into the brick wash house, a dull black and orange rectangle with three foggy windows offering a glimpse of the soapy procedure.

"Look!" he pointed out. "We're almost there!"

Then he spied something he hadn't seen before. Thick, round brushes rotated behind those glass windows, each one armed with thousands of fabric whips destined to beat the grime off the *Defiant*'s shiny frame – and perhaps the paint with it.

"Oh, Lord," James whispered in a chill rush of horror and trepidation. This wasn't a touch-free car wash at all!

Behind the Scenes...
Delving into The Debate — page 238

6

No Escape

James had all sorts of pent-up fears about brush car washes, mostly stemming from his father's sharp, repeated advice against using such things, yet Carla managed to disarm them all in one stroke. Gazing into the Camaro, she turned to her father and said, "You know, Dad, you don't have to try to look good to girls."

"I know," he said in mock seriousness. "I wouldn't look good no matter how hard I tried."

"That's right!" Carla assured him.

James bit back a smile. "Thanks," he whispered.

"No problem."

"Dad," put in Angela, "what would we do if aliens were hunting us right now?"

No matter how he tried to guide and nurture their growth, his daughters had the uncanny ability to stop everything with a simple question. That pleased him, for their inquiries often set up his most rewarding moments. The birds stopped their calls, the winds froze, his engine fell silent, and the Heavens opened. God listened.

"Why would aliens be hunting us?" he asked her.

"Well," said Angela, "you remember that episode of *The Next Generation* when Deanna Troi woke up one morning and she was a Romulan?"

James nodded, the image bringing him joy, though it paled to his rear-mirror view of Angela's imaginative smile.

"That's one of my favorite episodes," Carla said of the growing *Star Trek* catalogue.

Angela ignored her. "That could happen to us, couldn't it?"

"Well, I suppose it could. If you believe in aliens."

The 11-year-old leaned back, her eyes lost in thought.

"That would be so cool," Angela whispered.

His mind opened to the idea, James found the whole concept intriguing. "Of course, something like that could happen here."

"I hope I get to ride in a starship someday," Carla wished.

"It wouldn't have to be aliens," James continued.

"They've just got to do that," Angela told her sister.

"I mean, anyone can kidnap you," the reporter thought aloud, his speech slowing as he pondered it all. "That's what that story was about. It could happen anywhere, at any time, by a stranger secretly observing your every move, or someone you thought you'd known all your life."

"If they don't build those starships," continued Angela, "why, I don't know what I'll do. It just makes so much sense!"

"Yeah," Carla agreed.

"And the cosmetic surgery wouldn't be too hard," James went on, not realizing his girls weren't listening. "Although I doubt they could make it happen overnight, like they did to Deanna, and I bet it would be hard to keep someone unconscious that long. Although they can brainwash you."

"That'd hurt!" Carla exclaimed.

A car horn honked. Snapping back into the real world, James saw a hand wave from the truck in his rearview mirror. Then he realized the Camaro had pulled into the car wash.

"Hallelujah!" he whispered. They were almost there!

Behind the Scenes...
Aliens among us — page 239

His youngest daughter shuddered so hard, her car seat rattled.

"What's wrong?" James asked, shifting the *Defiant* into gear.

"Having your brain pulled out and washed," Carla groaned. "Augh!"

"Just think what it'd do to your hair," Angela remarked.

"What if they put it back in upside-down?" Carla wondered. "Just think how hard it'd be to watch TV?"

"I bet you'd see everything upside-down," Angela guessed.

"And how'd you eat your cereal?" Carla said. "Mom'd hit me for spilling each spoonful, I'd bet!"

"Oh, your mom doesn't hit you!" James stated. Then he added, "Does she?"

"Oh, no!" Angela said. "Though I think she did try to brainwash us."

"What?"

"Well, she used to rub those washcloths into our ears real hard," Angela told him. As Carla nodded, Angela said, "She might've been trying to reach our brains then."

James kept himself to a muted chuckle, thinking the girls were actually talking about him, since he'd given them most of their early baths.

"Is this where the receipt goes?" Carla inquired.

That caught James off-guard. Seeing her delicate hand pointing to a keypad on the driver's side, the reporter scrambled for the receipt he'd dropped – wondering all the while how he'd forgotten the cashier's ominous message. Yet in his heart, he knew the answer.

"Eyes full of fluorescent pink latex," he scolded himself. "Dumb move, James."

Unfolding the receipt for the first time, he couldn't see why he'd ever bothered. In faded letters from a weary ribbon were all the facts of his purchase: the store number, address, phone number, and a promotional blurb, plus instructions and a five-digit code for the automated car wash. Rolling down his window to punch in that code, he started to toss the receipt – only to discover, lightly scribbled in pencil, a vertical series of descending numbers on the back of the paper:

10
15
8
14
20
8
18
5
5
19
9
24
20
5
5
14

"Strange," James whispered.

"What's it mean?" wondered Angela.

"I have no idea," he admitted. He started to toss it aside once more, then thought better of it and shoved the receipt into his breast pocket. He would worry about it later.

He couldn't see much of the Camaro now, with the brushes whirling and the suds flying. That drew a longing sadness from the strange part of him that had sought a beer – a brew James hadn't touched since that bitter introductory sip encouraged by a neighborhood friend back in third grade. But his heart placed more interest in the two-line disclaimer printed in one-inch-tall white letters across a fiery red board nailed to the car wash entrance: *No campers, vans, minivans, trucks, or smaller vehicles. Station operator is not responsible for damage.*

"Which one of those are we, Daddy?" asked Angela, who had leaned over his left shoulder to read the print.

"One of the smaller vehicles, I guess."

"But isn't everything smaller than a camper or van?"

"Everything you could get in there," James agreed.

"So nothing can use this car wash?"

"A starship's not a smaller vehicle," Carla remarked.

"But it'd be too big to get in there," Angela reminded her.

"Oh, yeah," Carla agreed. "So, the only things that may use this thing are too big to get into it?"

"Maybe not," James threw out. "It doesn't say anything about people."

"Yeah, Carla!" Angela jumped in. "You ride on the hood!"

"No!" the nine-year-old snapped.

A loud blower roared before them. As James looked forward, the Camaro inched through the exit.

The empty washer beckoned him – a mechanical array of upper and lower spin brushes, water jets, and blinking lights, all built upon a U-shaped aluminum platform determined to encircle his vehicle. In a rush, James remembered all the fears his father had ever taught him about what these thousands of spinning whips could do to his car's finish. He wondered if he'd have any paint left on his precious *Defiant*, or how even the tiniest scratch would glow on its black surface.

Once more the impatient truck honked. James felt like cursing, then prayed his apology to God. Girding his concerns, James inched his Metro forward.

"Dad," asked Angela, "what's it mean by 'damage?'"

"It means you've got to trust God that everything will turn out all right. Maybe we'd better pray right now."

7

Starships Have Nothing on This

The girls squealed with delight at the blanket of thick white suds sprayed across the *Defiant*'s blackened windows. James chuckled, realizing they'd never been through one of these things before. *Maybe everything will be all right*, he wished. Then the brushes started whirling about like angry bees, defying their eyes to keep pace. The Metro lurched under their assault to the splashing sound one might hear within a massive dishwasher.

"Wow!" Angela exclaimed. "This is better than a roller coaster!"

James didn't think so. The brushes seemed far too close to him, pounding the Geo's polished jet sheet metal in tense waves he could feel through the steering wheel and floorboard. His worried eyes glanced to either side, hoping he'd parked the car in the center of the contraption. But it didn't matter.

For a moment the *Defiant* seemed to lean right. James gripped his seat. Through the passenger window he saw the cause: fabric whips on the huge right brush had snagged his outside mirror. The assembly tried to press onward, yanking the snared whips with enough force to rock the Metro from side to side. Just that quick, the mood in the car shifted.

"I've got a bad feeling about this," said Carla, quoting her favorite line from each of the first three *Star Wars* films.

Sounds of popping firecrackers rippled around the mirror. With an abrupt surge, the whirling brush resumed its journey around his compact Geo.

"I don't like this anymore," Angela whispered.

"Can we get out of here?" Carla spat out, her eyes quivering in fear.

James considered it, though he'd never seen anyone drive out of a car wash in progress. Through the rearview mirror he saw the brushes now spun in wild abandon through empty space. Nothing blocked his exit path. But an inner calm urged him to be patient. The wash was already half-over.

Something snapped outside the *Defiant*. Water hoses roared to life. Through the rinse cycle James saw the now-resting brushes start forward.

Again the whipping whirlwinds came to life, flailing his car's black sheet metal. James whispered prayers for all to turn out well. But like a great steel trap, his right mirror once more ensnared the great and powerful brush.

"Oh, no!" Angela cried. Carla screamed. As the mechanism squealed and whined, struggling to do its duty, James could only wait for the worst to happen.

Resolution came with a heartbreaking pop that echoed through the cabin. Freed of its trap, the mindless brush continued on its way along the *Defiant*, but James knew the damage was done. He didn't care that the rest of the wash went fine. All he could think of was the repair bill sure to follow – and of his foolishness for ever going through this in the first place.

Behind the Scenes...
"I've got a bad feeling about this." — page 240

That Was Quick

When the drying cycle finished, James pulled the Metro to a stop along the parking lot curb and inspected the right mirror. The top half of its charcoal black plastic casing had been yanked from the car's frame.

"Is it going to flop?" asked Angela, who'd crawled into the front seat and rolled down her window to watch.

"I have no idea," James admitted.

His oldest daughter sensed his dejection. "So, what do we do now?"

"We complain," he decided. Shoving his loose shirttail into his pants, James put on his best "Dirty Harry" scowl and started for the Easy Go. Then he came to his senses and turned back. "You girls stay here. Roll up that window and lock the doors."

With each step towards the convenience store, James prayed he'd not go through another runaround like he had before. Imagine his surprise when, upon entering the Easy Go, he found the cashiers had changed. In the place of the

---

Behind the Scenes...
Dirty Harry — page 240

---

youthful talker stood a middle-aged giant. If he'd not worn the orange Easy Go apron, James would have guessed him a banker or lawyer from his sharp eyes, black swept-back hair, and fair complexion.

"May I help you, sir?" the man put forward.

James was pleased to see they were alone. Walking up to the caged counter, curiosity got the best of him.

"What happened to the other guy?"

A flicker of uncertainty swept across the clerk's countenance, but it soon disappeared. "Why, I've been here all along, sir."

"No," insisted James, "the young man who was back here before, just a few minutes ago. Where's he?"

"Oh. We had to let him go."

"Wow. That was sudden."

"Well, I probably shouldn't say this, but it had been building up for a long time. He was inefficient. Talked too much. Kind of too friendly for an environment such as this, if you know what I mean. Slowed people down."

Though he understood everything the man said, it saddened James to hear it. He didn't want to think just being friendly to customers would not fit today's fast-paced world.

"May I help you, sir?" the man again put forth.

"Why, yes, you may. I need to file a complaint. The car wash brush snagged my outside mirror and yanked it loose."

The clerk pulled a clipboard from below the counter and handed it to James, asking the reporter to fill out the top form on the attached pad with the tethered black ballpoint pen. James tackled the paperwork as other customers came and went, glancing on occasion at the *Defiant* to make sure his girls were safe.

"All this information would sure make it easy on the aliens," he whispered.

"I'm sorry," said the cashier. "Could you repeat that? I did not hear you."

James grinned. "Just talking to myself."

Glancing over the form, the clerk handed Harrigan a Polaroid instamatic camera. "I'll need you to take a picture of the damage. I cannot leave this counter."

James hadn't expected that, though it made sense. "You're not afraid I'll run off with this?"

"Oh, I assume the car repairs will cost far more than the camera."

On that disturbing thought, Harrigan hurried back to his wounded vehicle. Having photographed auto accidents for the *Beaver Beacon*, James had a good idea how to capture on film a black mirror pulled away from the car's black frame. Taking a straw bound in white paper, he slipped it deep into the crevice the car wash had created. The edges of that paper-wrapped bar stuck out either side.

Angela lowered her window just as James prepared his shot.

"What are you doing?" she wondered aloud.

"Photographing the damage. Roll your window back up."

"Can you take one of me next?" Carla yelled from the back seat.

"This isn't my camera," James replied.

"What do you think they'd sell it for?"

"I don't want to buy it! I just want to shoot the straw. Now roll the window up!"

"How'd that straw get there?" Carla asked, even as Angela closed the portal.

With a click, Harrigan got the photo he wanted – an image of a white bar seemingly piercing the black mirror housing. The clerk was impressed.

"When do you think I'll hear about this?" James put to him.

"I don't know. Corporate handles these things. But I'd go ahead and get the car repaired if I were you. The owners here, they're not in the habit of fixing incidental damage."

"But the car wash did it!"

"I understand. But did you read the disclaimer as you drove in?"

Behind the Scenes...
Instant cameras — page 240

40

"Of course! I'm not stupid."

"Well, that should explain it then. Oh, there's one more thing. I'll need to have the receipt."

That caught James off-guard. "I thought I would hang onto that. It has the time I purchased the wash and everything."

"No," the clerk stated. "I must include it with your complaint to prove you actually paid for and used the car wash when you said you did. After all, who's to say you didn't pull up with a damaged car and tried to bum the repairs off on us? I didn't sell you the service."

"No – the clerk who was here before did!"

"Yes, of course. But he's no longer here." The man paused as if studying Harrigan. From his breast pocket he withdrew a pair of black, thick-rimmed glasses. Like Clark Kent transforming into Superman, the bifocals made James re-evaluate everything he knew of this man. Where once stood a simple, efficient clerk, James now saw a steely-eyed CPA.

Danger! Danger!

"The receipt," the tall clerk demanded.

James fished through his pants pockets, grimacing all the while. But the crumpled paper was missing.

"I don't know where it is," he admitted.

The cashier considered that. In a quiet voice he asked, "Did you happen to notice if it had any writing on it? Anything at all?"

Now Harrigan didn't know the lad who'd waited upon him before, but from the menacing aura this character threw off, James began to think that friendly, over-talkative boy had been dismissed for more than just inefficiency.

"No," James said, praying God would forgive this lie as He had Rahab.

The clerk took a deep breath, letting that pause lower the tension building between them.

"Good," he decided. "I would not worry about it then."

The way this calculating man uttered that dismissal ruffled

the hairs from James's knuckles to that little spot right above his left big toe that annoyed him so on cold nights. He glanced once more at the cashier, who was pulling another cigar from a breast pocket under his smock, and decided he didn't want to talk to this man any longer. Harrigan was pushing the door open when the cashier called, "If you find it —"

James stopped. This man was poking a hole in the cigar with a sharp pencil… just like all those eerie episodes of *Nowhere Man*.

"If you find that receipt," the clerk restated, "please bring it by. It'll save us from calling on you."

A strange quiet settled around them.

"What do you mean?" James wanted to know.

With a dominating smirk, the calculator pointed at the form on his clipboard.

"After all," he noted, "we know where you live."

Behind the Scenes...
Rahab — page 241
Nowhere Man — page 241

By Kirby Lee Davis

9

Sidetracked

"So now can we go to the zoo?" Carla demanded to know.

James settled into his bucket seat. The clock flashed "5:19." If they were to drive straight to the zoo, they'd barely get there before it closed.

He'd failed his girls.

"I'm sorry," he said, "but I'm worried about the car. If that mirror fell off, it might hurt something."

Settled in comfort within the front passenger seat, Angela assured him that she understood. Carla fell into a silent pout.

"I guess the thing to do right now," James thought aloud, "is to go to Leo Heavy Chevy Geo."

"But I'm hungry!" Carla exclaimed.

"Then eat your snack," James told her. "We'll go out for supper right after Heavy Chevy."

"But shouldn't we go to Leo Geo?" Angela countered with a smile.

"It's the same place," James laughed.

As his oldest daughter crawled into the back seat, James

Behind the Scenes...
Silly names — page 242

turned on the radio – only to switch it off when he heard Carolyn Danvers' silky voice slide over the KLOD airwaves. He didn't need that sort of temptation now, even if it was just an ad for her morning talk show. So, James stuck Carolyn Arends' *I Can Hear You* cassette into the dash slot. That album always proved a good fallback device, for her thought-provoking poetry inspired him in troubled times – which he had aplenty. The girls also liked Arends' sweet harmonies.

Leo Heavy Chevy Geo was one of three dealerships in the Franklin area. James appreciated its long service hours, from 7 a.m. to midnight on weekdays, 7 a.m. to 5 p.m. on Saturdays. With his reporter's lifestyle, he needed such versatility.

As the service department's colossal aluminum door cranked open, James glided the *Defiant* into the first empty berth beside the customer representative desks. Before he could get out, a young lady in a white golf shirt and blue slacks came to his door. Her shiny name tag read *Teresa Brown*.

"You wait here," he told his girls. Then he gave his full attention to the young blonde gazing into his eyes.

"What's troubling your Metro?" she said.

James started around to the right side of the car, thinking it best to show her. The move also saved him from staring into her cute face.

"I just had a run-in with a car wash brush," he said. "It snagged on this mirror and pulled it loose."

Trapping her clipboard under her right arm, Brown slipped her fingers inside the opened crevice and probed the wound. "I'm sorry to say this, but we're rather booked up right now for something like this. It might be better if you came back in the morning."

The back-door window sank into its frame. "It's broken,"

Behind the Scenes...
One uplifting album — page 242
Two Carolyns — page 243

Carla said, motioning to the mirror with her head.

"I see that," the service representative replied with a bright smile.

"We're afraid it might fall off," Carla told her.

"I was just getting to that," James cut in. "Roll the window back up."

"Oh, she's all right," Teresa said. But James ignored her.

"Roll it up," he insisted.

Mumbling and grumbling, Carla did as she was told.

"That's a sweet girl," Brown said.

"Takes after their mother," James answered, as he usually did such things. "Do you think it'll fall off? While we're driving around, I mean?"

"Oh, I doubt it. Just bring your car back first thing tomorrow."

James pondered that. He had his regular beat runs and another column to write that morning, plus a feature or two to start, an appointment of a very personal nature for the afternoon, and a city council meeting to cover that evening.

"You're sure you can't get it done tonight?"

Brown flipped to the last page of her clipboard pad.

"Well, if you want to wait around for about 10 minutes, we'll know for sure. But I don't think it's likely."

James heard the window descending. "Daddy," said Carla, "I have to go."

That decided things. "We'll wait," James told the charming lady. "Where's the restroom?"

Behind the Scenes...
Endearing conversations — page 243

10

Breakfast in Spandex

James almost broke into laughter. Someone with Leo Heavy Chevy Geo must love mirrors.

Huge, spotless reflections dominated every wall in the hexagon-shaped waiting room, so that no matter where he looked, James could see the somewhat overweight, shaggy-haired reporter with a nose that in a pinch could substitute for Franklin's early warning system. He could suck in his gut if he desired, but nothing short of a gallon of Vitalis could keep his obstinate cattail hairs from flaring before the heavens.

James sometimes thought gluing little pendants on the auburn offshoots would be cute – like a head full of mini bicycle flags. Perhaps if he embarrassed the hairs enough, they'd lie down as they were supposed to. But every time James considered something drastic, he'd put his hair problems in perspective with his nasal helicopter platform, his drifting waist, much less his constant, squeezing loneliness, and he'd decide taming those hairs just wasn't

---

Behind the Scenes...
The answer to cattail hairs? — page 243

---

worth it. After all, when you had a schnoz the size of a Cadillac, as Charlotte had once dubbed it, you stopped worrying about making yourself attractive.

Returning from the restroom, Angela and Carla fell in love with the magical illusions a near circle of mirrors could create. Charging to the center of the hexagon, his girls started their version of *The Dance of the Sugar Plum Fairies*. It struck James quite strange, since he couldn't recall the fairies stepping on each other's feet, knocking one another to the ground, or slapping their comrades senseless. When his girls reached that point, he determined it'd gone far enough.

Carla didn't mind. Once she realized trying to talk her father out of stopping them was impossible, Carla decided she was too tired to continue the dance anyway. But Angela had enjoyed herself and didn't want to stop.

"Why can't we go on, Dad?" she argued. "We're all alone here."

"That's because everyone else fled when you two fell into the chairs," James reminded her. "I should've stopped you then."

"You did," Angela said. "And I'm sorry. But this is so fun!"

"I'm bored," Carla decided. "I want to go home."

"I don't," Angela countered. "I want to play!"

"There's nothing to do here!" Carla moaned.

"Well, if you wouldn't have started fighting," James told her, "you could've continued exercising."

"Has it been 10 minutes yet?" Carla wondered.

"We weren't exercising," Angela told him.

"Playing is exercise, either for your body or your mind," James explained. "Or both. What you were doing was great. You'd be surprised what some people get paid just for doing that."

That got Carla's attention. "Paid?" she inquired, her eyes

Behind the Scenes...
That's *Fairy*, not *Fairies* — page 244

excited by images of dollars and what they could buy.

"I know," James said, leaning back. "It always surprises me. But then, there's much I don't understand in this world. Your mother, sometimes."

"I don't understand the divorce," Carla said in a hushed voice.

The wound revealed in her words pierced his heart. Running his fingers across her forehead, James knew he had to do something to cheer her up.

"You know what Tad would say he didn't understand?" he asked his youngest daughter. "Spiders."

"I sure don't understand spiders," Angela declared.

"I don't either," James admitted, "though they sure know how to eat breakfast."

"Dad, they eat bugs!" Carla exclaimed.

"I'm not suggesting we eat bugs for breakfast," James assured her. "If it could be done delicately, we'd already have a cereal on it."

"Augh!" Carla screamed.

James put on his most clownish face. "Just imagine – 'Yes, kiddies, a prize in each and every box of Super Critter Crisp, the cereal you chase with a spoon.' Or, how about, 'Captain Cockroach – you can't get away with the crunch, 'cause the crunch always gets in the way.'"

"I know it would with me," Angela told them, gagging.

"Dad, that's sickening," stated Carla.

"And besides, spiders are supposed to eat bugs," Angela reflected. "After all, what's a spider?"

"So you say, my most logical daughter. But at least the spiders know enough to not eat breakfast in spandex tights. Unlike some TV programmers around here."

Angela and Carla shared looks of puzzlement. James loved it. Anything that took their minds off their sorrow was good.

"You see, I enjoy a good, informative TV show while I eat breakfast," he explained. "Naturally, I tune into *Dudley Do-Right* and *Bullwinkle*. But to reach *Dudley*, my television always happens to cross the *20-Minute Workout*."

"What's that?" Carla wondered.

James almost stumbled.

He hadn't expected to have to explain that.

"It's an exercise show with girls… well, skinny ladies, bouncing around in colorful tights."

"Do they bounce better in the tights?" Carla asked.

James started to note, "Well, parts of them do," but then he realized exactly what he was saying and cut it off at the source.

"Tights are exercise clothes," Angela informed her. "Made out of rubber. It kind of sticks hard to all your skin, so that your blood rushes around and you can't hardly stand still."

James considered that for a moment before deciding it was best he didn't.

"Anyway," he stressed, just to get back to his story, "I ask you – who at 6:30 in the morning is ready for a workout? I step into the living room with a bowl of Wheaties in one hand and a spoon in the other, and then those young vixens come on the air, their soft voices purring compliments, and they start hopping up and down, waving their arms and legs back and forth like they were made of springs. And they talk to you with suggestive reassurance. Before you know it, you're on your feet, bouncing up and down, rattling the windows and cracking the floor. And if you're like me, you've got Wheaties thrown all over the room."

"Oh, wow," Carla said. "Mom's not going to like that."

"There's nothing that makes your breakfast take longer to finish than eating Wheaties off the floor," James told them. "If you've never tried it, watch the show. You'll be surprised how many flakes there are in a bowl of cereal."

"More than the dandruff on a giant, I'd bet," said Carla.

"How would you know how much dandruff a giant has?" Angela wanted to know.

"I saw it on the Disney Channel!" Carla snapped back.

"You did not!"

Behind the Scenes…

Rocky and His Friends — page 245
20 Minute Workout — page 245

"Girls!" James cut in. "Don't fight!"

"We're not fighting," Angela corrected him.

"Dad," interrupted Carla, "I'm trying to say something and you're not letting me!"

"Oh… well, I'm sorry. What is it?"

The nine-year-old took a deep breath and pulled her long black hair behind her shoulders. She always did that when plotting strategy.

"Well," she tried to articulate, "I don't understand just what these ladies are doing?"

"Exercising," Angela said.

"I asked Dad!" Carla snapped.

James knew what that retort meant. His daughters were getting hungry and irritable. Deciding to wait on the car might have been a bad idea after all.

"Angela's right," he said, "though you're not the only one to ask that question. You see, those young ladies stand there like female Mr. Rogers without the sideburns, among other things, and they ask those stupid questions like, 'Are you sweating?' and 'Doesn't sweating feel good?' Like I'm sure I could do an exercise routine for 10 minutes and not be sweating. Sure I'm sweating. I'm wondering what my landlord would think if he were to walk in and see soggy Wheaties hanging all over the walls. Or what my editor's going to do when I come in 20 minutes late due to a late shower to get the milk and wheat flakes out of my hair."

James had hoped his girls would be laughing right about now. Instead, their eyes were stern.

"Perhaps," offered Angela, "if you used some other kind of cereal, you wouldn't have that problem."

"No, it doesn't matter what other cereals you substitute. Raisin Bran falls apart faster when it flies from the milk, and although the raisins stay in the bowl longer, you find they don't taste so good without the flakes. And the sweet cereals like Quisp just get lost in the carpet, and so you walk around the living room hearing faint crunching noises all week."

"So that's what that is!" Carla exclaimed.

"After their strange workout," James said, eyeing his youngest one, "these ladies sit in front of the screen, their damp suits even more clingy than normal, and they're saying how sweating is wonderful, working out a body's muscles and making people breathe deeply. Before the show ends, they comment on how they enjoy stretching and hearing heavy breathing. I for one had long since given up the exercise, yet strangely, I was still breathing quite heavy."

I must be getting tired, James thought. *Why else would I be telling such a story to my daughters?*

With a quick breath, he asked God to forgive him. It was time to end this.

"Now *Bullwinkle* never had that effect on me," he revealed, "but then, that moose never practiced Winklecise, or I might now be accustomed to eating my cereal off the floor. Just like the spiders do."

As he did when he finished any story, James leaned back to see what effect it had on his audience. He saw amusement in Angela's chocolate eyes, but Carla's sky-blue orbs appeared enjoyably outraged.

"Oh, Daddy!" she almost screamed. "That's disgusting!"

"It certainly is," came a new voice.

James twisted about to see their service attendant leaning against the wall, her eyes aglow in the soft fluorescent light, her left arm propped against her angled hips. Her mischievous smile completely changed the way he perceived her. Standing as she did, James suddenly saw an attractive woman where before she'd been just... something else. An anonymous representative of a soulless corporation, he supposed.

"About your car," she said, straightening. "Unfortunately, I was right. You're going to have to bring it back tomorrow. We can't get to it tonight."

James rose with a sigh. His neck and back ached.

"It looks like you could use a workout," Brown commented.

"It looks like you could lead them," he countered, walking towards her.

"Once, perhaps," she allowed. "Not too long ago." Her words trailed to a whisper. "I'm surprised a decent columnist like you would tell your daughters a story like that! What are you going to do when your girls figure out why you were watching that show?"

James almost stumbled. Her words mirrored his conscience.

"You know who I am?"

"I remember that column," she said, smiling. "You told it well, although in print I think you referred to your wife instead of your landlord. Do you remember every story you write word-for-word like that?"

"No," he admitted, warmed and embarrassed by her attention. "Just some of the columns. The ones I think worked well."

"That one did." With her right hand, she reached for the cross hanging from his neck, lifting it gingerly from his chest. "But I wonder if that's really the kind of message you want to be spreading – or is that truly where your heart lies, after all?"

A playful retort came to mind, but James almost choked on the words as new meaning came from her questions. With a sly grin, she allowed his cross to tumble back into place.

"Daddy," interrupted Carla, "I'm hungry."

"I am, too," Angela said.

"I know," he replied, still lost in thought. "Just wait a minute. We'll get something shortly."

Brown led them down a short staircase to the Service Department, where James saw the *Defiant* awaiting them.

"I think what you were doing was very sweet," she said. "Not many divorced fathers spend such time with their daughters. Just take a little more care on what stories you tell them, okay? You may think of them as little girls, but they're growing up. They may understand more than you guess."

"I'll keep that in mind," James said. He found his interests for this young lady growing far beyond his car… a woman whose wit and charm matched her beauty. But he couldn't dwell on such feelings. His girls were hungry, and so was he. More important, the wounds he still bore would not allow him a chance at romance. He couldn't risk another betrayal.

"You're sure they can take care of it tomorrow?" he asked. "Tomorrow morning?"

By Kirby Lee Davis

"If you get here by 7 a.m., you'll have no problem," she assured him.

11

A Rude Awakening

None of them wanted to admit it, but they were all just too tired to enjoy the rest of the night. James knew he should've expected that, with all the stress that ended their afternoon, but still, that knowledge didn't lessen his disappointment. James cherished Wednesdays. It was the only evening of the week he could count on to enjoy time with his daughters, and he'd blown it.

By the time they'd finished their cheesy pie at Pizza Hut, the clock read 8:20. There was just enough time to get the girls home by 9. Carla complained once about missing choir – a time when she got to see friends the divorce had splintered away from her – but his youngest limited herself to a single sentence. Even his dynamo was too exhausted to rant too much after such a day.

Returning home to his empty apartment, James took a quick shower, doused the lights, and slumped into bed in his white cotton briefs. It defied his routine, not staying up for *Star Trek*, but he had an early schedule to meet. And after a day like this, he could hardly bear his daughters' absence.

It was like magic, being with Angela and Carla. Just standing in their presence created a portal of love, transporting him back to the fourteen years he'd given a marriage he'd mistakenly thought worked. In such times his

54

life had meaning. Without them....

In the depths of his soul, James choked on the arid wasteland that was divorce. Everything mocked him. His shirts and slacks were favorites Charlotte had chosen long ago. His books often told tales they'd read together, his albums spun tunes they'd sung in harmony, his paintings and photos reflected places they'd visited and treasured. Even the barest necessities of life, his plates, cups, and silverware, had been shared between the two of them. From all those things and more James beheld precious memories of a life his daughters now lived without him. A life Charlotte rejected.

If fleeing these things could save him, James would've done so long ago. He didn't want to be in this one-bedroom apartment, except he had nowhere else to go. He didn't want to live this life, yet it was the only one The Lord provided. So despairing was his time that thoughts of suicide sometimes slipped into his conscious, and while he rejected them – knowing that while he breathed, his Lord still had a purpose for his life – thriving often proved a bitter endeavor. Though he prayed daily for guidance, no answers came forth. God forced him to be patient.

As James crossed his thirty-seventh year of walking this earth, bleeding inside with every step, he could see his body and mind decaying from lack of purpose. The mirror revealed the truth: his faith was weak. He voiced his love of God, yet lacked the motivation to maintain his muscle tone, his body weight. His discipline. Desires that once filled his hopes and ambitions – experiencing the love of Christ through his family, his music, or the written word, admiring God's wondrous power in nature, participating in His church – such things now paled against his isolated life, his longing for companionship. Someone who loved him for who he was, without compromise or deception. Someone to renew his heart with the light of The Lord.

But could he risk such betrayal again?

James felt so twisted inside, he couldn't really tell. All he knew was that every time some such opportunity suggested itself, like at Leo Heavy Chevy Geo, fear turned him aside.

At least, it seemed like fear.

Only one thing gave him a moment's respite from his agony. As he peeled off his shirt, Harrigan rediscovered the cryptic receipt. Unfolding it in the bright bathroom light, James pondered its scribbled string of numbers. But weariness soon overcame his curiosity, so he set the folded paper in a little-used drawer and forgot it. His shower and bed waited.

Barely toweled off, he threw himself into his cold, lonely sheets, seeking escape in numbing sleep. His heart cried out to God, and yet when exhaustion drew him at last to slumber, existence remained a corrosive prison.

Somewhere in the night, he awoke to a throbbing dryness in his throat. The air was cold; true winter had returned. In the dim moonlight he stumbled to the sink, poured some tap water into a thick plastic glass, and drank his fill. Then he muddled his way between his kitchen counter and bed, his mind seeking little more than sweet slumber. He'd almost made it when a whisper blacker than night froze him in his tracks.

Breathing became quite difficult. "What?" James managed to say.

"Shut up, damn it!"

His sight still adjusting to the all-prevailing shadows, James could make out nothing but the outlines of his furniture. He couldn't tell where the voice came from.

Sharp-edged fear shredded his exhaustion. James wanted to scream, but he dared not. This intruder must have heard him in the kitchen, so he had not investigated their bedrooms. He probably didn't know of Charlotte or the girls. James meant to keep it that way. That ruled out calling the dog, but James doubted their aged, loving beast would be much help.

All at once, in a cascade of shock and despair, James remembered the divorce. Despite all he'd been through, it

---

Behind the Scenes...
Crude language — page 246

struck like a stunning revelation. He wasn't in his old family home! He had no wife or girls to protect, no elderly German shepherd to summon.

He was alone. All alone.

"Oh, God," he whimpered. Would this nightmare ever end?

The voice returned, its tone cold with sarcasm. "What you doin' up?"

James took one quick breath, then another, and yet another, all hoping to mask his fear. His limbs chilled in the brisk air.

"Getting a drink," he answered.

"Hold still!"

James stiffened, only then realizing he had been pacing from foot to foot.

"Shouldn't be up so late," the youthful voice said.

"Well, it was a long day –"

"Shut up!"

"Sorry." That word had escaped his talkative lips before James realized he was starting a conversation with a burglar. The retort educated him somewhat, but not enough.

Lord, help me!

"Man, you think that helps?"

"Well, I don't –"

"Shut the hell up, damn it! Shit! Man, you couldn't just go to bed. Noooooo! Had to get a drink. Shit! Could've been in and out. Nobody seen me."

James didn't know what to make of that. "Look… look. I know it's hard –"

"Drop it!"

James let go of his glass. It bounced against a bar stool, issuing a loud crack as it tumbled to the carpet.

"What was that?"

"A cup. My water."

"You're spilling water on the carpet? This late? God damn it! Why'd it have to be this place?"

"Don't say that."

"I said shut up! You want me to shoot you?"

"No."

"Then shut up, man! Shit!"

A brittle silence followed. Harrigan didn't know what to do. His every breath rumbled as an angry thunderclap.

"Oh, man," stirred the voice, "this is shit. This is really shit. Man, what'm I gonna do with you?"

James shivered. "Do with –"

"Gotta do somethin', ya know?" The stranger rambled through hopeless ideas James only half heard before his anger flared. "God damn it!"

For someone like James, such swearing drew forth an instinctive response: "Don't do that." And that earned a hard reply – the cold steel circlet of a gun barrel pressed into his back.

"You say what?" his intruder snarled.

James fought back his fear. "You used… you said my Lord's name in vain."

"So?"

"Don't. Please."

The barrel pushed further into his flesh. James winced.

"What… you some mighty Christian or somethin'?"

"No."

"You gonna call some angels, smite me down?"

"Wish I could, but no."

"Then shut up, damn it!"

James swallowed hard. "I just can't allow –"

"Allow?" The voice twisted in angry amazement. "Shut up! You're slowin' me down, man! Shit!"

"I just wish you wouldn't talk like that."

The intruder snorted. "You sound like my mother."

"You should listen to her."

"Oh, just shut up! I can't think!"

James endured another moment of silence, fearful the gun might go off. Sweat stung his eyes. He shook his head and was surprised to feel thin streams of cold liquid run down his

---

Behind the Scenes…
At gunpoint — page 246

---

back and shoulders. His sandy brown hair must've been wetter than he'd supposed.

The gun pulled back. "Oh man, you're leakin' on me!"

"Sorry."

"That does it! Take 'em off."

James hesitated, not knowing what he meant. The clock bell rang twelve times.

"Oh, shit," groaned the voice.

James felt his legs growing heavy. He stutter-stepped. The gun barrel returned.

"I said drop 'em," snapped the voice.

"Drop what?"

"Your clothes, man!"

"What clothes?"

The voice swore. "The ones you're wearin', man!"

"You mean my shorts?"

Irritation crept in. "You think I'm talkin' to anyone else here?"

"No," James whispered. But something spurred him to resist. "Why," he stumbled to say, "why would I want, well... to do that?"

The intruder hardened. "Because I said to."

"But... I don't want to."

"You don't?"

"No, not really."

The barrel bit deeper into James's soft middle. He prayed in silent desperation for God's protection.

"You think I care?" his assailant spat.

James took a deep breath. The air seemed like ice.

"I just," he began, "well, I don't like to disrobe before strangers."

"Shit, man! I can't even see you!"

That peaked James' curiosity. "Then why should I do it?"

"Why? You want me to shoot you?"

"I don't think you would."

Like most things he ever said, the words were out before James had considered them. He took a deep breath when he realized, this time at least, the arrogance of how he spoke. As the trigger inched backward, each click a bolt through the stillness, James prayed through his fear for Christ to empower his speech.

"Shit, man. You think I want you dead?"

James shivered. "Please don't talk like that."

"Oh, come on! You're worse than my mother, man!"

"She sounds like a good Christian."

"Good Christian? Jesus Christ! She could've wrote the book, man! But the book don't pay the bills!"

James detected something different in that. The man's hard, brutal edge had given away to hurt. It rang of desperation and despair, feelings James understood well.

"It can," he offered, "if you follow it."

"Oh, shut up, man! Just shut up! I don't care what you look like! Just drop the shorts, OK?"

"But why do you want me to?"

"Why? Now you're asking me questions?"

"Well, you're asking me to disrobe."

"Look – I ain't no gay boy, OK? Shit. Now I've had it. Just do it."

But James was no longer intimidated enough to give in. What they had in common had stirred up his compassion, which disarmed his fears.

"No," he decided.

"Do it, man!"

"I can't."

"Shit! Just who the hell do you think you are, man! I'm the one with the gun!"

"I know."

The intruder paused. "You know I have a gun?"

"You've stuck it in my back twice now."

"Oh, yeah. So do what I say, OK?"

"You know I'd like to, but I just can't."

The voice stiffened. "You can't?"

"No."

"I've got a gun on you, and you say you can't."

"Yeah. I guess so."

James heard a dejected sigh. "Jesus Christ. How'd I ever get sent to your place?"

"That's how. He led you."

"Oh, shut up, man!"

"But that's how He works! I know. My life's been crazy –"

"Just shut up!"

But James couldn't be quiet.

"Look," he said, deciding to take a different path. "If you told me why you want me to disrobe, well, I might be able to."

"What? You mean it?"

"Maybe. We could try."

"Well, I just thought… oh, man, I can't shoot you! I ain't never shot anyone! I just thought that if, well, you were naked like, you might not try to stop me."

"Stop you from what?"

"From what? Man, I'm here scopin' out your place, and you ask from what?"

That made James step back to reflect. He still didn't know exactly where the voice was coming from, but that didn't matter now.

"Well, I've never really had anything of value," James said, thinking of all he and Charlotte ever owned. "Just my wife – I mean my ex-wife – our girls, the dog, and cats."

"Oh shit!" Fear spun the voice into dire paranoia. "You have a dog? In here?"

For the second time in one day, James felt it appropriate to lie – just a little.

"Yes," he whispered, hoping God would forgive him.

"Damn it! That's not fair! They never said you had a dog! Man, you're supposed to put 'Beware of Dog' signs on your windows, man! Shit! You think I would've even tried your place had I known you had a dog?"

"I'm sorry," James found himself saying. "I didn't know."

"They must think I'm some kind of fool or somethin'." Without pause, the voice turned fearful. "Oh, man… the dog's in here now, right?"

"Well… she sleeps in the girls' bedroom."

"The bedroom? Shit! I was just about to go there!"

"Don't worry about her. If she wakes up, I'll keep her off you."

"You bet you will, man! I don't like dogs!"

"It'll be all right. If she wakes up, I'll hold her down."

"Look, man, I don't need no favors!" All at once the intruder chuckled at the irony of it all. "You doin' me favors. Just what are you anyway, some kind of super Christian or somethin'?"

For some reason James took offense at that. "No!"

"Then why aren't you mad, man? I broke into your place! Could've stole you blind if you hadn't walked in! Doesn't that burn your toast?"

"Well, yes."

"Hah! You gonna say all this stuff you have don't mean nothin' to you!"

"No, I wouldn't lie to you. But my family's more important."

"Damn, you sound like Ma."

"She must be a nice woman."

"She's a good Christian, man. It works for her. But never has for me."

"It's not supposed to, you know."

"Oh, shut up already!"

"Maybe you've never tried hard enough."

The voice sighed. "Damn it all – just my luck to get sent to a minister's house."

James winced. Sent?

"I'm no minister," he mumbled.

Or am I?

"Oh, hell. A priest then."

"I'm no different than you."

"The hell you say. Whatever you are, you're blind, man! Your life's padded!"

James almost stumbled. The man had a point. No matter how bad James considered his existence, he was managing to survive with more than the necessities of life. God was watching over him, even now.

"That may be," he said. "We all come into God's world different. But you still have to work at achieving His grace. You have to try and have faith in Him."

"Easy for you to say. Maybe I've never got a chance, man! World's full of hate!"

"Sometimes. But that doesn't mean you have to be."

"Oh, shit! You think I've never tried?"

"I wouldn't know. But it wouldn't matter anyway if you're just doing it for yourself."

"Myself?"

"Following Christ has nothing to do with making a living."

"Don't want a living, man. I want cash."

"That's what I mean – doing it for yourself. I don't follow Jesus for a reward. We follow Christ because we love Him, and He loves us."

James heard his words as if someone else had spoken them. He felt a hypocrite, thriving as he did in so much despair.

"Oh, hell. Love's nothin'."

"No," James whispered. "It's everything."

If only I'd understood that when I'd had it. But now it's gone. Charlotte's gone.

A blast of wind broke through the vents as the furnace came on. A door creaked opened, then flapped shut.

James stood as cold stone in his living room, waiting in stark, brittle fear for a response that never came. Only as he heard the front door shift, and felt the brisk winter breeze against his spine, did James dare search the apartment for the gunman. But the intruder was gone.

In a frantic rush the reporter checked his apartment once more, then again, just to make sure. Then he bowed before God, humbled and alive, thanking Him for his deliverance, and even more, for forgiveness – both for himself, and his unwanted and departed guest.

Still, behind it all, Harrigan couldn't help wondering just what had happened this night, and what he'd have to do to find out.

12

Marks in the Dark

It took more than ninety minutes for the police to finish their initial crime scene investigation. Few prints turned up, and to the naked eye they looked quite alike. Harrigan suspected they might all be his, but no one could say that yet. Interviews revealed no other damage in the area, and none of his neighbors had heard or seen anything unusual.

"Don't know what to tell you, James," Franklin Police Sergeant Patrick Haskins said as he gazed across the parking lot from the stairway entrance to Harrigan's second-story apartment. "You made anyone mad lately?"

Harrigan leaned against the railing beside the cop, shuffling from foot to foot to keep warm in the chill night. His eyes hung on the maintenance worker installing a new door to his home, one with a deadbolt. As this marked the first break-in at that complex in almost two years, the apartment manager made a swift response – a reassuring message to everyone else living there, much less the member of the press.

"Mad?" James said, tightening his arms about his thick wool jacket.

"You know, in that column of yours," the cop smirked. "Have you called another councilman... what was it, Daffy Duck? Have you made another crack about Franklin High's mascot? Brought up your marriage? That sort of thing."

"I've never written anything bad about Charlotte."

"Well, maybe not," the former '81 Beaver linebacker said, adjusting his stance against the cold railing. "But think about it. 'Cause this wasn't someone cherry-picking the area."

"Unless I was his first stop," the reporter suggested.

"I doubt it. Most burglars wouldn't start on an upper floor. They want to get in and out quick if something goes wrong. No, this one came here on purpose."

A second policeman walked along the sidewalk with a flashlight, while a third checked nearby vehicles. At times curious bystanders offered some advice or other comments, which the police took in accustomed stride.

Haskins stiffened. "Seriously. Have you done anything to tick someone off lately?"

"Well, just the normal stuff. You know I don't go around bothering people."

"You're a reporter. Who wouldn't you bother?"

The patrolman who'd responded first – James recalled her name as Jesse Sutton – shined her halogen flashlight into the *Defiant*. She circled twice, roaming the beam across each seat and the rear cargo area.

"OK then," said Haskins, "how are you going to report this?"

The cop at the sidewalk, whose name James didn't recall, started checking the grass. Sutton knelt at the cub alongside the *Defiant*.

"Depends on how you guys write it up," James stated. "We'll handle it just like all the other police reports."

Sutton stood. "I've found it," she called.

Haskins nodded. "Come on," he told Harrigan.

The patrolman hovered over a narrow peninsula of grass dividing the forward parking spaces. Her circle of light illuminated three parallel crimson chalk lines on the concrete curb.

Behind the Scenes...
Crime reporting — page 246

James groaned in exhaustion. Stepping from the staircase exposed him to the biting winds and the inviting scent of a warm fireplace. He couldn't help feeling somewhat envious.

"Not quite like those on the door," reflected Haskins, "but close enough."

"On the door?" James wondered.

"Your old door had three similar scratches in the lower left corner," Sutton told him.

"What do you mean? You're saying someone marked my apartment?"

"These could be directions," Haskins allowed. "Mind you – we don't know for sure. Yet. But it could be."

James could hardly believe it. "You mean, like for a hit man or something?"

"Or for someone who wanted to steal something in particular, yet didn't want to do it himself," Haskins explained. "Could have hired a stooge, told him how to get there, what to get. But I want to remind you, Mr. James Harrigan, that we don't know anything for sure. Nothing. So, if you have it in your head to write about this, you leave my name out of it."

"And mine," put in Sutton.

It always amazed James how often people assumed he was going to print every little thing he ever heard.

"And if you do write anything, you'd better let the chief see it first," Haskins added.

"Don't be crazy," James snapped.

"We don't need this kind of story in Franklin," Haskins stressed. "It'll just cause trouble, James. You hear me? Trouble."

James nodded. He knew when he was being intimidated. Not that it mattered to him, of course.

By Kirby Lee Davis

13

j-col34.wpd

Marriage certainly offers many advantages – companionship, cooking, in-laws, and other assorted things that can't always be discussed in a family newspaper. Yet the adaptations I've made to settle into this state of loving servitude are truly startling.

For example, I noticed the other week that my wife was changing the sheets on our bed again. She apparently does this about twice a week. When I was in college, I changed them once or twice a semester. After all, I took a shower each morning, so I figured, what's the difference?

I also kept a can of Lysol handy in those days, to manage the odors. It was amazing just how many smells we had running around our dorm. Now I keep a can handy for the cat odors. I don't spray the cat himself, of course. That would be like throwing a water balloon at Arnold Schwarzenegger. Some things just aren't done.

All these issues hit home when my wife left me for five days to visit her family. Before departing, she spent an entire

Behind the Scenes...
Lysol everywhere — page 247

week lining things out for me to do, with frequent scoldings, or perhaps I should say reminders, that I must eat hot meals each night. Of course, I agreed to all she said; I've learned to save my arguments for when I really need them. That proved a wise move, foreseeing her return. Or perhaps it was a lucky move, since I didn't.

Anyway, eventually she left, and I had the house all to myself. Believe it or not, things went as normal. Sure, our cat knocked just about everything off the walls and shelves, punishing me for leaving him alone all day, but I didn't mind. I could walk around these obstacles easily enough, so I figured, why pick them up when he'll just knock them down again?

I didn't fold the afghan back up, but I did leave it in a nice, friendly pile. And I made sure not to use too many dishes so that my wife wouldn't have too much washing to do when she got home.

You would think all that consideration would make her happy upon her return. But was she?

Need I tell you?

So I had newspapers laying on the couch and floor. I usually keep a pile under the table anyway. And why dust the furniture when it's the dust on the TV screen that really matters?

Seriously now, what's the point of vacuuming the floor when you can just wear your shoes around the house and forget about it? When it cuts through your shoes is when you vacuum. And why wash the windows when our cat's the only one who ever gets in them, much less looks outside. If those windows are good enough for him, they're good enough for me.

I never worried about such things when I was single, at least not more than once a month or year. Or two. And yet, she wasn't happy.

It's like I've always told her. With a spray of Lysol and a good, stout paper towel, you can do all the cleaning you need. Somehow, she never catches on.

But I guess that's beside the point. Really, it's not, but there's no way I can debate it further. My hands are too raw from forced dishwashing, scrubbing, vacuuming, and all sorts of other things.

14

Then Why Are You Selling It?

After all was said and done, between memories of that invading voice and his disturbing dreams of housekeeping, James managed just two hours of restless sleep. He started his new day with a fervent prayer of thanks for his deliverance, and yet he emerged in conflict. No comfort came with that morning's frosted wheat biscuits crunched to the beat of Rocky and Bullwinkle. No Fractured Fairy Tale or cinnamon cereal could get that voice out of his mind. His burglar had sounded so desperate, so broken, and so strangely familiar.

As he prepped for work, James pondered how he might help that young fellow. By keeping pace with the police investigation and county sheriff reports, and checking in with youth centers, high school counselors, and others, James felt he might just be able to find the kid.

"And if I do," James whispered more than once, "what then? What should I do?"

Behind the Scenes...
Poetry in motion — page 247

That marked Harrigan's conflict. He felt moved to reach out, and yet part of him resisted. He held vivid memories of that cold steel gun barrel pressed into his back. Those marks on his door and curb gnawed on his heart. He wondered if the culprit might return, to finish what he'd started. And behind all that, there was that wounded part of his soul fearing to open itself for anyone ever again.

Such were his concerns that chill morning. It was only as he slipped into his overcoat and ice-cold Metro that James recalled just how difficult this day's schedule promised to be – especially with his afternoon off. A juggling act, to be sure. But the drive to Leo Heavy Chevy Geo proved a blessing, giving James twelve uninterrupted minutes to settle his thoughts within the harmonious wisdom of Carolyn Arends. Singing with her through the end of *Alter of Ego*, his heart felt less burdened. Its last notes faded just outside the Franklin city limits, where the dealership waited. His clock reached 7 a.m. as Harrigan guided the jet black *Defiant* into Leo's huge metal Service Department. A balding man in a white dress shirt and gray slacks approached as James got out.

"I'm Walton Prescott," the interloper announced. "What's wrong with your Geo?"

Even though he'd only explained it twice, James was already tired of revealing the *Defiant*'s ills. So, he edited his tale with something close to surgical precision as Prescott inspected the right-side mirror. The summary gave James some satisfaction, for if he'd left out any vital facts, Heavy's attentive representative didn't show it.

"I don't know what to tell you," Prescott began, running his fingertips around the damaged plastic unit. "I don't know too much about Geos. Don't know if anyone here knows a lot about 'em. Tell you the truth, I don't even know if we can get to it today. You realize your warranty won't cover this?"

"I expected that," James said, girding his financial hopes.

Behind the Scenes...
"I don't know what to tell you" — page 248

"How much do you think it'll cost?"

"Oh, I don't know. I don't know too much about these little Geos. They make these things so disposably high-tech nowadays –"

"It was manually adjusted," James said of the mirror. "Not high-tech."

"– that even if it has no computer chips or wiring to check, they might have to replace the whole thing. And we're still kind of booked up from the start of the week. Spring came early, you know."

Images of pink latex flashed through James's mind.

"Oh yes," he said, shaking his head like an Etch a Sketch in hopes of finally erasing that thought. "How well I know."

Prescott rambled on as if James hadn't said a thing.

"You'd be surprised how many people think speeding limits only apply in storms and such. You take my wife. With that nice weather, she drives the interstate on-ramps like she's leaving the pits in the Indy 500. Our speedometer wasn't working –"

"Wait a minute," James interrupted. "You work here, in a service department, and your car's broken?"

That drew a blush from the middle-aged man. "Well, you know, it costs a lot of money nowadays to get even the simple things done."

Oh, Lord! James almost moaned. "Just what I wanted to hear."

"Anyway," Prescott went on, "I was timing her going up a hill, you know? And I discovered she was going excessively fast. I mean, like twenty to thirty miles above the limit, from what I could tell. She said she needed the extra speed to go up the hill, and she passed two other cars doing it. Timing her going down the hill, I found she was still speeding. She said inertia carried her downhill and held her foot on the gas pedal. But at least she showed some respect for the other

---

Behind the Scenes...
Shaking his head like an Etch A Sketch — page 249

---

drivers, getting back on our side of the median like she finally did. But then she saw that wonderful sunset, and so she turned around to watch it – just as a bridge support seemed to leap out of the embankment and right into our way. 'Don't you just love the clouds, curling in the sky like that?' she said. 'They look just like Robert Redford's nose.' Now, since I hadn't seen Redford since he got shot up with Butch, I grabbed the wheel and headed us back over the crumbling shoulder to the freeway. Feeling me reach over, my wife turns just so nonchalantly around and asks, 'Don't you think so?' as if I always went around ripping the steering wheel from her grasp. So I said something like, 'Wish he'd blow it,' speaking of course of Sundance, you know, and my wife… do you know what she does? She turns around and says plainly, 'Why, then it would lose all its color.' That's what this Spring-like weather does, Mr. Harrigan."

"What? Reveal stuffed noses in the sky?"

"No! It gets women out driving more. Accident rates soar, you know."

From a stare of mock seriousness, Prescott allowed a sly smile to break across his rubbery face. "Of course, she'd probably say I was the one actually driving then, but it sounds a whole lot better when I say she's the one turning around, don't you think?"

James didn't know or care. A greater reality grabbed his attention.

He had about $60 to spare in his checkbook. If that didn't cover his repairs, he'd have to break down and tap the couple of hundred he'd set aside for the IRS, since the divorce had stripped away most of his tax deductions. Then he'd really be in agony, for he feared his tax bill could far exceed his savings.

"Of course, with the cold breaking back in this morning, we've got our share of winterizing woes again," Prescott said. "Gaskets, hoses, blower drums. One lady's brought her Impala in for the third time. It seems her doors keep freezing up. This morning, when rubbing alcohol didn't loosen up her door lock, she tried salad dressing. Thousand Island! I swear – she pulled her window weather stripping back and poured that stuff into her door! She thought it would lubricate it. But I'll give her some credit – that door sure does smell better. Though it might not a few days from now. Might stink awful bad, you know?"

Heavy Chevy's talkative service rep clutched his rolling belly as he laughed at his own joke, but James wasn't amused. "Look – I need this done this morning. I have the afternoon off, and I don't want to lose it."

Prescott glanced at his clipboard, frowned, then looked down the service bay. Following his gaze, James almost despaired. He didn't see one empty berth.

"I don't know," Prescott said. "I don't understand too much about these Geos, you understand, so I don't know how long it'll take to fix. But we certainly seem stacked up. Do you think you could bring it back tonight?"

"I brought it in last night. They told me to bring it in today."

"Oh. Well, I don't know if they should have done that."

"What does that matter? They did! And I'm tired of the runaround. I don't want to have to come back again!"

"Well, you'll probably have to do that anyway," Prescott said with a grim smile. "Unless you're planning to wait here for your car."

"No! Listen – I've got stories to write, police reports to check, a damage claim to track down, a somewhat private appointment this afternoon that I don't want to talk about, and the city council meeting to cover tonight. I don't have time to fool around running my car back and forth here!"

"Well, I don't blame you." Prescott glanced once more down the service bay, then at the mirror. "I really don't know what it's going to take, though. Do you think you could leave the keys with us?"

"That's what I was planning to do all along! In fact, I need a ride to work."

"That I can arrange."

With a soft chuckle, the Leo Heavy representative led James back to his desk, which was little more than a podium standing alongside four others at the Service Department entrance. Sensing with relief that this irritating repair episode might finally be drawing to a close, Harrigan decided it was time to get serious.

"What do you think it's going to cost?"

"Oh, I don't know. Maybe $20 to $40 for labor, another $20 to $60 for parts. But I don't know too much about these Geos, so I don't know if I'd put too much stock in that if I were you. I don't know if anyone here really knows about Geos."

Then why do you sell them? James almost barked.

"I don't even know if we've got parts for Geos," the service rep went on. "Not for this, anyway. Not everyone goes around ripping his mirror off, you know."

Stepping behind his podium, Prescott slipped a pair of thick-framed glasses of the purest jet from his breast pocket. His gaze tightened.

"Because they lower our MPG ratings," he stated.

James felt a chill fear spread from his toes to his fingernails. How had this man guessed his unspoken retort?

"Do you read minds or something?" he whispered.

The man smiled, but his eyes took on a sinister glow.

"Or something," he said.

15

I Know What You Mean

Prescott told James to wait in the lounge for a driver to take him to work. James accepted that task with a reluctant nod, knowing just how full of smoking bystanders that room of mirrors could get this close to the Service Department's opening hour. But he didn't expect to find its couches filled by four portly middle-aged farmers, if Harrigan judged them correctly by their mud-caked boots, well-patched denim overalls, and flannel work shirts. With a smoldering cigarette in one hand and a steaming foam coffee mug in the other, these four engaged in a stifling battle of wits dwarfing anything James would have imagined. He leaned against the wall, loosened his overcoat, and resigned himself to the role of the eavesdropping fly. For he never knew where a good story lead might develop.

"Heard it on one of them morning *Journal* ads," said one of the farmers, a rather round fellow with an almost hairless head the size and malleability of a sponge rubber basketball. "Said trees actually communicate by odor."

Behind the Scenes...
A fly on the wall — page 249

"What's new 'bout that?" said the man opposite him. "I mean, when my boy comes home from school, I don't have to ask him what he et for lunch, you know? We all smells it."

James understood that. Some of his female friends had mastered subliminal conversation many years ago, using perfume to suggest their cauliflower ears had the same texture as port wine cheese.

"My ninth grade English teacher," interjected a barrel-chested farmer, "she used to ask why we never showered after gym class. I used to think that was quite astute of her, but I guess she was just thinking like a tree."

"Just imagine it – all these years, we've been kind of callous to our fellow man," said the fourth farmer, waving his coffee to the rhythm of his speech.

"What you mean?" asked the third.

"Well, each night we wash ourselves off, and we spread these fancy colognes all over, just blocking off our natural odors from the world. Kind of mean, isn't it? Limiting our lines of communication like that?"

James chuckled, then cut it off with a snort as he realized how much he enjoyed this eavesdropping. Why didn't he bring a book?

"I might not use my deodorant for a week!" the first farmer exclaimed.

"You never did!" the fourth replied.

"Why should we?" the second grumbled, shoving his rotunda-sized waist forward to make his point. "Damn cosmetics! It's just a commie plot to distract us!"

That surprised Harrigan. He hadn't heard a Red-fearing patriot speak his piece for quite some time.

Perhaps he didn't need a book after all.

"I'll tell you what I find distracting," said the first planter, using his smoldering cigarette as a pointer. "It's them *Journal* ads. I don't think I'll ever subscribe – not when they wake me

Behind the Scenes...
Talking trees — page 250

up every morning, telling me just what they think I need to know to survive that day. I mean, if they're going to just come out and tell me, why should I pay for it?"

"Costs an arm and a leg!" the fourth bellowed.

"That's what's wrong with society right now," interjected the third.

"Reading!" trumpeted the second.

"I thought he meant arms and legs," said the fourth.

"Nah," said the third. "This need we seem to have to grind everything up into brief roundups. No one's got time for the details nowadays!"

"I know what you mean," said the fourth, rolling his sharp-edged head toward each of them as if, like a jigsaw, his razor-like jaw could carve his point right into their blubbery scalps. "I know exactly what you mean. Last night I stayed up to see the 10 p.m. news, you know? Everything they had was either some crime going on who knows where, or some sort of silly corporate espionage stuff, government put-downs, or some kiddy stories – and each one wrapped up in three long sentences or less."

The third warmed up to the discussion. "And then these talking heads always have to try to say something that supposed to be witty between each item, as if we're tuning in just to hear their boring repartee."

"Damned TV people," grumbled the second, wiping his lips upon his grimy sleeve. "Work for the government, they do. They're in on it."

"It's all this high-tech business," said the first. "All these newfangled things they've got out now – TVs with more channels than you can shoot, microwaves that don't blow up tatters if you poke 'em, laser-guided eyebrow pluckers and self-sharpening combination can opener/fingernail clippers. They fill all these things with buttons that don't do nothin' at all that I can see, and the instructions are written in Chinese that just don't decipher in American."

"Damned Japanese," said the second.

"I know what you mean," replied the third. "I can remember when my parents got an emery board for opening a checking account. An emery board!"

By Kirby Lee Davis

With a soft, proud grin, the farmer leaned forward as if to share a deep secret. "I've still got that," he almost whispered. "You can't buy emery boards nowadays like they made 'em back then."

The farmers all nodded. James bit back laughter.

"But nowadays," the third continued, letting his voice rise again, "my wife opens a checking account at one of them recovering thrifts and she gets a food processor. A food processor! One that not only chops and dices, but it cleans and washes, dumps out the seeds, goes down to the store and picks up some sirloin, browns it, pours the grease off for gravy, and then whips up a nice casserole!"

"What – no biscuits?" the fourth chuckled.

"If we open another IRA, they'll give us the breadmaker for that."

"Don't," the second snapped.

"Not gonna," the third farmer said. "My wife – she couldn't make heads nor tails out of it all. She plugged that processor in, and it begins to ask her questions, you know? Things it says it needs to know to prepare her food the way she likes it. Like the day she was born, her weight at the end of each of the last five years, her celestial cycle, the number of white carbuncles in her blood, our Visa limit… all sorts of private things. Why, we got so fed up we just chucked it in the garbage then and there!"

"Good for you!" the second man exclaimed, waving his coffee mug before them. "Don't trust that stuff for a second. You hear me now! Touch them buttons, and them computer chips inside all that stuff, they start broadcastin' secret signals like they do off them bees, an' pretty soon they even know when you're going to the john, they do!"

"Bees?" asked the fourth.

"I know what you mean," said the first, so happy to get his

Behind the Scenes…
Banking on emery boards — page 250
"Off them bees" — page 251

79

two cents back into their conversation that he ignored the fourth farmer completely. "It's like trying to cross that downtown intersection on Choctaw."

"What?" asked the fourth and third together.

"Choctaw and Fourth," said the first. "You know, trying to cross to the diner."

"And that cobbler!" the fourth said through a wide grin. "I know you, Bernie!"

They all laughed at that. James couldn't help joining in.

"Yeah, well. Them buttons," the first – Bernie – finally went on, "they read one way and the walk signs face another. You can't tell if they're trying to tell you which way to walk or if they're actually aimed at City Hall, where the mayor controls what they say."

"Damned females!" spat the second. "You can't keep 'em quiet, no sir! Just talk on an' on 'bout things that don't make no difference to nobody!"

"And the truckers," continued the first, "they seem to roll down Choctaw like runaway locomotives. I have to look two miles down the road – two, I tell you! – just to make sure one of them truckers ain't on the horizon, and even then, I ask my feet if they're sure they can get me out of the way when I step out there and a trucker suddenly pops out to run me down! And I don't always like their answer!"

"Getting too much cobbler," laughed the third.

"Damned truckers!" spat the second, winding up his backbone. "Never was as cheap as trains. Tearin' up the roads and such, and not paying no taxes, no, not a dime – just passing the costs onto us. I'll bet 'ya that's their corporate secrets that's getting' out. Them commies –"

"I'll tell you what it is," said the fourth man, pulling his great bulk to the edge of the couch. James half-wondered if the worn furniture would tip, so huge was the mammoth gut leaning from it. "I'll bet your feet are just as tired as I am, being awakened by them unwanted *Journal* ads!"

"Who wouldn't be?" the third pondered aloud. "Hearing business news that early just takes the zest from the day."

The farming quartet laughed deep from the heart. James leaned out to stretch his aching back. That's when he spied a huge pink nose and two hazel eyes peek around the corner beneath a red mop of bushy hair.

"Anyone here need a ride to work?" the furry man called in a squeaky voice.

To his eternal joy, James discovered he was the only person waiting for a ride. *Finally, I'll get out of here!* he thought, offering a silent thanks to God. But his pleasure soon twisted into agony.

16

Did You Ever Really Wonder...

James had never seen a dealer use such a beaten wreck for a cab. By all accounts it had once been a 1974 Chevy, almost identical to the one Harrigan's father had driven his family in for two California vacations. The land boat's cocoa brown paint job was certainly the same. But rust had eaten massive bites out of the fenders. The chrome trim was missing. Something had scraped that broad hood down to its bare metal and replaced the driver's side door with a sky-blue number from some junkyard. Only tattered threads remained of the tan vinyl roof.

"Oh, you poor thing," James mourned, pulling his coat tight around his shoulders.

"Ain't she a beaut?" exclaimed the driver as he stepped past the reporter. "Got an eight-banger under the hood. When she decides to run, look out!"

"Yeah. Impala, isn't it?"

"Close, but no cigar. Caprice – '74."

At least I got the year right, James noted.

The driver was one of the best excuses for a hobbit Harrigan had ever seen. Short and fat to the point of being round, this shaggy copper-haired man whistled *That Thing*

You Do! as his furry hands unlocked the passenger side door. James drew it open and almost fainted from a released cloud of stench that could stifle rotten eggs. Luckily the safe arms of the Oklahoma winds came to his rescue, for though the foul odor pursued him, the brisk breeze proved the stronger. With a silent prayer of thanks, the reporter inched back to the open door, finding a wide bench seat re-upholstered with dirty green and white plastic strips resembling woven lawn furniture coverings. Eroding dunes of reddish dust flowed in circular waves across the sun-bleached dashboard. At his feet James thought he'd seen roaches scurrying in the shadows. One slipped beneath remnants of black-stained carpet, only to disappear through a hole in the exposed metal. The asphalt parking lot glared through the cavity.

"Lord help me," James whispered, even as the driver yanked open his door. "How do you stand this?"

"Oh, I love it!" the hobbit exclaimed, pulling a seatbelt across his cracked, fake leather biker duds and baggy Harley T-shirt. "Think of it! Being able to drive all day, stopping whenever I want to use the john. This is the life!"

This is the bravest thing you'll ever do, James decided, winding up his courage. *Just one step – no, two – you want both feet in the car, you know. Both feet – yes, that's good. Now open your eyes, James. Open your eyes, boy! Don't be a pansy!*

Harrigan decided that if he just locked his hands on his knees, and he didn't touch anything, and he kept his feet hovering above the floor, and he ignored the hole down to the street – and by all means, if he held his breath the whole way – he might just survive this journey. His pants might get stained, and his coat ruined, but he doubted anything would eat through to his shirt and skin. And he could always get Bennigan to brush off his back if necessary – the sports reporter never showed much concern about what he touched.

Behind the Scenes...
One hellish ride — page 252
Timeline hints — page 252

But closing the door proved a problem.

"No desks for me!" the hobbit continued. "Just the freedom of the open road – once I get her started, mind you."

By instinct James had grasped the aged armrest before he'd ever looked at it. Now the loose contraption clung to his fingers like five-day-old fruit chews left sitting in the hot Oklahoma sun. Aggravated, he slammed the door shut. The armrest rattled in his grip, as did the door.

"Oh, them hinges are loose," said the hobbit. The engine belched as he turned the key. "Just give her another couple of slams. Don't worry; you'll get it."

Since he couldn't get his fingers loose anyway, James pushed the door back out and rammed it home. At the same time the rust-bearded driver – who James had to admit was somewhat taller than a hobbit, though to reach the pedals he did keep the driver's seat pushed so far forward, the steering wheel nestled into his spongy gut like a sleepy kitten clinging to its mother – slapped his hairy left palm against the dash as he cranked the engine. The aerial concussion of the slammed door combined with the bucking reluctance of the V-8 to throw James deep into the seat. His hand flew free, but something else clung to his hair. James turned his head to see this new menace. The headrest latched onto his scalp like it had been glued there.

"That's a girl!" the driver bellowed, laughing in satisfaction at his rumbling engine. Turning on the heater, he said, "See? I told 'ya this old gal could haul. Now you'll see some action!"

Throwing the transmission into reverse, the hobbit jammed his foot against the gas pedal. James endured sharp, snapping pains as inertia yanked him from his seat. The rascally driver shifted gears and accelerated. His old Caprice almost exploded forward, throwing Harrigan back into the hungry headrest. Vinyl seemingly dipped in molasses gripped James's left cheek, his ear, and all the hair in between.

"So where are we headin'?" the driver asked, slowing as he reached the street entrance.

"The *Beaver Beacon*," James struggled to say. It's hard to

move one's lips when one's cheeks are attached to an immovable object.

"Sounds like some kind of porno bar," the driver commented. Then he rushed to add, "Hope that doesn't offend you. I'm not from here."

"Neither am I," Harrigan mumbled. But he'd long since stopped trying to make fun of Franklin High's moniker. Most inferences only led to trouble.

James tried to work his hand between his head and the headrest. His hairs cried out for mercy.

The Caprice surged forward, arching left for the heart of Franklin. James felt his skull being pulled irresistibly into the headrest.

Something crawled onto James's forehead. He screamed. The headrest held fast. Whatever insect he'd felt slipped down the oily surface of his nose like a high-flying skier, only to hang on for all it was worth at the tip of his snout. Like some hypnotic 3D film, James couldn't help staring cross-eyed down his facial bridge. Giant antenna extended from under his horizon. Out of the shadows inched a bulbous pair of bronze eyes surrounded by a thick chocolate exoskeleton. Two pinchers rose before him, opening and closing. Biting.

Harrigan's desperate shrieks rolled from window to window. James nearly went into convulsions trying to shed the half-inch roach.

"Oh, rats!" the hobbit exclaimed. "Hate them cab cooties."

Reaching backward, the driver slammed his right fist into the back of Harrigan's seat. James rocketed free of the headrest, striking his head on the dash. His forehead left a deep gouge in the dust eddies that had built up there for perhaps decades. But Harrigan didn't care about destroying that natural phenomenon. Again and again he swept his palms over his face, shaking loose whatever insects might be nesting there. Then he gave the headrest an angry glance, but the safety device wasn't there. His tormenter had vanished.

"You aren't supposed to use that," the hobbit remarked.

"I didn't mean to!" James snapped. "It grabbed me."

"Yeah, well, I'm not surprised. It's always doing something like that. Some things, they just go bad with time, you know? In the head. But it knows I'm the master. It knows I won't let it eat anyone when I'm here. But it can't resist trying."

All at once the driver thrust his head back to stare behind James's seat.

"Give it up!" he screamed to whatever lurked in those shadows. "You're not going to get anyone while I'm here. So there!"

James' left cheek felt ripped asunder, but that pain soon lessened as he massaged the wound, which opened the mental doors of his fearful curiosity. Keeping a wary eye on the overgrown hobbit as that jolly soul resumed his driving, Harrigan couldn't help wondering just what sort of dementia held sway in that furry head.

"Mind if I smoke?" the driver asked, shaking loose his beard. "You can roll the window down if you don't like it."

His mind still somewhat numb, James lowered himself back to the seat, keeping his head cocked forward.

"Cigarette smoke makes me sick," he mumbled.

"Oh," said the disappointed hobbit. "Oh, well. I can wait. I don't want to offend you. But if the smoke gets too strong, just roll down the window. Some drivers don't like that, but I don't mind."

A stop sign loomed on the horizon, marking the first major street in Franklin.

"Have you ever wondered –"

The hobbit stopped, glancing at James even as he slowed for a red light.

"Don't you believe in seat belts?" he said.

So caught up had he been in the Battle of the Headrest, James forgot to buckle up. He hesitated, wondering just what sort of surprise the metal-tipped strap might hold for him. But other than his gummy-stained hands sticking to the clip, the seat belt gave Harrigan no trouble.

The Caprice surged forward. James gripped the crumbling edge of his seat to keep from rocking back. Decaying chunks of foam rubber clung to his fingers.

James thought he heard a deep, malicious sigh of disappointment from the back seat.

"So," began the hobbit once more, "have you ever wondered what *It's a Wonderful Life* might have been like if James Stewart had been a vampire?"

Harrigan just kind of froze. This trip was one of the strangest he'd ever experienced.

"I mean, it would change the whole nature of the film," spoke the hobbit. "Not that Stewart couldn't do it – I think he could maybe, possibly, make an interesting vampire, you know? But it makes more sense, you know, creating that town of homes those people didn't really deserve if George could go and tap a pint of blood from his customers whenever he needed it. Kind of farm it out, you know? Or imagine what it'd be like if he'd played a vampire in *Mr. Smith Goes to Washington*. Just think what kind of boy's camp he'd create then. Why, it would change the whole face of the nation."

God help me! James almost whispered aloud. For to his great fear, the hobbit was beginning to make a weird sort of sense.

"Why…" said James, grasping for something to redirect their conversation, "oh… well, why don't you try to imagine what the film would've been like if, for example, Stewart had played a Christian?"

The hobbit shrugged. "Who says he wasn't? But what's the point of that? We've had our share of Bible thumpers in Congress. And look where we are."

James bit back a retort, for the hobbit had a point. Sort of.

Nine blocks of multistory brick structures reared before them. The driver sped into downtown with frightful ease. Not one eye seemed on the lookout for the oh-so-common jaywalkers.

"I'm sorry," the hobbit said. "I didn't mean to offend you."

James took a deep, loud breath through his mouth as they came to the corner of Fourth and Choctaw. He half-expected

Behind the Scenes…
Jimmy the Vampire — page 252

to see a rotund farmer in mud-encrusted overalls across the street from Greta's Diner, searching two miles down the road for hell-bent eighteen-wheelers.

"Didn't mean it," the driver added.

"You didn't mean what?" asked James, who was still half-pondering just what his fellow believers had accomplished in Congress over the last two centuries.

"To offend you," explained the hobbit, stroking his beard.

"You didn't."

"Cause that wasn't my intent," continued the driver, turning off the highway on Sixth. The ancient red brick warehouse housing Franklin's *Beaver Beacon* loomed at the end of the block. "But I imagine you'd be more intrigued if Donna Reed had been the vampire. You seem the type."

His last words sank in as James pondered how he could get out of the car without becoming attached to something. "What kind of type is that?" he asked.

"Oh, you know… the kind more interested in girls."

That's it, James decided. Not wanting to hear anything else, he whispered a prayer for help as he yanked on the door handle. With a metallic squawk, the door came loose and dropped, remaining attached to the Caprice by one blackened bolt. But James didn't care. Gracious to be out, free, and alive, he thanked God even as he shoved the aging portal back on.

As the door swung shut, James thought he'd spied the headrest rolling forward, as if to make one last desperate lunge for his scalp.

By Kirby Lee Davis

17

Back to Work

Pulling his coat tight around him – hoping all the while it didn't reek of the Caprice from hell – James took one breath of the frigid air and yanked open the greasy glass door to the *Beaver Beacon*. Only as his hand clung to the frozen handle did he recall the curse of the sticky armrest.

"Morning, Harrigan," Reynolds called from around the corner. "Sleep well?"

"No."

"Close the door!" Bennigan bellowed.

As if sensing competition, Reynolds shouted, "And then get in here. I've got a story for you to check out."

"In a minute," James cried back. Closing the door was easy; freeing his hand was not.

"And lock it," added the sports reporter.

Seeing his breath form a cool mist, James understood why Bennigan wanted the door kept closed. As one of three entrances to the drafty old warehouse-turned-newspaper headquarters, lodged right between the managing editor's office and the sports desk, just opening the door destroyed a half-hour's effort by their under-powered furnace to warm that cavernous room.

"Now," Reynolds commanded.

"I've just got to wash my hands," James called, stepping

off for the restroom before Reynolds could say anything else. But with three steps he thought better of it and stopped at the numerous piles of mislaid folders and media guides topping Bennigan's sports desk. The college dropout with the oversized gut able to digest anything sat as usual before his PC, reading through last night's sports wire. Even in this, the return of what was the coldest winter of memory, Jason bound himself in his favorite pair of patched blue jeans and a University of Oklahoma sweatshirt, his Oklahoma State University jacket hanging from his chair's back. An open can of Dr. Pepper sat beside his keyboard, waiting for his soft, round fingers to lift it once more to the bushy curls and thick lips that were Jason's trademarks.

"Ran into one of your fans," James said, trying to get Jason's attention.

"What else's new?" Bennigan replied, not looking from his screen. "They're everywhere. You know that."

With a sly smile, James turned his back towards his arms-length friend. "Could you brush me off?"

Jason grumbled, but gave the council reporter his full eye. "My Lord, James! What have you been doing?"

"Why?" Harrigan yelped. "What's it look like?"

"Like maybe you've been lubing a fire truck or something… whoa! Make that a hog truck. My, but this jacket stinks! What were you – no, wait! What's this we've got here? A cockroach?"

"Augh! Get it off me! Kill it! Kill it!"

Never was James more glad to feel a hard palm slamming into his back. He rocked forehead-first into Reynolds's outer wall, but he didn't mind.

Why oh why did I have to ride with that hobbit?

"Did you get it?" he whispered.

"Yeah, I think so."

James twisted about to see Jason wiping his left hand against his pants leg.

"What are you two doing?" Reynolds snapped as he stomped into the hall.

"James is breeding roaches," Bennigan said.

The editor nodded. "Looks like you've interviewed

another mud wrestler," he said, glancing down Harrigan's back. Then he took a deep breath and grimaced. "Make that a pig wrestler."

"Ha, ha. Nothing close," James mumbled.

Shaking himself off, he hurried past the sports desk to the side hall and restroom, ignoring their sparkling conversation on what could make such a stain and smell. It took three raw washings to get his hands feeling somewhat clean, and he destroyed two bird's nests (and three teeth on his comb) straightening his frazzled hair, but James didn't mind. He only wished there was some way he could clean his overcoat. But since there wasn't, and two people had already commented on its foul odor, he left it hanging outside the restroom.

The bachelor Bennigan had returned to his first love, the sports wire, while Reynolds had stepped back into his office. Society Reporter Janice Smithpeter was fast at work, cradling her phone against her slouching left shoulder as she typed. James thought it too early to see so much activity from their oh-so-short, coffee-loving, usually 9-to-5 reporter – until he spied Pricilla Underwood hovering with an impatient glare at the corner of Smithpeter's semi-orderly desk. The stern and stout Underwood – who James felt could, with just a touch of leather, substitute for a menacing tavern doorman – kept Smithpeter updated with events in that unincorporated Franklin suburb named Tortoise, her all-important hometown of 27 people that James suspected was just now advancing from party line telephones.

"Time for another Fat Mama Brown tale," he whispered.

As usual this time of day, Education and Religion Reporter Thomas Middleton was out, making his morning rounds to Franklin's nine churches and four schools. Middleton, like James, kept a fairly orderly desk, for while there where piles of papers and books just about everywhere he could stack

Behind the Scenes...
Gossip columns — page 253

them, each one had a specific purpose – unlike the sports desk, where chaos ruled the day.

Business Reporter, Photographer, and Webmaster Samuel Hernandez also was out, though James had no clue why. Nor did he get one from the nearly bare oak slab that comprised the ever-pert Mexican's desk, immaculately clean but for a few issues of *Wired*. With the expanding world wide web at his disposal, Hernandez saw no need for books – and his strategy seemed to work. James often wondered how.

"Harrigan!"

James walked straight to the editor's office. Reynolds handed him a printout of some wire story.

"Seems some local firms may be involved in a crackdown of sorts," he said. "Employees handing out corporate secrets and stuff. Why don't you see what you can find about it?"

"Ooo-kay," James said, glancing once at the paper before folding it in his left hand. "You do remember I have the afternoon off?"

Reynolds nodded, returning his attention to the overnight wire.

"And I've got the council tonight?"

"Yeah, yeah. Try to work this in. And I need two columns – one for Sunday, and one for the special tab. And one for the web page."

"No problem," James said, thinking they might be able to link to a reprint on the web. "And I've got a couple of things of my own to check. My car got damaged in a car wash yesterday."

"That's gonna happen," Reynolds mumbled. "I don't use them myself."

"Well, that's why I got a ride in. That's why my coat smells like it does. The *Defiant*'s at Leo Heavy Chevy getting fixed, I hope. They drove me to work – in a wreck that needs delousing! I might have to leave early to get my car, 'cause I don't want to ride in their cab again… and I've got to check on my damage claim. And I was nearly robbed last night."

That last note drew Dick from his PC screen, which is what James expected. But to his surprise, he spied genuine concern in his editor's stare.

"Someone broke in around midnight," Harrigan continued, happy to see signs that someone cared. "I just happened to be up, getting a drink. Surprised him, I guess."

"Probably surprised each other."

"Yeah, you could say that."

"You all right, then?"

"Yeah. I was scared, but we talked, mostly. He put a gun to my back a couple of times."

"A gun? A real gun?"

"Well, I think so. I didn't see it. I didn't actually see him."

Reynolds drew up in his chair. "You mean they didn't catch him?"

"No. He just kind of fled. I didn't even realize he was gone until he was *gone*, if you know what I mean. The police checked out the apartment and got some prints, but they didn't seem too optimistic."

That drew a grunt. "He get anything?"

"Not that I can tell. I didn't have too much time last night to check."

"Damn hoodlums," Reynolds snarled, leaning back. His hands fumbled around his chest as he pondered the possibilities. "You think you can write something up on it?"

James shivered. The constant cold made him long for a heavier shirt.

"Can't we do something about this heat, or lack thereof?" he asked for what now seemed the hundredth time.

"I've called Henry," Reynolds said, dismissing the question. "I'm more interested in that break-in."

"So... you mean beyond the basic," James half-asked, referring to the one-paragraph summaries he penned on each police and sheriff's report filed in Franklin. "I don't know. I haven't thought about it."

"Well, do. A lot of our readers would like to hear what you've been through, James. And I don't mean a humor column. A real thought piece."

"Everything I do requires thought."

"About as much as a doorknob. Think about this! You may consider your life a series of Laurel and Hardy skits, but this wasn't one of them."

"I don't know," James said, weighing the possibilities. "You weren't there."

"I don't have to be. Damn it, Harrigan! Think!"

James couldn't help smiling. "Please don't talk like that."

Reynolds threw his hands up in futility. "Listen to me, just this once. Please. Don't you know how stupidly asinine that sounds, asking someone not to swear?"

"You feel you have the right to offend me?"

Rolling his eyes in frustration, Reynolds turned away, but James couldn't let the point go. "If you'd said a racist comment –"

"Oh, hell! Just get out! And think about what I said as you gather the reports. I'd like to see something. I mean it!"

Behind the Scenes...
The right to use profanity — page 253
Wearing a cross to work — page 255

18

Just Pile It On

Walking the central hall through the newsroom took James to the main entrance and front desk, where the receptionist tried to help everyone who didn't enter via the other two doors. On a podium beside a visitor's couch and coffee table rested a stack of that day's edition. James grabbed the Thursday *Beaver Beacon* with little trepidation, knowing Reynolds rarely changed his prose.

"Good column!" called Janice Pendleton, their perky hazel-eyed receptionist. "I always loved those talking Coke machines."

James never tired of talking to Pendleton, who like most receptionists combined uncountable biological attractions with an irrepressible spirit to make one incredibly frustrating lady for a lonely man to be stuck in an elevator with, especially since she was married and thus amounted to one tantalizing yet off-limits temptation. Luckily for James, he didn't have to worry about such entanglements, or so he told himself. The divorce had cleaved that side of his heart.

"Why do you still write about your wife?" she asked, shivering as her question formed a mist in the chill air.

James stopped in mid-step. That was one thing he had expected Reynolds to change.

"I'm not really writing about her," he said, struggling as

ever over that point. "And I've written ahead –"

"Eleven months ahead?" injected Janice, amused in her doubts.

"Well, kinda," James whispered, folding the paper beneath his left arm. Now he didn't want to read it anymore. Burn it for heat, maybe, but not read it.

"Oh, well," she said, letting him off the hook. "Cold enough for you?"

Jason whispered his thanks for changing the subject. "Is it ever cold enough?"

Janice laughed. "All I know is, I'll quit if we have another week like Christmas."

Jason could understand that. He didn't think many of the proud and decent citizens of Franklin realized what the employees of the *Beacon* were going through, enduring the bitter winter indoors as well as out. But Jason had a theory.

"I don't know; maybe we should feel privileged," he told her. "It seems to me Reynolds was using those three weeks to test his latest cure for stress."

"Oh, yeah? And what would that be?"

"Why, you already know. Extreme cold."

Jason couldn't help laughing as Janice mumbled something awful. She was no different than any other employee of the *Beacon*. Few were especially fond of Reynolds for allowing them to learn firsthand just what it's like when hell freezes over, as the old brick warehouse's 52-year-old heating system couldn't handle those frigid blasts of arctic air that swept through the Sooner State during the holidays. But to James, it had been enlightening in an almost spiritual way, for when you work in a state of suspended animation, where spoken words must first be thawed in the microwave before people ever know what they've said, you simply don't have the energy to be upset with anything. Indeed, one barely has the energy to be anything at all.

"Think of it," James continued. "There are advantages to being frozen assets."

"Name one."

"Well, you can type and type all day, since you can't keep your fingers still anyway. The words might be full of misspellings – they might not even be words – but then, no one in Franklin's ever expected the *Beacon* to be picture perfect. Indeed, reducing our abundance in typos would only offend the Wayne Street Bridge Club, which uses the twenty or thirty new words created weekly in the *Beacon* for extra points in Scrabble. And I don't know about you, but my typing speed actually improved in the frigid climate, since my fingers were so numb, I couldn't feel any pain anywhere. I could just pound away, you know? Even if my fingertips burst, as I found flesh tends to do in such subzero atmosphere, my blood conveniently froze on contact with the liquid oxygen in the misty air."

"James!" she exclaimed in a playful protest.

"What? Didn't your fingers split?"

"No!"

"Oh. Well, mine did. But like I said, it didn't seem to matter. Once I managed to pry my ice-bonded skin from the congealed typewriter keys, I just typed on my merry arctic way."

Pendleton threw James a shrug of mock disgust.

"That's sickening! Where do you come up with this stuff?"

"What stuff? That was nothing unusual. I'm sure none of this was any surprise to Reynolds."

"It wasn't?"

"Of course not! He knew the old furnace couldn't hack it before the cold winds arrived. It never has in the forty-three years anyone's ever tried to put out a paper from this red brick blockhouse."

Each time it froze up, Reynolds would pry himself into his extra thick layer of camouflage hunter coveralls and say once more how the next time his lease came up, he'd move out of that drafty old place. Somehow just saying it made him feel better, since he was not even in the middle of his twenty-year lease and so couldn't move out even if he'd wanted to. And he didn't, for as Reynolds had once confided to James, the long-term stability of that lease was what he desired. With that worry lifted from him, Reynolds felt pretty secure.

"Frozen, but secure," James whispered aloud.

He looked back to their receptionist, but she'd switched

her attention to an incoming call – which was what she was supposed to do, James reminded himself. So with a farewell wave, he strode back to his desk, hiding his gaze from "Fat Mama" Underwood in hopes she wouldn't try to start a conversation with him. The effort succeeded, partly because Reverend Jim Bob Wilson had arrived – probably to drop off a Sunday School notice.

James had always admired the good pastor, even with his quirks. A lover of gardening, the snowy-haired Wilson had a habit of seeing biblical characters (and sometimes whole scenes) in gourds and squash, which he would then anoint with a rather stringent oil drawn from the fifteen blessed gallons Evelyn Stanley had brought back from her trip to the Holy Land some twenty-two years before. The olive oil had long since gone bad, of course, but since it was from the Holy Land, everyone seemed to think it a blasphemy to not use it in some devout capacity. So, they decorated Wilson's church with shiny if smelly sweet potatoes, sugar beets, and cucumbers that he deemed held the shape of the Apostles – which always gave newcomers something to talk about weeks after they'd forgotten his sermon.

With Wilson occupying Underwood, James managed to slip past Bennigan's desk and the corner to Reynolds's office to reach the hallowed confines of his own terminal. There, shuffling through Harrigan's collected sheriff reports, stood Frank Cobb – mud-caked overalls, overly thick trifocals, and all the rest.

James sighed. He knew why the scraggly old tree root of a rancher was there: to make sure Harrigan wasn't reporting yet another animal massacre story. Cobb came in almost every Thursday for just that purpose.

"Howdy, Frank," Harrigan called, walking around the stout rancher to reach his seat. It wasn't easy; Cobb wore scuffed Wrangler boots the size of Kansas.

"Hi, James," said Cobb, not taking his eyes from the reports.

Slipping into his armless chair, James activated his PC and fed it the passwords necessary to satisfy Hernandez's security measures. When all was up and running, James slid a Word

Perfect file from his "C" drive bank of stashed away extras – columns he'd written in advance, whenever he had a spare minute – and moved it to the server file for Sunday's edition. This particular column was one of his favorites, written from his experiences when Charlotte had gone to visit her parents for a week.

From the corner of his eye, James saw his phone's voicemail light was on. "Perhaps they've already got an estimate," he whispered, hoping Leo Heavy Chevy might have some idea how much it would cost to repair his dislocated mirror. He had to have that estimate soon if there was any hope of getting the *Defiant* back by noon.

Cobb let the Xerox copies fall, the pages fluttering in aimless abandon to his desktop. James couldn't help smiling, though he felt sadness at the rancher's frustration.

"Why don't you tell me what you're looking for," Harrigan asked.

Cobb ran his thick, callused fingers through what remained of his sandy hair. Then, with a grunt of resignation, he folded his glasses, slipped them into his breast pocket, and latched his thumbs in his overall suspenders for safe keeping.

"I shot my dog yesterday," he admitted.

James nodded, having expected something like that. "Was he mad?" he said, just to be polite.

"Well, he didn't much care for it at the time," Frank replied in a subdued tone. "Kept crawling out of the hole I dug him, too."

James allowed himself a compassionate smile. Though Cobb loved hunting, Harrigan knew the paranoid old rancher clung to the notion that every pheasant he shot was actually out to get him. At least five times the nearsighted Cobb had seen downed birds rise up and charge him, but unafraid, Cobb had stood his ground, stared through the ever-present fog in his trifocals, and emptied three or four rounds into his attacker, which unfortunately would kill the faithful hound retrieving his bird. Yes, it was sad, but Harrigan liked the gruff old farmer who couldn't see the wart at the tip of his nose, and so James never criticized him – although Harrigan was forced to print each dog massacre, to the distress of

Franklin's animal rights activists.

"Well, I'll tell you: I haven't seen any report on that," James told him. "But you know, if I do, I've got to report it."

"I know. And I know you're fair. Guess I'm just tired of getting hollered at."

"Can't say I blame you." James shivered, then stood in hopes of signaling the rancher to leave. Harrigan didn't mean to be rude, but he had a busy morning ahead.

"Well, if you do get something, could you give me a call?" Cobb said. "My wife hates being surprised."

"Sure," James agreed. They shook hands, and Cobb turned to leave. Then he glanced back.

"Say, is everything all right with you?" the rancher said.

"All right?"

"Well, yeah. I don't mean to be nosy, you know, but you've always been fair with me, and I appreciate that. And since I've heard some scuttlebutt that you're in some sort of trouble –"

"What? When did you hear this?"

"Oh, this morning, at the diner. Some people was talkin' about you. Don't rightly recall what was said."

"Well, I wish you did!"

"I'm sorry about that. But I'm not sure anyone really said anything, you know? It was just talk."

James settled back in his seat. "Just talk."

That's what newspaper writers were supposed to generate – talk. Get people interested in the community and buying their product. But it was always unsettling when the reporters themselves became the subjects.

"Well, would you give me a call if you hear more?"

"You bet," Cobb answered with a friendly nod. "Take care now."

"You do the same," James whispered, pondering the unknown omen left by the rancher. Then his eyes spied the phone message light once more.

"I need two columns," Reynolds shouted from his office.

"I haven't forgotten," James yelled back. With a flick of his mouse, he moved j-col27.wpd from his "C" drive to the server. Then he picked up his telephone receiver, tapped in his code, and found a single message left from early that morning.

"Mr. Harrigan? This is Donna with Fester Coop's office. We have your results back. Removing your left upper wisdom tooth will be covered by your insurance, but the lower two will not. They should each run about $225. Could you call me to set up an appointment? Thanks."

"Rats," James whispered, erasing the message. The two cavity-scarred teeth were painful enough, but this would be worse. How was he going to afford it?

Pulling back from the edge of despair, Harrigan reached for his public records notebook and two pens, all needed weapons in his daily gathering of police, fire, and sheriff rounds. Only then, as he debated whether he could last another year or so with occasionally deadly tooth pain, did he find himself the target of Pricilla Underwood's menacing gaze.

James nearly cowered beneath his desk. Underwood's frozen stare was so antagonistic, Harrigan doubted even the sun's nuclear fire could withstand her assault.

"I know what you're up to, young man," Fat Mama growled. "I know what you're doing. I'm watching you. And I never forget. Never."

"Lord in Heaven," James whispered.

"Yes – pray. You'd better!"

Behind the Scenes...
Foreshadowing through extras — page 255

19

j-col27.wpd

Here's another news story you'll never read...

...Sludgepond-Sloop City News, by Fat Mama Brown

Mr. and Mrs. Frederick Blumenwinchel returned to their rundown shack of a home last week after spending two weeks visiting his mother, Mrs. Martha Blumenwinchel, in the hospital. They had first visited her after her first operation three weeks earlier, when she became Mr. Mark Blumenwinchel. Two weeks ago, he decided he didn't like the change, so he had surgery to return to Mrs. Martha Blumenwinchel. The operation was designed to decrease confusion and tension. Mr. Frederick Blumenwinchel, formerly Frances, commented, "It couldn't help everyone."

Big Ted Tinkle and his wife Bluto left their three brats Wallo, Whale, and Whoopee with his grandmother, Mr. and Mrs. Willow Splatter. The Tinkles left Tuesday and haven't been seen since.

Over 42 and a half members enjoyed the church supper Wednesday night in the fellowship room. The 42 and a half cooks each baked scrumptious desserts and tested their flavor, managing to eat all the food. The other 140 members present danced around on the tables, scraping the silverware with their shoes, devouring the tablecloth and napkins, and generally chewing up the walls and candleholders in a raving fit of hunger. At its end the carpet showed numerous nibble marks, the standard church paintings of bread and fruit baskets had been baked and served, the drapes holes dripped chocolate syrup and catsup, and a good time was had by all.

Visitors Sunday of Mr. and Mrs. Hedgehog Snorts included no one. Saturday, they had no visitors either. In fact, they haven't had visitors for weeks.

A meeting was called Tuesday at 12:47 a.m. by Mrs. Fat Mama Brown of the Obesity Society. After a roll call, they had a biscuit call, then a gravy call, after which they planned ice cream socials and cake walks once a week for the next 10 years. Brown then plans a one-week diet to maintain her weight.

Mr. and Mrs. Tinsil Springwater returned home Wednesday after going to work that morning.

Genghis Khan, the Mongol conqueror who once welcomed Marco Polo, arrived for a formal visit with the Sludgepond mayor Friday. Mayor Friday gave Khan a key to the city as the town high school band played *Santa Claus Is Coming to Town*, to which the high school choir sang, *Genghis, You Smell Like a Nice Guy*. Khan then sold Sludgepond citizens more than $5,620 in valuable Mongol savings bonds before making a quick exit down pothole highway in his 1983 Cadillac, escorted with honor by the Sludgepond police car.

No future date was set for the next meeting of the Jolly Rodgers Society, a boating club that boards and pirates other yachts on the Tabasco River. Roger Hampster, president of the club, said formal dates were unadvisable, as the county sheriff always showed up and arrested the group. Rodger Topple, the treasurer, suggested inviting the sheriff to join the club, but as the sheriff's name was Ted, and not Rodger, the motion failed. Rodger then instructed the Rodgers to not

---

Behind the Scenes...
Absurdities — page 256

roger in their agreement until the roger-wilco sign was given.

Mr. and Mrs. Tim Belch visited their son, Mr. and Mrs. Tim Belch Jr. Tim and Tim talked with Mrs. Tim while Mrs. Tim Jr. made tea. Mr. and Mrs. Belch then left the Belch home, arriving at the Belch home later that night. The Belches supposedly aired their differences, and so all is well.

20

Loose Ends

After jotting down the who, what, when, where, and why for each of the seven calls investigated by the Franklin Police Department over the last 24 hours, James could picture how the all-important one would read.

"12:02 a.m. Thursday. An unidentified man entered the apartment of Mr. James Harrigan. After some discussion, the intruder fled. Summoning the police at 12:22, Harrigan reported nothing missing. Detectives investigating the scene found no evidence or witnesses. The police have no suspects."

James knew that wasn't entirely correct. Fingerprints had indeed turned up, if the patrolmen at the scene knew what they were talking about. But no one would confirm anything, either on or off the record. Nor would they say if anyone else was pursuing it.

If Harrigan gained anything in this visit, it was the knowledge that these department employees had all decided to shy away from him. James could see only two reasons for it. Either someone had told them to shush, or they feared talking would give James the right to print their names in forty-eight-point type on Page One.

As if this event was worth something like that.

So, with his pen and notepad in hand, James sought

permission to go back and see Chief Isaac Jacobs. His request was denied.

"Why? I just want to ask him some questions."

"Of course you do," said the dispatcher, a dark-skinned woman with eyes hard enough to chisel granite. "And maybe poke fun at the way he combs his hair or slurs his Ts. But you're out of luck. He's not available."

"Look… it's nothing like that."

"Of course not, but he's not here."

"Well why didn't you say so?"

"I did," the dispatcher snapped. "So you might as well head on back to your little dumpster and dig up some more garbage."

James didn't know how to respond to that. He couldn't imagine what he'd done to tick her off, though he realized some people just didn't like reporters. By instinct he resorted to humor, saying, "I don't want to go. It's warm here." But the words seemed hollow and unappealing. In the end, he departed as the dispatcher turned away to take an incoming call. Even so, he felt eyes following him as he slipped out the door.

As luck or fate would have it, up drove Franklin Patrol Car No. 41. Jacobs's personal chariot.

James kind of admired the chief. The retired Marine kept himself in good shape, he practiced his craft with schooled professionalism, and he handled himself well under scrutiny – including that brought on by a few councilmen (probably Army grunts, James had always hypothesized) who didn't like his straightforward style. Even better, Jacobs kept good relations with the media – no matter what mud occasionally darkened the waters. He managed this even while hating Harrigan's guts, which many people seemed to do these days.

Seeing he couldn't avoid the reporter, Jacobs got out with a

Behind the Scenes…
Systemic distrust — page 257

hard slam of his car door. James couldn't help envying the clean black vinyl and shiny brass of that warm police jacket.

"Don't you have something important to do?" Jacobs grumbled as he stepped onto the sidewalk.

"Some would think the police beat important."

"Reynolds obviously doesn't, or he wouldn't have Pauly Shore covering it."

"Ha, ha. Very funny. But Pauly Shore has a good reason for being here, chief. Could you comment on what happened last night?"

Jacobs ignored the question, striding past Harrigan to yank open the main door. But as the barred glass swung outward, a wave of frustration flowed across the chief's face. With a sigh, he turned to acknowledge Harrigan. Anger simmered in his gaze.

"You mean about your call? About your attempt to create news copy by summoning three of my men to your apartment at midnight? Disturbing about 100 other residents unnecessarily?"

James couldn't believe what he'd heard. "Unnecessarily?"

"Unnecessarily. Or should I say unlawfully."

"That's not true!"

Jacobs didn't back down. "You do realize it's against the law to file false reports?"

"I didn't!"

"And to lie to an investigating officer?"

"I didn't do that!"

"You know, Harrigan, you really tempt me. All my life I've wanted to arrest a reporter. To put one away. If I just had one shred of evidence –"

"But you have! What of those fingerprints?"

"What fingerprints? All we found were yours, your daughters, and those of the apartment maintenance man."

Behind the Scenes...
Pauly Shore — page 259
Idle threats? — page 259

"That's it? What about the marks?"

"What marks?"

"The marks on the street – and my door!"

"What do they prove, Harrigan? That someone owns some chalk? Is that a crime? And that was only used on the gutter – not your door. You could've scratched that when you moved in, or brought in groceries, or just kicked it. So you see, my friend, nothing substantiates your story. Nothing."

Through all his years, Harrigan had never felt his integrity so questioned. The onslaught swept him into the grip of a strange, unaccustomed panic.

"Now you know me," James stressed. "You know I've never misquoted you or written falsehoods. I'm not saying I've not made mistakes –"

"Mistakes?" Jacobs seemed amazed James would even suggest otherwise. "Mister, you've alienated every person who works for this city. Twice we've been forced to cut our staff by 10 percent or more. Twice – in just two years! But did you ever really dig into that?"

"Every month I've reported the declining tax collections, and what the city's done about it!"

"Did you ever question the councilmen on why we're patrolling some areas so vigorously and others not, or extending our water lines where so few people live, or paving certain less-traveled roads?"

"I've recorded every action the council's taken!"

"You never truly dig, James! Covering meetings isn't enough!"

Those words gnawed at Harrigan's heart. Was Jacobs suggesting something corrupt was going on?

"And I backed the sales tax hike!" James offered, not wanting to give up just yet.

"Yes… and when it passed, what did you write? Let's see…."

From his wallet, Jacobs withdrew a ragged, much-folded clipping from the *Beacon*. "I kept this one because it especially infuriated me. Let's see…."

Bending back in exaggerated pomposity, Jacobs deepened his voice to read from the wrinkled paper: "'So, the voters adopt a higher sales tax rate. What then? It seems to me that very few people have taken this contingency very far, in a practical manner. After all, we're talking $1 million a year here. That's an even $83,333.33 a month, except for the month when it's $83,333.34. That month the city manager can go out and buy a gumball or something.'"

James choked off a laugh. He still liked that line! But the chief only snarled.

"'Just think of it – $83,333.33. The city general fund was only short $18,669.98 for December, though it would have been much higher without those unfortunate-yet-necessary personnel cuts. So, if it continues like this, that leaves $64,666.35 per month. The yearly total approaches $775,996. And that's one good down payment on the Dallas Cowboys.'"

Jacobs turned his steely eyes on Harrigan.

"The Dallas Cowboys?" the cop exclaimed.

James struggled not to smile. "Well, it'd be funnier if they were still for sale."

"Oh, it gets funnier all right." Stretching forth the clipping, Jacobs read on. "'Consider all the implications. What great majority in Franklin would vote against buying the Cowboys? Why, just from marketing alone, the city would earn back its money. Plus, you get nearly 50 players who could be trained to be firemen, policemen, weed trimmers, any number of city jobs. So what if they play football on weekends! They could use a good, honest job to keep them in shape between games.'"

Jacobs shoved the clipping into Harrigan's face. For a moment James feared the chief of police would punch him.

"As if just anyone could be a cop!" Jacobs spat.

"Now wait," James countered. "Some of those players have college degrees!"

"Harrigan, you insulted the voters, telling them they'd just passed a huge tax increase with apparently little need. You had the perfect opportunity to call for the council to reverse their firings, to maybe even increase these piddling wages they give us. But do you? No! You tell them the new tax wasn't even needed. 'Unfortunate-yet-necessary personnel cuts'? James, you're a fool. Even worse, you're a fool pretending he's a fool, and doing so good a job he's even fooling himself. This city's worse off for having you."

James had no idea how to respond to that. Part of him urged a strategic retreat, while another side tried to buck up his backbone. Even his usual urge to fall back on satire seemed to betray him. But as Jacobs started to pull away, James knew he had to act. Desperate, he pulled out the wire article Reynolds had given him.

"Wait," he called. "Do you know anything about corporate secrets being spread in Franklin?"

Jacobs swung around with an incredulous stare. "What?"

"We've had this wire story," James blurted out, shoving the paper forward, "of some firms in this area trying to squelch employees giving out some type of corporate secrets."

With a grunting sigh, the chief scanned over the story. Then he tossed it back to Harrigan.

"Use your head, James. We've only got 22,000 people living in Franklin, not counting the outer areas. This isn't a corporate town. Oklahoma City could see this, maybe, but not here. Wise up, boy! Put your head to better use."

With a nod of dismissal, Jacobs stepped into the police department building. James held his ground, stunned by the whole exchange. Chill winds swirled around him. If possible, it seemed even colder now than before.

The door swung open. Jacobs stuck his head out.

"And by the way," he told Harrigan, "you'd better keep your nose clean from now on. You pull another stunt like that, and I'll haul you in, so help me God."

James felt a groundswell of anger. "I'm going to tell you for the last time. I didn't stage anything. It was real."

"Yeah. Sure. Listen, Harrigan. You've irritated a lot of people since you started with the *Beacon*. Now you'll have to

Behind the Scenes...
Vital elements — page 259

110

pay for all those seeds you've planted. Then you'll see who your friends are."

21

We've Been Warned

It was a cold, lonely walk back to the *Beacon*.

Outside of two brush fires, the fire department had enjoyed a lax day. Even the Emergency Medical Services (EMS) line remained quiet. At the county sheriff's office, reports proved equally slow in coming. Over the last 24 hours, deputies had rounded up three loose cattle, caged a rabid dog, and hauled away an abandoned car. As for the other issues grinding on James, the deputies had little light to throw on anything – and not because their electricity was out. They agreed with Jacobs on the wire story, but while they mumbled that they'd heard of the burglary attempt on Harrigan's apartment, they didn't want to discuss it.

James left each place sensing they were glad to see him go – and that left him pondering just about everything. Was he doing his job right if it alienated everyone? If it was the job that bothered people, was it something he wanted to be involved in? Or as Cobb suggested, were others spreading stories about him? Was someone out to get him? Or was he just a fool, as Jacobs believed?

And did his jacket still reek?

With each corner, he asked God to guide him. A frigid gust of wind answered his silent words.

James scrambled into the *Beacon* just before 10 a.m. Most

everyone had fled the icebox. Hernandez left Harrigan a request for a third column, something never published. "I prefer unique items for the website," he'd noted. Reynolds was busy composing Sunday inside pages in Quark XPress, so James proceeded to his desk, hoping to see his voicemail light on. It was.

"Come on, Leo Heavy," he whispered, punching in his access code. To his delight, James found he had three messages. He dialed up the first.

"Hello, James," came a soft whisper. "This is Haskins. Keep quiet for a while, OK? There are some delicate things going down. Please; it will do us both some good."

James drew little meaning out of that until he recalled Sergeant Patrick Haskins, the first responder to his police call. The man who'd suggested someone might have ordered the break-in.

The next thing James knew, Reynolds was glowering at him from over the four-foot workstation divider.

"Didn't you hear me?" Reynolds yelled.

"I guess not," James admitted. "Must have been lost in thought."

"I'm glad I came out here to see it," Dick quipped. Then he turned serious. "I just got a call from Jacobs. He thinks you were lying about the break-in."

James grimaced. "He told you that, too?"

Reynolds nodded. "Not in so many words. He did say he thinks you're irresponsible."

"That's what he told me. And when I got back, I found this message on my machine."

Reynolds listened as James replayed his first piece of voicemail over his phone's loudspeaker.

"Interesting," the editor said.

James took a deep breath. "Isn't it?"

"Well, I know you've got a lot to do, and just a little time to get it done in. So, let's talk tomorrow about this story."

Harrigan felt a surprising burst of joy. Even though James hadn't given much thought to what he'd write about the break-in, he'd half-expected Reynolds to cancel the piece after talking to Jacobs.

"And let's try to get some idea about what Haskins is afraid of," Reynolds continued. "Quietly, though. Let's be careful."

"Isn't it obvious?" James said, warming up to the subject. But Reynolds cut him off.

"Few things are obvious," the editor snapped. "Expected, yes. Telegraphed, often. But if you start out thinking you know what's going on, you're setting yourself up for a big surprise. We've been warned, James. Let's be careful on this one."

Reynolds locked eyes with Harrigan, making sure James fully understood what was expected of him. Harrigan held his gaze, unafraid. That brought a smile to the editor's often-rascally lips. Satisfied, he turned away, only to pivot three steps later.

"Oh… Samuel would like a fresh column for the web," Reynolds said. "Not one we've run before."

"I'll see if one's ripe."

Behind the Scenes...
Juggling wisdom — page 260

By Kirby Lee Davis

22

Poor Communication

James felt a twinge of hunger – the kind he usually detected when thoughts of real investigative journalism came to his head.

It never failed. All the romantic icons of a hot phone tip, the editor rushing out to confirm a story, the drive to spring for your jacket and hit the road… all that stuff naturally made James hungry for a Snickers, that historic snack bar of peanuts and caramel which modern ad campaigns long ago enshrined as the true sustenance for newshounds. He almost leaped out of his chair for the vending machines – but then he saw once more his phone's flashing voicemail light and drew himself back to earth. He still had two messages to hear.

Erasing the first, the second message played: "Hi, James. This is Sandy. Sorry I didn't see you at choir. I've finished *Beyond the Shores of Mars*. To be quite honest, it's got some big holes. I should be downtown later today or more probably tomorrow; maybe we can talk about it. See ya."

James erased that one without a moment's pause. *Beyond*

Behind the Scenes…
A reporter's candy bar — page 261

the Shores of Mars was his latest novel; the first he'd written since the divorce. For that reason alone it was dear to him, representing a step back into his former life. And the social relevance of the tale appealed to him, even if it was something of an extravagant comic fantasy.

"But then, who wouldn't be enamored," James thought in a whisper, "reading of a giant rabbit gaining superhuman powers to fight for justice and the American way?"

The whole concept appealed to him, though he half-feared some crazed zealot group might find cryptic biblical references in its near-apocalyptic ending. After all, it's not every day someone sees a huge hare in green and orange leotards stopping Arabian terrorists from bombing the Statue of Liberty and the Prince of Wales, speaking there to illegal immigrants rescued from a modern sweatshop.

And Sandy Travis thought she'd found holes is such a tale? How was that possible?

"It's not," James decided then and there. Travis was obviously going bonkers.

The intensity of that thought drew cautious feedback. Harrigan didn't want to lose Sandy as a proofreader. She was way too good at catching typos, and other developmental problems. She was just way too good, period – at just about everything. And she was a close friend. Perhaps his best. But that, too, was not a subject James wished to tread upon. Or even think about.

Friendship? Love? Bah, humbug!

Yeah, that's the ticket.

James sighed. The third and last message waited. If his day was to improve at all, it had to be from Leo Heavy Chevy Geo.

"Hi, James. This is Carol at Riverside. Sorry about this late warning, but it can't be helped. The insecticide crew will

---

Behind the Scenes...
Superhero hares — page 261
Voicemail anguish — page 261

come by tomorrow morning to spray your apartment for bugs, so be sure and clear out all the cabinets in your kitchen and bathroom, cover any plants and food items, and if you've picked up any pets since we last talked, make sure they're secure. Thanks."

James almost slammed the phone down after erasing that one. He hated that quarterly routine of emptying out about everything he owned, just so the bug murderers could come and find there weren't any six-legged crawlers camping anywhere near James since he never kept anything in his apartment even close to what they'd like to eat – or what he craved, for that matter. He had no plants or animals, and hardly any eatables not wrapped in something that could only be penetrated by Damascus steel (or its laser equivalent). But try to tell that to the Riverside Apartments cockroach hunters and what do you get? A good laugh.

For someone who loved painting smiles on faces, that hurt – especially since Harrigan wasn't trying to make them laugh.

Flexing his sluggish legs, James stood once more, but now the thought of crossing the wide wasteland of the composing department (or was that composting? He was never quite sure) to reach the vending machines no longer appealed to him. And as his subconscious reminded him, the day was getting late and he had a lot to do. So, reaching into his Yellow Pages, Harrigan began his Don Quixote quest for salvation from a ravenous car wash. Finding the phone number of the Easy Come, Easy Go, he gave it a call. The phone crackled to life after two fruitless rings.

"Yes?" came a hard voice.

James hesitated. "Is this the Easy Come, Easy Go?"

"It's one of them. Which one did you want?"

"Oh… well, the one on Harley Studley Drive."

"Sorry. We're on 43rd. Good day."

With that, the man hung up.

Behind the Scenes…
Reaching into his Yellow Pages — page 262

Frustrated that he'd called the wrong station, James let his fingers do the walking once again. Three Easy Comes were listed: One on Rivendell Road, which James recalled was near the Church of Hellfire and Damnation in the Happy Valley addition; one at Seventh and Choctaw, not too far from the *Beacon*; and one at 43rd and Harley Studley. And that was the only one even close to Charlotte and the girls. So, in a twisted rage of being both vindicated and cheated, James called it again.

"Yes?" answered the same tired voice.

"This is the Easy Come, Easy Go, isn't it?"

"Oh, I suppose so."

"Well then, you ought to say so."

"You ought to know who you're calling before you dial it."

"I did!"

"Then why did you ask?"

"Because... it just seems polite for you to identify yourself first!"

"Why? Have you identified yourself?"

James stopped to consider that.

"No, I guess not."

"Not very polite of you, is it?"

"Look – I never said I was polite!"

"No, but you're good at saying I'm not polite. That's not polite, if you ask me."

"I didn't ask you!"

"Well, why did you call then?"

"Because I wanted to know if this was the Easy Come, Easy Go on Harley Studley!"

"But you said you already knew that before you'd dialed."

"Well... that isn't all I wanted to know!"

"Well, do you know this other stuff already, too?"

"What other stuff?"

"The stuff you don't already know that you're going to ask about. That other stuff."

"How could I already know about it if I don't already know about it? That's why I'm calling!"

"So? You already knew what station you were calling, and yet you asked about it. How am I supposed to know? I mean,

I still don't even know who you are."

"I haven't told you!"

"Then why should I help you?"

"Because I'm calling for help!"

"And that's why I'm here."

James took a deep breath, all the while wondering, *Why me, Lord?*

"Look," he started again, "I filed a damage claim at your station yesterday."

"You damaged our station?"

"No! Your car wash liked to rip the mirror off my car!"

"Oh. Was it self-defense?"

"Self-defense? What are you talking about?"

"Or was the car wash provoked?"

"Hello? Are we talking about the same thing?"

"Well, yeah. Was your vehicle taunting the car wash?"

"Taunting the car wash? Are you crazy?"

"Of course I'm crazy. I'm working here, aren't I? I'm talking to you! Man, you are one impolite dude."

Knowing he had to calm down right this instant, James took a second deep breath, then a third. Neither helped. He considered reciting the books of the Old Testament backwards, but he didn't think he had the patience, time, or knowledge to do it well.

"OK," he allowed, not wanting to have to call again. "How could my car taunt your car wash?"

"Well, I don't know. They're both just machines, after all. But I bet it gets pretty frustrating, watching all those cars just come and go wherever they please, and that car wash is stuck in one place its entire life, just soaping things down, then rinsing them off. Not much ambition there. Got to be frustrating."

"I wouldn't know. All I wanted was some idea when I might expect some decision on my car!"

"What kind of decision do you want?"

"Like whether my repair costs will be covered!"

"Why would you expect them to be?"

"Because your car wash damaged my car!"

"So."

Now this, James felt sure, was an excellent example of justified anger.

"Did you read the disclaimer before you drove in?" the man interjected.

"Well... yes."

"The red sign printed on the front of the car wash?"

James suddenly sensed he was defeated.

"Yes," he repeated, not wanting to give up.

"Well then, there's your answer."

"But my car was damaged, and I filled out a claim!"

"So? We're not an insurance company. We're not in the business of fulfilling damage claims."

"You shouldn't be in business period, with that attitude."

"Look – I'm just being honest with you. You wouldn't want me to deceive you, would you?"

"No," James had to admit.

"Good. That would be impolite."

Harrigan felt close to swearing. *If you say that one more time...*

"But you shouldn't ask me this anyway," the man continued, "since I'm not the one who decides these things. All that is done at corporate."

"What? Why didn't you say that before?"

"You didn't ask. I was just trying to answer your questions."

Harrigan almost exploded. His ears popped. It hurt. He didn't care.

"Well, when will corporate decide?" James demanded to know.

"Once they get the report. I sent it in this morning. I thought the picture turned out well."

"Thanks."

"If you want to know who to talk to at corporate, call Jeannie Francis Hallivard Johnston Smertz. And jot that down; she likes it when people use her full name. She'll make the decision."

Setting aside his frustration, James asked the name be repeated, scribbled the 1-800 number down, and said a quick goodbye. He'd already talked to whoever that person was longer than he'd ever wanted to. Swallowing hard, he dialed up Smertz. A soothing voice picked up the first ring.

"Hello. This is customer service. How may I help you?"

James issued a long sigh of relief. Finally, a nice person!

"Hello. I'm James Hooligan – No! I'm sorry, that's James *Harrigan*. I'd like to speak to Jeannie Francis Hallivard Johnston Smertz, please."

"Sure. Let me transfer you."

James waited as the phone dialed. On the third round, someone picked it up.

"Hello," came the soothing voice. "This is customer service. How may I help you?"

"You were transferring me to Mrs. Smertz."

"You mean Ms. Smertz?"

James pondered that for a second. "Did you say Ms. Smertz or Miss Smertz?"

"I don't know. Let me transfer you."

With a click, the phone started dialing again. Someone picked it up immediately.

"Hello. This is customer service. How may I help you?"

James switched the phone to his other ear, just to see if doing something that stupid might help resolve this.

"You were switching me to Mrs. Smertz," he said.

"We don't have a Mrs. Smertz. Unless you mean Miss Smertz."

"Oh. I don't know. You said before it might be Ms. Smertz."

"I did?"

"That's what I thought you'd said."

"Oh. Well, I'm sorry, but whoever she is, she's not here right now. Would you like to speak to her voicemail?"

James almost laughed. *Will it talk back to me?* he considered asking. Instead, he gave her a simple "Yes," and when the taped message came on, he asked it to give him a call at her earliest opportunity.

"And Heaven help me," he whispered.

It was now almost 11 a.m. Finally! One hour to endure before reaching lunch and his afternoon off. But James knew he still couldn't relax. In that hour, he could either go over that night's council agenda, so that he wouldn't be surprised by anything, or he could make a few more inquiries on that silly wire story, or he could continue on his search for the anonymous intruder. In his heart, there was no doubt which he'd choose. Even though the police and sheriff departments had proven uncooperative, he still had the counseling centers and churches he could call.

He started to reach for his Yellow Pages once more when his phone rang. To his joy, it was Walton Prescott at Leo Heavy Chevy Geo.

"Congratulations, Mr. Harrigan," he declared with pride. "We've got your car ready for you."

"Ready? Already?"

"Just check in with the cashier and she'll get your keys."

"But you said you'd call me with an estimate before you did any work!"

"I did?" Prescott flipped through some paperwork. "Didn't anybody call you?"

"No!"

"Oh. Well, I'm sorry about that. But your car's ready now."

Something in that didn't sound good. James girded his pocketbook and asked, "How much did it cost?"

"Let's see... a total of $146.87."

An overhead collision of Haley's Comet and a B-2 loaded with 24 thermonuclear warheads wouldn't have broken through Harrigan's falling curtain of melancholy. Ebbing throbs of his sudden deep despair left him with nightmares for years thereafter.

"How much?" he stammered.

"Well, that's $96 for two hours labor and just over $40 for the mirror. You're lucky we had one in stock. Otherwise, we'd have to had one trucked in from Tulsa. Might have cost more."

"Really," Harrigan moaned. "I feel so fortunate."

Behind the Scenes...
Phone runarounds — page 263

"I can tell," Prescott said with a laugh. "Would you like me to have Chester come back out and get you?"

"NO! I mean, no, I don't need a ride, out there, right now. I'll... I'll get one here... somehow."

"Oh. All right then. See you soon!"

"Yes. I'll see you. Soon." But as he hung up, his lips whispered, "When hell freezes over."

As his breath fell about his hands in a cold mist, Harrigan realized that foul time might not be so far away.

Behind the Scenes...
Comparing yesterday and today — page 264

23

The Stage Is Set

Vowing to turn in a third column Friday, James tightened his jacket and took off for his less-important bank, all the while fighting off a dazed emptiness threatening to engulf his heart. In truth, it didn't require much thought to walk to either of his banks, as both were within a short trot of the *Beacon*. He kept a savings account for the taxman's bill at Bean Brothers Bank, which used a three-bean salad as its mascot since there were three Bean brothers. His ATM and checking account James maintained at Sooner National Bank, which used Oklahoma State University's orange and black colors in all its paperwork to overcome animosity Cowboy fans held towards the word *Sooner*.

It was to see the Beans that James headed now. He dreaded having to tap his savings to pay this car bill, yet Harrigan knew he had no choice. Over that loomed the greater dilemma: how would he cover the IRS, his dentist, and whatever emergencies followed with this depleted fund? Would he end up with rotting teeth in debtor's prison?

Behind the Scenes...
Two accounts, two banks — page 265

Would anyone come to visit him?

Would they bring ice cream? came a carrot-spitting voice.

What flavor?

Would they even know he only liked chocolate, although if it had almonds in it, that would be all right?

Or peanuts?

Yes, that would be wonderful!

Would his guards eat it all before James even got a taste?

Stepping into the generous warmth of Bean Brothers' rustic lobby, James decided then and there that he'd talk to the warden, if he ended up in prison, and make sure those guards knew not to touch any ice cream guests brought him. Unless it wasn't chocolate. Or vanilla. Or chocolate chip, for that matter. Indeed, they should eat strawberry, or any sherbet. Although frozen yogurt wouldn't be so bad.

"May I help you, sir?" said a voice piercing his self-inflicted satire.

James glanced up to see a sweet old lady bank teller trying to hide the fact that something hideous repulsed her. She leaned back, straightened the white lace collar on her lavender dress, then tilted her head forward. That move unbalanced the bulbous brunette pouf atop her scalp. Its momentum summoned an embarrassed smile while she breathed through her mouth, her nostrils having clenched to keep her from gagging.

Everyone else in that two-story lobby fled to the side walls. Harrigan studied them but a moment before settling at the teller's window.

"I need to withdraw $150 from my savings," he told the lady, wondering what had set everything off.

She nodded in agony, her honey-scented beehive hairdo

Behind the Scenes...
Scary hair — page 266

---

leaning with malice towards him before arching back in a
near freefall. James feared that towering hulk might
overwhelm her spindle neck and carry her skull to the dark
void behind the bank counter, but somehow the sniffling
teller mastered both inertia and gravity, much less the sway
of that beautician's fortress of solitude.

"Have you filled out a withdrawal slip?" she spat between
her improvisational balancing moves.

"Oh… I'm sorry. I must have forgot."

Too busy worrying about ice cream, James admonished
himself. *But that's better than pink latex fantasies, I guess.*

"Oh, that's all right, son," the teller assured him, though
her eyes sank into an unforgiving squint. "If you could give
me your account number, I'll fill it out for you."

Grateful for her reluctant kindness, wondering all the
while why his phone conversations couldn't have gone this
well, James dug out his wallet.

"You sure you won't steal me blind?" he joked, hoping to
lighten her mood as he revealed his bank card.

From the corner of her wrinkled lips peeked the sly scowl
of a scheming carnivore.

"Why would I need to do that, Mr. Harrigan, when I could
just as easily have our claims department put a lien on your
possessions and strip you of every asset you've ever hoped to
acquire – in perpetuity, no less?"

James pondered if he should laugh at that – and indeed, he
started to – but his mirth dissolved when her chalky face
showed no sign of jest. Humbled before such wit, he folded
up his wallet, realizing she might be one of those old ladies
who didn't cherish satire. Perhaps even a friend of Fat
Mama's.

A strange contentment settled over the woman as she
completed his transaction. Her money drawer opened with a
sigh.

"And if you decide to write me into one of your columns,"
she said while counting out his cash, "be sure to spell my
name correctly: B - A - N - K - T - E - L - L - E - R. And you'd
better not name this financial institution."

With one firm stroke, this balanced bundle jammed his

funds into a Bean Brothers Bank envelope and thrust it towards Harrigan. James folded the packet into his breast pocket and beat a graceful retreat. That was easy, as no one stood anywhere close to him. Indeed, that whole side of the bank seemed deserted.

Only as he stepped free of that hundred-year-old sandstone fortress did James remember he'd nearly liquidated his savings. Any accidents or mistakes now would place him in grave financial danger. But what else could he do? Already he felt the call of his checking account from the modern brick stronghold of Franklin's financial community, its striking edifice looming just across the way. The sooner Harrigan deposited that wad of cash, the better.

At the "Go" sign James stumbled into the four-lane street, dodging some old yellow Dodge pickup intent on running the red. Someone shouted something he couldn't quite hear, but since its legible fragments sounded somewhat vile, James assumed that message was meant for him and thus he ignored it. The sounds rose anew. On the center stripe James twisted about, expecting to find someone sending curses his way. He didn't – until the signal changed. In a flash the five waiting cars roared to life and sped by, even as two trucks and a van crossed the intersection behind him.

James breathed deep of that frigid air. He'd become an island in Fifth Street's sea of traffic.

"The mayor must have pushed the button," he thought aloud.

"Harrigan!" came a distant shout.

Once that initial wave of drivers passed, James found he could pick his way across the street without much trouble. Only when he did so, coming to rest just before the polished oak doors fronting Sooner National Bank's main entrance, did he look again to find whoever shouted at him. James turned, and turned, and turned once more – until he ended up facing those two wide doors that had been his objective all along. Not once did he spy anyone who might desire his attention.

Indecision mounted. James moved towards the corner entryway, then stepped back. Those shouts formed a mental

itch demanding scratching. He scanned the busy corner yet
again amidst his mounting frustration. A curious band of
downtown denizens eyed James from the bench outside
Ruby's Diner, the glass-fronted eatery neighboring his bank.
Not one of those staring eyes looked familiar. Across the
street he watched four people head for Bean Brothers; he
didn't recognize any of them, either. On the far corner stood a
young African American in worn denim, frozen as a statue.

No one showed a bit of interest in him.

"You're getting paranoid," James whispered to himself.
"Hearing things."

In his heart, the broke reporter didn't buy that.

It is wise to be cautious in the face of uncertainty, a flat voice
argued within him. **Consider what you know. Someone breaks
into your home. You receive warnings of suspicious rumors
concerning your wellbeing. An officer of the law suggests the
police chief withheld facts from you – and perhaps about you.**

A sharp breeze swept around him. Shivering, James let
that debate die in the warmth of Sooner National's earth-tone
entryway. After all, he had money to deposit.

With its frontier heritage, Bean Brothers clung to all things
antique. The Beans took pride in their lobby's century-old
brass customer tables, marble teller counters, wood-burning
heat stoves, and bronze oil lamps. Sooner National chose the
opposite approach. Granting the Beans the nostalgia market
dominated by farmers and retirees, the corporate head of
Sooner National – born of a thrift closed eight years earlier –
invested in more "happening" fields like consumer banking,
financial planning, and asset management. The lender
abandoned lobby traditions for an outer ring of glass-lined
offices overlooking a circular walnut-trimmed core manned
by four tellers. Customer traffic wandered the lane between
these structures, guided in part by a ring of stone-topped
benches and service tables starting and ending at the walnut-

---

Behind the Scenes...
Banking heritage — page 268

---

paneled entryway, home to downtown Franklin's only automated teller. For a brief moment Harrigan considered using that machine, which to this date had never spoken a word to him of any kind, but then his paranoia kicked in and James stepped toward the center island, determined to see a living, breathing person.

Without the visions of ice cream to blind him, James witnessed in action the phenomenon that could only be called "The Stench Coat Effect," for with every person in his path, Harrigan observed a look of surprise and astonishment, which in a breath morphed into nausea. Survival instincts soon forced these reek victims to flee his presence before they even realized what they were doing. Thus the lobby's farthest reaches filled with everyone not duty-bound to a desk. Such victims cringed as the stench drew near. All four tellers crossed themselves – and not one was Catholic.

The most unfortunate one – i.e., the youthful teller James chose – brushed her curling auburn hair from her face, took a deep breath, and tried to smile.

"May I help you?" her faint voice wheezed.

"I need to make a deposit," James monotoned. Handing her the folded money envelope, Harrigan reached for a tethered pen and blank bank slip. But as he filled out the appropriate slots, a robotic call straight out of *Lost in Space* warned of danger. James glanced up to see the teller's pearl blue eyes holding one of his $20 bills against a bright desk lamp.

"Is something wrong?" James wondered. "There should be $150 there."

"Just a minute," the teller said. Backing her sharp-suited form to the center of the circular desk, she showed the bill to an older woman James could only guess was her supervisor. With one swift view at that $20, the dark-haired officer nodded.

Behind the Scenes...
The Stench Coat Effect — page 267

Harrigan felt his nose hairs stiffen. That signaled one thing: This is going to be bad.

"What's wrong?" he said, hoping his speaking first would confirm his innocence in whatever scheme they imagined.

The two women turned to face James. All at once the two-story lobby seemed so much smaller.

"Where did you get this?" the supervisor asked.

"Just across the street." James picked up the empty Bean Brothers envelope to prove his point. "I just withdrew this from my savings."

"Uh-huh. So you don't remember where you got it?"

"I just told you!"

"May I see your withdrawal slip?"

James reached for his breast pocket, but it was empty.

"Oh, Lord! Isn't it in the envelope?"

The young lady held the empty packet open for him to see.

"Then she didn't give me one," James whispered.

The ladies shared a dubious look. With a deep breath of resignation, the supervisor asked James to accompany her.

"Why?" Harrigan blurted out. "What's wrong?"

"This bill's counterfeit," the young lady answered.

"Counterfeit?"

James couldn't believe it. A bank had given him a counterfeit bill? His bank?

I've passed a counterfeit bill?

Behind the Scenes...
I've passed a counterfeit bill? — page 268

By Kirby Lee Davis

24

What Next?

Trapped within a constricting fog of despair, James allowed himself to be led into one of the glass cubicles. Seated at a small oak table before the two tellers – and an unidentified balding man in the far corner, standing like a statue in an unwrinkled black suit – James autographed a statement for the Federal Reserve that admitted he'd passed a counterfeit bill. The tellers asked once more how he'd received the bill. Under their unforgiving stares James recounted the whole wretched tale of his damaged mirror on the *Defiant*, the high repair bill, and his depleted savings, right up to his imprisonment in their transparent cell.

It was difficult, revealing such things. All those events weighed so heavy on his soul, magnified many times over by the threat of the break-in and ever-present heartache of divorce – but those tales Harrigan kept to himself.

A respectful moment of silence followed his story's corrupted end. With care reserved for the most delicate of operations, the young woman lifted the counterfeit bill by one corner and slipped it into a wax paper envelope. Then she handed James a deposit slip totaling $130.

"I'm sorry, but we cannot credit you for the phony bill," she said. "Do you understand?"

Numb from the whole experience, James could only nod.

He didn't blame these ladies. This was his fault as much as anyone else's. He'd never examined the money that Bean Brothers teller gave him. He hadn't even bothered to count it.

Only then did their shadowy observer come to life. Stepping to the table, he leaned his left arm against the polished oak top and focused his trained gaze on Harrigan's forehead. James couldn't see a bit of color in those black eyes.

"Are you sure you don't know how you got it?" the man grumbled.

Harrigan felt his heart could burst at any moment. "I've already told you this how many times? Why don't you believe me?"

The man didn't move, didn't blink. His penetrating stare never relented.

James was dumbfounded.

"I know this sounds strange," he allowed. "I understand that. If I could tell you some other answer, I would. But I can't. It feels like my whole life's collapsing right now, but I'm stuck with this. It happened! This, this whole thing… it can't be that uncommon!"

The two women smiled in their confidence. James felt trapped between them.

"Then tell me," he demanded. "Just how rare is this?"

"Very," the supervising teller assured him.

"We're trained to spot them," interjected the younger lady.

"All bank tellers undergo training to learn about the distinctive feel of U.S. currency, the colors," said the supervisor. "They get very good at accessing what a bill should weigh, how it should feel."

"I'm not surprised," James said. "But I know one teller that didn't spot it – and she gave it to me!"

"So you say," the man replied.

"That's how it happened! Go ask her! She's right across the street!"

The man stepped back, a cynical smile brightening his lips. "Very well. You may leave. But be aware the Secret Service will be calling you."

"The Secret Service? The guys who protect the president?"

The man nodded. "They investigate these things."

"But why me?"

"You have just committed a federal offense. This will go down in your file."

James almost choked. My file? *I have a file at the Secret Service?*

"But it wasn't my fault!"

"So you say," the man grumbled, though the two women looked more sympathetic.

"I'm sorry," one whispered.

James barely heard her.

"This is so crazy," he said to no one in particular. "All I wanted to do was wash my car – and now Big Brother's going to watch over me for the rest of my life? Do I deserve that?"

25

It's Not Over, Son

Stepping back into the free world, Harrigan felt like a marked man. There on the sunny sidewalk he whispered a prayer for guidance and protection, but at its end, he sensed only the cold winter winds.

"Why me, Lord?" he moaned.

A sky-blue Mercury Sable honked as it drove past. James heard its welcome and recalled discussing the car wash disclaimer with his daughters. The memory mocked him. Why, oh why had he not heeded those quiet whisperings? None of this would have happened!

"Tough, isn't it?" came a hard voice.

James didn't bother to answer. He didn't wish to talk to anyone right now. He just wanted to crawl into a hole and die.

"I can see it in your face," spoke the interloper. "Life's turned on 'ya."

In desperation, James reached for that side of him able to laugh in the midst of adversity, but even his vain, cavalier self remained silent. There was no escape.

"What am I going to do?" he whispered.

"You think livin' good's the answer," continued the voice. "That's what we're told, ain't it? His road's easy, His burden's light... isn't that just what The Good Book says? But it's a crock, man. Being God's man just makes it worse."

Frustrated beyond his endurance, James slammed his fist into the crossing signal button. Pain flared from the impact, but that searing blast made little headway against his aurora of fateful dejection. Then he heard a faint call. The quiet song held both a melody and a purpose. Within them he sensed hope. Its notes took shape, finding unity in harmony. From its depths awakened a pulsing light.

"I've tried it all, man," the interloper went on, oblivious to the music. "Dope, sex. Booze. Nearly popped a man once. Got locked up more times than I can count – and I wasn't even 16. Then I found Christ, you know? And I thought, 'Wow! Maybe Ma's right!' There's truth there, to be sure. But people – especially Christians, those hypocrite Christians! – man, they don't let you forget, you know? And they don't let go."

The light coalesced with other forms, other colors, mixing into the world about him. James saw it in that busy traffic, the "Don't Walk" sign, the afternoon sun.

Like a man rising from deep sleep to instant peril, so did James emerge from his despair. He heard yet another call…

Awake! The enemy's at the gates!

Pulling his coat tight, James listened.

"Ain't nothin' you can do about it, neither," the outsider rambled on. "Hang low, and they'll find you. Button up, and they'll pry you out, or shoot you up. No, man, there ain't but one way out. One way. And it ain't no upraised finger, either. You think about that."

Something about that voice seemed familiar. James almost recognized it, or felt he did, although he couldn't quite place anything there.

The way the man said "Ma." Where had he heard that before?

The "Walk" sign flashed on. Harrigan pivoted instead.

Behind the Scenes…
Being God's man — page 269
One way — page 271

Walking towards the diner, hardly five steps ahead of him, passed a tall black youth bound in ragged denim, his hands stuffed in the shallow pockets of his thin Levi's jacket. His black hair was trimmed so short, his dark scalp showed through.

James shivered within the cold winds, pondering how that tall, skinny kid stayed warm – and where James had seen him before.

"Hey!" he shouted.

The lad twisted about for only a second as he strode towards the diner. Still, that proved all Harrigan needed. Even without the orange and green smock, he remembered the cashier fired at the Easy Come, Easy Go.

"Wait!" James called. "I want to talk to you!"

The youth broke into a run.

"James! James Harrigan!"

Few things irritated the reporter more than being sidetracked. Every voice in his head urged James to pursue the kid, but one – the part that would recognize Sandy Travis's speech even if it were filtered through a Halloween sound processor. The warmth he felt for her was enough to hold him in place, at the corner, until she reached his side – which took but a wink or two. A daily jogger, she bounded up unencumbered by her long overcoat. Her light brown hair flowed like a pendant in her wake.

Harrigan took a deep breath. The kid was long gone.

"Imagine running into you here!" Sandy said, giving James a hug.

"It's not too hard to picture," he replied, "since you just did it."

He returned her embrace, comforted by her glow, but then he scolded himself for his selfishness and stepped back. She didn't seem to notice.

"I stopped by the paper, but they'd said you'd already gone. Just lucky I drove by and saw you!"

"Isn't it?" James allowed, hoping beyond hope that the kid might appear again, somewhere beyond the diner. But it didn't happen.

Travis switched from playful enthusiasm to bridled

concern. "Is something wrong?"

James looked deep into her harvest gold eyes, always so warm and open. It was ever risky, exposing himself to such beautiful honesty, in all its many forms, and yet he loved taking the chance.

But this wasn't the time for such thoughts – if there ever was one. For he'd had the kid in his sights, then let him go. An important piece of the puzzle... gone.

"Yeah," he whispered. "A whole lot of things."

This drew Sandy's complete attention. "Like what?"

"Well, it's a long story. A long story." He took a deep breath, considered his options, then gave in and asked, "Could you give me a ride to Leo Heavy Chevy Geo? I need to pick up my car."

"OK," she agreed, pointing the way to her Mercury Sable. "But you've got to start talking, buster!"

"No problem – though before we're done, you might wish you hadn't asked. You see, I'm a criminal now."

26

The Paradox

The short drive to Heavy Chevy should've been quite easy, but it wasn't – at least for James.

With their doors unlocked by remote, he slid into the passenger seat before Sandy got behind the wheel. Closing the door, she stiffened, took a deep breath, and started a frantic search about the floorboard.

"What's wrong?" James pondered before distraction struck. He couldn't help noticing her coat parted, revealing a fabulous pair of legs stretching from a shiny set of running shorts to her well-worn sneakers. The sight verified one truth: if Coke could manufacture a bottle that shapely, Pepsi would be out of business.

Embarrassed he'd thought such a thing, James turned away – even though part of him considered such concerns quite silly. It wasn't like he hadn't seen those legs before. Despite being the mother of two teenage boys, she'd managed to build upon her beauty by keeping in near-decathlon shape. James had experienced that firsthand, when

---

Behind the Scenes…
Coke bottle legs — page 272

---

one brisk morning he'd tried jogging with Sandy and her husband Jack, only to drop to the ground before the first mile ended.

"This is just who she is," he said, thinking aloud.

Most days, Sandy's usual attire was T-shirts and shorts. It fit her casual lifestyle, one known to seize a chance to run or join a soccer match at an opportune whim. And no matter how hard she worked or played, her eyes ever sparkled with Christ's vibrant love, and her long brown hair ever flowed about her sprightly form with all the flair of the Breck Girls of old.

Even now, as she was wrapped up by concern for something else.

Trying to keep his gaze away from her, James turned towards the back seat as if he had joined the search.

"Looking for anything in particular?" he asked over his shoulder.

Sandy straightened. "Don't you smell it?"

That drew a slow moan from James's heart. Sandy didn't notice.

"It smells like something died in here!" she exclaimed. "I don't get it. That wasn't here before!"

"I know what it is," Harrigan admitted. Stepping out, he removed his jacket, rolled it into a fabric log, and hurled that cylinder against the Sooner National Bank's back wall. Girding his shivers, James then returned to her sky-blue Sable.

Sandy watched him in disbelief. "That was stupid," she scolded him.

James laughed. Throughout the divorce, Sandy had been his closest confidante, his adviser and friend. He loved her as a sister... perhaps even more. And yet he feared her, or rather, he feared himself.

"Take a whiff," he urged, repeating that when she

Behind the Scenes...
Breck Girls — page 274

hesitated. So she took a deep breath – and marveled at the astonishing change.

"Well," she said through a smile, "it may stink, but you need that jacket."

"Not that one. I've had enough of it."

"Maybe so, but it can be cleaned, you know?" Stretching her car door open, Sandy retrieved the coat before that door could close behind her. Throwing the dank roll into the trunk, Sandy hurried back behind the wheel, started the engine, and cranked up the heater.

"You didn't have to do that," James couldn't help saying.

"Oh, like I want you to catch a cold!"

"I wouldn't catch a cold."

"You would, exposing yourself like that."

"Exposing myself? Look who's talking!"

Puzzled, Sandy glanced down at her bare legs. "So?"

James couldn't help noticing her overcoat had fallen open clear to her neckline, revealing a simple athletic T-shirt.

"Should have known," he said, risking one more glance at her shifting thighs before turning away. "Let me guess: an indoor soccer game."

"No, basketball," Sandy answered as if surprised he would ask. Then she saw his fleeting eyes and broke into a stifled laugh. "Really? I'm embarrassing you?"

James stared out the window. "No… of course not! I just think it's a little hypocritical, you worrying about me getting overexposed when you go around practically naked under your winter coat."

"Practically naked? This?"

"It is February!"

"Oh, pah! You should see me swimming!"

"I don't want to."

On that James was adamant. *Never. Never ever.*

Sandy enjoyed his modesty. "Ha! Admit it! You are embarrassed!"

James realized he was squirming and tried to stop. But he couldn't look long her way, either – not with Sandy focusing on him so.

It was such a terrible paradox. Throughout his life, he'd

always had more female friends than male, since so few men seemed to read these days, and he'd never been much on hunting, boating, or most other outdoor sports. While he was married, such relationships worked. But now, with his status twisted to divorced and single, all those ties seemed so... electric. For loneliness did strange things, changing the essence of incidental contact and familiarity, all while making him long for companionship. Now James found it difficult to be near most any women he found attractive – which impacted about all members of the female species. The slightest innuendo could conjure up temptations he wasn't used to dealing with.

Among his longtime friends, this was agony.

"Or is it me?" Sandy asked in a mock pout. "Do I look that bad?"

James had to meet her gaze now, if only to see the playful light in her eyes.

"Of course not!" he exclaimed.

"You don't like looking at my legs, then? Or do you just not like legs in general?"

"You know better than that. Now you're teasing me."

"I know. And I know you're too chivalrous to even imagine anything. But tell me the truth, James – since I think you really are embarrassed, aren't you. I don't want to make someone sin. Do you find this suit too suggestive? Too revealing?"

"No," James had to admit. "You're dressed modestly for what you're doing, though I bet it gives Jack fits. I just don't know how you can go around like that in the winter."

"Well, I'd already phoned you that I'd stop by when I realized what time my game started. I didn't think I'd have time to change."

"Makes sense. And you're in the car, so it's not like you're strutting down the street or something."

Behind the Scenes...
The terrible paradox — page 274

"Strutting down the street! Sometimes your sense of shock –"

"Well, come on, Sandy! It's not your fault you're a beautiful woman – or that people take one look at you and wish..."

"What? That you could sleep with me?"

James hesitated. "You shock pretty well yourself."

If anyone else had suggested that, James might have run away. But he'd shared everything about the divorce with Sandy. Such subjects were not new between them.

"No," he said. "Divorce tempts you with far greater sins than lust."

Sandy leaned against the steering wheel, her eyes sparkling as she considered this, ever pleased to match him at intellectual word play. "Name one."

"That's easy. Envy."

"You envy my legs?"

He chuckled, but chose a more honest answer. "I envy the man who can claim you for his own. I envy Jack for winning your heart. I envy you, for you've found the love of your life. Mine… mine turned out to be a mirage."

Sandy fell back into her crushed velvet seat.

"I think Charlotte loved you," she pondered aloud. "At first, anyway."

"So did I. But after what she's told me, after what she's done.... You know, I wonder now if I'll ever know what real love is. I lie awake sometimes afraid, really afraid, that I'll die having never shared the kind of bonding you and Jack have."

Sandy bowed her head. Her long hair fell like a curtain around her face, hiding away her clenched eyes. James heard her whisper, "Lord, speak through me!" as her hands pulled that loose overcoat over her knees.

"Don't think that Jack and I don't have our problems," she whispered.

"I know. Everyone goes through hardships of some kind. Nobody's perfect."

Though you're about as close as they come.

For to James, Sandy Travis remained just about the perfect example of the Good Samaritan.

By Kirby Lee Davis

They'd known each other since Harrigan had first brought his young family to Franklin, becoming fast friends at the First Baptist Church. By fate or God's hand, the Harrigans bought a house within two blocks of the Travis home, so their families played together often. And when Charlotte would go to visit her parents, Sandy brought meals to his door. She'd babysat his girls, and let James borrow a car when his battery had died. When he unwittingly shared his curiosity about jogging, she'd volunteered to join him – at 5 in the morning. When a neighboring house burned down, she ran through a pouring rain – without a jacket or umbrella – to make sure everyone in the Harrigan household was all right.

She'd sacrificed for him – again and again and again. Just as she was doing now.

"James, you know that God understands these needs we have? It doesn't diminish our love for Him – not if it's honest and true to our faith. This was His plan, James! He created us with this drive to take a mate to love and cherish. It's not bad."

"I know it's not bad." *Though Charlotte...*

"Then why do you have such a problem with it?"

"I never said I had a problem! It's just that, well, you know what the Bible says about divorce."

Sandy nodded.

"I've already had my shot at marriage, if you know what I mean, and I blew it," Harrigan mumbled. "Doesn't that mean –"

"No," she declared. "You didn't ask for the divorce. You didn't desire it. And correct me if I'm wrong here, but you only granted it because that's what she wanted."

"Well, I didn't think I could try to hold her to –"

"– A vow she couldn't keep," Sandy interrupted. "Right; we've been through that. And you're right: God doesn't want

Behind the Scenes...
The Good Samaritan — page 273
One shot at marriage? — page 275

marriages to end in divorce. But He doesn't want us to be alone, either. That's why He created Eve! So that Adam, even in God's presence, in the perfection of the Garden, wouldn't be lonely. Just like you are now."

James rocked backward. He hadn't quite considered it that way.

"God understands loneliness, James. Remember what Christ yelled on the cross? 'My God, my God, why hast Thou forsaken me?' Haven't you pondered that same thing?"

Harrigan held vivid memories of such thoughts. His last year seemed filled with them.

Sandy stretched a warm arm across his shoulder, gently scratching his back. James almost swooned.

"It's hard to imagine being lonely when you're the Son of God, and yet Christ surrounded Himself with the disciples and took them just about everywhere. Remember, He even wanted them around when He was praying His heart out in the garden! And on that, you know, it's remarkable to imagine anyone being lonely in God's presence at Eden, yet the Bible says Adam was, and God understood. He *understood*, James! So, don't you think He would understand you, too?"

Harrigan had to look away. His eyes grew annoyingly wet.

"I suppose so," he whispered.

"There's no supposing about it!" With a light laugh, Sandy made some comment on the time and pulled away from the curb. Accelerating for the highway and Leo Heavy Chevy Geo, she couldn't help saying, "I think you've handled things pretty well up till now."

James wiped his eyes on his sleeves. "I don't know. It doesn't feel like that to me."

"It never does."

"Now you're sounding like Charlotte."

"Well, she was right about some things. Like that."

"What?"

"How hard you are on yourself, for one."

James started to smile, then cut it off. He didn't want anyone to see them driving around like that, having what some might see as a good time during working hours – or any other time, for that matter. He didn't want to start any rumors.

A huge, silly grin flashed across Sandy's face. "Oh – I forgot your book. Sorry! I'll bring it back tomorrow."

"It's no problem. It'll give you another chance to uncover more holes."

"Good. Now let's get to something important. Just what law did you break?"

27

j-col32.wpd

SUGGESTED HEAD: A Midcouncil Night's Dream

I must admit to a tremendous error… one I hope will not crush your faith in me.

You see, I fell asleep during a city council meeting.

It was the marathon executive session of January – the one that ended in February. The council stepped into the clerk's office with five items on its agenda. The door closed, beginning the test of wills.

Now you must understand this fact. When you're sitting in that tiny casket of a press box, all alone but for the spiders and lice, looking for things to do becomes an obsession. Some of the time you can kill with the battle of thumbs, especially if one or both combatants have earned a brown or black belt. But as it goes, my car has three black belts, my thumbs none. So they wrestled, and my left one was pinned twice. Knocking over two trash cans in its anger, it then spat garbage to whatever was laying around the desktop until the wooden rim hanging across the table got sick of it all and gave it a good paddling. Meanwhile, my right thumb was pinned by a wisp of cigar smoke, which of course thrives in the Franklin Council Chambers.

Somewhere along the line that night, my defenses broke.

As the meeting dragged on and on, the great test of stamina overcame my will.

I can imagine what the council members were saying... "Is he dead?"

In a grisly transformation from human to troll, one's envious tongue licked its lips over its lower fangs, six-inch incisors able to crunch the thickest bones in a single bound.

"Let's cook 'em in a stew 'n finds out," the somewhat female voice croaked in hideous laughter.

The council members grumbled and groaned as they rose from their shredded chairs, revealing themselves as scab-encrusted goblins. Then came the central titan. He stood as a robust carving of primeval man, head and shoulders above them all, holding aloft in his fur-covered arms a rustic iron hammer capable of pummeling mountains. The Nordic godling cracked his massive mallet against the table with thunderous fury. Accented by a terse growl, his eyes crisscrossed the hazy arena from beneath the curled ivory horns of his bronze helmet. The chamber grew silent.

"Unhand the lout, ye maties. Abast, I say! He's but ink ribbon and calcium – mere words. More devilish evil canst we pass on his head than a skewer!"

"We can?" the members wondered, their minds aghast that such things could be accomplished during my slumber. "Tell us!"

The bearded Viking snorted. "What, pray tell, is his position here?"

A disfigured man hobbled forward, his muddy hair falling in lumps against his tattered cloak, his left shoulder bent so low that his wrist drug through the grime and dust on the molding ground. Rambling to the table, he tapped against the microphone, then spat, "To guard the public against the council menace!"

The storm deity bellowed laughter. "Exactly!" He leaned forward in all his power, the long bristles of his black beard scraping clean the podium varnish. "So let us defy his high calling! As he sleeps, let us pass a plague upon the peasants – a most high water rate, new sewer system bonds, computer console acquisitions, personnel cuts...." His eyes flaring as

wide as the mouths gaping around him, the titan's voice rose
to a high crescendo matching the lightning of his hammer.
"Let our city break even financially!"

The audience roared its approval.

"I still says we should stew 'em," said a disgruntled
council goblin. "K-bobs with his own pen. You know, K-
bobs? I make joke, I do!"

The Asgardian prince squared his fur-bound shoulders
toward the man-sized rodent, his eyes blazing with fury.
With long breaths the godling pondered how to handle the
dissident – whether to fry her with the electric wrath of his
storm, pound her into orc chow with that imposing mallet, or
whisk her away to the cornfield. His lips rumbled, and
everyone cringed.

"Perhaps ye's right," he decided.

With a whirl of his hammer, the storm god flew to the
press table. His hands twisted around my neck.

I stirred.

Awkward feet started scurrying about.

"Hurry – back to your normal voices!" I heard a man
whisper.

"But what of our clothes? Our human bodies?"

"There's no time!"

"But he'll notice we're different! What then?"

"Why – then we'll skewer him like the scoundrel deserves,
ye maties!"

"No! You must remember to talk normally! We're elected
councilmen."

Thus I awoke, found my pen lodged in my cheek, pulled it
out, and resumed taking notes. Things seemed to advance
from there as if nothing unusual had happened. Strange, but
true.

Behind the Scenes...
j-col32.wpd — page 277

By Kirby Lee Davis

28

Motivation

With a deep, steadying breath, James rushed out the doors of Leo Heavy Chevy Geo. At once winter's welcome settled around him like an icy blanket, but he hardly noticed, having already frozen inside when he'd watched that $140-plus check slide into Leo's cashier drawer. With it disappeared all the money he had built up to finally get a television or stereo, to pay his taxes or fix his teeth... money he needed to get ahead. All because of a stupid decision at a car wash.

For a brief moment, James looked with earnest upon the sunny afternoon, but he felt no warmth there, seeing only the anguish of a cloudy horizon beyond. Despair burned within him – born of the divorce, ignited by a spark of suds and spray, inflamed by the break-in, fed by the banks. And though Sandy had attempted to douse that wildfire with a deluge of spiritual common sense, seeing that check change hands knocked into oblivion the words she'd urged him to follow. Sorrow raged within him, a force unto itself – yet it bubbled and churned in restless abandon, cold and shapeless, without purpose.

Thus came the next step in his guiding destiny.

Gazing into the vast depths of the Oklahoma prairie, only one thing gave James hope. Luckily – or so he optimistically assumed – his Metro sat parked just outside the entrance.

With it, and his free afternoon, perhaps he might escape this mess, for a while at least. Extending his shaking hand into his pocket, he withdrew his keys and froze.

In a hole in the wall, there stood the hobbit. Not a dry, sandy hole, but one of red Oklahoma brick outfitted for a double-bolt security door. It would have provided comfort to the portly furball if the hobbit had kept something close to a welcome disposition. As it was, the overgrown mass in fake motorcycle garb drew no pleasure from the shade granted him. Spying James, he waddled into the afternoon sunshine with an air of consternation usually reserved for taking overly ripe hamburger to the dumpster.

Out of politeness, James drew his arms tight around him, enduring the cold to greet the hobbit. He'd soon wished he hadn't.

"So… couldn't bear to let me pick you up, huh?" that squeaky voice accosted him. The defiant one parked his feet less than two feet from the Metro's front bumper. "I'm not good enough for you?"

"I never said that!" James snapped.

"You just as much did, telling them you didn't want me to come get you! Have you ever wondered how that makes me look?"

"Well, like someone who's available to pick up someone else."

"Oh, no! That's not how it works! More like Jimmy Stewart, when he's got that guy by the throat in *Winchester '73.*"

In the blink of an eye, a mad fever gripped that pudgy hobbit face, twisting it into a rabid grimace of anguish Lon Chaney would've been hard-pressed to match. It soon passed, returning to the quirky, aimless serenity the hobbit had cast before – and yet James couldn't get the vile hunger

---

Behind the Scenes…
Paying homage — page 278
Famous faces — page 278

---

of that stare out of his mind.

"When a customer turns down a return ride, it's a reject!" the hobbit told James. "You're one of them, so you just might not understand. But that's how it goes down."

Harrigan hesitated. A nervous fascination held him in place, yet urged him to flee.

"Well," he meandered, "I don't know if that's fair."

"You bet your donuts it's not fair! I bust a gut getting Ole' Bertha ready for business – and that's not easy, you know?"

"I should think not."

The hobbit reared. "What's that supposed to mean?"

"Well...." James fidgeted, not wanting to tell what he really thought about that filthy car. "It's just that... she's old."

"Now you sound like them."

"Who?"

"Them! They're all against me!"

Not understanding, yet afraid to admit it, James spread his palms wide to the cosmos. The hobbit didn't miss a beat.

"Don't you think I'd tweak her a little more if I could? I mean, you can only do so much on taxi fares. But they don't care about that. They'd really rather have their own employees ferrying people around in their own cars. Another chance to show new models off – all clean and perky and that! Ha! It's a conspiracy, I tell you!"

James felt left far, far behind. "How?"

"Oh, don't tell me that! Don't you get it?"

"Get what?"

"Why, they're trying to get me to buy a car, man! They're trying to get you to buy a car! They're trying to get everyone to buy a car!"

The hobbit flared his eyes to James as if he'd just revealed the secrets of God Himself, but the reporter still didn't understand. The hobbit sighed.

"Well? Don't you see what that means?"

"No," James admitted.

"Augh! Wake up, man! You're deep in it! It's a racket – a conspiracy, I tell you! That's what it is – a conspiracy!"

Harrigan took a step back. His hand slipped against his car door handle. He yanked it open, feeling a strange need to put something between him and the beefy man-thing.

"You mean, this auto dealership… that they're actually trying to... well, sell autos?"

The hobbit nearly jumped out of his furry feet. "Yes! But that's only the beginning."

"The beginning," James muttered. "Oh, I see. You're right. It's diabolical."

"Yes!"

"They not only sell you the cars, but they repair them, too."

"Yes!"

"And the cars – they look nice, and drive well, but the way they're made, sooner or later they break down. And they're made so that only the dealerships can fix them."

"Yes!"

"And they bleed you dry doing it!"

"YES!"

James found himself enjoying this tirade. He couldn't help wondering why, except that the hobbit made such an enthusiastic audience, Harrigan felt he could do no wrong.

Or was there something more to it?

"And even then," he continued, whipping his voice into a delightful frenzy, "they'll only drive for so long until they break down again – and thus the whole cycle starts over, breaking and repairing and replacing – until you have to buy a new car!"

The hobbit's eyes came alive. "You do understand!"

Harrigan nodded. "And it never stops! All your life you'll be in their clutches, making car payments, then repair payments, then car and repair payments…."

My Lord, James realized, *there's a whole lot of truth to this!*

In triumph, the hobbit folded his arms across his rotund chest. His vinyl sleeves crackled.

"Now, if I were a vampire, I'd know how to take care of these ghouls," he stated. "But I think I know the next best thing."

James took a deep breath. His head was starting to ache. "What's that?"

"Why, keep Ole' Bertha runnin'!" the hobbit beamed. "It's

expensive, but as long as I can fulfill my taxi contract, they can't fire me. So, if I keep repairing her, I'm doin' fine – as long as more people don't cancel out on me, like you!"

"I didn't mean for it to look like that," James interjected, though he felt dishonest saying it.

"Oh, I can tell you didn't," the hobbit said. "But it gets expensive, though, fighting the battle. You wouldn't have a couple hundred I could borrow, would you?"

Harrigan shook his head. That question required no thought at all.

The hobbit sighed with shared sorrow. "Oh, I forgot. They've already got your money, don't they? You're hooked."

29

It All Fits

You're hooked.

The words tripped back and forth through his thoughts, masking the gusts of wind buffeting the *Defiant*, the grinding echoes of his tires on the pitted road, even the melodic logic of Arends.

"Paranoia," James thought aloud. "He's got it bad."

Yet Harrigan couldn't let it rest. Something within his heart clung to the hobbit's fears – and with good reason, for James shared these concerns. He felt trapped by a world shrinking about him, constricting him.

And why not? Harrigan couldn't help wondering. *Hasn't rotten luck dogged my every step?*

Luck wasn't a concept James usually took to, and yet here, it fit. In less than 24 hours, he'd managed to nearly destroy his life.

Yes, it was bad luck. Extremely bad luck. On the level of Job.

Or was it?

"I'm a target," he realized.

Half the town must be spying on him, or so he guessed from the diner rumors and Fat Mama Brown's foul omen. Wasn't that what the police chief had warned – that he'd be watched from now on?

And now his name was being reported to the Secret Service.

James sucked in a deep breath. This was almost unreal.

Imagine – now he shared something with all the kooks who'd ever threatened the president's life. James Harrigan – the target of a federal investigation!

And perhaps a hit man, he realized, recalling the chalk marks.

Was that possible? Stupid question! He'd felt the gun in his back! That had been real!

His skin chilled. That guy was still out there. Probably looking for him.

"I'm being hunted," Harrigan whispered. *Just like Deanna Troi.* "But why me?"

You're hooked.

A police car sped by as James headed the *Defiant* back into Franklin. Harrigan almost swore. What was that cop doing patrolling the streets when someone was trying to kill him?

But the police wouldn't help him, would they? Noooooo… Jacobs had made that clear.

Harrigan wiped his forehead. What had Haskins suggested – that James had offended someone? The thought almost made him laugh. It could be anyone, Reynolds would argue – starting with Charlotte.

That pierced Harrigan to his soul.

As much as James wished he could put the divorce behind him, he doubted that would ever work. At least, not until his girls were grown up and on their own… if even then.

But that was a matter of pain, between Charlotte and himself. It was separate from this, right? It had to be.

"No question," James stated, slowing as he came into downtown. This went far beyond the divorce. It was almost as if someone was assaulting him, in the most insidious ways possible. Undermining his work with his boss, his time with

---

Behind the Scenes…
Pursuing counterfeiters — page 279

155

his girls, his very ability to survive… to believe in himself.

Like Job.

But that was ridiculous, wasn't it?

Sandy had told him so. "Trust God," suggested this friend whose presence taunted him – by his own weakness, not hers.

"And what does that indicate?" James asked the windshield. "I'm a sinner."

But who isn't? came a clear voice. *All she said was to give this problem to Christ. What better advice could you follow?*

Tis a shallow, short-sighted answer, claimed a frequent counter. *James must still live this life on his own. He is responsible for it.*

If he did as she urged, what could go wrong?

James grimaced at the answers that swarmed his head. The break-in, for one. The runaround at Leo Heavy Chevy Geo. The stories being spread, and strangers telling him to beware. The gasoline distributor that refused to help him. The counterfeit bill. The harassment by the police, by Fat Mama – though James felt sure Fat Mama didn't actually know who she was; by that he meant, he felt sure Underwood didn't realize she was Fat Mama.

You're hooked.

"I'm caught up in it all," Harrigan whispered, heading into downtown with little but his eyes on the road. "Just like a conspiracy."

That was the word the hobbit used, time and time again. James had considered it simple paranoia, just like the jargon from those four right-wing farmers at Leo Heavy. But what if, just perhaps, there was something to their fears? What if James had indeed stumbled into something… something big?

It didn't make sense… and yet, why else would someone want to kill him?

That's overstating it, James knew – but not by much.

What if the car wash had been set up to damage his car? After all, several other vehicles – all larger than his – passed through that device just before the *Defiant* entered it, and they'd not been hurt. And it was computer-operated, so someone could, conceivably, program it to come in tight for that one wash, just to damage his vehicle.

But why?

Perhaps the Easy Come characters purposely tried to confuse him, to slow him down. Perhaps the dealership intentionally gave him a runaround, just to keep him off-track.

But why?

Perhaps even the police were sabotaging him! Undercutting his reporting, accusing him of lies!

James had to slam on the brakes for an almost-missed red light. His distracted driving had made the signal but a blip in his thoughts.

"Wait a minute." What was it Jacobs had said about investigating the council?

James had needled the panel's members for months in his column. Could one of them be setting him up?

Perhaps the counterfeit bill had been planted on him to destroy his credibility... to get him fired!

That was possible, wasn't it? Wouldn't a councilman count the bankers among his intimates?

The light flashed green. Through pattern driving he turned left, finding himself back at the *Beaver Beacon*. Realizing that hit him like a splash of freezing water.

"This is crazy," he mumbled. "I'm not thinking clearly... I'm getting tired."

There was truth in that. Like looking through a Coke bottle, he realized weariness mutated all his perceptions.

Still, such logic seemed a half-hearted attempt to dismiss the extremist views, with all the cloak-and-dagger theories reverberating through his head.

As he parked, James couldn't help staring long and hard at all the other vehicles settled around him. He half-expected to find a dark-windowed Suburban sitting nearby, full of Secret Service workers armed with binoculars and shotguns.

You're hooked.

Behind the Scenes...
"You're hooked" — page 279

"Conspiracy," he spat. "How? What's the connection?"

A trio of grade school youth ran past the *Beacon*, laughing all the while. James watched them in a state of amazement, as if he'd never seen anyone run before. Then he rushed into his office.

30

No Luck

"What's so wrong with castration?" he heard Reynolds bellow.

James didn't bother looking to discover who his editor was talking to, or if anyone else was around. Gathering his afternoon mail off the seat of his cold, ragged chair, Harrigan hit the phones. His objective: to find the fired cashier.

He started with the Easy Go, just to see if anyone there would help him. When that effort failed, as he'd expected, he tried to describe the kid to Franklin High's counselors and all the area churches, youth centers, and counseling agencies he could think of.

Not one person seemed capable of linking any living person to the best portrait James could offer of the lad.

After fourteen calls, taking up more than ninety-eight minutes – not counting two brief interruptions and a break to swallow some aspirin for a growing headache – Harrigan's lunch-starved stomach started growling for attention. Yet his heart pressed him to continue, to track down some school yearbooks, church membership rosters, whatever was necessary to identify the lad. For James knew that disgruntled youth was the key to everything.

Through it all, Harrigan felt a deep weariness pervading his every thought. The last twenty-four hours were catching up with him. Slowing his reactions, numbing his alertness.

Impairing my judgment, he realized.

"So," proclaimed Reynolds, coming around his office corner. "What's so important that you'd work through your afternoon off?"

James laid the phone back in its cradle. He'd expected this interruption would come, sooner or later.

"I had some ideas on finding the kid," he said.

"What kid?"

"The one that tried to rob me."

"You're sure it's a kid?"

Something in Reynolds' tone bothered James.

"Look – I may not have seen him, but I heard him. I'm not stupid."

"Uh-huh."

The editor settled himself against a filing cabinet. His eyes had all the affection of someone chasing spiders with a can of Raid.

With that thought, James recalled he had yet to empty his kitchen and bathrooms. The very idea frustrated him.

"Let me ask you something," interjected Reynolds. "Did you read my editorial on that Texas rapist?"

James nodded. Reynolds had a habit of chatting whenever he wasn't on deadline. Usually James just leaned back and endured it, since few things were so pressing he couldn't burn some time here or there. But now....

"You think I was too hard?" his boss asked.

James took a deep, steadying breath, then shrugged. His eyes fell upon the stack of mail he still hadn't touched. By impulse he grabbed the top piece, a long envelope with the red and blue state seal, and ripped it open – thinking the move might discourage Reynolds and get him to leave.

It didn't.

Behind the Scenes...
A global killer — page 282
Castration — page 280

Rats!

The letter contained advance notice of a radio address planned by the governor, along with its complete text. Unfortunately, this announcement arrived two weeks after the broadcast date.

"Truly vital information," James mumbled, tossing the letter away. Then he dared lift his eyes.

Reynolds still hadn't moved.

"Rats," Harrigan whispered.

Girding his soul, James decided to tackle the bull by its horns. He took another deep breath, looked Reynolds straight in the eye, and said, "You were foolish."

His publisher stiffened. His brow ruffled.

"People like him are responsible for their actions, not biologically driven," Harrigan continued. "Do you truly think that fruitcake's sex glands drove him to hurt people?"

"Yes," Dick answered, ever stubborn, with just a touch of resentment.

"No way! Some people just desire to dominate, to inflict pain – that's what tempted him. Like Leopold and Loeb. And that urge is still there, whether he's castrated or not. He can hurt people in other ways... even worse ways."

"You don't think a chemical imbalance can influence behavior?"

"Of course it can! But does it cause all such behavior – with rational people?"

"Yes!"

"No."

"Of course it does!"

"No, it doesn't."

"James, there are millions of insane people out there who need drugs just to function."

"The term's 'mentally ill,' not 'insane,' and those are cases where the brain is so impaired it can't function on its own.

Behind the Scenes...
Leopold and Loeb — page 280

But that's a minority. With most people, rational people, with this rapist –"

"How come you think he's not impaired?" Reynolds interrupted.

"Did you hear him in the interviews? In testimony?"

"That doesn't prove anything."

"Dick, castration's no different than knocking the gun out of a robber's hands. The intent to rob is still there!"

Reynolds put on that haughty grin that Harrigan hated. "I bet you don't believe in the death penalty, either."

"What does that have to do with anything?"

"Do you?"

Harrigan hesitated. His cross necklace glittered in the dim light.

"If we can't do like Heinlein once suggested," he began, "and just export everyone determined to do evil –"

"Evil? Does everything for you come down to your faith?"

"What else?"

"Oh, you make me want to laugh! James, when are you going to accept that your Judeo-Christian dogma's been dismissed from our world?"

"Never."

"Are you going to tell me everything you do's based on the Bible?"

"Well, I wish it was."

"You admit it's not?"

Harrigan's tenor phone rang through the chill air. As he yanked the receiver up, James asked God's blessing for whoever had provided the timely interruption.

"Newsroom," he said. "Harrigan here. Who's there?"

"Don't be sassy," Reynolds whispered.

A gentle voice spoke up. "Who is this?"

"James Harrigan, of the *Beaver Beacon*."

"Harrigan, did you say? Not Hooligan?"

Behind the Scenes...
"Like Heinlein once suggested" — page 282

James took a deep breath. "Harrigan, mam."

"Oh. This looks like Hooligan."

"Fitting," Reynolds commented.

"Anyway, Mr. Hooligan –"

"That's Harrigan," James interjected.

"Oh, yes… so you said. I'm sorry. Anyway, Mr. Hooligan, I've just spoken with our boys at the station on Harley Studley, there in Franklin. They confirmed that you did indeed file a damage claim for a 1996 Geo Metro, in regard to our car wash."

His chair groaned as James lurched forward. This was the customer service representative for Easy Come, Easy Go!

"Now, I cannot comment on your complaint until I see the paperwork," she continued, "but I think it only fair to warn you that we're not in the insurance business."

A nauseating chill gripped him. Hadn't he heard this before?

"If you read the disclaimer we post on each car wash, you assume responsibility for the actions of your vehicle on our premises, Mr. Hooligan. Do you understand that?"

"My name's Harrigan, and yes, I understand. But that doesn't change the fact that your car wash damaged my car."

"I cannot comment on that until I see your claim, Mr. Hooligan. When I see it, I'll give you another call. Thank you for doing business with us. Have a good day."

Stunned at the dismissal, James slipped the phone into its cradle. "Strike three," he whispered. "I'm out."

Wiping his face with his sleeve, Harrigan was surprised to see his publisher still standing there, his face grim, his eyes tight and aware – as if waiting for something.

James leaned back. A sigh of weary despair slipped from his lips.

"I'm not perfect, Richard," he said, using Reynolds's proper name for reasons he couldn't begin to explain. His editor shifted his feet at the word. "I fail myself more often than not. I failed today."

That kid's still out there somewhere. Lord, help me find him!

Reynolds leaned against the filing cabinet, scrutinizing Harrigan.

"Oh, I see," he said. "Is that what happened at the bank?"

That hurt. James folded his hands against his chest, growing angry just thinking about the counterfeit incident. "You've heard about that?"

"Yes. Some people are naturally concerned."

"Some people?"

"Ted Carbuncle at Sooner National, for one."

"Carmichael," James corrected him.

A tarnished image took shape in his mind: a crusty, balding bludgeon of a man, the vice president at the bank and Franklin's Ward 3 councilman. A Depression economics graduate who desired to cut taxes above all else, although when tax benefits could be proven in dollars and sense, he would embrace the modern world. As he had the facilities at his bank.

"Oh, yes," chuckled Reynolds, "that is his name, isn't it? How did I ever get it mixed up?"

James didn't have to answer that. They both knew Harrigan had made the switch in one of his council parodies, when Carmichael had resisted the city manager's efforts to upgrade Franklin's ancient TRS-80 computer system.

"I get the point," he stressed.

"Maybe you do," Reynolds allowed, "and maybe you don't. Today I've heard questions of your character from three different city officials."

"Three? Who's the third?"

"Never you mind. Now I've handled plenty of complaints about your judgment in the past, James, but never before on whether you, as a person, were right for this job. I don't like that. It's bad for our image, and it gives me a major headache."

"I understand," Harrigan growled.

"I don't think you do."

"Look – I'm not a counterfeiter!"

Behind the Scenes…
Trash-80 — page 282

"I'd like to believe that. But do you know what Carmichael told me?"

"I have no idea."

"He said all it takes is someone who knows how to run a scanner and a decent image processor. Just like you."

"So? Half the people here know how to do that!"

"How many have divorced in the last year? Declared bankruptcy?"

James almost swore. How did Carmichael learn the divorce had forced him to seek bankruptcy protection? Was he probing Harrigan's private records?

Was he in on the conspiracy?

"Oh, get off it!"

"You fit the Secret Service trends. The patterns they investigate. That's what Carmichael says, anyway. Do you know, James, that you've given the Treasury Department reason to impound our computers? To shut us down?"

Resurgent anger gripped Harrigan. Shooting to his feet, he stuck his finger in Reynolds's face and spat, "Do you think I did it? That I'm that desperate?"

The hulking editor didn't back down. James met his stare, realized the full meaning of what he was doing – confronting this linebacker of a man who could fire him at a whim, much less knock him clear through the wall – and began to doubt himself anew.

Reynolds softened. "No. I just want you to be a little more careful, son. We're all walking a tightrope now."

31

No Escape

Seeing his anguish, Reynolds sent James home to get some rest before the council meeting. Indeed, he tried to talk Harrigan into letting someone else cover the panel, but James refused. He only agreed to go home after first calling his daughters – to remind them of his love, since he'd be at the council meeting that night, and wouldn't see them this weekend. Then he called the Bean Brothers, to report the counterfeit bill they'd given him. To his surprise, their customer relations representative credited $20 to his account.

"We don't play those sorts of games with people," she explained.

Well then, who do you play those games with? James almost asked.

"We realize it's just our word against yours," she continued, "but you've been a good Three Bean customer and we'd like to have more of your business. Why do you have your checking account across the street in the first place?"

That caught him off-guard. Why indeed?

Behind the Scenes...
Corporate kindness — page 283

"Because, well, I've always been afraid a deposit would end up in the wrong place, if both my savings and checking accounts were at the same bank."

"Oh, that's highly unlikely. A lot of our more paranoid old-timers share that fear, but it doesn't happen. I can assure you of that."

With that official confirmation that he was paranoid, Harrigan hung up and went home. And felt awful. Everywhere he looked, James saw shadows of someone approaching, or heard noises of someone creeping. Listening perhaps for the first time to the cracks and moans of the apartment block itself, twice he thought someone must be opening the front door or prying open a window. It was maddening. After a half hour of such ghosts, he decided enough was enough. He had to get out.

Locking his door behind him, James almost ran down the outside stairs to the *Defiant*, which as usual he'd parked in the same corner slot. In the street behind it, a trio of elementary school-aged girls played some bizarre combination of bowling and baseball. He started to yell at them, concerned they might somehow damage his car swinging their garden hoe bat, but when the girls began squealing in their triumph, he realized he had no idea what they were doing.

Then it dawned upon him.

Recording a score, the brunette bent to the curb in her bright spring dress and, with a piece of chalk, placed another stroke alongside those the police had found.

32

We're Live

After eating an aimless, stomach-leveling supper at McDonald's – his thoughts all the while pondering anew the uncertain path his life had taken and the vastness of this mounting conspiracy, that it could involve young girls – James arrived early at the council chambers, pen and paper in hand, determined to scan over the agenda before the meeting began. A good thirty people were in the audience, broken into groups of three or four per row, most talking of nothing anyone else would care about.

"Must be something good coming," he said to himself. His head pounded like a rap fan's earthquake-imitating sub-woofer.

James felt a strange disappointment as he threaded through the chairs. Against all logic, at the back of his mind he'd hoped to find the kid there. He knew it had been unlikely, yet he'd still wished it so.

The council chamber was arranged like a small auditorium. On the stage lay a curved table seating nine: Franklin's eight council members and, in their center, the mayor. Between the table's two ends, just in front of a podium for the public to address the panel, rested a small extension seating five – the city manager, fire chief, city attorney, treasurer/secretary, and chief of police. Behind that,

to the right, stood the small oak press table and its two slots –
one for the *Beaver Beacon*, and one for Franklin's one radio
station.

Carolyn was already there, in a crimson turtleneck,
running tests on the mike.

James hesitated. Usually KLOD sent renegade hippie Mike
Paris, the ever-silent sound engineer whose task was to
coordinate the broadcast of each council meeting. The spunky
Alaskan Carolyn Danvers rarely ever took his place, for she
ran the morning shift and, more importantly, had a knack of
commenting on just about everything the panel did – as they
did it. The council hated that, although from what James
understood, the audience loved it.

"Hi, sleepyhead!" she called across the room.

James's hand flittered in a sheepish wave. Ever since
Charlotte spat a sour remark about the overly friendly DJ,
he'd made a habit of avoiding Carolyn. The divorce didn't
change that. For though he liked the tightly cropped brunette,
he couldn't help questioning how someone who kept a live-in
boyfriend could be such an excessive flirt. Still, those
concerns disappeared whenever he ended up in her bubbly
presence. And besides, he couldn't ignore her proud ivory
figure in winter's clingy sweaters and second-skin leather.

As he approached the table, she raised a hand for him to
stop.

"I've got just one question for you, Harrigan. Why didn't
you mention me in that thumb-duel column of yours? I mean,
I beat you three times!"

"Yeah, yeah, yeah. And you know why."

That brought a pleasing smile to her lips. "I can't help
being a woman."

A male voice erupted from the headset laying on the table.
"What'd she do – brush her chest up against you?"

James jerked his head back. "Are we live?"

Behind the Scenes...
Foreshadowing — page 284

"Always, sugar," she purred. "I'd be glad to prove it."

Sliding into the seat beside her – and adjusting his chair so that their knees wouldn't ever mingle – James was surprised to see the eight council members start parading in from the neighboring executive chamber. Five men and three women, all in their forties or beyond, plus Mayor McCheese – that is, Mayor Sam McDuff. Each one laughed as they looked his way. James couldn't help wondering why.

"They've been talking about me," he whispered, "about either the counterfeit or the snoring tales."

Or could it be something else?

"Yes, go," he heard Carolyn say.

From the street entrance came their hefty city manager, the chain cigar smoker James Hertz, along with the chief of police, City Attorney Patrick Pallen, and City Treasurer Sharon Pulaski. The fire chief was absent, as usual, but Jacobs looked razor sharp in his dress uniform. Like he was trying to make a point.

"With the council members all piling in," stated Danvers, "it's time we begin tonight's episode of 'Who's Going to Curse the Police Chief This Time?' or as it's more commonly known, the weekly Franklin City Council meeting. Your host tonight is Carolyn Danvers, star of radioland from here to the next block over, and with me, talking to himself once more, is our favorite satirist, the *Franklin Beaver Beacon's* own James Harrigan. What's going on, James?"

Hearing his name, James whispered, "Is it time already?"

Danvers laughed. "I guess Mr. Harrigan is still a little droopy from our last snore session – in which he quite literally participated. Someday, James, you're going to realize that we're always waiting on you."

Sudden awareness swept through Harrigan. Twisting to his left, he found Danvers ready for action in her tiny headset, her eyes wide and sparkling.

"Fifteen seconds," announced the engineer at the station.

"Gotcha," she replied. "Next time you'd better include me. In everything."

By Kirby Lee Davis

33

Breakdown Countdown

Following the prayer and reading of the minutes, McDuff opened the floor to new business. A grizzled old man in patched denim overalls stepped to the public's podium. His words came in sputtered links as he considered just what he was saying.

"I'd like to know why," he spat into the microphone, "why it is you all don't open the city's books. Open them for us to see, now, in a public meeting."

James flipped his small notepad to the first available page. Sometimes good stories came out of the public comments.

"Please state your name for the record," monotoned the secretary.

"I says, I'd been wondering why you all don't open the city's books?"

"Where have we heard that before?" Carolyn whispered to her listeners. "Seems a logical request, doesn't it? Especially with the personnel cuts we've endured, the sales tax passing, and the water rate discussion yet to come?"

"Let'm come to the City Hall to check the books!" the city manager spouted forth, smirking to the council and the city treasurer.

Only one panel member joined in that politically reckless humor.

"What – take time off work?" the speaker asked.

"We all have to sometimes," offered McDuff. "Besides, you wouldn't understand them. I don't understand them. I have a gopher who I show them to during the spring thaw, and if he comes out of his hole, I know they're sound."

Snuffed chuckles meandered around the council table. Some audience members joined in. The speaker seemed annoyed.

"That gopher died a year ago," he snapped.

"I've been trying to tell you we had problems!" McDuff replied with a smile. "That's why we've voted for all this stuff."

"Oh," the speaker said, pondering that. "OK then. I was just wondering, was all."

"If you're done," interrupted Ward 6 Councilman Furtis Page, who at 46 was the youngest man on the panel, "I'd like to ask the city manager a question."

"Go ahead," said Hertz, rolling his large body around to view Page, who sat to McDuff's right.

"This ought to be good," whispered Carolyn. Her black leather pants crinkled as she slid forward. James resisted the urge to look down, though he couldn't help smiling. He loved that sound. To be honest, he loved leather… on women, at least.

His conscience scolded him for that slip, but James was just too weary to care.

"Mr. Hertz," began Page, "would you ask that person why he's running his patrols the way he is?"

This time it was the audience's turn to chuckle. By "that person," everyone knew Page referred to the chief of police, Isaac Jacobs.

"I would be glad to do that," replied Hertz, "although you do realize that all patrol routes are matters of internal policy, to be determined solely by my office?"

"Are you saying I don't have the right to ask you about your job?"

"No, Mr. Page."

"Then ask him!"

Smiling, Hertz turned to the man sitting next to him – who

in his polished uniform was staring directly at Page.

"Chief Jacobs, why are you running your patrols the way you do?"

"We talked about that this morning," said Jacobs, never taking his eyes off Page.

"Oh, that's right. We did, didn't we?"

"They will be handled as per official policy – decided by me, with the city manager's input, and only his input," Jacobs stated, never flinching under Page's hostile gaze. "If you want to ask any more questions, I believe my attorney will be glad to answer them."

Page leaned forward, his eyes sharp as a buzzard spying its kill.

"Mr. Hertz," he began, never once looking away from Jacobs, "what did that man just say?"

Hertz sighed. "I'm sorry, Chief Jacobs. What did you say again?"

"If you want to ask any more questions, I believe my attorney will be glad to answer them."

"Can't you just tell me?"

"I am telling you."

"OK then, tell me."

"I believe my attorney will be glad to answer them."

"Oh, come on, Isaac! Can't you tell me?"

"I just did!"

"Are you threatening me?" Page interrupted.

"Threatening us," another councilman clarified, weary of the ongoing tension.

"On that note," entered an exasperated McDuff, "I think we should skip ahead on our agenda and go directly to our executive session – if there are no objections."

James heard plenty of mumbles, but no objections.

"Soooooo," said Carolyn as the council members rose. "Only five minutes in and they're already into an executive session." She shoved the spare mike in front of James. "Must be a new record, huh, Harrigan?"

James leaned forward, giving Hertz plenty of room to squeeze past in his walk toward the executive chambers. Even so, Hertz had to shove James hard against the table to get by. Harrigan couldn't help gasping.

"That's putting it well," Carolyn remarked. "Small-town politics; gotta love it!" Then she turned her eyes squarely on Harrigan. "So, I guess that means it's just you and me, James, for the next few minutes at least. I've got you all to myself at last."

Harrigan shoved his chair back, taking a deep breath. "Bet he did that on purpose," James muttered. *Hertz's probably in on it.*

A nervous chill spiked through the reporter. In the corner he spied a dark-suited, square-jawed man in black sunglasses – staring straight at him.

"Secret Service," he thought aloud. They're watching me already!

Carolyn leaned into him, slipping a warm, gentle hand on his arm. "Listen, sugar, we're at a commercial now. Do you think you could tell a story during the next few minutes? I'd rather us talk than have them play music."

It took a moment for James to realize she'd asked him something. Then he nodded, his thoughts still on the suit observing him. The man was reaching for something in his pocket… a pencil – no doubt to shove into his cigar! *Just like Nowhere Man!*

Harrigan swabbed his eyes with his shirtsleeve. His headache felt worse.

Lord, help me!

"Welcome back," Carolyn started.

"I think I need something to eat," James blurted out. "You want something?"

Danvers frowned. "For those of you just joining us, the Franklin City Council has already retreated into its executive chambers to discuss what I believe is a matter of policy with the city manager and the chief of police. So, I'm here with James Harrigan, the resident wit of the *Beaver Beacon* –"

Behind the Scenes…
Insights on the city council — page 284

James slid his chair back. She pointed her gorgeous index finger toward the mike, but he stood instead.

"– Who's about to satisfy his stomach with a Snickers, I would guess," Carolyn told her audience. "Mike, let's replay the opening of the council meeting. I'd like to go over some points with our audience."

"Sure thing, Carolyn," replied the studio engineer.

"And when James gets back," Danvers continued, giving Harrigan a wink, "we'll hear how his week's been so far."

James nodded. His head ached from the effort.

34

Confrontation

Closing the door behind him, James thanked God for the foresight of whoever designed Franklin's municipal building. For only great wisdom could have led that nameless architect to place the City Hall break room right behind the council chambers.

Unfortunately, that still left him to deal with the nemesis of all sugar-parched humans.

Switching on the light, James found himself alone in a small plaster cubical lined with a folding card table, a large trash can filled with worn magazines, a smoked glass door to the rest of City Hall, and three vending machines of various sizes. One offered cigarettes, one canned soda, and one snacks. Not one of them accepted dollar bills.

Wiping the weariness from his forehead, Harrigan worked his wedged-in billfold from his back pocket and counted his change. The column of Snickers in that metal monolith of corkscrew-hung confections displayed a price of 65 cents. But James knew he needed at least a quarter extra to satisfy this money-hungry device.

Since his first recollections, James carried a suspicion that all such contraptions considered him a patsy willing, if not aching, to be exploited. Whether it was the newspaper racks that ate quarters like he did M&Ms, or the rod-yankers that

forced you to win a tug-of-war with a pulley able to lift a
two-ton truck before it released anything, or those
automatons that made you prove your worth by entering the
exact value of Pi into their numerical interfaces, or the bully
display chests that expected you to shake their refrigerator-
sized bulks for five minutes before they surrendered the
object of your desire... not one vending machine he'd ever
encountered seemed willing to give up freely what he'd paid
good metal money for.

The worst offenders strung items on corkscrews.

Though it had a friendly appearance, this City Hall vendor
ever toyed with consumers. In theory, all you had to do was
press a numbered button and the corresponding item would
fall free from its corkscrew to a thin trap door, where its
weight would send it plummeting into the long well where
James could retrieve it. But he had used this evil construct
before. He knew it wasn't just content to see people squirm
from not getting what they'd paid for. No, this one had a
much greater imagination. It wanted your money, your
merchandise, your hand – everything.

Seeing his cross reflected in the vender's transparent
plastic cover, James knew the dangers before him. But with
his head pounding, his stomach growling, and his limbs
aching ever more with every breath, James didn't care. He
cast his coins into the slot and punched in the number for the
lowest hanging Snickers. And at first, all seemed well. Gears
came alive, worn metal cogs ground in their movement, the
appropriate metal curlicue revolved, and his chosen Snickers
fell free – only to get stuck in its descent between two rows of
bagged Cheese Doodles.

Growling in outrage, James slapped the sides of the
machine several times. Nothing happened. He pressed the
coin return. No luck.

"I knew it," he grimaced, twisting free his billfold once
more. Having just enough change to buy one of the accursed
Cheese Doodles – potential leftovers of the Disco era, or so he
assumed from the dust on the bags – Harrigan shoved his
coins into the slot and pressed the right number. The correct
corkscrew turned, but the bag of Doodles seemed to roll with

it, sliding backward instead of forward. His stomach's betrothed Snickers remained a hostage.

𝕾𝖍𝖆𝖐𝖊 𝖙𝖍𝖊 𝖉𝖆𝖓𝖌-𝖇𝖚𝖗𝖓 𝖙𝖍𝖎𝖓𝖌! came a rascally voice. So, James wrapped his arms around the broad front of that monolith and, with a great yank that could only come from his near-mastodonian anger, somehow rolled the back legs of that foul contraption off the floor. And after it pounded with excruciating pain against his forehead – and almost came toppling down upon him – James decided never to do anything so stupid again.

The Snickers, meanwhile, clung ever so close to the dairy puffs.

Despair settled around Harrigan. "Lord," he whispered, "is everything against me?"

His frustrations made good use of these mechanical pirates. *This machine's in on it! Obviously! Just like the car wash!*

But from that shallow darkness came a ray of hope. In a moment of inspiration, James realized the Snickers wasn't that far above the long well trap – just three rows of corkscrews. If he could wedge something up through that door, he might be able to knock the candy bar free.

Drawing a ragged issue of *Sports Illustrated* from the trash, James found that if he kept his left hand flat against the bottom of the well, he could slip his fingernails under the lip of the trap and pull it down. That allowed him to work the rolled-up magazine through the gap with his right hand. But try as he might, he couldn't get close to the imprisoned Snickers – even with his right forearm thoroughly wedged in the machine. The magazine just wasn't long enough.

Slipping his arm free, James searched the room for some tool he might use. Finding none, he tried the room's other door, thinking this building's ever-wise architect surely placed a sink or some sort of storage or supply options there for people to use after they'd eaten. Such a room would naturally offer some tool, even if just a flyswatter! But his hope proved fruitless, the door locked.

Long, dejected strides carried him back into the council chambers. The rambling buzz of small talk hit his ears, the much-reduced audience all a-chatter with the panel still in executive session. Carolyn, her headset on, playfully extended her right hand to Harrigan, motioning with a long, sinuous finger for James to return. He started to obey until his eyes fell upon the mayor's rosewood gavel – with a handle longer than his trashed *Sports Illustrated*.

James ran back to the cursed machine, swinging the gavel from hand to hand. It required some nudging to get the polished mallet past the trap, but James managed it. With gentle patience he worked the wooden hammer up with his right hand, penetrating the corkscrew rows. Its soft rubber tip soon brushed against the enemy Cheese Doodles.

The candy bar didn't move.

James stretched out his right hand once, then again, but try as he might, Harrigan couldn't nudge the gavel hard enough to knock the Snickers free. He attempted different variations of handle movements, sure the next twist would dislodge that stubborn chocolate delight, but it never happened. In desperation he let the heavy rosewood head roll down, then with a sharp twist of his wrist, Harrigan swung the mallet high. Flying from his grasp, the gavel soared for the Cheese Doodles. As it reached the bags, the rubber tip struck the vending machine's transparent cover and rocked back – where it came to settle upon corkscrews holding bagged peanuts and peanut butter crackers.

Harrigan's drooling mouth hung free. He couldn't believe it. He'd lost the mayor's gavel!

"Oh Lord, help me!" James moaned, working his arms loose. He took one shaky step back, then another.

It still didn't seem real. He actually lost Mayor McDuff's favorite gavel in the vending machine! The one McDuff's grandmother carved him for his eighth birthday!

Hard newspaper instincts gripped Harrigan. Foreshadowing headlines flashed across the wall:

Behind the Scenes...
Vending machines and smokescreens — page 285

Counterfeiter convicted in great gavel caper... Mayor minces renegade reporter... 'I enjoyed every minute of it!' McDuff boasts....

Who wouldn't believe it, the way things were going?

Twisting for the door, James found himself face to face with Carolyn. Her eyes glowed with devilish intent.

"So," she purred, stepping into him. Anticipation outlined her sly smile. "We're alone at last."

35

Taking a Stand

By instinct James stepped backwards. Carolyn followed. Her supple form leaned into him, charging him with sensual electricity that overwhelmed his senses like an onrushing tidal wave. Yet as exciting as her flesh was, almost more than he could bear, it was the beauty of her face that truly captivated him. Having never stood that close before, James felt mesmerized by the elegant curves of her pink cheeks, the flare of her delicate nostrils, the damp hint of a tongue waiting behind her shiny red lips. The invitation of her open stare.

Had he ever experienced such desire from anyone? Even Charlotte?

"Did you get everything you wanted?" she whispered, meeting his gaze with a passionate fire.

Something within him resisted. "No," he stuttered, his thoughts sluggish within the tempest of temptations. He inched away from her – and found that corkscrew nemesis at his back.

Carolyn filled the void, pressing her rose-scented turtleneck against him. Her lips met his. They embraced.

Newfound awareness energized Harrigan, yet left him reeling, his TSRs at record levels and climbing. James felt his hands sweeping over her as if they had minds of their own.

Suggestions flared through his heart, swooning him with realities in black leather and soft cotton that he couldn't ignore. Nor could he deny delighting in the exquisite pleasure he drew from contact with such a beauty. But as he slid his fingers along the sensuous lines of her back, reveling finally in the soft bounce of her autumn brown hair, James gently, with deep-felt reluctance, pushed her shoulders away.

Carolyn smiled in triumph.

"Ready now?" she said, swaying to and fro ever so slow.

James took a deep breath. Holding her at arm's length gave him a full view of her enchanting femininity.

You're crazy to resist! came an eager, almost frantic voice. *She wants you!*

"You're already seeing someone," James said, almost as a defense.

"You're not."

"That doesn't matter."

"You're right. None of that matters. I don't think he'd care anyway. He's probably got girls in other towns."

James flinched. He didn't know her boyfriend, but the man sounded like an utter fool.

"Then why do you stay with him?"

"Well, life's cheaper that way. And he's good to me, though not like you'd be, I'm sure."

"Oh, stop that."

"What?"

"Taunting me. You know what I mean. And stop moving."

"What, this?" With a flirty sigh she pulsated in ways James felt sure would make a belly dancer envious. And just that quick she stopped, grinning a sheepish smile that almost melted his heart.

"I'm sorry. I know I'm coming on strong. It's just… well, I like the power, you know? To take you. Because I could, if I wanted. But I want more than that. I've always liked you,

Behind the Scenes…
TSRs — page 286

James. Couldn't you tell? I mean… well, I think we could be so great together!"

Not knowing what else he could do, James felt a deep, desperate need to put some distance between them. But when he tried once more to step away, he found that dreaded corkscrew criminal still had him cornered.

"I know," he admitted. "You may be right. But I want more than that."

Puzzlement invaded her playfulness. "More than what?"

"This… this kind of thing."

Carolyn fought to keep from laughing. "What – sex?"

Her amusement only embarrassed James further.

"Can't you even say it?" she giggled.

"I, well, I probably could… if I wanted to."

"If you can spell it, you can say it. But that's beside the point. Why would you automatically think my innocent kiss means I want to seduce you?"

Harrigan almost gagged on that logic. What did make him think that? His exhaustion? His loneliness? His desires? Or the fact that she had all his nerves on edge?

Could he be that wrong?

"Well, that is what you're doing, isn't it?"

"Of course! But I'm disturbed you didn't get that a long time ago. Either I'm a little rusty, or for a smart guy, you're rather slow."

James looked down, hoping to avoid her eyes. Then he realized what he was staring at and turned away.

"What do you think I'm after," she probed with a luscious smile. "A one-night stand? Oh, I've got much more in mind!"

Her wild amusement chilled him. "Lord, help me!" he whispered.

Get a grip, Harrigan!

"Maybe so," he told her, "but sex is the end result with me, not the beginning."

A questioning glare flashed across her brow. James feared he'd insulted her.

"What are you saying?" she pressed. "You think I sleep with just anyone?"

"I didn't say that!"

"Now see here! I'm very choosy about this sort of thing, Mr. Harrigan!"

"I know that. But I don't –"

"I've only gone to bed with men I've really cared about. And that's just three people, if you must know. Well, maybe four, or five."

"Look… I'm sorry if I've –"

"So don't hold your hang-ups against me, Mr. High and Mighty!"

James couldn't help smiling. That was the second time she'd said that to him.

"Well put," he told her. "Are you satisfied?"

Carolyn blushed, her anger heightened by his sudden humor, but it soon gave away to gentle appreciation.

"James, you're so different. You're like no one I've ever met."

"Yeah, right. I doubt that."

"I don't," she said, drawing close once more. The scent of fresh-cut roses was so intoxicating. James thought it fit her – elegant in its beauty, innocent and still seductive, even when barbed to the hilt.

"Charlotte was a fool to leave you," Carolyn continued. "You know, I told her that once."

That sent a shock through his system. "You what?"

"I ran into her in the supermarket parking lot," Carolyn answered, wrapping her arms about his chest. James felt a rush to caress her. He resisted.

"I said anyone who'd divorce you was insane," she finished.

Picturing that encounter sobered James. He could only imagine what his ex would have thought, since Charlotte always labeled Carolyn a headhunter… and correctly, he now realized.

Carolyn swept her hands around his hips, drawing him

Behind the Scenes…
Mr. High and Mighty — page 287

near. Harrigan tried to squirm free. Part of him hoped she'd battle back, but Carolyn gave away with but a sly grin.

"Please," he protested, "don't do this!"

"I'm sorry, but I don't give up easily."

"Look, Carolyn. I don't begin relationships with sex. I might end them that way, if I'm in love – and married."

"But why wait, if two people love each other?"

"You love me? Just like that – you really love me?"

"Well, I could. In time."

Settling her palms against the soft leather clinging to her hips, Carolyn offered Harrigan a figure Barbie would die for. James could not look upon her without thinking himself an old-fashioned fool.

You're just afraid, went his internal debate. *So what if you've never done anything like this before. Take her! Enjoy yourself!*

Sensing his hesitation, she stepped into him once more. Harrigan couldn't help gazing down at the inviting contact. Shining bright from the crimson canyon between her proud breasts was his silver cross.

That settled things.

"If, and when, that happens," he began, "and I feel the same way, then perhaps."

"You know, if my boyfriend's the issue, I could change that. I could get my own apartment."

James sighed. "That's not it. Not that that's not a concern."

"Or I could move in with you!"

"No!" With firm resolution, he pushed Carolyn an arm's length away. "Listen. I'm a Christian. I can't do this sort of thing. I just can't."

Folding her arms against her chest, Carolyn took a deep, resolute breath. "Well then, maybe we should start things properly. Would you go out some time with me? See a movie or something?"

James thanked God for her understanding. "I'd love to, once you're no longer involved with someone else."

She laughed. "That again?"

This beat seemed an opportune time to flee. Harrigan leaped at the chance, squirting by her for the door.

She pinched him as he passed.

36

Going Public

"What have we here?" asked Cloretta Brown.

James hesitated, afraid he'd thrust open the door in Brown's face, but the kind, retired librarian representing Ward 4 only laughed as she walked past him into the break room.

"Thought I'd find you here, dear," she told Carolyn, nodding once towards James with a wry smile.

Glad to see the Franklin City Council returning from its executive session, James stepped out to discover Mayor McDuff in an animated conversation with the city manager and Ward 3's Ted Carmichael, even as Simon Bernard, Christopher Davis, and Jessica Derkins slid past for their seats on the far side of the table. Ward 7 Councilman Stan Land was already in his swiveling chair, alongside Ward 8's Shirley Jackson. Having listened to the mayor for a second, Furtis Page was heading for his seat when he stopped beside James. A huge smile blossomed on his face.

"I see someone's been doing some probing of his own," he said, giving Harrigan's forearm a not-so-gentle punch as Carolyn emerged from the break room, her face aglow in a sheepish grin.

Stunned by the absurdity of that observation, James could only ask, "What?"

With a nod to Danvers, Page wiped Harrigan's cheek with the handkerchief this councilman always kept in his breast pocket. Revealed on the white cloth was the crimson smear of Carolyn's lipstick.

James felt himself turning beet red. Carolyn giggled.

Brown stuck her head through the doorway, her gray beehive hairdo bouncing in her excitement. "Sam," she called, "you ought to see what they're selling in here these days!"

"No wonder you're falling asleep up here," Page said, giving Harrigan a second nudge. "Is that how you two spend your time?"

"Oh, it gets much better than that," the disc jockey boasted with a step towards her radio set.

"Carolyn!" James yelped.

Curiosity sparked the mayor's eyes as he walked to Harrigan's side, having seen Danvers smile in passing. But that didn't surprise James; the men on the council always kept their eyes on Carolyn whenever she moved.

"It's nothing like that," he told Page.

"Look what I got for my forty-five cents," proclaimed Brown, stepping up to McDuff's chair. "Thought I'd get a pack of Juicy Fruit, you know? But low and behold, that machine not only gives me my gum, but a Snickers, two packs of Cheese Doodles, some peanut butter crackers, and a gavel. And a quarter to boot!"

"What's that?" the mayor exclaimed.

James decided the time was right to retreat.

"Now how do you think your gavel got in there?" he heard Page ask.

"Don't know," said McDuff, laying the long-handled hammer down at his spot. "But it looks all right."

James sighed in grateful praise. *Thank you, Lord!*

"What about that scratch there?" asked Brown.

"And that one?" added Page.

"And that long –"

"All right," sighed McDuff, cutting them off. "I see it."

Sliding into his seat, Harrigan could hear Danvers chuckling.

"Wonder how it got there?" Page repeated.

"Wouldn't they like to know!" Carolyn whispered.

"Twenty seconds," came the radio loudspeaker.

"Shush," James told her, adjusting his chair away from hers.

"All right, all right," said McDuff, striking his gavel with newly opened eyes. "If we'd all take our seats, I think we could pick up our agenda."

"Let's do a roll call," offered the city treasurer, speaking in her secondary role as the secretary.

"A roll call," Carolyn said to her audience. "Now let's all recite these together: cinnamon, crescent, clover, hot cross, biscuit. Any others, James?"

Deciding he'd better play along if he didn't want Carolyn to start on him anew, Harrigan leaned into his microphone. "I always thought a roll call would be Furtis standing up to yell, 'Roll! Roll!'"

"And then the audience would roll all around the floor!" Danvers whispered. "I love it!"

Lifted high by her animated talk, Carolyn's right hand fell on Harrigan's left arm. For virtue's sake he casually brushed it off.

"I think we can see we're all here," McDuff told Pulaski. "Let's move forward."

"How do we stand on the minutes?" the secretary asked.

"Let's just sit on them," laughed Brown. "My feet are killing me."

"I think we'll go on to the departmental contract," the mayor decided. "Is our negotiator here?"

"Which department is it?" asked Ward 8's Shirley Jackson, a rather large African American barbecue shack owner, proud of her Civil War heritage, with a stare that could melt battleship plate armor.

"I don't think we want to go into that," said Land. Turning to McDuff, he stressed, "I want to say once more, this is something we should do in executive session."

"Oh no!" snapped Ward 5 Councilwoman Jessica Derkins. "I can't stand another minute in that room. It's so hot and stuffy!"

"We'll just discuss the basics out here," said McDuff, "and

then, if we get technical, we can go back in there."

As that went on, James watched a somewhat bent man open his briefcase at the public podium. With his shiny scalp, long beard, sharp nose, and large, round glasses, James thought he looked rather rodentish. Like a balding chipmunk, to be precise. Yet his eyes had that steely stare of a calculator.

"Oh, yes," said McDuff, noticing the negotiator. "Tell us, sir, how is this department contract different from the last?"

"Well," said the chipmunk, stretching out each syllable in a shrill voice, "it's about the same, except it's bigger."

"How much bigger?" asked Page.

"Oh, about ten pages."

The council murmurs seemed to indicate that was acceptable.

James felt a hand caress his left thigh. He almost jumped out of his chair.

"But what's the cost?" asked Carmichael.

"Of the ten pages?"

"Of the contract!"

"Oh," said the chipmunk with a pause, "well, it's about the same, except it's bigger."

"How much bigger?"

"Oh, a few million dollars here and there. Petty cash funds."

Glancing around to make sure no one noticed, James tried to ease his shoulders around so that he could get both of his hands on Carolyn's soft, smooth paw and pry her lovely fingers off his leg without creating too much of a scene.

Her nails dug in. Her eyes sparkled in playful glee.

James sought to wedge his fingers under her palm. She slid her hand higher. By instinct he started to scoot back, only to hear his chair slide against the tile floor. The squeal almost unnerved him.

"Don't you ever give up?" he whispered.

"What would I give up? I haven't got anything yet."

"Carolyn! This isn't the place!"

"Then just tell me where, sugar."

"Hey guys," came the subdued loudspeaker. "You're on the air."

Ward 2's rather sluggard councilman, Simon Bernard, chose that moment to stand. "Well, I think we should leave the minimum water rates about the same –"

"This isn't the water rate study," Page said, interrupting the seventy-year-old grocer.

Bernard winced. "Must have remembered the wrong speech. I can feel it back here," he said, motioning to the base of his skull. "Sam, could you give me a sharp tap?"

Leaning to his left, McDuff slammed his gavel into that soft spot just behind Bernard's left ear. The balding man adjusted his jaw, tested it, then smiled.

"There now… yes, that's good. Anyway, I think this contract could be much better done in-house." A few council members rustled in protest, but Bernard waved them down. "Our typists do a much better job on things than we give them credit for."

"I make a motion we adjourn," said someone on the panel. James couldn't tell who, his panic binding his thoughts to the spidery hand creeping up his leg.

"I second it."

"You can't make a motion to adjourn," the mayor protested.

"Now, now. A motion's been made," came Brown's distinctive voice. James couldn't help smiling at the pleasure dripping through her words. He knew she'd always enjoyed the council vaudeville.

The warm retort amused Carolyn as well. Thus distracted, with a twisting motion Harrigan managed to dislodge Danvers' firm grip. Carolyn immediately sank her fingers between his. To his surprise, James found he liked it.

"Hard to keep notes like this," he remarked.

"Sometimes you don't have much imagination," Carolyn replied. "I could make it so much harder."

James couldn't help smiling. "Is sex all you think about?"

Behind the Scenes…
Government shenanigans — page 288

"That's supposed to be my line. You're the man, after all."

Councilman Christopher Davis leaned into his mike. "I make a motion we agree to the contract except for the part that says, 'The Ward 1 councilman is a rat fink.'"

"You can't change a contract!" snapped the chipmunk.

"Now I'm from Ward 1," replied Davis, "and I know I'm not a rat fink, or at least I wasn't when I was voted one."

With a great display of frustration and a muttered "Complaints, complaints," the chipmunk grabbed his eraser and rubbed the offending passage from his Big Chief tablet. He then turned to Page and said, "I guess you want to change the part about rezoning your home for environmental waste?"

James couldn't take his eyes off the graceful hand embracing his own. Something didn't seem right.

"Why me?"

Carolyn offered an innocent smile.

"I mean, look at me," James whispered. "I'm not muscular or handsome or anything like that."

"So?"

"You could have anyone! You're gorgeous! There are models who'd die to look like you!"

"Harrigan," Carolyn said with a sigh, "you really are a sexist pig. Do you know that?"

With a sharp jerk, she drew her hand from his.

"I've just about had enough of your blind self-righteousness. You think just because I'm so beautiful, I can't be attracted to anyone who's not some kind of muscle-bulging, kinky Greek god? Or do you think I'm a dumb brunette… all bod and no brains, is that it?"

"No!"

Through a fog, James heard the mayor beat his gavel. "A motion's on the floor."

"Pick it up," said Brown.

Behind the Scenes…
Big Chief tablets — page 289

Carolyn reared like a snake, only slightly hindered by her headphones. "Listen, Mr. High and Mighty Right-wing Christian Moralizer. Stop judging me by my looks!"

James recoiled. "I'm just trying to understand!"

"I think I've made myself clear."

"But why me? You could have anyone you wanted!"

"God damn you, James!"

Harrigan cringed. "Don't talk like that!"

"Why not? I meant every word. I want God to do it. What do you think I am – some sex-starved wench, setting my claws in whoever meets my fancy?"

The gavel struck. "I said, we have a motion –"

"Oh, shush!" whispered Brown. "I can't hear them."

Carolyn ignored it all. "I don't use people. You should know me well enough to know that. I don't seduce men I want favors from, lie about their performance, or fake orgasms. I know what I want in life, and I'm 100-percent honest. And if that scares you or your Christian sensibilities, I'm sorry, but I'm not going to change."

Once more the gavel cried out.

"I'm the one who's sorry," McDuff said, "but we are trying to have a meeting here."

"Who cares?" asked Brown.

"I do," the mayor replied. "Some others might. And as much as I don't want to do it, I think we'll have to vote on the motion just so that we can forget it."

"I'll second that," said someone.

"I didn't ask for one," the mayor snapped.

James took a deep breath. Leaning back, he was surprised to see half the council watching him. To his horror, the audience did as well.

Or perhaps they're just ogling Carolyn, he considered.

She wore a smile on her face that would light up the Statue of Liberty in the depths of an eclipse. With a wink, she

---

Behind the Scenes...
Sex and Christian fiction boundaries — page 290

slipped her right hand up his arm to the back of his neck. Her long nails rolled against his spine, massaging him. Relaxing him. Arousing him.

"Sex is a gift," she whispered. "An expression of love. You don't have to run from it."

James didn't know how much more he could take. He felt a growing power within urging him to embrace this, and yet there remained, as always, a voice he'd long before come to trust. Usually calm and content, but it was different now. For the first time he could remember, that voice had lost its soft, reassuring posture, adapting almost the fearful electronic omens of the *Lost in Space* robot.

Carolyn drew her hand away. "You know, it's common for divorced men to be scared. Of women, commitments. Contact. But I can help you with that."

"Damn it, Carolyn!" interrupted the loudspeaker. "How many times do I have to say you're on the air?"

"Oh, pooh," she told the studio engineer. "Our morning show's livelier than this!"

"But this is a council meeting!"

"On the air," James whispered.

Before the whole city.

That realization nearly flattened him. Here he was, trying to do his job, and Hertz, Jacobs, Page, Brown – all of them watched him, struggling not to laugh. They knew what was going on! Others like Carmichael glared with eyes of fire. They would crucify him.

James Harrigan, a representative of the *Beaver Beacon*, gallivanting around with a flirty woman on live radio during a public meeting. Despite the warnings from his boss, the city leaders complaining about his attitude, the counterfeiting incident, the police obstruction claims, he'd shamed and disgraced his newspaper, and himself.

Carolyn's soft, welcome hand enveloped his own, squeezing his palm. Her eyes sparkled. Her stare invited him in.

In his heart he wanted to accept, to dive in and partake all she offered, and yet he believed he couldn't do it. Indeed, that he must not.

That division threatened to rip him apart. It was just too much.

Without a word James fled, not stopping until he reached his apartment. In cold, lonely darkness he threw himself onto his bed and wept, praying for guidance.

By Kirby Lee Davis

37

j-col-flushot.wpd

Some of you may disagree, but for my money, there's no worse way to experience the glorious nausea of the flu than with a flu shot.

Imagine the economy burning up $3 billion a year combating something that has stopped up noses since the dawn of time. That tops a trillion bucks in my lifetime alone. And where did it get me? Rolling up my sleeve at the local grocery store.

That's right – my supermarket had a counter for influenza vaccinations, administered right between the Ritz crackers and Ragu Garden Style Spaghetti Sauce.

No wonder the Chinese have traded in their little red books to make Happy Meal toys for McDonald's. You just can't top modern capitalism.

Not that I didn't try.

"Give me your arm," repeated the white-gowned nurse, a black-haired linebacker of a woman tired of competing for

---

Behind the Scenes…
Bad math — page 292
Capitalism and Happy Meals — page 293

my attention with a counter full of Chickens on a Biscuit cracker boxes. But then, I'm sure I'm not the only one often caught pondering the biblical significance of how we can transform poultry into teensy snacks that by some quirk of fate is called a biscuit. I mean, contemplating the chemical processes required to make something edible of those stringy feathers can occupy my mind for days. But at that moment I didn't have the time. For with one look at the nurse's impassioned scowl, I knew her M&M dispenser must have run dry years ago.

"Your arm," she repeated.

"Well, OK," I allowed, "but it seems like a high price to pay, especially since I've already written you a check."

Now that may sound like an old joke to you, but deep in the recesses of my noggin' I've always considered that had to be one of the best pick-up lines ever concocted. But did it work on Nursezilla?

Nooooooo.

"Don't mess with me, funny boy," she growled, all the while scouring the top of my right arm with something that smelled like a mixture of Alka Selzer and turpentine. "I've got a gob of geezers lined up behind you and nothing to do about it except impale this nice little needle into your scrawny carcass."

At that instant, the process of turning feathers into tea-time delicacies no longer intrigued me. Indeed, as a long aqua syringe appeared like magic within her right hand, I began to think that risking glands the size of watermelons might not be such a bad thing after all.

Like a gunslinger she leveled the menacing injection device at my chest. With a flip of her thumb she kicked off the safety cap, exposing the two-inch needle to my alarmed gaze.

Her green eyes glowed with almost beastly delight.

"I know what you're thinking," she whispered. "Sure, you're only 30 feet from the door. You might be able to make a break for it. And if you do, you might only miss a few days of work with the flu. But since I'm standing here, right now, armed with perhaps the most effective syringe known to man, a 22-gauge, 3.5cc Abbott Luer Lock that I could ram right through your puny bones into that concrete wall, you have to ask yourself one question: Do you feel lucky? Well, do you? Punk?"

Less than six hours later I relished the onset of the shot-induced watermelon glands, thankful I wasn't digging smashed concrete pebbles out of my ears. And even though the vaccine made me feel about as warm and cuddly as the blob, I can look forward to the fact that (hopefully) I'll not be spending as much time sick from the dreaded influenza bug. But I haven't yet gotten my courage up to revisit that cracker aisle.

So much for my return on a trillion bucks.

Behind the Scenes...
Ragu, Ritz, and flu shots — page 290
The cost of battling the flu — page 291

38

The Summons

Awakened but not alert, his dreams clogged by the appealing spices sprung free when opening a fresh box of Chicken on a Biscuit crackers, James managed to crawl out of bed and catch the phone on its fourth ring. He still didn't know if answering that high-tech interloper was wise – for after propping a chair against his front door, he'd gone to bed last night thinking Reynolds wouldn't wait for Harrigan to come in before firing him – but in the end, James figured he had to face whatever resulted from his on-air dance with Carolyn.

To his surprise, the caller wasn't Reynolds, but Sergeant Patrick Haskins.

"James, I need you to come to the Fourth Street Overpass," he all but commanded. "I think we've found your burglar."

Talk about the power of words! Those two sentences changed everything for Harrigan.

"All right! I'll be there!"

"Now, James. And don't say I called."

Harrigan hesitated. "Well, OK. Is there anything else I need to know?"

"Just hurry."

With that, Haskins hung up.

The finality in those words punctured the reporter's

balloon of instant energy. Confronting a rush of weariness, James bit back his muddled emotions as he returned the phone to its cradle. Part of him still felt giddy. This signaled the police had investigated the break-in after all. Maybe Jacobs wasn't out to get him. Maybe all his worries were overblown… just like the marks on the curb, or his door. Yet he couldn't understand why Haskins didn't want his name dropped, unless someone in the department still disliked Harrigan.

Perhaps someone was still out to get him.

Fears of his firing returned as another call interrupted James' stiff efforts to button his shirt. Without hesitation he skipped for the phone, which he caught on the fifth ring.

This one wasn't Reynolds either.

"Hello, Mr. Harrigan," came a subdued Southern voice. "I'm Sandra Woods, a receptionist with the Riverside Baptist Church. You called yesterday seeking information on a young man, correct?"

James felt his spine go taut. His soul followed suit. He knew little of that African American church east of the railroad track. It was a rather quaint, if somewhat under-maintained facility of old brick, with a charming bell tower of ragged oak.

"That's right," he answered. "A young black man."

"Yes. Well, we think we know who it was. I must know, though, Mr. Harrigan, why you want this information."

James almost told her about the robbery, but fearing she might not aid him, he only admitted, "I think he's in some trouble."

"He has been for a while."

"Thought so. Look, Mrs. Woods, I want to help."

"You're not checking up on him?"

"Yes, I am! That's why I called."

"Oh. I'm afraid then I can't talk to you."

"Why?"

"You're with the *Beaver Beacon*, right? You're probably working on some story, right? Well, I don't want him dragged out in public any further. Him or his mom. She's suffered enough."

"I don't want to hurt them."

"No, of course not. You just want to print what you think's the truth. And each time you do, our people come out looking like hoodlums. Why don't you ever print anything good about us?"

"Mam, I don't –"

"He's been trying to do good, Mr. Harrigan. He's tried to turn his life around. He doesn't need your abuse."

"Look," James stated before taking a deep breath to plot out his next words. He didn't want to say anything about the sergeant's call, but he had to learn more about the lad. "I'm trying to help. I met him at the Easy Come, Easy Go. He seems like a nice kid."

"If you met him there," she replied, controlling the pace of her words, "you must know what happened."

"He was fired."

"But why?"

Harrigan checked himself. Why indeed? Because of the conspiracy? Because someone had told him to break into Harrigan's home? Or simply because he was a thief?

Thinking anew about the lad – who was such an integral part of Harrigan's problems – James began to wonder how he ever could have imagined such a conspiracy.

"I don't know," James admitted. "But he seemed a nice kid at the store. He talked to me a long time."

"I'm not surprised. He'd turned his life over to Christ about half a year ago, after being heavy into drugs. He worked at three different places, trying to make his mom happy, and trying to talk to people about God in his own way. He passed notes to some, witnessed openly to others. He gave away those tiny Bibles to customers. But his old friends rejected him for it, and the kids at school, and even our church, they shied from him – you might say they still feared him – and the places he worked didn't like him talking

> ## Behind the Scenes...
> ### Reporting on racism — page 293

about God so much. Fired him for it."

"Notes?" James wondered aloud, feeling a sudden chill. "Like on the receipts?"

Excitement entered her voice. "He gave you one?"

"In some sort of code."

"That's how he did it at the convenience store, since they'd told him to stop. But he was desperate to witness, however he could, and he felt sure God would provide. So when they canned him, and his mom jumped all over him, he ran away. Thought his faith was all wrong. She's not seen him since."

Woods paused. James dared not let go.

"If you know where he is, we'd like to know," his caller said. "We're afraid he might do something bad."

Harrigan felt he had reached a dangerous precipice.

"Was he, well, suicidal?" James said, fearing the answer.

"He tried once before."

Harrigan endured a flash wave of nausea. What had the kid said on the street – there was only one way out?

"Look, Mrs. Woods. I need to check something. I may know where he is. If I do, who should I call?"

"Me… here at the church. And I'd like to see that note."

"Why?"

"Because the Easy Come folks have been trying to get their hands on them – for evidence, I think. They probably feared… well, that the boy… that he would sue them. Discrimination or wrongful termination or something else."

James recalled the steel-eyed manager asking about the receipt.

"But why a code?"

"Because the Easy Come folks didn't want him talking to customers about Christ, so he'd put things in simple codes. Usually based on the alphabet. But they didn't cut him any slack. And after the firing, the Easy Come manager called the state police, saying company secrets were being given out. Trying to cover their tails, I think, even as they tried to gather back all those notes. Our police chief laughed in their face, God bless him. Yes sir, Mr. Isaac Jacobs is worthy of his names!"

Desperate excitement washed over James. So Jacobs wasn't

trying to harass Harrigan… he was trying to protect someone!

"Look, I have to go," James decided.

"You'll call?"

"Count on it," he said, hanging up.

Somehow he remembered just where the receipt was – in a small drawer by his bathroom sink. Unfolding that crumpled paper, James tried a simple code from his childhood, numbering each letter in the alphabet: A=1, B=2 and so on. That method translated the code as JOHNTHREESIXTEEN.

Harrigan started shaking.

John 3:16. "For God so loved the world that He gave His only begotten Son, that whosoever believes in Him should not perish, but have everlasting life."

Despair descended around Harrigan. For James feared the lad who'd written this had given up on life – and Harrigan couldn't help feeling it was his fault.

By Kirby Lee Davis

39

Failure

Girding himself didn't help against the cold that sunny morning. But the bite of winter was nothing compared to the unnerving realities before him.

It saddened James to find a crowd forming around the Fourth Street Overpass. Threading his way through the murmuring throng, he drew the attention of a patrolman at the edge of the highway.

"You're Harrigan?" His words condensed into a chill fog, only to be swept into oblivion by the shifting winds. "Where's your camera?"

"I didn't bring one," James said, hesitating in his answer. The Franklin police didn't ask reporters for cameras unless they had a body they needed photographed.

"Boy, look at that," someone whispered.

A frigid breeze broke around them. James hardly felt it.

A corpse. *Oh, God! He is dead!*

"It's all right, Johnson," called Haskins from atop the old bridge. "Let him come."

Without a word, the patrolman waved James forward.

"He sure got his," came a gruff voice from the crowd.

Fear spread within Harrigan. Praying in silence for guidance, he took a deep breath and pressed on up the manmade hill, passing two parked Franklin squad cars, their lights flashing. The breeze slapped him. With the rising elevation he could see the ever-increasing number of onlookers had surrounded this side of the overpass. For most, the effort to gawk had to be useless. He doubted few would even catch a glimpse of what was going on.

"What is it?" James said to no one. "Why does this sort of thing attract us so?"

Stupid question. He knew the age-old answer. Bloodlust. Death.

Dread weighed heavy upon him. This was the one side of his job he hated.

To be forced to see a man's last moments never seemed right, but to have to describe it to others... to be paid to do it ... to find people wanting to read and see all the grizzly details....

The winds howled. At the crest of the concrete ribbon, Harrigan came upon a dank trail of crimson drying in the foul air. Over a half circle of about five feet, marked by a single tire track, there was an initial splattering of what he could only guess was blood, pocked with a few marble-sized bits of raw, shattered flesh.

A drag trail between fresh skid marks ground about forty feet across the highway, displaying the driver's last-minute attempt to miss the victim. At its end lay the deceased under a forbidding black tarp. Some fifty feet beyond two abandoned patrol cars rested an unmarked semi. Its driver, a huge bear of a man, sat propped against the left front wheel, his face buried within his gloved hands.

"Lord, have mercy on him," James prayed aloud.

And on me. Oh, God, I think I'm going to be sick!

"Amen," came a second.

"Who is it?" Harrigan managed to ask, nodding with a roll of his head to the corpse. He wanted to twist away, to look upon Haskins and nothing else, but something within him refused to budge. Something both drawn and repelled by this scene. Something that felt somehow responsible.

Oh, Lord! Why? Why?

"James," said the sergeant, stepping to the reporter's right side, "I need to ask you something once more, and it's critical.

You did or did not see him during the break-in?"

"You know I didn't."

With firm determination, James turned his back on the hidden corpse. An icy breeze struck him full in the face. He coughed from a dry throat. His eyes watered.

"I only heard his voice," he continued. "But I'd seen him before."

Harrigan could tell this was difficult for Haskins, despite his years of experience. Dark circles outlined the patrolman's bloodshot eyes. His hands shook as his gloved fingers clicked upon a Bic pen, scribbling notes on a torn gray pad.

"When?" the cop asked, his voice weary in its despair.

"Earlier that day. At the Easy Come, Easy Go on Harley Studley. And I ran into him yesterday, downtown. I recognized his voice."

"You're sure?"

"Yes! He approached me, just in front of Sooner National Bank. Talking in real negative terms."

Haskins stepped away, looking across the crowd far below. *Debating himself,* James figured.

"Why didn't you call me?" the cop inquired.

"I tried to talk to you yesterday morning when I made my rounds. Jacobs, too, though he didn't want to listen."

"I know all about that. OK then." Haskins paused once more, reconsidering things. "This isn't a pretty sight, James, and since you didn't bring a camera... Look. I have an old photo we'd kept on file. Since you think you've seen him before, I'd rather show you that. See if you recognize him."

Harrigan nodded, preferring it that way. He didn't want to face death.

From the back of his notepad, the sergeant slid free a wrinkled wallet-sized studio portrait. Jason needed but a glance to be sure. His hair was somewhat longer in this old shot, and his smile seemed forced, but otherwise it was the lad who'd dogged Harrigan's last days.

"God help him," James whispered. "That's him."

"You're sure?"

The reporter nodded. There was no doubt.

"Well then," sighed Haskins, "that solves your case at

least. We only had one helpful print from your place, a fragment that somewhat matched his, though not enough to do anything with. But with your I.D., that should do it – since he's dead."

James pulled his arms tight about his chest. With the wind ripping through his thin London Fog overcoat, he had a new reason to hope he ran into Sandy – to see if she'd cleaned his winter jacket. But such sidetracked thoughts whimpered and died in the sterile realities confronting him now.

The mass crescendo of all his woes took shape within the lifeless husk at his feet. All his exaggerated fears of damaged cars and break-ins, counterfeits and conspiracies, they all meant absolutely nothing when considered alongside the immediacy and finality of death.

Bitter rain broke from the dark clouds of despair shadowing his soul. This kid had James pegged right from their first meeting. For someone who'd considered himself ruined by bankruptcy and divorce, James had managed to rebuild a home for himself. He may have been isolated from those he loved, but he never wanted for food or clothing or shelter or even companionship, if he'd so chosen. And despite all the criticisms Reynolds had fielded, James knew his job had never been endangered. For in all the darkness, God had blessed him. Like Job.

Yet even within such grace, James felt not love, but a deep, condemning guilt. For when his life's path had led to someone who truly needed a strong witness, how had James repaid his Lord? With apathy and paranoia.

What was it the kid had said? *There ain't but one way out. One way. And it ain't no upraised finger, either.*

Desperate echoes flogged his soul. Why oh why had he not contested such misbegotten logic? How had he allowed himself to be so corrupted by self-centered fears that he'd not heard that boy's heart crying out for guidance?

Behind the Scenes...
Questions of Job — page 294

Even under prosecution by his boss and peers, this young lad had tried to reach out to him. *Why couldn't I have done the same?*

Before him lay the bitter results of his failure.

The kid's found his answer, James realized in his swelling bitterness. *And I drove him there.*

Demands to flee overwhelmed his thoughts. And yet, James couldn't leave. He still had questions he needed answered.

"So," he forced himself to put forward, "you know who he is?"

Haskins released a deep breath of regret. "This wasn't his first attempt, you know. He tried twice before to step in front of trucks. Right here on this bridge. But those times, he always did it too early, as if he wanted to give the driver time to miss. This time, he just launched himself into its grill. The driver... he didn't have a chance. And this was only his second run. Can you imagine how he must feel? He may never drive a rig again. Hell, he might not be able to do much of anything for quite a while."

James felt a kinship with the nameless behemoth truck driver – almost as great as that he shared with the deceased.

"Where's he from?" James asked.

"He's an independent out of Arizona. Wife's on her way, but it's going to take her a day to get out here. Can't imagine what this will do to his insurance, but it can't be pretty."

"Insurance?" Harrigan choked off sarcastic laughter. *You think he's worried about that now?*

A handset kicked in, warning about the growing crowd. Lifting his radio from his belt, Haskins made some comment about the "vultures," then asked the dispatcher why the coroner's unit hadn't arrived yet. The supervisor didn't know.

"Typical," Haskins spat.

"Look," James said, "I need to be getting to work. Do you know who he is?"

"Yeah," the sergeant said. "Terrance Jackson."

James stiffened. "Shirley's child?"

40

Sorting

Loose ends sometimes tied themselves together, or so it seemed to James. In the hazy aftermath of the boy's attempted suicides, it made sense that the police chief would take a strong personal interest in protecting the Ward 8 councilwoman's wayward son, even if the lad had a history of significant problems. It might also explain another councilman's desire to persecute the police chief, if the council members in question were enemies of sorts – or if one just disagreed with coddling the son of another. And it could explain how a sergeant might feel forced into silence, even if he felt duty-bound to help James.

Wrapped into a neat package, it made one juicy story – but not one James would ever write. Even if some elements of the public might benefit from such coverage – and a gossipy few, like those in the bloodthirsty crowd, would eat it up – Harrigan knew putting his thoughts in print would damage just about everyone involved. He wasn't prepared to do that. He wouldn't give anyone such satisfaction.

What Reynolds would think about this, James couldn't guess – though it wouldn't matter once Harrigan was fired.

Not that *that* mattered, either. Indeed, with images of death clouding his thoughts, James wondered if anything mattered.

Leaving the *Defiant* in the *Beacon's* parking lot, Harrigan was disappointed to find the building's heating system still dysfunctional. His editor always seemed more hyper in a deep freeze. But the staff appeared busy, and Reynolds was not in his office, so Harrigan was able to slip to his desk undetected. There he found a small bundle of mail, which he resettled upon his chair seat, and his lit phone message light indicator. Harrigan switched on his computer and tapped in his voicemail access code. His jaws clenched. On such a day, one message was stressful enough, but three....

"Hello, Mr. Harriman. This is Milo Steward, a customer service rep at Leo Heavy Chevy Geo. I'm just calling to let you know that the estimate on your mirror is... is.... (Where is that, Jane? I can't find it anywhere.... Yes, I looked on my chair! Do you think I'd be stupid enough to leave things lying on his chair?) I'm sorry, Mr. Harrison, but it seems I've misplaced the estimate on your... well, your car. If I remember right, it was around.... (No, not the Corvette. It wasn't a Vette! You think I'd be calling on a $140 bill for a Vette?) Anyway, Mr. Halogen, please give me a call about your, well.... It was a car, wasn't it? Yes, so I recall. Well, thank you, Mr.... What's that?... Hooligan."

On any other day, James might have written a column about all the comic foolery that car wash caused him. But there was no joy in his life now. Taking a deep breath in a vain effort to clear his muddled thoughts, he erased the message with two keystrokes and went on.

"Hello, James. This is Carol at Riverside. You didn't clean out your cabinets today."

Harrigan almost slumped into his mail-laden chair. *Oh, God help me! I forgot!*

"I needn't remind you," the recording continued, "how periodic treatments are not only required to keep our apartments free of dangerous infestations, but also they're

---

Behind the Scenes...
Writing tactics — page 295

required as part of your lease. Now, I can arrange for the exterminator crew to come back to your place by four this afternoon. Call me if you can't have your cabinets cleared out by then. It's important, James. Thanks."

Imagining the bug mercenaries on their missions of insecticide made Harrigan shudder. For no matter how he looked at it, or how necessary it was, the Riverside mission was just another slice of death.

Snapping his index finger into the "3" and "#" keys, James sent Carol's message to Davy Jones's phone locker.

"I wonder if Micky, Peter, or Mike have lockers," he thought aloud – never questioning what personality quirk would send his rattled thoughts tripping from Hades to the Monkees. Not that he had time to ponder it, with the third recording upon him.

"Hello, Mr. Harrybear. This is Milo Steward, a customer service rep at Leo Heavy Chevy Geo. I'm just calling to tell you, the estimate on replacing your mirror is... is.... (What's that? What do you mean I've already called him?) Oh. I'm sorry. I have the wrong number. Thanks."

Harrigan enjoyed erasing that message, though it didn't last.

"James!" came the voice of power at the *Beacon*. "I need to talk to you – now."

Reynolds stood leaning against the corner to his office, sharply dressed in his gray no-wrinkle slacks and white dress shirt. A hard glare ground into his face. As they made eye contact, Reynolds lingered but a second before rolling away, bound for his desk.

Releasing a deep sigh, Harrigan followed his boss into The Furnace. James expected a first-class roasting, and he didn't really care.

Reynolds was lighting a thick stogie as Harrigan took a

Behind the Scenes...

Silly messages and memories — page 296
From Hades to the Monkees — page 297

seat. Pulling deep on his smoldering cigar, Dick blew out a rolling ring of stringent smoke and watched it float to the ceiling. When he turned to James, his eyes settled in open curiosity.

"What's wrong?"

James fidgeted. This wasn't how he imagined his boss would begin.

"You look as white as a sheet," Reynolds continued. "You feeling OK?"

"Well, I've not been sleeping well," James admitted. He felt his heartbeat accelerate, his breaths grow shallow. He was at a loss to know what he could do about it – or why it had even happened.

"A-ha." Reynolds exhaled a cloud of hot gas from the side of his mouth. He watched it rise but a moment before focusing once more on his reporter.

"So," said the editor, "what exactly happened last night?"

James stiffened, waiting for the bricks to fall. "What do you mean?"

"Well, I accidentally hit my wife's button for KLOD on the way in. Danvers was speaking about the sexual tensions at last night's city council meeting, of all things."

James clamped his fingers around the armrests. A drop of cold sweat stung his left eye.

It seemed so obvious now that Carolyn would bring up last night's meeting on this morning's show. That was her shtick, after all – revealing her private life for anyone who dared listen. But he hadn't expected it. And yet, even as he imagined all the embarrassment she could cause him, it paled against other specters haunting him. The mystery of death. Imminent death. And his role in it all.

A glittering light ignited his chest. James took his cross in his hands and squeezed.

"And then I get this call from Jacobs," continued Reynolds, "asking if you're alright. Said he was quite impressed with you last night, but he was concerned when you left early."

It took a few moments for James to even consider the call from Jacobs.

"He said what?"

"That you didn't even stay for the water rates debate," Reynolds answered. "Though from what I could tell, it didn't sound like much. The debate, I mean."

James nodded, sorting through his editor's earlier response. It sounded like the first kind thing the police chief had ever uttered about him.

"You didn't stay?" Reynolds said.

Only after considering his options did Harrigan nod. He hadn't anticipated this. Indeed, it didn't quite seem real. Nothing did.

"Well," reflected the curious publisher, "I don't mind telling you, this sure has kicked up a lot of interest. McDuff called, as did Hertz and others. Whatever happened last night, they all seem to think highly of the way you handled it. And envious… some of them, anyway. Strange situation."

James took a series of deep breaths, trying to relax. His system rebelled. He could feel the anxiety coursing through him, pressing against his flesh like deep sea waters.

And images of death lay all around.

"Are you sure you're alright?" Reynolds repeated.

"No," James said, deciding things had gone far enough. "I received a call early this morning from Haskins."

"The sergeant who'd called yesterday."

"Right. He'd found my burglar. The kid committed suicide this morning."

"Oh, God."

"Just jumped in front of a truck. Killed instantly."

Reynolds nodded. "Fourth Street Overpass?"

"That's the one."

"Yeah. I couldn't get you at home, so I sent Samuel there."

"Yeah, well… I beat him there. It's on my mind a lot, and I've got to admit, I'm feeling really confused right now. A lot of things don't seem right."

Reynolds held his cigar perched next to his lips. "This your first run-in with death?"

"Like this, I guess. I mean, I was around my grandmother as she was dying. I've been a pallbearer more times than I can remember – or want to remember. But, to actually see… and the crowd!"

James doubted he'd ever forget the gawkers – people who were supposed to be friendly, sympathetic neighbors.

Who was actually in more need of help – a man who tries time after time to kill himself, and finally succeeds, or the man who comes to watch and says with a smile, "He sure got his."

Drawing such a reaction in death, James wondered what the young Jackson had faced in life. It might explain many things.

And when I had a chance to witness to him, to help him, I didn't. God forgive me!

Reynolds glided his chair backward. "Don't blame yourself. Every beat reporter goes through it. Hell, you never get over it, James. And you can't prepare for it. I saw a veteran war correspondent gag at a traffic accident once, so don't beat yourself up."

A chill breeze flowed through the office. Harrigan pulled his arms tight but felt no warmer. He shivered, grit his teeth, and settled into frozen asset frustration.

It seemed obvious now he wasn't getting fired today. That, at least, was something. But it changed nothing of the hell he now lived – and gave him no reason to live it. For he'd failed everyone… even God. Especially God.

A phone rang. Reynolds yanked his receiver up, grunted acknowledgment, and hung up.

"You've got a visitor," he grumbled, "and a deadline. The city pages go in today, you know."

A small sparrow flew by the window. James watched it twist about in mid-flight, enjoying the morning breeze as it soared from the shadows into the rising sun. Harrigan wondered how that bird could feel such pleasure in this harsh cold.

A smoke ring obscured his view.

"Look, James, I'd like to give you the day off, but… oh, hell, Hernandez isn't busy today. Tell me: if he brushed over last night's minutes, could he write up a council story? Did anything important happen?"

Harrigan leaned his chin against his left fist. *Oh, nothing much*, he almost answered. *Just another tragic twist in my life.*

"No," he muttered.

"Good. That'd still give you tomorrow to write that story we've talked about."

Recalling that made James cringe. It was apparent now that the break-in was not a simple tale of irony, but one step in the deadly trail of something determined to destroy him. And it wasn't over.

"No," he whispered to himself, "that's paranoia raising its head again. Get a grip!"

Janice shoved her lovely head into the doorway. "Someone's here to see James."

"I remember," Reynolds said. Then he motioned for Harrigan to leave with a thrust of his right hand that flicked cigar ash across his desk.

James worked himself to his feet, wondering who would wish to see him today, of all days. Cobb, perhaps, having heard more scuttlebutt at the diner. Or Fat Mama, ready to grind his bones to make her bread. He could readily imagine that if Underwood caught Carolyn's show – which he remembered would remain on the air for yet another hour.

Sliding around the corner, James came to a sudden stop before a long pair of bare designer legs resting on a freshly pressed coat folded atop his desk. There, with her nose buried in the last pages of his manuscript, awaited Sandy Travis.

"I'm sorry," she said, not taking her eyes from the book, "but that scene where the prince bounces off the hare's front teeth… it just cracks me up!"

"I'm glad," he said, only to find gravity taunting him. For leaning back in his chair had pulled open her long, unbuttoned jacket, revealing Sandy in all her sleeveless jogging suit glory.

"Another sight to make Jack jealous," he mumbled.

Behind the Scenes…
Radio personalities — page 298

By Kirby Lee Davis

41

The Meaning of It All

It didn't require much coaxing for Sandy to talk James into a late breakfast at the diner – she simply proposed they discuss his manuscript. But James entered the eatery feeling as inconspicuous as a blimp. It was one thing to talk with another woman at church, on the phone, or even in her car… but to meet a woman alone in a public place – a married woman, no less! – where everyone and their dog could see them.

Dare he place an innocent friend under such scrutiny? He knew the bitter results of divorce. How could he put anyone to such an emotional risk?

And for it to be Sandy!

With his first step in the door, James found himself scanning the eatery's twelve booths and its eight-stool counter, just to see if he recognized anyone. He didn't, to his good fortune, though that didn't shake his fears. It didn't help that the waitress guided them towards a booth to the strains of Elton John's *Goodbye Yellow Brick Road*. Bernie

---

Behind the Scenes…
Goodbye Yellow Brick Road — page 299

Taupin's haunting words seemed so incriminating, even though James had never really taken the time to figure out just what Elton was singing about.

"You're sure that was him?" Sandy asked, sliding across the crimson vinyl bench seat. Harrigan took the opposite one, positioning himself to not sit over any of the three jagged tears in its aging cover.

"No doubt," he mumbled, finishing the tale he'd begun in the short drive over.

"And you feel responsible."

James struggled to meet her golden eyes. Sandy cradled her tanned face within her propped-up hands, her arms hidden down to the tabletop by her long auburn hair. The strands pooled elegantly around her elbows.

Even the bounce of her hair seems orderly, James thought.

"I am responsible," he answered, pausing as the waitress laid before each lap a glass of ice water, an old-fashioned coffee cup overturned on its chipped saucer, and a set of weathered stainless-steel silverware bound by a white paper napkin.

"Because you didn't witness to him," Sandy reflected.

"Yes! He reached out to me, didn't he?"

"So it seems, though it was a rather cryptic way."

"The only way he could. I mean, he had been fired twice for talking about Christ, and yet he still did it."

"Until the third time."

"Yeah, well. At least he tried. And me, the best I do is wear this cross."

"That's not true. I'm sure your example moves a lot of people, seeing how you've handled things."

Harrigan shrugged that off.

With a warm smile, Sandy slipped her hands over his. James welcomed the touch, longing for more – and then pulled away.

Behind the Scenes…
Christian witnessing — page 300

"Why are you so worried about what other people think?" she said.

Harrigan snapped his head up. "I'm not."

"Then why do I bother you?"

"Well, because... I'm worried about what other people might think."

She laughed. It proved a hearty pleasure. James couldn't help joining her.

Looking at his friend was like eating fine chocolate. She radiated the relaxing warmth of true beauty – not from her physical attributes, though they were coaxing, but from inner confidence. The kind built on faith.

The kind James so often lacked.

"Felt good, didn't it?" she asked him. "Laughter, I mean."

James nodded, glad she'd explained.

"Where's the joy in your life?" she inquired. "Not that fake satire you put in your columns. Where's your happiness?"

Something inside him didn't want to answer that, much less think about it. A wisecrack came to mind, and he started to voice it – only to feel the dart wither on his tongue under her compassionate gaze. He couldn't lie to her.

"What reason do I have to feel joy? So much of me is gone. Inside, Sandy. I have nothing left. My wife's rejected me. My kids were stripped from me. I mean, you don't know how hard it's been, being unable to see my girls three out of every four weeks."

And with all that's happened, I've hardly given them a second thought these last few days. Some father I am.

She took his hands in hers. "James, let's pray about it. Right now."

James wondered if he dared open his heart to God in such a public place. His thoughts pivoted around the boy, from that old silent photo to his convenience store gaiety, that street corner desperation, the bloody bridge.

"Oh, Sandy. So many times I've wondered if it's worth it. Living this life."

"Of course it is!"

"Have you ever been there, drowning in such heartache and hopelessness? I look at what this kid's done and I can sympathize so much with how he felt. If I'd just listened to the pain in his voice. If I'd just said something friendly to him."

"Things might have ended the very same way. We just don't know, do we?"

"I think I have a pretty good idea."

"Oh, you're God now?"

James didn't know how to answer that. There was an edge to what she said, almost an attack. He didn't want to face that. He couldn't. So, he changed tracks.

"You know, all my life I've taken the easy way out of things."

"Not all!"

"Well, it seems like it. My parents wanted me to become a doctor. I had the grades for it. But I didn't want to have someone's life hanging on my hands. I thought, if I went into journalism, I wouldn't have to see someone die. The easy way out, you see? Marrying Charlotte was the same thing – she pursued me, and I was so amused that someone actually was attracted to me that I went along with it. I'd never really allowed myself to, well, to open up to a woman before."

"But you love her."

"Yes," he admitted. *Deeply.*

As the radio broke into *Superstar* by the Carpenters, the waitress arrived to get their order. Embarrassed by the attention, James asked for a glass of orange juice. Sandy did the same.

A forgiving smile lit up her face. The sight brought Harrigan pleasure – and he felt guilty for it.

"James, you remember that man Peter healed outside the Temple? The cripple in Acts? The Bible says he'd laid outside the Temple for years, so Christ surely had seen him – and yet Jesus let him go on with his painful life."

Behind the Scenes...
Superstar — page 303
A healing story — page 304

James leaned back as far as he could go. "So?"

"So, we are bound to run across people, hurting people, who we can't help. I mean, if you read about all the multitudes that gathered around Christ, that must have happened all the time. There had to have been hundreds who sought help and didn't get it. The difficulties that some people went to just to reach Him are sometimes why we even remember their healing. The man lowered through the roof, or the lady who had the faith to touch His robe. I mean, He made a point of letting Lazarus die, just to make his healing more dramatic."

"What are you saying – that we just shouldn't care about anyone unless they get in our way?"

"You know better than that. It's just that… well, sometimes we go through hard times. Life's a test, after all. We learn from it. How we handle it defines our character. And yes, you might have been able to help this young man, but it was his choice to kill himself, James, not yours. I don't know what shaped his life, but I know how hard yours has been, and you've not given up. He didn't have to, either. So don't beat yourself up over it."

"I'm not beating myself up."

"You're not?"

"No! It's just…."

James felt himself stumbling. He heard Carolyn's voice over the ceiling speakers introducing Three Dog Night's *Easy to Be Hard*, even as the waitress returned with their drinks. Sandy sat across from him, attentive, caring, giving her time to Harrigan even though by her garb she had been bound for some athletic contest.

She was as he'd always known her: a loving disciple of Christ. Her sacrifice numbed him.

"It's selfish, I suppose," James said. "You know, when you

Behind the Scenes…
Stories of faith — page 306
Easy to Be Hard — page 303

get right down to it, I see myself in that kid. I look back at how I've handled my life, and I see all the ways I could have ministered to people, and yet I didn't. All the mistakes I've made. All the things I thought were just so important, and yet are nothing when you get down to the basics."

James sipped from his juice glass. The pulp tickled his tongue.

"Some of the things I've guided my life by… sometimes I can't help but question everything I've done. You know, these last days, I've caught myself telling little lies, just to ease out of certain problems. It was so easy, you know? And I'm so lonely. I actually bought a *Playboy* book the other day. I was intrigued by the histories it promised –"

"And the pictures?" Sandy interjected.

James squirmed. "Well, there was that, but to be honest – honest, Sandy – I mean, haven't you always wondered how people who pursued lifestyles we frown upon could claim to be so happy?"

"No."

"Well, I did. Do. And this book had histories of every playmate the magazine's run – and what they've done since they posed. Several told of turning to Christ since appearing in the magazine, and some even condemned the *Playboy* lifestyle. Others had some tragic turns. But it amazed me how many took great joy in what they did, twenty, thirty, even forty years after appearing."

"Keep in mind most of those women haven't lived that long. They don't really know what impact it'll have."

"I think just the opposite. Their lives are so immersed in that culture, they learn rather quickly what impact it'll have. I mean, *Playboy's* fifty years old. There's at least one woman in there, Sandy, who claims to have been a Christian when she posed – and another who'd taught Sunday school before she posed. And they embraced that life."

James saw his friend harden.

"They're mistaken," she stated.

"I know that. I do! But it taught me something. We go around thinking God wants us to be happy – and I truly believe that – but I'm only now understanding how His concept of happiness is so different than mine – or at least, from what mine was. How simply living a life in Christ, by itself, should provide all the happiness we ever need – whether we go through a divorce or a car wash that thrusts you into a federal investigation."

Sandy choked off laughter.

"What?" she blurted out.

"Well, I mean, my old views of a happy life were so worldly. So wrong. Cars, house and home, fine clothes, all that worthless stuff. That's not what life's about. I know that, and yet, it's so hard to give up. And it's so easy to forget what God would have us do when our world's collapsing around us… or for that matter, when everything's golden and we're prospering. Sandy, I've failed so many things."

As the radio played harmonies having nothing to do with three sleeping canines, Sandy took a long, patient drink, all the while smiling with such warmth that Harrigan half-expected her to break out in laughter. In the end she put down her glass, wiped her lips, and said, "You know, sometimes I think I'm wasting my time with you."

If he'd been standing, James would've collapsed.

"You're such a smart guy," she continued. "You should be so full of joy!"

"Joy?" *Sandy, I'm dying inside!*

"Yes. Joy. Tell me: why are we here?"

The obviousness of her question made him stumble for an answer.

"Because you suggested it," he decided, punting the ball away.

"No, James! Why are we *here* – on Earth? What's our point in being here?"

Realization crept over him. She's talking about truth. Spiritual truth.

"To worship God," he said.

"Good boy. Through all of our lives, we have only one important decision to make. Do we believe in Christ, or don't we? If we do, we live and die for Him, as the Bible instructs us, and the Spirit leads us. And if we don't accept Him, then we just live and die. Right? Can we both agree on that?"

James felt himself back in Vacation Bible School. "Yes, I guess so."

Sandy cast him a whimsical nod that told him there was no "guess so" about it.

"And which choice did you make?" she said.

"You know!"

"So, tell me anyway."

"I believe in Christ."

"And who's he?"

"The Son of God. Jesus. Our Savior, who died on the cross for our sins."

"That's right. *The* Man. The *perfect* Man, spiritually, intellectually – who gave up that perfect life for us. How does that make you feel?"

Bitter shame crept through Harrigan's flesh.

"Thankful," he mumbled.

"It should make you feel happy, James! Every morning you should wake up with such happiness! We're not slaves of this world anymore! Every time we take a breath, we should rejoice. We're free of sin! Hallelujah!"

Harrigan drained his glass dry. The vibrant liquid offered no help with the emotional conflict within him, the chastising soul that embraced her words, the wounded heart intolerant of hope.

"It's not that easy," he moaned, feeling a burden to defend himself.

"Oh, yes, it is!"

"No, it's not! Look, I know what you're saying. I know it's true. But for me, right now, I just don't feel it. I don't!"

In a slow, painful stretch of time and breath, James watched the pleasure drain from Sandy's face. It wounded him… another burden on his soul. But in her eyes burned determined flames.

"You know, Peter and James wrote to you, in the Bible, those hundreds of years ago. How to cope with the hardships we face. Upholding Christ in the midst of this sinful world. The day-to-day ministry of our lives."

"Day to day," Harrigan echoed. "That's where I failed."

The waitress stopped in her rounds to see if they wanted

anything else. Halfway through asking, she giggled.

"This is so cool," she whispered. "I guess he's not going to call."

"Who?" Sandy wanted to know.

"On Danvers' show," said the waitress, a middle-aged blonde with tight curls bound by a white bonnet. "She's been asking her lover to call all morning. Listen."

James wished he could disappear.

"Well, it's 9 a.m.," Carolyn said, "so I guess he's not turned in. That's what I choose to believe, anyway. But if you are listening, I want you to know, I'm sorry I put on such a show last night. Sometimes I get carried away with myself. I'm a clown, and a flirt – always have been – and sometimes I go too far. I'm sorry. It was… inappropriate. I'm just lucky I have such a good friend in the studio."

"What – the engineer?" Sandy wondered aloud.

"I guess their council broadcast last night was edited," the waitress said with a smile.

Thank you, Lord! James prayed.

"But more than that," Carolyn continued, "on the other things, I want you to know… you were right, all along. People sometimes wonder what sort of impact their example has on others. Well, what you did last night changed my life. It's made me do a lot of thinking. And I've come to the conclusion that I really want to know you better. So, I'm moving out. I'm getting a place of my own.

"And also… some of my steady listeners might not believe this, but I'm going to study this God you've built your life around. I must admit that, well, I'm intrigued. I want to see for myself what you think's better than sex. And that, for the rest of you listening in, is all you're going to hear about that – for now, at least. So have a good day, Franklin! I'll see you next week."

The waitress walked off, chuckling a little more with each

Behind the Scenes…
Joy in difficulties — page 308

step. James hid his face in his hands. Sandy pulled them away.

"You were at that meeting, weren't you?"

Ashamed, reluctant to admit anything, James allowed himself a brief nod.

"Well," Sandy reflected, "it sounds to me like you've had a greater impact on someone than you'd ever like to admit."

"Perhaps."

"And maybe that's your answer, James. For all these things you're facing. Think about it."

By Kirby Lee Davis

42

j-newcol.wpd

I need to step down from my humor soapbox today.

It's strange to imagine living on this earth for only a day or so, and yet, I can't help feeling that if we honestly sifted through our lives, discarding all the time burned on mindless diversions and earthly pleasures – all the selfish, trivial things that dominate our culture – we'd have left only a handful of hours spent in heartfelt toil and sacrifice to actually improve this world.

Unsettling?

It gets worse.

For of those few hours, it's safe to bet tragedy is the all-too-common element igniting, connecting, and compounding them. In this commercialized, self-absorbed society that we cherish, it is in the swirl of the tempest that we truly define our character. All too often we come out the poorer for our efforts.

This must stop.

How can Christ's work be completed in this grand society we've built to shelter and defend us?

In the same way it has been done over most of the last two millennia – through not just divine will, but the hands and hearts of believers.

And yet it seems so much harder now, in this world where

high technology and modern government help us isolate and encase ourselves in imaginary fortresses, aloft from the messy things in life. It's so easy to lose sight of our fellow man in the jungle of our personal ambitions and schedules. Where our exposure to pain is nothing more than driving by a car accident – all the while angry that traffic has slowed – or serving food at a homeless shelter once a quarter, somehow feeling satisfied that we've done enough for those less fortunate than ourselves.

How much better would we be – how much stronger would our society be – if our lives were not so sanitized? If we had to deal daily with the real human problems of hunger, despair, hopelessness, rejection, and death?

Don't tune this out as the ranting of some self-righteous televangelist. These are my problems, I'm sorry to say.

Through the last months I've seen the innards of my life turned inside out. Habits exposed as diseases. Beliefs challenged as crutches. I've confronted changes I've been fighting, refusing to let go. Dreams that were crushed, and missions left undone. And through it all, I've discovered the foundation upon which I'd pledged my soul lays incomplete – not due to His negligence, but my own. I've talked fast and furious about The Message, but I'd not even tried to work all His promises in my life. I've not even bothered to learn how.

So, I'm going to make you a pledge. From this moment I've set a new goal for my life.

To truly study and apply the Bible.

To open my eyes to all the different ways this world needs Christ.

To magnify what God's done for me.

To share His love.

To live the life I profess – every day, every hour, every second.

Pray for me, that when this focusing moment fades, I will have the strength to fulfill this vow. I will do the same for you.

Together, we will make a difference.

By Kirby Lee Davis

Afterward

Thank you for reading this book. I hope it spoke to your heart. If you find yourself identifying with, or suffering like, one or more of the characters you've just met, don't brush that aside. You are a beautiful creation of God – beloved, whether you believe it or not. Seek help. Many organizations stand ready and willing to aid you. Your area churches, cathedrals, tabernacles, and synagogues offer countless resources to meet your needs. Engage them. Above all, open yourself to God. Set aside all doubts and skepticism, worries and fears, so that the Father, the Son, and the Holy Spirit may work in you and through you. Allow yourself to be forgiven, and to forgive... to love, and to be loved. For you are not alone, no matter how much this world may tell you otherwise. Many around you share similar pains and anguish, strangers and friends alike, and they too may be saved, with you, perhaps through you. God works in such ways, leading us all along the road to renewal.

Behind the Scenes...
This is the end... — page 310
Self-deception and redemption — page 314

The Road to Renewal

By Kirby Lee Davis

Behind the Scenes

This section provides background information on the history and culture of this novel's 1990s setting, my writing strategies, and theology. Hopefully these will hold you over until you find more authoritative sources. Tackling this turned into an interesting self-examination, one where I often debated what topics needed explanation. Breck Girls made the cut, along with Elton John's *Goodbye Yellow Brick Road*, the biblical concepts of joy, and many other subjects. A good number earn brief summaries; others draw essays and comparative analyses. After some debate I decided readers probably knew enough about Spaghetti-Os, Robert Redford's nose, and the Gettysburg Address, among others. And some references, like Queeg and his marbles (from *The Caine Mutiny* novel and film, for those who don't know), I'll probably ponder their inclusion for the rest of my life.

By my personal preference, all biblical quotes draw from the New King James Version, published by Thomas Nelson. Several websites offer easy ways to examine these verses in other translations. I often use biblegateway.com.

j-col47.wpd

That code identifies several things:
• The title of this novel's first chapter.
• The file name of a column (which is that chapter) our lead character – reporter James Harrigan – wrote for his newspaper.

The "j" denotes the author's name, while "col47" refers to this being his 47th column. That ".wpd" reveals the firm's use of Word Perfect software, a popular word processing program in the 1990s.

I developed this coding as part of a filing system for when my employer switched our newsroom from a Mycro-Tek platform to networked personal computers. I thought my spur-of-the-moment improvisations could serve as a stop-gap solution until we came up with something better. We ended up using my system for well over a decade.

I wrote many a column, review, and social commentary through my 40-year newspaper career. Nearly all of them sampled my broad sense of humor, one honed as I grew up with the Marx Brothers and *Monty Python's Flying Circus*, Bugs Bunny and *Green Acres*, Don Rickles and *All in the Family*. At times I drew criticism for my sometimes reckless absurdity. One high school teacher threw me out of class for including one of his jokes in an article for my school paper (which just happened to run inside our town's weekly newspaper). Another time our school superintendent grilled me for a bit of satire I included on a scholarship application. Perhaps the biggest hit came when I self-published *The Spawn of Fashan*, drawing attacks for mixing elements I found funny into something others took quite seriously. Over time I learned a few lessons on how and when to contain these impulses… you'll encounter some of these in this novel!

"Try me! I'm a new talking Coke machine!"

That line in Chapter 1 introduces readers to a talking Coca-Cola vending machine. These actually existed. Coke distributed 3,100 such devices around the United States in the early 1980s, according to a 1982 *Washington Post* article. A computer system developed by Sanyo allowed these monoliths to synthesize speech in English, Spanish, or Japanese. Those I encountered opened with my novel's introductory line. They mixed in other statements as you made your purchase. Still more dialogue or music emerged while the machine waited for someone to push its buttons or drop in coins. Fun but expensive to install and repair, technicians I spoke to said Coke and its distributors generally phased out these machines before the decade's end.

"Halfway through the picture, my seat buzzed."

Moviegoers today are familiar with high-tech seats that recline, shake in time with the action, or allow you to order food. Such was not the case in the 1990s, when this novel takes place. But theaters did experiment with the literal electric shocks discussed in Chapter 1… only it happened in 1959, capping a decade when U.S. film distributors, desperate to compete with surging home television usage, tried everything from wider screens and 3D to smell-o-vision… and seats that shocked people at key moments. Director William Castle hoped such stimulation would enhance the thrill aspects of his film *The Tingler*. While his system did not survive the moment, its legacy did stimulate my imagination enough to impact this novel…

Future Shock

Chapter 1 opens with a humor column written by the protagonist, a newspaper reporter demonstrating some fear of evolving technology. Since *The Road to Renewal* takes place in the 1990s, both those fears and technologies may seem rather quaint today. But the "writer" acknowledges this in his playful use of the term "future shock." That was the title of a landmark 1970 bestseller by futurist Alvin Toffler. Though I was only 11 years old when that hardcover emerged, I read its paperback four years later. His cautionary words (some still valid) played upon concerns heightened by Watergate, the space race, and the Vietnam War, and yet his cultural theories also drew resistance and disbelief from my faith and love of absurd satire. This echoes throughout the novel…

Talking cars

The talking Coca-Cola vending machine of Chapter 1 was not the only such innovation of the 1980s. While Ford may not have delivered the talking Mustang my novel features, other automakers did experiment with voice simulations in their dashboard operating systems. Rather than let a computer speak, Nissan installed small phonographs in some models to play recorded female voice warnings for certain driving and system alerts. Chrysler went a different route, adapting Texas Instruments technologies (remember the Speak & Spell?) to provide up to 24 different synthesized vocal warnings or reminders. Mercury, Buick, and Oldsmobile also tested these waters, but consumers balked at them all. Not one survived into the 1990s.

Talking Coke cans

Besides talking vending machines and cars, Chapter 1 also features a talking Coke can. Like the others, this has some roots in reality!

After its New Coke fiasco, in 1990 the Coca-Cola Co. tried to boost its restored Coke Classic brand with unique packaging: a limited-edition can that held cash prizes within ill-flavored water used to disguise its contents and discourage drinking. Unfortunately, the patented "MagiCan" sometimes failed to work, and a health scare over its safe-yet-foul fluid led to this marketing campaign's early demise. But other beverage companies soon offered high-tech can contests of their own, encouraged by aluminum manufacturers threatened by increased plastic bottling. Coors Light joined the fray in 1992 with a microchip-enhanced can that told consumers of their prize as they drank its beer.

Perspective

In Chapter 2, readers learn that Chapter 1 was a humor column written by the book's protagonist, newspaper reporter James Harrigan. *The Road to Renewal* includes many of his columns, which fulfill several purposes.

• In a few cases, these usually absurd excerpts serve the same function in the book as in that small-town newspaper: to amuse and entertain… hopefully. That's a debated point among some characters, just as my humor columns often were during my newspaper career.

• These pieces work as bridges between scenes or gaps in time.

• These transitions provide insights on the characters and culture, with information the reader may need to know later.

• Several columns foreshadow events to come.

These excerpts also inject different voices into the novel's third-person point of view. That structural element sets *The Road to Renewal* apart from my other books – which fits my goal to approach each one with a different style.

All four novels in The Jonah Cycle utilize limited first-person narrative, with the viewpoint characters changing from book to book. *The Prophet and the Dove* is told by an old slave. He also narrates book four, though from a far different standpoint. Book three draws from a tortured shepherd who first appeared in book two, while that title, *Lions of Judah*, comes through the eyes of … you'll find out.

I know some readers prefer multiple viewpoints. The marketplace embraces this, with many books and films sharing diverse protagonist and antagonist positions that reveal vital plot secrets. As Hitchcock often noted, this helps generate audience sympathy and tension. But I prefer writing with a more limited perspective, where only God knows what everyone is thinking. Since I live with but one viewpoint – my own line of sight – I find maintaining this keeps my writing more realistic. *The Road to Renewal* provides a good example. Using a limited third-person perspective best retains the mystery and uncertainty of life, and it helps explain why honesty, trust, and love are crucial to daily survival.

God's Furry Angels is my exception. Since I wrote that for my kids, *GFA* employs a classic storyteller format where a central narrator juggles many different viewpoints to weave his tale. The most-remembered character in *God's Furry Angels* is a youngster excited by discovery and learning, so to her, unraveling the mystery and uncertainty of life is but one aspect of growing up. This differs from *The Road to Renewal*, where faith represents our best – and sometimes only – bulwark when facing the unknown, as Harrigan discovers.

Franklin, OK, and the University of Football

When I finished The Jonah Cycle, my mind crafted a modern sequel to the third book's horror story. I set this tale in rural Oklahoma, a land I knew fairly well. To camouflage some areas I wrote about, I created the fictional Oklahoma City suburb of Franklin. Little did I know there once was such a town, settled south of OKC shortly after the Land Run of 1889. Franklin survived until 1906, when its fourth-class post office was taken over by mail operations in nearby Norman. Franklin residents soon became part of that growing city, home of the University of Oklahoma – my alma mater, which I often referred to then as "the University of Football." This fondness carried over as I wrote *The Road to Renewal*, with my Franklin as its setting.

Hot topics in small-town journalism

Chapter 2 introduces readers to James Harrigan, a reporter and humor columnist for the *Beaver Beacon* newspaper in Franklin, a "suburb" of Oklahoma City. Harrigan serves as the central figure in this novel's three-day comic tragedy. Readers also meet Harrigan's boss, Managing Editor Dick Reynolds, and view a small newsroom in the days before the web, when no book of information was ever discarded, no matter how old or trivial, and employees spent hours clipping, dating, and filing multiple copies of almost every article and photo to see print, along with some that didn't.

I painted this picture from personal experience, having worked in nine different Oklahoma newspaper offices from the 1970s to '90s. The novel's mid-1990s setting captures newsroom transitions from dedicated word-processing systems to networked personal computers (usually disk operating systems, known as DOS). That move's high cost, factoring in hardware and software, often taxed the financial resources of small papers. This led many publishers to invest in generic PCs, frequently pre-owned, which explains the condition of the *Beacon* terminals.

This exchange between Harrigan and Reynolds hints at divisive cultural issues the Oklahoma press sometimes tiptoed around in that era.

Reynolds warns that Harrigan's satirical columns often struck the wrong chord with Bible-belt readers. I ran into similar complaints with the slapstick parodies I penned back then, even though Oklahoma public television helped lead the way in bringing *Monty Python's Flying Circus* to mainstream America. Go figure.

Such concerns also underscore why Reynolds criticizes Harrigan's frequent writing about marriage when *Beacon* readers knew of his divorce. Unstated but inferred were editorial concerns about offending conservative audiences that frowned upon divorce, even though more and more marriages ended that way. I encountered such feelings after my divorce, and not just in the newsroom.

This grilling peaked when Reynolds questioned Harrigan's wearing a Christian cross while on the job. Though spoken in jest, our protagonist recognizes the threats behind those barbs.

While I never faced such pressure from my employers – the issue came up only a few times through my career, and then from people I interviewed – I had heard of such challenges in more populated settings. They are far more frequent today, marking just one hot topic where this novel parallels modern times. In later chapters Harrigan will face protests over racial injustice, journalistic integrity, judicial punishments, sexual orientation, religious freedom, and offensive language – which started in Chapter 2 with Reynolds' frequent swearing on the job. These draw from my own experiences in the '80s and '90s, unfortunately illustrating how some things never change.

The *Defiant*

Chapter 3 introduces readers to James Harrigan's Geo Metro, a two-door hatchback General Motors adapted from Suzuki's Cultus minicar. Suzuki produced this model from 1983 to 2016. GM launched its version in 1989 as one of three vehicles bearing the Geo logo. GM hoped that new Chevrolet sub-brand would finally give its North American dealers some popular and efficient fuel-sippers. The low-tech, no-frills Metro mostly delivered on that promise, even when Oklahoma dealers slapped an air conditioner onto its three-cylinder engine.

The Geo nameplate survived until 1997. Its evolving models continued into the next decade as Chevys.

Forced by divorce to find cheap, reliable wheels, I picked up a jet-black Metro in 1996. It averaged 33 to 43 miles per gallon even with that AC. My two daughters had plenty of room in the back seat, and the hatch opened to sizable storage space.

Outside of mountain climbs, that tiny engine provided enough power for most driving situations. Its small size proved easy to maneuver and park, although the light body tended to slide even in the rain. Once I added a cassette deck, that motorcycle with a cabin worked out pretty well.

We named it the *Defiant* – from the newest ship in *Star Trek: Deep Space Nine*, our favorite show at that time. With its dark paint, tinted windows, and slim front end, that Metro actually resembled the nose of Star Fleet's tiny battleship, and its runabout handling strengthened that illusion. My oldest daughter gladly hung her toy Micro Machines *Defiant* from the Metro's rearview mirror, where it swung for two years.

But as 1998 drew to a close, I received a message from God (yes, honestly – I will write a blog on that someday) to trade my Metro for something larger. After a bit of soul-searching, I found a Plymouth Neon at a price I could stomach. Completing the deal in December, I drove that sparkling emerald green compact less than a month before it became the second entry in a nine-car pileup. That black ice nightmare totaled my beautiful Neon but left its passenger crash box intact (I *have* blogged on this – twice). Lacking such protection, no doubt my Geo would have been crushed, taking me with it.

Unfortunately, my daughter's toy didn't survive the ordeal. As you might imagine, with my purchase I transferred that tiny ship to the Neon. When the accident blew out my windshield, the *Defiant* disappeared. We never saw it again.

Willy Wonka and the blueberry girl

This pop culture reference emerged as James and his young daughters started on their trip to the Oklahoma City Zoo. Somehow they went from discussing gasoline to digestive gases to the blueberry girl who exploded in the 1971 film *Willy Wonka and the Chocolate Factory*. Like many scenes with James and his daughters, I drew this from lively discussions with my own kids.

Easy Come, Easy Go

The Easy Come, Easy Go convenience store plays a prominent role in *The Road to Renewal*. I dreamt up this thrifty chain from several shops I frequented in my youth, weaving together actual conversations held among their isles to complete those depicted in this novel. One revolved around how much candy each store sold and how scanning each piece impacted the chain's inventory. Another time a cashier scribbled a coded message on the back of my sales slip. And numerous unseasonably warm winter days at neighboring stores confronted me with "the Call of Spring" while I gassed up my cars. More to come…

Kelvin Sampson

Kelvin Sampson became the head basketball coach for the University of Oklahoma men's program in April 1994. His first squad finished its season with a 23-9 record and a 15-0 home court run, spurring three organizations to pick him as the NCAA's coach of the year. Sampson guided the Sooners through nine straight 20-win seasons, three Big 12 tournament titles, and 12 postseason tournament births, all but one in the NCAA's big dance. His era ended in 2006 when Sampson accepted the head coaching post at Indiana University. He guided the Hoosiers to a pair of 20-win seasons and the 2007 NCAA tournament before resigning

under allegations of multiple recruiting violations. He
jumped to the National Basketball Association, serving first
the Milwaukee Bucks, then the Houston Rockets. That post
may have touched his heart, for in 2014 Sampson returned to
college ball to coach the University of Houston men's team.
In his first eight years, Sampson led the Cougars to seven
straight 20-win seasons, five American Athletic Conference
titles, and four consecutive NCAA tournament appearances –
including the 2021 Final Four.

Delving into The Debate

When I wrote this two decades ago, Chapter 5 proved a
polarizing force among my proofreaders. Some drew lines
over what I termed "the Call of Spring." They feared that
sexy turn pushed the boundaries of Christian fiction too far.
Others were confused and confounded by James' response to
it all.

To best tackle these divergent topics, let's set aside the
issue of sex until later chapters, where it truly takes center
stage, and focus instead on The Debate.

This mental argument impacted my publishing options for
this novel, for its use of different fonts and point sizes does
not fit most e-book formats. I adopted that tactic to depict
different voice characterization without delving into lengthy
descriptions that could reduce this chapter's rhythm to a slow
grind. I also felt revealing an onslaught of voices best
captured how hard it can be to keep up with fast-flowing
thoughts.

At its core, The Debate illustrates how the diverse ideas we
ingest, even the seemingly innocent ones, may actively
impact our thought and decision processes, especially in a
crisis. I suspect impressions from entertainment products
often play prominent roles due to the importance we give
messages in songs, films, television, books, video games,
etc. Other sources could include historical tales, family
heritage, morality lessons… the options are endless,
depending on personal education, culture, and interests.

In breaking down James' mental exchange, we encounter

17 different voices that draw from his (and my) background in radio, TV, and cinema. Some characters may identify themselves through iconic lines: Jack Benny's shouts of "Wait a minute!" and his wife's sarcastic response, the "Danger!" warnings by the *Lost in Space* robot, Bond's nomenclature. Here are others, for those who couldn't guess them all.

The calm, steady voice represents the Holy Spirit… an identity that may help you recognize the speaker in italic. Considering the author, this debate naturally attracts a Vulcan devoid of emotion, *Star Trek's* Mr. Spock, and an erratic Looney Tunes counterpart, Bugs Bunny. Their entrance brings in frequent foes – Dr. McCoy, Elmer Fudd, Daffy Duck – with the Riddler crashing the party just because he wants to. That's when two anarcho-syndicalist peasants step in from *Monty Python and the Holy Grail*, only to get shoved out of the way as Archie Bunker summons his wife for a beer. That reveals 007 and his counterpart from the minds of Mel Brooks and Buck Henry, the indomitable Maxwell Smart. From *Get Smart* we also draw the Cone of Silence.

Those looking for logic in all this should remember who dreamed it up. The Debate offers signs on how James thinks, along with some indications of how and when this novel will turn. Readers will find echoes of The Debate in the most unexpected places. But it's good to remember what draws this mental chaos to a close: an interruption from James' daughters. That points to what truly holds his attention and heart.

Aliens among us

"Dad," put in Angela, "what would we do if aliens were hunting us right now?"

That Chapter 6 question from James Harrigan's 11-year-old daughter draws from the *Star Trek: The Next Generation* season 6 episode *Face of the Enemy*. Originally aired Feb. 6, 1993, that exciting tale involved Romulan rebels kidnapping and surgically altering counsellor Deanna Troi. Angela's question spurs an amusing discussion on whether such things could happen to their family… foreshadowing events that will soon rock James to his core.

"I've got a bad feeling about this."

"I've got a bad feeling about this," said Carla, quoting her favorite line from each of the first three Star Wars *films.*

James' youngest daughter drew her quote from the original theatrical trilogy by George Lucas. James also thinks of these as "the first three *Star Wars* films" because he included the two Ewok television movies, although 9-year-old Carla had yet to see them. The first of the prequels did not hit theaters until 1999, just after this novel's setting and the time period when I wrote *The Road to Renewal*.

Dirty Harry

It surprises me that *The Road to Renewal* taps "Dirty" Harry Callahan a few times. While he's one of actor Clint Eastwood's most iconic characters, I have never seen one of those films. I learned of Harry in nauseating detail from one of my high school friends. A huge Eastwood fan, he followed Harry's exploits from his 1971 debut through four sequels. His enthusiasm led me to see *Kelly's Heroes*, which I loved. I later caught a few Eastwood films at my movie theater (as projectionist/manager, I put them together). But I never caught up with Harry.

Instant cameras

Chapter 8 tells us how the Easy Come, Easy Go manager made James photograph his damaged car with a Polaroid instamatic camera. I could have capitalized "Instamatic" as a proper name had I made the manufacturer Kodak, for in 1963, that photographic giant introduced its popular Instamatic line of easy-to-use film cartridge cameras. But Kodak crafted that name in a play on the instant-picture technology Polaroid introduced in 1948.

Those consumer-friendly cameras used self-developing film to give users actual photo prints within seconds. This led to several popular products with both advancing model numbers and stylish names – the Swinger, the Pathfinder, the Memory Maker, the Spectra, the Captiva.

Kodak introduced its own self-developing film and camera system in 1976. Though it used a separate and incompatible process, Polaroid eventually won a lawsuit to block its rival. But long before that happened, the word "instamatic" became somewhat synonymous in popular culture for instant-developing film and cartridge cameras, no matter the manufacturer.

These ever-evolving systems remain entertaining curiosities to this day, which helps explain how James' young daughter could become so captivated with the instant film process.

Rahab

"No," James said, praying God would forgive this lie as He had Rahab.

This Chapter 8 excerpt takes readers back to the Israelites entering the Promised Land. Before crossing the Jordan River, Joshua sent spies to study its inhabitants and landscape. Enemy soldiers almost caught those scouring the city of Jericho, but a prostitute named Rahab hid the Hebrews in her house, lied to their pursuers, and helped the spies escape. Joshua spared her life when Jericho was destroyed, allowing Rahab to join the Israeli people.

Her story raises an interesting conundrum for followers of the 10 Commandments, which discourage lying. An article at thegospelcoalition.org suggests God apparently approved not just what Rahab did but the Israelite use of spies, which thrive by deception. The New Testament books of Hebrews and James mention Rahab's acts as examples of good works drawn from faith.

Nowhere Man

On Aug. 28, 1995, the conspiracy television series *Nowhere Man* made its debut on the new UPN network. Although this serialized anthology ran just one season, *Nowhere Man* drew praise for storylines questioning our nation's culture, identity, and purpose. Bruce Greenwood led an ever-changing cast that boasted several established and emerging stars, including Bryan Cranston, Dean Stockwell, Maria Bello, Carrie-Anne Moss, Dwight Schultz, Hal Linden, and Dean Jones. This series gave me several lasting memories. Among them: never trust anyone who uses a pencil to cut his cigar… a distinctive habit I extended into *The Road to Renewal*.

Silly names

Chapter 9 demonstrates my love of *Mad Magazine*-styled absurdities. Take KLOD, which I always considered a great radio call sign. And now it is! I concocted the name "Leo Heavy Chevy Geo" from my Metro shopping days. I love the rhythms in those rhymes! The novel's newspaper carries this word play to the edge. You see, I once worked in a town where the high school mascot's name raised sexist and blood sport connotations, and yet, when I lampooned that fact in my newspaper column, their fans publicly lambasted me! So I took a similar path with Franklin High's figurehead, with a twist: I inserted the mascot into the newspaper mast.

One uplifting album

Chapter 9 introduces readers to a singer and album dear to my heart. This also establishes a landmark on this novel's timeline.

On Aug. 15, 1995, Reunion Records released *I Can Hear You* by Carolyn Arends, a new Christian recording artist from Canada. I discovered that debut CD during the worst week of my life. Forlorn, wandering aimlessly through a Christian retail store, I popped the album into a listening station hoping to find some refuge from my broken heart. With its opening acoustic guitar burst, Carolyn's wholesome optimism lifted my soul. I loved the sentimentality in her songs *This Is the Stuff* and the title track, the striking truths in *Reaching* and *The Altar of Ego*, the reassurances of God's grace in *Love Is Always There* and *The Power of Love*, the longings for yesterday in *What I Wouldn't Give*, the wonderful reimagining of a beloved hymn in *All Is Well*. Every track struck home as I reeled under the threatened loss of my family – especially the simple charms of *Seize the Day*, which shares the engaging story of a would-be novelist. These tunes fueled so much hope, I asked my wife to listen with me, believing Carolyn's harmonic wisdom might help change her mind about the divorce. Although that dream collapsed, Carolyn's uplifting messages strengthened my faith and heart as I built a new life – which explains its role in *The Road to Renewal*.

Two Carolyns

Some readers may wonder if my novel phases into the Marvel Cinematic Universe when Carolyn Danvers enters the scene. This represents more word games on my part. While I did draw her name from Marvel Comics, as something of a twist on another Carolyn (Arends) introduced in that same Chapter 9 paragraph, my Danvers is a flirty radio DJ, not a superhero. The MCU didn't exist when I wrote this novel, and Ms. Marvel was a minor character at that time, making only sporadic comics appearances through the 1990s (when this novel takes place). My Danvers takes center stage in Day 2 of *The Road to Renewal*…

Endearing conversations

The first third of this novel revolves around protagonist James Harrigan's bungled efforts to take his two young daughters to the Oklahoma City Zoo. His compounding problems spur amusing commentary and debate, and yet the most charming exchanges spring from the girls' natural curiosity and shared experiences with their dad. I drew many of these conversations from my life, the situations sometimes compressed and adapted to fit within the novel's narrative.

The answer to cattail hairs?

The admired and lampooned hair product Vitalis first appeared a century ago. Lewis Brothers Inc. trademarked the brand in 1924, according to the website baybottles.com.

Although initially marketed to both sexes, Lewis Brothers soon focused on men, claiming Vitalis helped stop hair loss and dandruff while serving as "a perfect vegetable dressing that has no stickiness." Advertising heightened after Bristol-Myers acquired the product in 1931, touting its ability to give your hair a "60-second workout."

In 1952, Bristol-Myers rejuvenated Vitalis by adding the "New Greaseless Grooming Discovery V-7." That's also when the product became known as a hair tonic. But as television's rising popularity made a star of Vitals, the product also gained a comic reputation for intoxication. Vince Staten's book *Did Trojans Use Trojans? A Trip Inside the Corner Drugstore* attributed that drinking joke to the tonic's main component: multiple forms of diluted alcohol, a common hair product ingredient valued for its ability to quickly evaporate. Bristol-Myers milked the brand for several decades before selling it to Helen of Troy. That conglomerate sold it to HRB Brands LLC in 2021.

That's *Fairy*, not *Fairies*

Since its initial 1892 performance, *The Nutcracker* ballet by Pyotr Iylich Tchaikovsky has become a Christmas season favorite. Children have long loved the segment *The Dance of the Sugar Plum Fairy* (not *Fairies*, a common and popular mistake). This features a dream sequence dance for young Clara, the narrative's protagonist. "The Sugar Plum Fairy is like a fairy godmother, dancing a numinous spell of contentment on Clara's behalf," notes an article at depthinsights.com. Tchaikovsky helped bring that dance to life by using a celesta, a piano-styled instrument invented in 1886. Enamored with its bright sound created by hammers striking orchestral bells, Tchaikovsky crafted a sharp, rhythmic melody reminiscent of falling rain. "At the premiere of *The Nutcracker* in Saint Petersburg, the Sugar Plum Fairy appeared on the stage and the magical sound of the celesta emerged from the (orchestra) pit," Thomas Kotcheff wrote in a blog at kusc.org. "The audience was in total awe, no one had ever heard this mysterious sound before and no one knew how the sound was being made!" As the new century took root, the ballet and instrument earned cherished places in history.

Rocky and His Friends

Chapter 10 tells readers about different television shows protagonist James Harrigan watched when eating breakfast. While the odd mix provides nice insight on his curious character, these reruns mirrored programs I sometimes caught during my mid-1980s morning starts.

Two of these shows originated in the late 1950s. Jay Ward Productions introduced USA viewers to the animated characters Rocky, Bullwinkle, Dudley Do-Right, Mr. Peabody, and others in *Rocky and His Friends*. This first aired on the ABC network in November 1959, a month before I was born. Switching to NBC in 1961, the show ran through 1964. Its many popular characters soon reappeared under other program titles, with Dudley getting his own show in 1969. Rocky and his friends achieved still more success in the '70s and '80s through home video sales and syndication to individual stations, which led to occasional competition against each other.

20 Minute Workout

The *20 Minute Workout* was a 1984-85 Canadian TV production designed to tap the growing home aerobics market. This syndicated show provided USA stations five episodes a week featuring a trio of young leotard-clad women tackling high-impact aerobics and stretching routines on a revolving platform. While instruction came from the leader or a narrator, the novel shares how the encouraging dialogue often broke down to benign comments like "Are you sweating?" and "Doesn't sweating feel good?" over an energetic soundtrack. The show drew a fair bit of attention for its attractive cast, staying in syndication long after its demise.

Crude language

Chapter 11's use of four-letter words drew fire from some proofreaders and reviewers. I understood their concerns, but felt the course language necessary to portray a violent situation as it happened. One of my goals in writing *The Road to Renewal* was to push the boundaries of Christian fiction. Unbelievers often scoff at how Christian stories and programs tone down or filter out unpleasant realities in life. I wanted to show a Christ follower honestly dealing with divorce, crime, and other hard situations, thinking this might spur skeptics to give my novel a chance. *The Road to Renewal* also may help believers take heart when facing their own trials.

At gunpoint

This novel's sense of childlike wonder comes to a jarring end as protagonist James Harrigan endures the heartache of his divorce. But that lonely, guilt-ridden night only heightens our shock when James finds himself at the end of an intruder's cold gun. His improvised debate with the novice burglar forces Harrigan to promote and defend his Christian faith in the face of eminent death. This darkly humorous chapter (11) revives and strengthens some early plot lines while bringing out new ones as James (and readers) enter Day 2 of *The Road to Renewal*....

Crime reporting

Chapter 12's crime scene investigation takes *The Road to Renewal* back to its journalism roots. I drew many of its observations and deductions from police reports I covered during my newspaper career. The comments to our protagonist also draw from personal experiences. Like Harrigan, I received many questions of my integrity – and sometimes actual accusations of bad intent – from rural Oklahoma law enforcement officers who didn't even know who I was. With these came frequent warnings to not use an officer's name or remarks in any article…

By Kirby Lee Davis

Lysol everywhere

In Chapter 13, humor columnist James Harrigan reveals how he used Lysol spray to neutralize his college dorm room odors. While some consumer advocates recommend against this, Harrigan's strategy mirrors my personal experience (which I drew from encouraging Lysol ads) in the 1970s, when the concept of an antiseptic disinfectant serving as an air freshener was still taking root. Many people back then limited their Lysol usage to countertops and toilet bowls, never realizing it could do wonders with bed sheets, blue jeans, and gassy visitors.

Lysol's history somewhat defends my example. Developed to combat Germany's 1889 cholera epidemic, the product proved its disinfectant value with 1918's Spanish flu pandemic. But that didn't stop manufacturers and retailers from seeking broader consumer applications – going so far as feminine hygiene and contraception.

Lysol's modern identity rose in 1930 when its producer introduced a disinfectant liquid to hospitals and drug stores. After the aerosol can took off in 1962, home bathroom cleansers came in '68, followed by an all-purpose cleanser in '85. Wipes debuted in 2000, hand soaps nine years later. Somewhere in all that came a laundry sanitizer. As for air freshening, Lysol countered naysayers with its Neutra Air spray, which also works on surfaces. I can't help wondering just how different it is from the regular spray, which many retailers still sell as an air freshener.

Poetry in motion

The rhyming cover teaser for *The Road to Renewal* hints of one dark plot. The front cover offers just the first two lines (and the last two, as it turns out) of this suggestive poem, but the back cover reveals it all:

Three days. Two guys.
One lives. One dies.
A father who struggles
To survive his divorce.

247

A son whose troubles
Allow no remorse.
A sinner who battles
To dig his way out.
A believer whose trials
Leave no room for doubt.
Three days. Two guys.
One lives. One dies.

While I thought that captured the book's spiritual scope within a nice bundle of riddles, I allowed myself to overlook the misdirection in this mystery. After all, the teaser offers no clue of the book's rampant, often absurd humor. Some observers did not recognize how the poem foreshadows Christian trials and tribulations. And many read a murder mystery between those lines, which brought further confusion when my novel's rolling plotline took until Chapter 14 (or so I'm told) before my comedy drama offers a hint of who that second "guy" might be.

Some readers didn't pick up on it until much later.

I see that as a good thing, for it heightened the mystery. This partly reflects my writing in a modified third-person narrative, which limits everyone to primarily one perspective. Since readers know no more of what's going on than our protagonist does, everyone remains in the dark about things not in Harrigan's line of sight. But this mystery also reflects all the distractions our protagonist endures in these three confusing days and James' struggles in coping with them. His growing weariness adds a natural smokescreen, one that often reflects my day-by-day experiences.

"I don't know what to tell you"

A crazy number of amusing things happened to me at car dealerships. Naturally I included several such tales in *The Road to Renewal*. Chapter 14 presents one of the more frustrating turns: a Geo representative warning me his mechanics had little expertise in repairing the Geo that dealer sold me. The rep tried to distract me by sharing his own amusing car woes. Among them: how one customer tried to deice a frozen window with Thousand Island salad dressing. Naturally such mirth sets up still more car toons for our protagonist… some of the lighter stepping stones in *The Road to Renewal*.

Shaking his head like an Etch A Sketch…

The Etch A Sketch was introduced to the world by the Ohio Art Company on July 12, 1960, just seven months after author Kirby Lee Davis came aboard this earth. Beloved as a simple yet dexterous drawing tool – a self-contained, durable device that operated without batteries, one easily reset by a fun shake of its red plastic frame – this stone-age precursor of today's tablet computer (not really, though it's fun to say that) sold more than a half-million units in its first year. In 1998 – nearly parallel to *The Road to Renewal* timeline – the Etch A Sketch was inducted into the National Toy Hall of Fame. By 2013, its worldwide sales topped 100 million units.

A fly on the wall

Chapter 15 finds protagonist James Harrigan stuck in an auto dealer's waiting room, forced to listen to four farmers rambling from subject to subject in an aimless gab session. This mirrors several experiences in my life, amplified no doubt by a 35-year newspaper reporting career that required I attend all sorts of press conferences, public meetings, lectures, conventions, and small-group sessions. Like Harrigan, I often found these conversations fueled or dominated by:
- Political wannabes promoting a position.
- Conspiracy theorists grousing about anything.

In rural Oklahoma, such grumbling often turned against all things metro or modern. *The Road to Renewal* shares many such discussions, often word for word (I had a memory like a steel trap when I wrote this… which leads into a joke *God's Furry Angels* fans might remember). My depictions may feature a bit more slapstick than you're used to, which may reflect our protagonist's weariness, his/my Looney Tunes/ Monty Python/Groucho way of thinking, or the Oklahoma setting, but this absurdity serves the message well.

Talking trees

Chapter 15 finds protagonist James Harrigan marveling at scuttlebutt in an auto dealer waiting room. The opening topic: a *Wall Street Journal* article suggesting trees talk to each other.

While James scoffs and chuckles at all the "chemical exchange" theories the old farmers discuss, scientists were a bit more openminded by this novel's 1990s setting. This was quite a change from 20 years earlier, when many researchers attacked the 1973 book *The Secret Life of Plants* for suggesting trees, herbs, and flowers had emotions and could communicate. While skeptics dismissed that book's 150+ years of research as pseudoscience and paranormal hype, supporting evidence soon developed.

By 1998, enough solid research existed for a *Plant Physiology* article to bluntly declare, "Plants are in constant communication with a multitude of diverse organisms." The 2013 book *What a Plant Knows* shared evidence showing plants send and respond to message smells from other vegetation. The 2016 book *The Hidden Life of Trees* said these perennials may use scents, leaf colors, and toxins to communicate with or manipulate plants, insects, or animals around them. Some scientists now cite growing evidence that trees not only talk with each other (via chemical, light, or electrical means), but also forge alliances and interactive relationships with neighbors. Some theorize about a possible *Avatar*-styled collective intelligence in forests.

Despite all this, many people still might laugh at these concepts – or at the idea rural farmers would ever read the *Wall Street Journal*. Such people would savor reading *The Road to Renewal*…

Banking on emery boards

Chapter 15 shares fun memories of when banks gave away appliances. As the U.S. economy expanded after World War

II, lenders invested in grand offices, branch networks, and colorful advertising campaigns, all to better stand out in the crowd. One tactic proved especially popular: offering free merchandise to consumers opening new checking or savings accounts. With home ownership rising and lender competition tightening, these freebies spread from practical items – like decorative pens, wall calendars, and road atlases – to larger, more valued products, such as coffee pots, took kits, and sporting goods. Kitchenware filled many promotions as more and more housewives responded.

That trend changed as the U.S. economy slowed in the '70s and '80s. Inflation rose, and waves of bank and thrift closures reduced competition. Lenders invested in automated teller machines and other high-tech advances to cut operating costs while aiding expansion. Many financial institutions trimmed or abandoned their expensive incentive programs, weary of watching customers frequently move their accounts to claim the next hot offer.

By the time of *The Road to Renewal*, older consumers would reminisce about their favorite giveaways. Some gifts became family heirlooms – even items as insignificant as emery boards and fingernail clippers, rewards from one of my parents' old banks.

"Off them bees"

"Don't trust that stuff for a second. You hear me now! Touch them buttons, and them computer chips inside all that stuff, they start broadcastin' secret signals like they do off them bees, an' pretty soon they even know when you're going to the john, they do!"

It's now quite common to tag bees, sharks, dogs, birds, etc., with computer chips as small as this "a." Testing today extends their function from radio frequency identification (RFID) tracking to manipulating limbs and actions. But this remained relatively new at the time of *The Road to Renewal*, as our Chapter 15 excerpt hints. The first RFID tag patents came in the 1970s. This led to the first usage of U.S. animal microchips, their size as small as a grain of rice. That's when an Oak Ridge National Laboratory research team adapted these technologies to track Africanized bees. According to a 2015 *Biosensors* article, they developed an electronic chip about the size of a half-carat diamond and glued it to a bee's thorax. Using solar collectors instead of batteries, that chip weighed less than 35 milligrams (i.e., a fraction of an ounce).

One hellish ride

Gooey headrests, cabin rust holes open to the street, roaches in the crumbling upholstery…. hopefully that's not your typical taxi ride, especially for auto dealer customers ferried to work. But that's the farcical setting for Chapter 16. Like many tales in *The Road to Renewal*, it draws from my personal experience – down to its most absurd details. The chapter also showcases our protagonist's habit of associating people with characters he appreciates – in this case, hobbits. It provides yet another example of this fiction's reality.

Timeline hints

As Chapter 16 introduces readers to the "hobbit" driving our protagonist to work, the text drops a solid clue on when exactly *The Road to Renewal* takes place. This comes from the tune this "shaggy copper-haired man" whistles – *That Thing You Do*. That song shares the name of the 1996 film it came from, a classic rock-and-roll musical written and directed by Tom Hanks. The whistling reflects my own habits at that time, for I fell in love with the film and its songs from the first moment I saw/heard them. They remain beloved favorites to this day!

Jimmy the vampire

Chapter 16 features one of my favorite jokes in *The Road to Renewal*. Here's an excerpt:

"So," began the hobbit once more, "have you ever wondered what It's a Wonderful Life *might have been like if James Stewart had been a vampire?"*

My mind dreamed this up while watching another Stewart favorite, *Winchester '73*. As Lin McAdam pins "Waco" Johnnie

Dean's gun arm, Stewart reveals a rage rarely seen on screen. Something in my noggin linked that facial wrath to how Jack Palance played *Dracula*... demonstrating how my mind works. Naturally I applied this vampire scenario to other Stewart classics....

Gossip columns

Before the internet revolutionized the communications sector and privacy became a global concern, gossip columns anchored many newspapers – especially in rural markets like my fictional Franklin, Oklahoma. Some papers printed one such roundup for each town they covered, or tried to, for people enjoyed reading and sharing tales of neighbor romances, parties, pranks, and other goings-on. Such edited gossip actually started as the printing press enabled the rise of pamphleteers, newspapers, and magazines. Many papers grew by adding society news from areas where they wished to expand their advertising, distribution, and subscription bases. As newspaper chains formed, they hired society columnists not just in their primary markets, but in popular regional or national destinations that interested readers. This helped create the correspondent sector. Papers also chased gossip about artists and the rich; those columnists who frequently scooped competitors gained nearly as much celebrity as those they reported on. While print media eventually lost much of that niche to radio and television networks, many newspapers continued to milk local society news into the '90s. Since most such writers were amateurs living in towns they covered, their prose often nauseated editors and reporters. During my years in rural Oklahoma markets, I frequently parodied such texts with my comedy columns. One such spoof appears in *The Road to Renewal*...

The right to use profanity

Chapter 17 finds our protagonist once more challenging his editor's frequent use of profanity. This is another example of how *The Road to Renewal*, while depicting rural Oklahoma societies in the 1990s, remains relevant today... and how some of today's politically correct issues have surprisingly long legs.

While linguists chart the history of swearing over hundreds of years – I suspect it goes back to the development of languages – questions over the legal right to use such words rose only as lawmakers sought to legalize free speech. The creation of the United States opened the door to such expression, which gradually lessened public resistance by making foul language more common. Traumatic experiences accelerated this, from the Revolution and settlement of the frontiers through the Civil War, Prohibition, the Depression, and the world wars. Such heartaches heightened the evolving use of swear words (and substitutes) in self-expression. Those choices challenged concepts of civil obedience and morality. As with many movements over the last century, American communication and entertainment mediums helped spread these practices into other cultures.

For a time, swearing fell in line with the social revolutions of the '60s. But in that era of enlightenment rose new concepts of life, liberty, and the pursuit of happiness, which led to beliefs in personal freedoms from disrespectful or objectionable policies and statements. Recent court cases in the United States, Canada, and other nations have limited perceived rights to not be offended. As for the right to offend, court rulings established a few situations where foul language may be regulated. Many states also maintain public safety and civil disobedience laws that limit using profanity in certain settings.

Swearing in the workplace remains a complicated issue, one highly dependent on the situation, environment, established policy, and management views. With profanity increasingly common, some analysts suggested its limited use may help build a sense of camaraderie and teamwork in certain cases. Thus, determining what constitutes unacceptable swearing may depend on how the audience receives that speech. Seeking legal consistencies breaks down to several factors, including what words were used, their context and tone, who or what the speech targeted, and what audience heard or read it.

Wearing a cross to work

Swearing wasn't the only work practice debated in *The Road to Renewal*. Our protagonist's cross necklace also proved a hot topic. This argument drew more from personal opinion than the law.

While applying religious principles to business practices remains a contested issue in some areas of the USA (where this novel takes place), labor regulations generally protect worker rights to wear symbols of their faith. "In most instances, employers are required by federal law to make exceptions to their usual rules or preferences to permit applicants and employees to observe religious dress and grooming practices," notes the U.S. Equal Employment Opportunity Commission website. This standard is little changed from the 1990s, the setting for *The Road to Renewal*. But the number of people wearing crosses has increased, jewelry analysts say. They attribute this to prevailing fashion styles and not (necessarily) to signs of faith. The many different cross shapes allow wearers to make statements of hope, security, and triumph without embracing any one belief.

Several Christian communities lean against wearing jewelry, including crosses. They urge believers to avoid ornamentation, pointing others to Christ through their actions. That was my personal standard until someone gave me a cross necklace and asked me to wear it. Though reluctant, I agreed. On that very first day, I met someone who had no idea what the cross symbolized. This opened the door to explaining my faith. I have worn a cross ever since – a practice I wrote into *The Road to Renewal*.

Foreshadowing through extras

Chapter 18 features four one-scene appearances (well, Fat Mama Brown actually came up in the previous chapter, but she didn't have any lines). These characters play vital roles in advancing the plot and providing background color while throwing light on protagonist James Harrigan's unique job.

First up: perky hazel-eyed receptionist Janice Pendleton.

Her discussion with Harrigan provide a nice continuity link back to Chapter 1. These talks also offer humorous looks at the *Beaver Beacon*'s winter chills, which mirrored a situation I experienced in one of my jobs. I love that "frozen asset" line!

The other three characters shine light on the eclectic environment Harrigan works in – which helps prepare readers for more comical chaos.

Reverend Jim Bob Wilson's imagination drew from a farmer I met who collected vegetables and gourds resembling biblical heroes (in his eyes, at least). Cobb's habit of anointing these figures with spoiled olive oil drew from a missionary I met who refused to discard souvenirs from his Holy Land travels, no matter their state of decay.

I based rancher Frank Cobb on a nearsighted farmer who told me how he accidentally shot his hunting dog. The "Was he mad?" joke, which leads readers into perhaps the most politically incorrect elements in this book, came from a Milton Berle humor book I read as a kid. It's the only borrowed quip in *The Road to Renewal*, one I almost took out before I recalled how Uncle Miltie frequently stole other people's lines, or so went the longest-running gag in his illustrious career.

Cobb's inquiries introduce readers to the county sheriff's crime reports and Harrigan's police beat, which the novel soon explores. Cobb also plants a seed of doubt in the reporter's head to complicate the plot.

That brings us to Pricilla Underwood, who Harrigan depicts as Fat Mama Brown in his column. She presents one of the more polarizing personalities for Harrigan. His satirical spin on her writing reveals how our hero perceives his community. Her vague accusations reinforce Cobb's hazy warnings, setting off Harrigan's reporter paranoia. This throws a wrinkle in the plot stream that echoes throughout the novel.

Absurdities

Sometimes things you develop work, and sometimes they don't. Chapter 19 features one of the zanier columns by *The Road to Renewal* protagonist James Harrigan. It's a parody I wrote in my newspaper days to poke fun at the small-town society columns I'd endured for years. Readers who recognized that satire loved the piece, while those who didn't make the connection, or had never read such newspaper copy, sometimes wondered just what was going on. Some readers of *The Road to Renewal* also responded that way, even though earlier chapters foreshadowed what lay ahead. I suspect some critics might enjoy this farcical text if they heard it out loud… this style of humor often works better when spoken. But then, I'm a bit biased, and not just as the writer. Having grown up in rural towns, I remember many amusing stories of life's twists and turns that reflected those I parodied. It felt nostalgic. And I savored the occasional lampoon news and articles featured in my old *Mad Magazine* collection.

The first line in this chapter – *"Here's another news story you'll never read…"* – echoes a recurring feature from *Mad*'s classic issues. The rest of the "column" mixes the styles of Dave Berg, Don Martin, and other legendary *Mad* contributors, along with the spirit of *Monty Python's Flying Circus*, the Marx Brothers, the Zucker/Abrahams/Zucker team, and the Looney Tunes/Tex Avery cartoon antics I still love.

I adored the column's plentiful silly names, the nonsense about family visits and trips that went nowhere, the church meals (I endured so many as a child), the roll call jokes (which foreshadow another turn in the novel), and the diet scheduling spoof. The red-carpet rollout offers one of my favorite jokes in the whole book: "Mayor Friday gave Khan a key to the city as the town high school band played *Santa Claus Is Coming to Town,* to which the high school choir sang, *Genghis, You Smell Like a Nice Guy.*" That just cracks me up. And it goes on from there…

Systemic distrust

"So you might as well head on back to your little dumpster and dig up some more garbage."

American trust in journalists and the media reportedly

reached an all-time low in late 2022, if you trust Gallup polls. But in my 40+ years of professional reporting and editing, I never saw a time when the public actually trusted the press.

Some publications and broadcasters held favor over the last century, especially in select fields. A few individuals like Walter Cronkite and Edward R. Murrow earned the public's confidence through years of solid work. Crises in the 1930s through '60s aided this by providing subjects – namely Axis and communist aggressors – most everyone could agree on. But by my estimation, the American press lost much of the public's respect by the '80s, if indeed it ever truly held it.

Many observers developed a general distrust of the "fifth estate" through its increasingly political coverage of Vietnam, Watergate, and their many ramifications. These same events spurred even stronger liberal, often disillusioned, outlooks among many journalism instructors, reporters, and editors. Several professionals I met forgot their publications and stations were businesses seeking profits. Others shaped their coverage to maximize marketability and profits.

The end result: systemic distrust on both sides. Instructors often taught students to seek controversy, while editors instructed reporters to identify and highlight conflict, even if they had to interpret or "create" that conflict. Many readers and viewers complained about how the press aggressively stressed negativity, though few people I met admitted to seeking out "positive" news.

Our opening quote, drawn from Chapter 20, came my way from a police department dispatcher irritated by my questions over case reports. Many patrolmen and civic execs offered similar opinions, which *The Road to Renewal* often shares. These hostile receptions diminished as my reputation grew, leading many subjects in recognized newsworthy stories to seek my involvement. But the only time people truly wanted my news coverage came in their promotional efforts. In most such cases they openly referred to my articles as "free publicity." Much of this originated with public relations executives who, having studied my work, determined I was a "safe" or "honest" reporter.

We'll come back to this…

Pauly Shore

In Chapter 20, Franklin's police chief mocks our protagonist/newspaper reporter by calling him "Pauly Shore." This refers to Paul Montgomery Shore, a USA comedian who rocketed to stardom in the early '90s through popular appearances on MTV and HBO. His 1992 hit film *Encino Man* drew still more spotlights, but then the public woke up. Shore's star plummeted as this one-note wonder released a series of cinematic flops over the next four years. "Shore was met with an increasingly hostile reception and his lunacy was dismissed as crude, tasteless, dumb and, for the most part, unfunny," notes imdb.com.

Idle threats?

"All my life I've wanted to arrest a reporter. To put one away."

That Chapter 20 quote by Franklin Police Chief Isaac Jacobs mirrors what an Oklahoma deputy said to me in week one of my first newspaper job. He pulled me over near midnight for driving a bit under 30 miles per hour through a rural downtown. I didn't realize its speed limit bounced from 30 to 10 to 30 in 10-MPH increments over five blocks, for each block had but one streetlight and one highly recessed sign, and I drove the only car on the road until his siren emerged. After repeating his threat a few times, the patrolman let me off with a warning.

Vital elements

With its confrontation between protagonist James Harrigan and Franklin Police Chief Isaac Jacobs, Chapter 20 performs several vital tasks. It shows readers how this rural newspaper reporter must juggle new and old stories at a moment's notice. It throws light on how unrelated events may blend, and how background or low-priority tasks, such as a humor column, may scar your reputation. The chapter waters seeds of discord in Harrigan's brain and foreshadows several turning points bound to complicate his future. And it adds yet another threat to Harrigan's life… all vital elements as we near the midway point in *The Road to Renewal*.

Juggling wisdom

Chapter 21 brings up more journalism points as it stirs the plot. The chapter reveals more about our protagonist's rural newspaper police beat, which also includes daily sheriff, fire, and ambulance activity checks. These he will write up in an abbreviated format for the public records newspaper section while monitoring each event for possible articles. All this comes on top of his assigned features and news events he must cover, along with his humor column. If that doesn't illustrate how much multitasking/article juggling a reporter may face, the police phone tip James Harrigan receives brings it home. Editor Dick Reynolds then shares a phone call of his own to heighten the pressure: a complaint by the police chief over Harrigan's actions.

What follows is a gem of wisdom that today's media may not pay much attention to, or so some people fear. Despite Harrigan's first-hand experience in his apartment break-in and the following police probe, Reynolds warns him to not pursue that story with any preconceptions:

"Few things are obvious," the editor snapped. "Expected, yes. Telegraphed, often. But if you start out thinking you know what's going on, you're setting yourself up for a big surprise. We've been warned, James. Let's be careful on this one."

That logic counters how some media outlets operate today. Instead of pursuing open, unbiased investigations – which can eat up background development time, something many papers and broadcasters simply cannot afford any longer – reporters and editors often start by identifying a conflict or controversy to target, then pursuing sources that support their opening thesis. And they can get rather stubborn about it in this politically correct age. I once worked under a set of editors who assigned me a news feature with a definite headline and message in mind. But as I investigated the issues and talked to authoritative sources, I found their premise in error. My editors disagreed, for changing that premise would disrupt their plans. They sent my article back seven times for rewriting, no matter how many respected professionals I added to identify and support other outlooks. After my eighth attempt, they rewrote my article to fit their preconceptions.

A reporter's candy bar

Chapter 22 finds reporter James Harrigan craving a Snickers, the alleged energy food of journalists. That mythology draws from a Mars Inc. marketing campaign depicting busy American reporters eating Snickers in times of stress. I saw my first such television commercial in the early 1970s, when the Pentagon Papers, Watergate, and other scandals gave the press a romantic image. Mars updated these messages in the 1980s and '90s before releasing an actual Snickers energy bar in the early 2000s. While I never felt this craving, Harrigan does, which leads to future headaches…

Superhero hares

Chapter 22 introduces a bit of silliness: a novel in development called *Beyond the Shores of Mars*. Like protagonist James Harrigan, I loved the concept of a rabbit gaining superhuman powers to fight for justice and the American way. More important, I understood Harrigan's need to get back into creative writing. *Beyond the Shores of Mars* was his first book start since his divorce… a step back into his former life, a step forward into what would come. I had a similar manuscript in my life… one that led me into *The Road to Renewal*.

Voicemail anguish

When entrepreneur Gordon Matthews developed the foundation for voicemail, I thought such tech would improve my life in many ways. His work started in '79, when only the rich (or secret agents) had wireless phones or answering machines. Yet even I, a lowly University of Football journalism student who happily lived without such toys, knew what wounds a missed call could bring. It didn't take long for voicemail systems to reach affordability and spread nationwide. That's when I discovered this tech caused as many headaches as it prevented – perhaps even more, since a voice message promised consequences where a missed call might earn a reprieve. *The Road to Renewal* presents abundant examples, all drawn from my actual experiences, some hilarious, some heartbreaking. Chapter 22 shares one recurring message I hated: last-minute notices by my apartment manager for pesticide appointments requiring empty cupboards and clear baseboards. But my greatest angst came from market competition. In the '90s, I built a treasure trove of saved messages my children left on my work phone. These recordings proved especially uplifting after my divorce. One day I arrived at my desk to discover my employer had changed voicemail systems – and since the new tech couldn't work with the old, they discarded all our messages, past and present.

Reaching into his Yellow Pages

Reaching into his Yellow Pages, Harrigan began his Don Quixote quest for salvation from a ravenous car wash.

In the days before web search engines and smartphones, most people looked up telephone numbers using regional compilation books known as the Yellow Pages. Legend links that colorful name to an 1883 supply snafu: a U.S. phone directory printer ran out of white paper and substituted yellow. That gained a purpose three years later when printer Reuben H. Donnelley started selling directory advertising. Donnelley and the American phone companies soon decided to print residential listings on white paper, business listings and ads on yellow. New England artist Henry Alexander developed the familiar three-finger Yellow Pages logo in 1962. AT&T adopted it nationwide a year later. The "let your fingers do the walking" slogan – alluded to soon after our Chapter 22 excerpt – came in the '70s. This tradition continued after 1982 phone deregulation efforts opened the directory sector to outside competitors. That industry thrived until the internet changed user habits.

Phone runarounds

Chapter 22 shares slightly edited versions of the silliest phone runarounds I've endured to date. Placing these irritating bumps in *The Road to Renewal* gives protagonist James Hartigan quite a headache. The first event happens when our intrepid reporter calls the Easy Come, Easy Go convenience store where a car wash pulled his car's side mirror loose (in Chapter 7). James seeks an update on his damage claim, but the cashier blows him off, saying Harrigan dialed the wrong number. When James calls again, the cashier admits Harrigan got it right after all, but blames the reporter's "impolite" attitude for why he made that lie.

Directed to the corporate office, the receptionist puts James on hold, forgets who he is and what he wants, then picks his button again. This process she repeats over and over…

"Hello," came the soothing voice. "This is customer service. How may I help you?"

"You were transferring me to Mrs. Smertz."

"You mean Ms. Smertz?"

James pondered that for a second. "Did you say Ms. Smertz or Miss Smertz?"

"I don't know. Let me transfer you."

The clincher comes when Leo Heavy Chevy Geo's service department phones to let James know he can pick up his car. Harrigan's moment of happiness comes and goes as he ponders aloud why no one got his approval on the repair costs.

"Didn't anybody call you?"

"No!"

"Oh. Well, I'm sorry about that. But your car's ready now."

That's when Harrigan learns the bill totals $146.87… quite a bit of money for a reporter at a rural newspaper back in the 1990s (this bill was the focus of a "Behind the Scenes" entry on the next page).

As for the repair estimate call, or lack of one, that question foreshadows phone messages still to come… more laughs drawn from my actual experiences!

Comparing yesterday and today

Reading tales of yesteryear naturally spur modern-day comparisons – so let's do that with a key plot point in *The Road to Renewal*, which takes place in the 1990s. In Chapter 14, protagonist James Harrigan fears how much it will cost to replace the broken side mirror on his subcompact Geo Metro. "Oh, I don't know," said the service department attendant at the Oklahoma dealership where James bought the car. "Maybe $20 to $40 for labor, another $20 to $60 for parts." Some three hours (and eight chapters) later, the bill came in at $146.87 – a big hit to our hero's pocketbook.

Since mirror designs have advanced quite a bit – many now include remote adjusting, proximity sensors, signal lights, etc. – we might expect modern repairs to cost far more. A December 2022 jdpower.com article said side mirror replacements average $299. Parts generally range from $139 to $328, while labor came in around $90. A September 2023 price check at autoservicecosts.com estimated side mirror replacement bills would fall between $139 and $328 for parts *and* labor, with the parts alone going from $35 to $90. While other insurer and repair websites generally agreed, a thecostguys.com article warns "installation costs are often the largest part."

What role would inflation play in this?

I drew *The Road to Renewal* car repair scenario from an extremely similar event I endured in 1997. If you plug that year and my $146.87 bill into www.usinflationcalculator.com, the website estimates our September 2023 equivalent at $279.73.

Since the Metro was a low-tech subcompact, those repair estimates appear to align well with what Harrigan paid. Perhaps improved design/manufacturing/distribution techniques helped contain inflation.

But recalling the Metro's ultra-small size brings back another memory: the Geo door mirror was a multipart component replaced as a unit. While this proves true for many vehicles today, it is not universal – a factor general repair estimates may dilute. Car/truck owners also may have more generic part options today to counter higher-cost original manufacturer parts – another issue general repair estimates may downplay.

Our inflation estimate also raises labor cost questions. My 1997 bill surely made a profit for that dealership, among the most expensive service providers then and now. Perhaps the difference between this constant-dollar calculation and our modern repair guesses points to other factors – higher regulatory costs, for example, or debt servicing burdens, infrastructure upkeep, declining brand loyalty…

Of course, today's web resources include part replacement cost estimates on seemingly any vehicle ever made, including the 1995 Geo Metro. Website repairpal.com suggests replacing our Geo door mirror would cost between $203 and $210. That doesn't break down as you might guess: repairpal.com projects labor at just $26 to $33, while the parts came in at $177. That website offers to set you up with a service provider in your area – almost certainly not a dealership – which reminds us how all such educated guesses may change from one part of the globe to another. We find similar variances from auto parts e-sellers, including Amazon, which offer our Geo replacement mirrors at a third to an eighth of these repairpal.com parts estimates.

Two accounts, two banks

In Chapter 23, our protagonist must withdraw money from his savings account to deposit in his checking account, all to pay that Geo Metro repair bill. That's when we discover James Harrigan keeps these accounts in different banks.

Using more than one bank has long been my practice, to limit potential account mix-ups and make me think twice before tapping both. While every bank and credit union I've used recommended against this tactic (as might be expected), apparently I'm not alone. A 2018 GOBankingRates.com survey of 2,000+ American bank customers found only 50 percent used one bank for all their needs. About 28% used two lenders, 11% three, 4% four, and 7% five or more.

Once you moved beyond convenience and flexibility, the primary reasons for using multiple banks revolved around different products offered, particularly no or low monthly fees. This resonates in today's volatile economy and higher inflation. Some money managers recommend my strategy to add "friction" between you and your money, as a 2021 CNBC.com article put it.

"If you don't see your savings account every time you log in to your checking, then you're much less likely to spend it," financial planner Sophia Bera said in a 2016 *Business Insider* article.

Of course, the "friction" argument is my second reason for keeping my savings and checking accounts at different banks. My first reason was to limit the impact of possible lender errors. Although little discussed publicly, this has become a much more significant issue in the years since *The Road to Renewal*'s 1990s setting. "Operational risk is elevated as cyber threats are elevated and continue to evolve, with an observed increase in attacks on the financial services industry," the U.S. Office of the Comptroller of the Currency said in its 2022 annual report. "Across key risk areas, banks are experiencing challenges retaining and replacing staff, especially those with specialized experience, due to increasing turnover."

I suffered problems in both areas last year. Luckily, I caught both errors within two days. It took my bank three weeks to restore funds stolen via cyber theft and two months to fix its internal error of deducting my monthly rent check twice. Customer service staff – a few of them trainees – said the bank's accounting error took that long to fix because the executive who usually handled such issues had retired, and the bank had yet to replace her.

Naturally, these turns irritated me greatly, but others told me their problems took far longer to resolve.

Scary hair

In Chapter 23, our protagonist watches an old bank teller struggle to keep her skyscraping locks from tumbling down.

She nodded in agony, her honey-scented beehive hairdo leaning with malice towards him before arching back in a near freefall. James feared that towering hulk might overwhelm her spindle neck and carry her skull to the dark void behind the bank counter, but somehow the sniffling teller mastered both inertia and gravity, much less the sway of that beautician's fortress of solitude.

This scenario draws from my '60s childhood, when big hair reigned. While most such 'dos dazzled the eye, the beehive unnerved me. Being a curious and imaginative kid, I feared women used those swirling towers to cover their mutated skulls. When I found myself around ladies bearing beehives, I watched in anticipation of their compounded tresses losing balance and plunging to the earth, carrying their heads with them.

I did what I could to safeguard myself when around such ladies, making sure to never sit beside pending catastrophes if I could help it. For with my *Mad Magazine*-trained mind, I suspected those bulges harbored spiders, wasps, mice, or other nasty predators. I never saw such denizens peeking from their hairy caverns, but in my mind, it was wiser to be safe than sorry.

The Stench Coat Effect

In Chapter 23, our protagonist notices how everyone moves away when he steps into a room – in this case, two rooms, as in two bank lobbies. He calls this response "the Stench Coat Effect." Like many elements of *The Road to Renewal*, this tale draws from something I endured. I don't recall how that disagreeable odor affixed itself to the back of my jacket, but once I became used to it – which didn't take long, since the weather required I wear that coat – it surprised and amused me how that foul scent drove most everyone as far away as they could get. It took a trip to my dry cleaner to make that jacket endurable once more. The shop manager chuckled when I picked it up, noting how they had to take extraordinary steps to cleanse its cloth. He wondered just what I'd done to get that coat so smelly. My answer drew a good laugh, though I couldn't tell if he believed me. All of which makes me wish I could recall the tale. When I wove my memories together for *The Road to Renewal*, I tied the Stench Coat Effect to that nasty taxi – which also marked my coat with a lingering odor. If you don't recognize what cabbie I'm talking about, you'll have to look up "One Hellish Ride" on page 252. It's worth it.

Banking heritage

Chapter 23 introduces two banks used by our protagonist – one embracing Oklahoma's turn-of-the-century architecture and antique fixtures, the other adopting all things modern. This typifies many competitive lending stances of the '90s, especially in rural areas of the Sooner state.

Part of this reflected common sense, for few Oklahoma towns at that time could boast of existing even 100 years. Thus, many of its bankers operated in classic brick, wood, and marble sanctuaries dating back to the state's heady oil boom days (roughly 1901-45, although some areas enjoyed strong activity for years after). It made economic sense to maintain these beautiful staterooms and bunkers that naturally shaped your business environment and identity. New institutions had the freedom to build homes tapping evolving architectural styles and construction materials. Older institutions experimented in such motifs in the 1980s as Oklahoma adopted new branch and interstate banking laws, but many lenders maintained their old cathedrals in a state that treasured its frontier heritage.

Technology proved the real game changer. Adapting to computer networks and automated teller machines reduced workforces and reshaped long-held security practices. With that went old conceptual needs for thick stone walls and bomb-shelter vaults. As e-banking advances reduced consumer foot traffic, many lenders repurposed or shed their soaring sanctuary lobbies along with many branches.

I've passed a counterfeit bill?

Chapter 23 ends with a major plot twist: our protagonist discovers he just passed a counterfeit $20 bill. This nightmare hangs on two outrageous ironies: he got that phony bill from a bank, and he tried to deposit it at a bank!

I can hear you saying that scenario's highly unlikely. I agree! The Oklahoma Banking Association's chief attorney laughed when I told her of this, noting how all bank tellers are trained to spot fakes and would never give one to a customer. I adapted her explanation in Chapter 24:

"All bank tellers undergo training to learn about the distinctive feel of U.S. currency, the colors," said the supervisor. "They get very good at accessing what a bill should weigh, how it should feel."

But like nearly all the jokes in *The Road to Renewal*, this scenario actually happened to me!

It worked like this in the novel: newspaper reporter James Harrigan withdrew $150 from his savings account to repair damage caused by an automated car wash. He walked across the street to his other bank – all without looking at the cash – and tried to deposit the money into his checking account. That's when the teller found a counterfeit among his bills.

In real life, I went through my home bank drive-thru to withdraw $150 from my savings account, all to pay for car repairs forced by a truly aggressive car wash. I then drove to work (where I was an editor) without looking at the cash, walked to the bank managing my checking account, and tried to deposit that money. The teller found a counterfeit among my bills. This led to my cross-examination by bank officials and an unidentified federal official, who warned me to expect a Secret Service investigation that would go into my permanent file… just as the novel relates. Chapter 24 ends with Harrigan uttering words that capture exactly how I felt:

"This is so crazy," he said to no one in particular. "All I wanted to do was wash my car – and now Big Brother's going to watch over me for the rest of my life? Do I deserve that?"

Being God's man

Chapter 25 opens with James Harrigan trying to deal with all the problems piling up in his life. He encounters a desperate soul whose offer of help reeks of despair:

"You think livin' good's the answer," continued the voice.

"That's what we're told, ain't it? His road's easy, His burden's light… isn't that just what The Good Book says? But it's a crock, man. Being God's man just makes it worse."

Though the youth twists his verses, a well-known Bible passage does support some of this. Using the New King James Version as our guide, Matthew 11:28-30 quotes Christ in words our interloper paraphrased: "Come to Me, all you who labor and are heavy laden, and I will give you rest. Take My yoke upon you and learn from Me, for I am gentle and lowly in heart, and you will find rest for your souls. For My yoke is easy and My burden is light."

Many would-be believers trip over these words because they simply do not listen or follow through. They do not truly come to Christ, take up His yoke, and learn from Him. Lingering on what they want to hear, they expect Christ to free them of trials or burdens, which is not what He said. Indeed, many Bible verses warn just the opposite. John 16:33 quotes Christ thus: "In the world you will have tribulation. But take heart; I have overcome the world."

Our desperate soul came closest to the truth with his complaint: *"Being God's man just makes it worse."* Christ followers often face trials due to their faith. Jesus warned of this in his Sermon on the Mount, saying, "Blessed are you when they revile and persecute you, and say all kinds of evil against you falsely for My sake. Rejoice and be exceedingly glad, for great is your reward in heaven, for so they persecuted the prophets who were before you."

Living without faith equates to tackling the world's challenges by trial and error, unaided, as this wounded soul admits:

"I've tried it all, man," the interloper went on, oblivious to the music. *"Dope, sex. Booze. Nearly popped a man once. Got locked up more times than I can count – and I wasn't even 16. Then I found Christ, you know? And I thought, 'Wow! Maybe Ma's right!' There's truth there, to be sure. But people – especially Christians, those hypocrite Christians! – man, they don't let you forget, you know? And they don't let go."*

That disturbing quote sets the stage for the second half of *The Road to Renewal…*

By Kirby Lee Davis

One way

Chapter 25's aggrieved interloper casually twists the meaning of a common worship practice of the late 20th Century (the novel's setting). Mentioning how "hypocrite Christians" often have a hard time forgiving his criminal past, he complains:

"Ain't nothin' you can do about it, neither," the outsider rambled on. "Hang low, and they'll find you. Button up, and they'll pry you out, or shoot you up. No, man, there ain't but one way out. One way. And it ain't no upraised finger, either. You think about that."

Combat terms rise in that rant. "Hang low" refers to keeping a low profile, among other things, while "button up" draws from army tank operators shutting hatches to shield them from gunfire, shrapnel, grenades, and ricochets.

Then our speaker drops the line *"there ain't but one way out."* Having already mentioned his knowledge of Jesus, this reference to "one way" touches upon a phrase Christians often used then and now: a biblical statement that mankind had only one way to God – through Jesus. To symbolize this, many charismatic worship leaders in the 1970s, '80s, and '90s would urge believers to lift high a hand, the index finger pointing to Heaven. Thus, when our disturbed advisor spouts, *"And it ain't no upraised finger, either,"* he's disavowing the Christian faith and pointing to death as his "one way" out.

All of this came to me from a pessimistic atheist who used these words to attack my faith. Discussing this, we found some common ground over the concepts and foundations of faith. He agreed that we both drew our world views from faith – his in science and the physical senses, mine in spiritual truths experienced through my physical senses. And he admitted that where my faith spawned hope in a future, his pointed only to death.

Some readers today may not recognize the practice of pointing to Heaven. It draws from biblical references for believers to lift high their hands in acknowledgement of God. Early Christians also used finger and hand signals to share messages and make statements of faith. Worshippers in other faiths have similar practices. Some common Islamic and Jewish hand signs parallel Christian symbols, though with different meanings and purposes.

Coke bottle legs

In Chapter 26, our protagonist compares his friend to a soda pop bottle:

He couldn't help noticing her coat parted, revealing a fabulous pair of legs stretching from a shiny set of running shorts to her well-worn sneakers. The sight verified one truth: if Coke could manufacture a bottle that shapely, Pepsi would be out of business.

I drew this from my childhood infatuation with cold soda. The 1960s proved a remarkable era in many ways, one being pop sold in glass bottles. While sellers also used plastic and aluminum, glass ruled due to its ease of recycling, attractive designs, and ability to not taint the drink with an aftertaste. Every brand boasted a distinctive shape, and sometimes colors, but Coke stood out with a swirling hourglass form reflecting feminine charms. Distributors developed that design in 1916 to set Coca-Cola apart from copycats. It worked so well, the "Mae West" bottle earned a cultural life all its own. Even as a kid, I understood why artists as diverse as Salvadore Dali, Agnez Mo, Jamie Uys, and Andy Warhol would tout the image in paint, film, and song. That bottle pleased the eye whether filled or empty, though everyone preferred light sparkling through that caramel cola.

I cherished the biting taste that came in a chilled bottle seemingly made for my grip. I loved watching condensation drip along those smooth curls, a curious counter to the bubbles floating to the top. Even the cap engaged my mind, the red metal flaring just so around that graceful oval. The whole experience was simply fun, from buying the brew to whistling into that empty flagon. Of course, as I got older, that contour made an even greater impression, as this *The Road to Renewal* reference illustrates. Marilyn Monroe and Raquel Welch would play a role in that, as did many friends.

Although glass lost its prominence in today's cost-driven

economy, that romantic bottle thrives in many forms. It's a wonderful reminder of how some things never change.

The Good Samaritan

In Chapter 26, our protagonist compares his friend to a beloved biblical character, the Good Samaritan. This draws from Luke 10:25-37, which for the uninitiated refers to the New Testament Book of Luke, one of four providing testimonies on the life of Jesus Christ. The "10" refers to the tenth chapter of Luke, while the other numbers denote specific passages in that chapter. These verses quote Jesus narrating the Good Samaritan's parable. Allow me to retell that tale and thus set the scene.

Seeking to test Jesus, a lawyer asked what he must do to gain eternal life. Christ asked a question in return: What did the law say was required? The attorney answered by quoting Deuteronomy 6:5 from the Torah, the Hebrew law handed down by Moses. That verse says: "You shall love The Lord your God with all your heart, with all your soul, and with all your strength." He then added the tail end of Leviticus 19:18, "love your neighbor as yourself."

I suspect Christ smiled when He heard the lawyer, for He Himself would use that same answer when a scribe asked what the greatest commandment was, as recorded in Mark 10:28-34. Christ told this smart lawyer that he had answered correctly, to which the lawyer said, "And who is my neighbor?" That's when Jesus shares the parable of the Good Samaritan.

This tale starts with thieves attacking an unnamed man on his way to Jericho. They leave him lying on the road naked and half-dead. A traveling priest comes upon the victim but moves on without offering help. Neither does a journeying Levite, a member of the Hebrew tribe of Levi who would assist priests during worship. Then a resident of Samaria finds the wounded one. Now, in normal situations a Hebrew would have little to do with Samaritans if they could help it, and visa versa. But this Samaritan had compassion for the victim. He tended to those wounds and took the man to an inn, leaving money and a note of support asking the innkeeper to take care of the victim.

Ending his tale, Jesus returned to the lawyer who had wondered "And who is my neighbor?" Christ asked this man which of those three travelers – the priest, the Levite, or the Samaritan – was the neighbor to that victim. The lawyer answered, "The one who showed mercy."

I imagine that brought another smile as Christ said, "Go and do the same thing."

Breck Girls

Chapter 26 makes a casual reference to one of the most successful advertising campaigns of the last century. Its tale starts in 1930, when Edward J. Breck joined his father's laboratory in Springfield, Mass. There he developed the first pH-balanced liquid shampoos, along with other hair/scalp treatments. To expand sales during the Great Depression, the manufacturer launched a color print advertising campaign in 1936 showcasing soft-focus pastel portraits of female shampoo users, all by commercial artist Charles Sheldon. This celebration of American hairstyles picked up steam in the '40s as the "Breck Girls" became romantic icons of feminine charm and purity. While Breck adapted the ads to television in the '50s, their identity remained tied to paintings featuring everyday women rather than professional models. Even so, several future stars emerged from the Breck Girl ranks, including Cheryl Tiegs, Jaclyn Smith, Cybill Shepherd, Kim Basinger, and Brooke Shields. The ad campaign ended in 1976 with the death of its second illustrator, Ralph William Williams. The Breck company later attempted to restart this campaign using photographs, but no efforts succeeded.

The terrible paradox

In Chapter 26, protagonist James Harrigan worries about having a close friend of the opposite sex – especially one both beautiful and married. He sees this as a "terrible paradox" of his faith… a description that somewhat fits his biblical standard.

God's word warns believers to resist temptation and flee sexual immorality. Paul's first letter to the Corinthians offers many insights on this. Christians should follow God's will and keep their lives above reproach to set good examples before others, as Paul notes in his first letter to Timothy, chapter 3, verses 1 to 7. In such ways, believers fulfill Christ's call to "Let your light so shine before men, that they may see your good works and glorify your Father in heaven" (Matthew 5:16, New King James Version).

The Bible also gives believers 59 "one another" orders that encourage friendship with everyone. Examples range from the obvious "love one another" of John 13:34/Romans 13:8 to "serve one another" in Galatians 5:13 and "encourage one another," 1 Thessalonians 4:18. Ephesians 2:19 reminds us that followers of Christ "are no longer strangers and foreigners, but fellow citizens with the saints and members of the household of God." Galatians 3:28 proves even more embracing: "There is neither Jew nor Greek, there is neither slave nor free, there is neither male nor female; for you are all one in Christ Jesus."

Thus we reach Harrigan's paradox. As Peter wrote in his first letter, chapter 5, we must shepherd all those around us while staying vigilant to resist temptation and sin. Struggling to walk that fine line leads Harrigan back to the heart of his faith and fellowship, as readers will see throughout the rest of *The Road to Renewal*.

One shot at marriage?

Let's discuss divorce, which shadows everything in this novel. In Chapter 26, protagonist James Harrigan shares his deepest fear with Sandy Travis, a close friend and fellow Christian: *"You know, I wonder now if I'll ever know what real love is. I lie awake sometimes afraid, really afraid, that I'll die having never shared the kind of bonding you and Jack have."*

This draws not just from his loneliness but the depths of his faith: *"I've already had my shot at marriage, if you know what I mean, and I blew it,"* Harrigan mumbled.

That "one shot" view may surprise or amuse readers

today, considering how nearly 80 percent of divorced Americans remarry, according to some analysts, and 40 percent or more of those unions fail. But Harrigan's view parallels conservative Christian standards in the novel's 1990s setting... and today.

To paraphrase, God's word defines marriage as a lifelong commitment between a man and a woman. While biblical law allows divorce in cases of sexual sin or desertion, it encourages forgiveness through faith and repentance. It does not sanction remarriage while the other partner lives, which reveals God's long-term hope to save that sacred commitment.

Christ eloquently explains all this in Matthew 19. In 1 Corinthians 7, the apostle Paul adds insight on how a spouse's faith – or lack thereof – may impact biblical law.

And thus, Harrigan's "one shot" comment rings true under his faith. But since American marriages fall under U.S. civil law, some Christians apply a bit of leeway when a believer remarries if his/her former spouse:

• Has wed someone outside biblical law.
• Is an unbeliever.
• Dies.

Even in these cases, only death makes marriage reconciliation impossible. Yet these issues might factor into Sandy's loving counterpoint. She tells James:

"You didn't ask for the divorce. You didn't desire it. And correct me if I'm wrong here, but you only granted it because that's what she wanted."

"Well, I didn't think I could try to hold her to –"

"– A vow she couldn't keep," Sandy interrupted. "Right; we've been through that. And you're right: God doesn't want marriages to end in divorce. But He doesn't want us to be alone, either. That's why He created Eve! So that Adam, even in God's presence, in the perfection of the Garden, wouldn't be lonely. Just like you are now."

Sandy drives that point home:

"God understands loneliness, James. Remember what Christ yelled on the cross? 'My God, my God, why hast Thou forsaken me?' Haven't you pondered that same thing?"

To this she adds...

By Kirby Lee Davis

"It's hard to imagine being lonely when you're the Son of God, and yet Christ surrounded Himself with the disciples and took them just about everywhere. Remember, He even wanted them around when He was praying His heart out in the garden! And on that, you know, it's remarkable to imagine anyone being lonely in God's presence at Eden, yet the Bible says Adam was, and God understood. He understood, James! So, don't you think He would understand you, too?"

This debate will continue as James advances along *The Road to Renewal…*

j-col32.wpd

After that emotional debate, Chapter 27 changes the tempo with a comedy column penned by our protagonist, newspaper reporter James Harrigan. *The Road to Renewal* "reprints" these humor pieces from its fictional newspaper for several reasons:

• The columns work as transitions between scenes or gaps in time.

• These bridges provide insights on the characters and culture, with information the reader will need to know later.

• These excerpts inject different voices into the novel's third-person point of view.

• Many of these columns – including this one – foreshadow events to come.

• Last but not least, these often-absurd texts serve the same function in the book as in that small-town newspaper: to amuse and entertain. Their effectiveness is a debated point among some characters, just as my own columns were in real life. This one makes a corny reference to *The Twilight Zone…* did you catch it?

I wrote this particular one based on something I really did: fall asleep while covering a city council meeting. Several readers (and city officials) got a big kick out of it, for local humor reasons I won't explain here. The column also becomes a hot topic among *The Road to Renewal* characters, who will soon bring up something else that happened in that sleepy council meeting.

Paying homage

In a hole in the wall, there stood the hobbit. Not a dry, sandy hole, but one of red Oklahoma brick outfitted for a double-bolt security door…

Savvy readers may recall how protagonist James Harrigan received a horrific taxi ride from a short, round driver James compares to a hobbit. Chapter 28 reintroduces that character with a playful twist on the iconic opening lines to *The Hobbit*. Tolkien had a way with words…

Famous faces

Chapter 28 recalls two legendary actors, James Stewart and Lon Chaney.

The latter, who died in 1930, thrilled and horrified audiences in such silent films as *The Hunchback of Notre Dame* (released in 1923) and *The Phantom of the Opera* (1925). He became a silver screen icon for his amazing performances and haunting makeup, using techniques Chaney developed during his stage days. His diverse masking efforts earned Chaney the nickname "The Man of a Thousand Faces." His legacy includes another Hollywood star: son Lon Chaney Jr., who died in 1973. He also carved out a horror film career, making his most significant mark while portraying *The Wolf Man* (1941).

Stewart, who died in 1997, remains one of Hollywood's most beloved stars due to his remarkable number of memorable performances. With his stumbling drawl and rambling pitch, Stewart was one of those actors who seemed at home in every genre. I suspect most people considered him a friend of the family… I certainly did, which may be why the "hobbit" taxi driver in *The Road to Renewal* brought Stewart up twice in talks with protagonist James Harrigan.

My personal favorites among Stewart's films include *You Can't Take It with You* (1938), *Mr. Smith Goes to Washington* (1939), *The Shop Around the Corner* and *The Philadelphia Story* (both 1940), *It's a Wonderful Life* (1946), *The Stratton Story* (1949), *Winchester '73* and *Harvey* (both 1950), *Bend of the River* (1952), *Rear Window*, *The Far Country*, and *The Glenn Miller*

Story (all 1954), *Vertigo* (1958), *Anatomy of a Murder* (1959, the year I entered this world), *How the West Was Won* and *The Man Who Shot Liberty Valance* (both 1962), and *The Cheyenne Social Club* (1970). They combine for a great binge weekend!

"You're hooked"

James Harrigan hears all sorts of conspiracy theories in *The Road to Renewal*. Chapters 28 and 29 bring this to a boil as "the hobbit" taxi driver shares his rebellion plan against Leo Heavy Chevy Geo. James plays along, diagnosing "conspiracy" realities in auto ownership cycles. But Harrigan finds some truth in this as he reaches a synopsis: *"All your life you'll be in their clutches, making car payments, then repair payments, then car and repair payments…."*

That's when the hobbit turns it all around, pegging our protagonist as a victim: *"They've already got your money, don't they? You're hooked."*

Harrigan spends Chapter 29 drifting ever closer to paranoia as he ponders what all this means. The weary reporter weaves together everything plaguing his life over the last two days: his painful divorce, that damaging car wash, the bungled break-in and resulting police antagonism, his depressing repair bill, the nasty taxi ride and stench coat affair, all the scuttlebutt, that counterfeiting debacle…. Harrigan begins to see himself as a hunted target, paralleling his daughter's *Star Trek* imagination.

This ties the whole book together as we head into the home stretch…

Pursuing counterfeiters

It may surprise readers that the U.S. Secret Service would investigate a rural Oklahoma counterfeiting incident. But Congress created that branch of the U.S. Treasury to handle all such cases across the nation. That started in 1865, at the close of the Civil War, when counterfeit bills comprised nearly a third of all currency in circulation.

Pursuing counterfeiters remains a priority of the Secret Service. With other nations also using the U.S. dollar as legal tender, this agency focuses on international investigations targeting counterfeiters and their distribution networks, according to the website secretservice.gov. The Secret Service also offers comprehensive forensic counterfeit detection training programs for banks and law enforcement agencies overseas. In 2022, the Secret Service prevented more than $2.6 billion in cyber financial crime losses around the globe, according to its annual report. The agency also seized more than $41.5 million in counterfeit currency.

Castration

Chapter 30 opens with a debate over using castration to punish rapists. This was a hot topic when the state of Texas adopted this option in June 1997 (a strong clue for dating this novel). Texas was not alone; three other states had already enacted laws allowing chemical or surgical castration for some convicted sex offenders. While this remains a contentious issue, with some case studies questioning castration's effectiveness in stopping repeat offenses, its legal use spread to eight states and some foreign countries by 2023. Over those years, the focus for determining a convict's motivation turned from malicious intent to chemical imbalances and mental illness. To better address prisoner rights and public safety needs, some states are testing various hormonal treatments and techniques. "State legislators continue to explore the use of surgical and chemical castration for sex offenders," according to a FindLaw.com report updated in August 2023. "Some states such as Oregon and Georgia, have stopped their use of chemical castration in sexual offenses and repealed these laws."

Leopold and Loeb

In a debate over castrating convicted rapists, protagonist James Harrigan raises the issue of free will by dropping the names Leopold and Loeb. This references a historic 1924 murder case brought against Nathan Freudenthal Leopold Jr. and Richard Albert Loeb.

Born into wealthy Illinois families, these two young friends (possibly lovers) admitted to doing numerous burglaries before deciding to commit a crime "that would set all of Chicago talking," as a 2008 *Smithsonian Magazine* article put it.

Since Loeb saw himself as a master criminal, and Leopold believed himself a superman who lived outside any moral code, the teens used the winter of 1923-24 to plot the kidnapping and murder of Loeb's 14-year-old cousin, Bobby Franks. The duo committed the deed on May 21, sending a ransom note the next day. But mistakes in their "perfect" crime – Leopold lost a pair of eyeglasses when they hid the body – led to their arrests after the corpse (and glasses) were found. Both culprits confessed their guilt on May 31, with Leopold saying they did the crime for thrills. As he allegedly told a newspaper reporter, "A thirst for knowledge is highly commendable, no matter what extreme pain or injury it may inflict upon others."

No doubt their plans and confessions led Harrigan to cite this murder as an example of criminal free will. But their convictions also presented legal arguments for the other side.

The Leopold and Loeb families hired renowned defense attorney Clarence Darrow, who saw their cases as stepping stones in his battle against capital punishment. Darrow had the two plead guilty to avoid a trial by jury. He then asked the judge to consider their pleas, ages, and mental condition before deciding on sentences. This opened the door to evolving psychological theories and hormonal studies suggesting human actions drew more from conditioning and chemical interactions than rational choices.

On Sept. 10, in a hearing broadcast by radio station WGN, the judge sentenced both defendants to 99 years in prison for the kidnapping charges and lifetime stays for the murder. Loeb would die twelve years later at age 30, stabbed to death at Stateville Prison. Leopold, paroled in 1958, sought anonymity by moving to Puerto Rico. He died there in 1971 at age 66, having used the intervening years to marry, study social work at the University of Puerto Rico, and make occasional trips back to Chicago. By then, this case had settled into history as the murder trial of the century.

A global killer

Chapter 30 casually cites one of the most successful brands of the last century. S.C. Johnson Co.'s historic 1955 launch of Raid House & Garden Bug Killer marked the family firm's first product release that wasn't made of wax or designed to polish a surface. But like Johnson Wax, the Raid brand soon became a powerhouse with more than 30 products. Raid held a 49-percent share of the $8.7 billion global home pesticide market in 2019, according to a *Wall Street Journal* article.

"Like Heinlein once suggested"

"If we can't do like Heinlein once suggested," he began, "and just export everyone determined to do evil —"

In that Chapter 30 quote, James Harrigan refers to the short story *Coventry* by noted science fiction writer Robert Heinlein. That tale first appeared in the July 1940 issue of *Astounding Science Fiction* magazine. As one of the first entries in Heinlein's "Future History" series, *Coventry* depicts a frontier reservation similar to Great Britain's Australian penal colony. "The Coventry of the title refers to land set aside for those citizens who do not want to abide by the Covenant, a future constitution of what the United States became after the Crazy Years," notes an article at classicsofsciencefiction.com. The Covenant guarantees all citizens the freedom to pursue happiness so long as they don't commit violent acts against another citizen. "Most people accept the big government of the Covenant, while the anti-government folks are sent to a reservation where anything goes."

Trash-80

Chapter 30 drops the cryptic name TRS-80. That refers to a computer line Tandy Corp. released in 1977 through its Radio Shack chain. Just that quick, the huge electronics retailer became a leader in the emerging personal computer sector, even though many stores started with just a display model.

Though TRS-80 hardware and software development suffered from Tandy's cost-cutting focus, growing demand in homes, small businesses, schools, and governments (like those in our fictional Franklin, OK) spurred the computer's evolution through several models and a laptop line. For a while, TRS-80 user needs helped support custom software-writing entrepreneurs in many cities.

I used two TRS-80 portable models at an Oklahoma City newspaper. Once you adjusted to the small screen, the light devices served writers well.

I also learned how to program the computer. Often I would go into Radio Shacks and set a TRS-80 to display and repeat the line "HELLO, YOU SILLY GOOSE!" over and over until the terminal was shut down. It amused me to find my program still running days after I had loaded it… a sign the clerks knew nothing about operating the machines.

TRS-80 development ended in the mid-1980s as competitors using Microsoft's disk-operating system (known as DOS) came to dominate the marketplace. These PCs could tap a growing number of popular "killer applications" like Lotus 1-2-3, which the TRS-80 could not run. Tandy also found itself squeezed by two irresistible forces:

• Tandy failed to keep pace with competitors' ever-improving hardware quality, which helped Radio Shack entries earn the nickname "Trash-80."

• Tandy suffered in competition from upstart generic PC makers, whose use of DOS and no-name, mix-and-match components helped their units outperform the TRS-80 while undercutting its prices.

Gaining antique status has not done the TRS-80 any favors. You may find old models selling today for around $50.

Corporate kindness

Chapter 31 reveals how the Bean Brothers Bank credited $20 to protagonist James Harrigan for the counterfeit bill one of its tellers gave him. The mirrors how my lender responded after I endured the same scenario. Our conversation followed that in *The Road to Renewal*, right down to the question of why James kept his savings and checking accounts in separate banks. That response marked the first time I was called an "old-timer." As that year ended, I received a letter from the U.S. Treasury Department announcing the conviction of an Oklahoma City man for counterfeiting. With it came a check for $20. I sent that back with the address of my savings bank – and a reminder of where I received my phony bill.

Foreshadowing

Readers first hear about KLOD Radio's silky-voiced Carolyn Danvers in Chapter 9. James Harrigan immediately switches the channel, for as the book notes, he didn't need that sort of temptation, even if it was just an ad for her morning talk show. That fun bit of foreshadowing grows long legs, for Danvers doesn't return until Chapter 32. That starts a long, sexy plotline as Carolyn demonstrates why our divorced protagonist fears this excessive flirt. She also throws new light on one of his comedy columns!

Insights on the city council

Chapter 32 sees our weary protagonist/newspaper reporter preparing to cover a Franklin City Council meeting. That council is a group of elected representatives that oversees Franklin's city manager-led government. It meets in the council chambers, a room inside City Hall, the building that houses most of Franklin's government offices.

Chapter 33 leaps into the meeting, which is presided over by the mayor. Following generally accepted procedures used in the 1990s (the setting of this novel), this meeting starts with a prayer asking God to bless and lead their rural Oklahoma community, its leaders, and their actions. The mayor then asks the council to vocally approve the "minutes" (activity record) of the last meeting. Council members usually back this to keep from having to hear the secretary read their past actions out loud.

The fun begins when the mayor opens "the floor" to "new business." This allows citizens to walk to the podium (thus the "open floor") and ask whatever questions they desire of their elected or appointed officials. (Council members also could raise topics this way if they missed the agenda

By Kirby Lee Davis

deadline.) This "new business" takes a somewhat zany turn in the novel when a voter asks city leaders to "open the city books." That means the appellant seeks to look at the city's financial records. Before the computer age, city treasurers often scheduled times when citizens could come to City Hall and personally look over the ledgers. This represented an early form of transparency in government.

While the responses of the mayor and city manager may sound a bit zany to readers, their comments somewhat parallel tongue-in-cheek turns I heard in council meetings in the 1980s. One must remember that these small-town governments were often made up of friends and neighbors, which could lead to informal quips and running jokes (along with bitter rivalries). It's one reason why I started writing my humor columns.

At some point the mayor cuts off hearing new business to start on a previously announced agenda of ongoing topics referred to as "old business." The council may pause the meeting at times to consider legally sensitive topics in private; this is called an "executive session."

Chapter 33's pointed conversation about the police chief and his patrol routes draws from actual city council meetings I covered decades ago. That hot exchange mixes well with our protagonist's growing fears over Secret Service probes, *Nowhere Man* agents, and flirty radio hosts.

Vending machines and smokescreens

One of our protagonist's main character themes is a simmering frustration with advancing technology. First seen in several amusing Chapter 1 turns, this motif rises again with James Harrigan's daughters, their car wash debacle, his repair woes, some troubling phone dialogues… the list goes on. Chapter 34 introduces a new mechanical foe: an overstuffed City Hall vending machine. Harrigan's resulting battle for a waylaid Snickers bar mirrors those I often endured while pursuing my journalism degree at the University of Football in Norman, OK.

On days when I didn't have time to reach the student

cafeteria, my lunch often consisted of a canned drink and a Twix candy bar. That United Kingdom-bred confection marked a new habit for me, for it entered the USA in 1979 during my freshman year. I usually bought my Twix from a J-school vending machine. That device also debuted in the '70s. Its design worked by hanging candy, chips, and other products from long, swirling bars.

Theoretically, a customer would find his desired snack among those numbered corkscrews, insert the correct coins to buy the treat, and tap the bar's number into the keypad. When satisfied, the machine would revolve the appropriate corkscrew once, so all the products hanging from that spiral bar would roll one turn forward. The snack nearest the buyer would fall off its bar to land in the pick-up area.

The process usually worked well, but sometimes an ornery item slipped backward on its corkscrew instead of forward. Or the snack would fall as desired, only to get caught on the way down against one or more still-dangling items.

Vending machine makers would solve these problems by using two corkscrews per product instead of one. Those bars sat below snacks instead of above them, so that the paired swirls always pushed the chosen item forward. The front snack plunged into an enlarged drop area that almost guaranteed they would reach the buyer.

It took time for owners to cycle through their old vending machines… especially in rural Oklahoma, where merchants often waited for these somewhat expensive devices to wear out before ever considering replacing them. That's why Harrigan faced one of the older monoliths in the Franklin City Hall Break Room.

In terms of writing, that snack machine battle provides readers a fun change of pace. It works like a smokescreen, dividing the Franklin City Council drama while setting the stage for Carolyn's pursuits.

TSRs

Chapter 35 drops an original *The Road to Renewal* term not mentioned since Chapter 5. We're talking about Temptation

Susceptibility Ratings, or TSRs. The subject first rises when protagonist/newspaper reporter James Harrigan endures the "Call of Spring" while waiting in line to wash his car. This threatened to push his TSRs "beyond the danger level." Carolyn's getting physical in Chapter 35 lifts his TSRs to "record levels and climbing" – which may explain why the subject never rises again, despite the heat…

Mr. High and Mighty

The seductive Carolyn Danvers slings the title "Mr. High and Mighty" – along with other choice words – at protagonist James Harrigan when she gets fed up with his morality and diversions. This wordplay taps an old English phrase sometimes used as an adverb, one targeting those who think or act as if they're better or more important than others.

According to writingexplained.org, the English Language roots of "high and mighty" go back to the 1400s, when only wealthy and influential members of European society could regularly afford to own and maintain horses. Perched atop their mounts or sitting comfortably in their coaches, these riders presented an enduring symbol of people who literally enjoyed positions above those individuals forced to travel on their own two feet.

Now, based upon my many years spent in the earnest study of *Mad Magazine* – I could have majored in that field had the University of Football offered such a degree – I've always considered this phrase drew more from a revisionist look at the airliner disaster film *The High and the Mighty*.

That John Wayne drama garnered widespread praise during its original 1954 release, only to be labeled superficial and pretentious by later film historians. Those very qualities helped *The High and the Mighty* earn another place in history as the basis for the classic 1980 spoof *Airplane!* and its satisfying, if not quite classic, '82 sequel.

I drew Carolyn's playful banter – and this attack, in all its forms – from verbal darts thrown my way by a few women I have known. More on that later…

Government shenanigans

Chapter 36 depicts some crazy goings-on during a city council meeting. We'll focus first on the actual actions by the panel and not the press table seductions that soon take the spotlight.

While considering a new departmental contract (we never learn what department it is for), the council takes a few procedural liberties to shortcut the system. Things escalate from there, at times resembling a Tex Avery cartoon. For example:

- A gavel blow to the head clears a lawmaker's mind.
- A contract addendum labels one councilman a rat fink.
- A different article seeks to rezone the city manager's home for storing environmental waste.

One proofreader (and I suspect at least one reviewer) saw no sense in all this. I asked my proofreader to consider the setting before passing judgment.

Our protagonist/newspaper reporter, whose viewpoint generally frames our novel, often sees his world through a slapstick filter. At times this encourages him to associate extreme people or actions with characters (or caricatures) he knows. His weariness elevates this, as do his fears of a pursuing conspiracy, which means his observations just might be a bit flavored. Throw upon all that the fact that his mind's not focused on his job, for the beautiful radio disc jockey sitting at his side is trying to seduce him – on the air, during the meeting. That commands his direct attention, leaving his backwater perceptions to monitor the council. And so, it's possible he got carried away by all this. His memories might not be entirely accurate.

Of course, there's another reason why it reads this way. This is a slapstick comedy staging a final big buildup before the fall!

And what a fall it will be… tragic.

As with most elements of *The Road to Renewal*, these tales draw from my life. Franklin's council topics and actions echo meetings I attended. The City Hall building layout recalls a few I worked in. Ditto that for the council room, though with this caveat: since that particular town had two newspapers and two radio stations, the city used separate tables for its broadcast and print reporters. Thus I often sat alone. Our competing weekly stopped covering the meetings, being unable to keep up with my daily coverage – or so I was often told. Naturally I want to believe that, even today. The "thumb battle" mentioned in Chapter 27 happened one rare moment when I actually had a comrade sharing the table. The snack machine adventure of Chapter 34 took place as depicted, during one council's executive session. As for Carolyn…

Big Chief tablets

During the Franklin City Council meeting, readers see the panel's unnamed contract negotiator (who reminds our protagonist of a chipmunk) using a Big Chief tablet to keep his notes. While some may (and hopefully will) see that as a joke, I observed many a lawyer, accountant, and other professional using Big Chiefs in the days before laptops became affordable – including one time by a city council's contract negotiator. These notepads didn't cost much and they got the job done – which points to one reason why the Big Chief dominated its American market for decades.

Like most folks, I first came to appreciate Big Chief tablets in grade school. That was one thing I probably shared with my parents, who attended elementary school in the Great Depression… which was not long after the Western Tablet Co. first released this historic product (surprisingly, no one seems to know exactly when that happened; it first came out sometime in the '20s, most records suggest).

Designed to meet school needs, Big Chief tablets came with plentiful large pages backed by a cardboard panel to support writing or drawing. These pages had big lines across open spaces to help kids learn to write, while their low prices appealed to parents and school systems with stretched budgets. Thus the Big Chief tablet became a national bestseller for decades, and since it primarily targeted the American educational system, the product changed little over that time… a strategy that allowed competitors to catch up and surpass it by the 1980s. Big Chief sales stopped in 2001, although not for long. Nostalgia trends led to renewed production in recent years.

Sex and Christian fiction boundaries

I smiled when some proofreaders suggested Chapter 5's sexy "Call of Spring" pushed Christian fiction boundaries too far. That scene foreshadowed much more to come… though it took 30 chapters and a few more hints before things grew truly hot. By then, *The Road to Renewal* had delved into job loss, bankruptcy, an expletive-laden confrontation at gunpoint, and other sensitive elements stretching that Christian fiction envelope.

This underscores why I wrote *The Road to Renewal*. As I suffered through my divorce and returned to a single life, I endured temptations and frustrations most Christian novels avoid. I wanted to share a humorous, heartfelt tale about real-world challenges believers face today. I wanted to show how we could use our faith, biblical principles, and prayer to work through the compromising situations life throws at us.

Like many other turns in *The Road to Renewal*, the seduction scenes in Chapters 35 and 36 weave together similar events I endured. That realism helped keep me grounded. It also led some readers to ask if I would become a romance writer…

Ragu, Ritz, and flu shots

It's common today to find a nurse, pharmacist, or medical clinic offering shots or tests in a supermarket or discount store. But in the 1990s, when *The Road to Renewal* takes place, this was a novel concept in most of America. Innovative capitalism at work!

I first ran into such a market test at my local grocery. I came across a nurse manning a portable card table between the Ritz crackers and Ragu Garden Style Spaghetti Sauce. Armed with a box of syringes, vaccine, and a notepad for jotting down patient info, this rather imposing caregiver administered flu shots to most anyone who walked up. That so amused me, I wrote about it first for a newspaper humor column and then this novel. Impressed by her firm stance as a nervous soul (namely, the guy before me) tried to back out, I adapted the nurse's words to fit a classic *Dirty Harry* quote:

"I know what you're thinking," she whispered. "Sure, you're only 30 feet from the door. You might be able to make a break for it. And if you do, you might only miss a few days of work with the flu. But since I'm standing here, right now, armed with perhaps the most effective syringe known to man, a 22-gauge, 3.5cc Abbott Luer Lock that I could ram right through your puny bones into that concrete wall, you have to ask yourself one question: Do you feel lucky? Well, do you? Punk?"

This marks one of those rare moments in writing *The Road to Renewal* that I sought a bit of help. Although the internet was rather young at that time, I was pretty good at researching information (and attracting computer viruses, but that's another story). Still, I needed an experienced hand for this quote, and so, seeking the kind of truly menacing syringe that a "Dirty Harry" nurse might use, I called my younger sister – who was a nurse of some renown – and asked for her opinion. I could tell she was wondering just what I was up to this time, but she hesitated only a moment before naming this Abbott product. The rest is history.

The cost of battling the flu

Around 1997, I ran across a press release estimating the flu cost Americans $3 billion a year in medicine sales, healthcare services, and work absentees. Intrigued, I used that figure in my newspaper healthcare column and one of this novel's humor columns.

That battle surged over the next two decades due in part to the rising U.S. population, increased international travel (which expanded the flu's spread and season), and simple inflation. Estimating these costs became harder as consumers used more over-the-counter (OTC) drugs – which some analysts said reduced spending on more expensive treatments – and COVID muddied the waters. But it's fun to identify the total cost of such an issue, so let's try.

A 2016 report by *Pharmacy Times* estimated Americans

spent $4 billion a year on OTC medications just to contain their coughing. A 2019 report in *Drug Store News* found Americans paid more than $8.6 billion in 2017 for OTC upper-respiratory products, with another $4.1 billion shelled out for flu-related pain relief meds.

According to a 2020 report compiled by the National Committee for Quality Assurance and the National Alliance of Healthcare Purchaser Coalitions, battling the flu costs Americans an estimated $11.2 billion annually in direct and indirect healthcare services. Direct medical costs – based on outpatient doctor visits, emergency department visits, and hospitalizations – came in at $3.2 billion. Adults diagnosed with the flu averaged losing 3.7 to 5.9 days of work, resulting in $8 billion in indirect costs.

As for the bigger problem, a 2022 report by the Centers for Disease Control and Prevention estimated 9 million Americans suffered flu illnesses during the 2021-22 influenza season. This resulted in 4 million medical visits, 10,000 hospital admissions, and 5,000 deaths.

Bad math

Our protagonist's flu shot column includes one instance of really bad math. To quote Chapter 37 in *The Road to Renewal*, which takes place in the late 1990s:

Imagine the economy burning up $3 billion a year combating something that has stopped up noses since the dawn of time. That tops a trillion bucks in my lifetime alone.

Let's set aside the issue of clogged noses and follow the money. At $3 billion a year, I would have to survive 333.33 revolutions around the sun to see our flu tally reach that trillion-dollar level. That's almost five times the average American male's lifespan, according to worlddata.info.

Now such errors might not matter when you're just trying to spur laughter, but this one still makes me cringe… and smile! For in the nearly 30 years since I wrote that – first for my metro daily newspaper, and then in this novel – no one questioned my trillion-dollar statement.

Of course, the whole equation hinges on how long I live.

At I type this, I'm 63.5 years old. If I survive another 269.83 Christmas seasons, my prose will prove correct.

So there's still a chance…

Capitalism and Happy Meals…

McDonald's U.S. eateries enjoyed some long customer lines back in the 1980s and early '90s due to several hot Happy Meal campaigns. As the collectable toys became ever more decorative and technical, McDonald's moved their manufacture to China to take advantage of its cheaper labor costs. *The Road to Renewal* made a casual reference to this in a humor column on capitalism and the flu. I quote:

No wonder the Chinese have traded in their little red books to make Happy Meal toys for McDonald's. You just can't top modern capitalism.

Ahh, the optimism of the 1990s. Let's overlook that, focusing instead on that excerpt's backstory – for toys were a small part of McDonald's China efforts. They started in the early 1980s under a patient plan to build a complete supply chain. When Mickey D's first China restaurant opened in 1990, they had just one local plant to service it (with burgers, naturally). Everything else had to be imported. But by 2006, McDonald's 43 China facilities supplied almost 96 percent of what its 770 China restaurants sold, according to a Reuters report. Those plants also created produce (and toys) for McDonald's locations in the Far East, Europe, and America.

Reporting on racism

While *The Road to Renewal* touches upon racism many times throughout its text, the novel doesn't directly address that subject until Chapter 38. That's when our protagonist's efforts to track down a suspected burglar draw a response from the receptionist of an African American church.

Their phone exchange mirrors complaints I fielded during my first-year reporting at a small Oklahoma daily newspaper. The truth in her remarks – and the regretful events they lead up to, which *The Road to Renewal* depicts – spurred me to dig deeper into this dark subject.

When possible, I continued this as my career advanced. It wasn't easy, for the business news focus of my next publication rarely touched upon such topics, and I spent many years behind an editor's desk doing little if any reporting. But with the Oklahoma City bombing and my move to Tulsa, I received more opportunities to research and write about (even live through) a few Sooner State tragedies.

I covered several Native American tribal advances and studied some bitter sorrows. I shuddered at Tulsa's violent history. I researched its legacy in slavery, the ex-Confederates who settled there, and the open role the Ku Klux Klan played in Oklahoma's early development. But no matter how many documents I read, historians I consulted, or survivors I interviewed, I never could understand what drove people to do these awful things.

I wrote *The Road to Renewal* just before the turn of the century (I could be more specific, but I rather enjoy letting readers guess when this novel takes place). When I re-edited the text in 2018, I was struck by how many elements echo today's hot topics… another sad reminder that some things never change.

Questions of Job

By the time we reach Chapter 39, James Harrigan has compared himself numerous times to the Old Testament patriarch Job. This underscores the depths of Harrigan's suffering, for Job was a classic character of antiquity, a wealthy, pious man who questioned God after losing his family, health, and possessions for no apparent reason.

That issue of undeserved suffering divides modern Western cultures. Indeed, many people who today reject God cite dissatisfaction with that seminal query, "Why do bad things happen to good people?"

While Job does not abandon his faith, this steadfast man proclaims his innocence while demanding to confront our Lord. After suffering condemnation and debate from onlookers, Job finally gets to face God. The Lord turns the tables on Job, confounding him with the truth of His sovereignty while throwing no light on Job's questions.

"Job came away with a deeper sense of God's power and splendor, trusting Him more," noted pastor Charles Swindoll in an article at insight.org. But Swindoll admitted the Book of Job may not satisfy today's readers. "God allows pain for good reason, but He may never reveal those reasons."

More on this to come…

Writing tactics

Chapters 38 and 39 mirror tragic events I experienced while serving my first daily newspaper. Chapter 40 outlines its aftermath. Elements adapted from this suicide tale include the phone calls and police conversations, those bloodthirsty gawkers, and that shattered truck driver. Into this I mixed that biblical note and the convenience store subterfuge, which drew from a different newspaper escapade in my past.

While earlier chapters offered strong teasers, it's in Chapter 38 where readers see the riddle poem parallels between our protagonist, newspaper reporter James Harrigan, and the fired convenience store cashier/bungling burglar. Chapter 39 provides the lad's name: Terrance Jackson. Note how most everything we learn of this conflicted young man comes from the observations of others. That was intentional. *The Road to Renewal* uses a limited third-person narrative to preserve its underlying mystery. Since readers know no more of what's going on than our protagonist does, everyone remains in the dark about things not in his or her line of sight. I appreciate the realism this brings and how it enhances the intrigue.

Discussions in Chapter 38 identify the hardships and racism Terrance endured. By staying in Harrigan's viewpoint, I do not attempt to put into words something I've never truly experienced. Instead, I allow readers to ponder this burden through their own reflections as Harrigan takes in the death scene and its barbaric audience.

In Chapter 40, our protagonist finally gets to fill in the missing pieces to his conspiracy. Those first two paragraphs summarize the heartbreaking political ramifications of a wayward child… a humbling turn of events mirroring incidents I experienced in my reporting days. It was the kind of political scoop many reporters might die for, but like Harrigan, I never told it in newsprint. Indeed, this sad tale is one reason I left the general news industry to take a reporting post with a daily legal/business newspaper. I enjoyed that field and publication, forging a 31-year career that included work in nearly every editorial staff post. But I never forgot the lessons of that suicide, or stopped examining my life for answers.

Silly messages and memories

Chapter 40 shares slightly edited versions of two hilarious phone messages I received concerning repairs to my damaged car mirror. As in *The Road to Renewal*, I found these in my work voicemail the day after I paid for the repairs and picked up my Geo Metro. Here's the first one, as made to protagonist James Harrigan:

"Hello, Mr. Harriman. This is Milo Steward, a customer service rep at Leo Heavy Chevy Geo. I'm just calling to let you know that the estimate on your mirror is… is…. (Where is that, Jane? I can't find it anywhere…. Yes, I looked on my chair! Do you think I'd be stupid enough to leave things lying on his chair?) I'm sorry, Mr. Harrison, but it seems I've misplaced the estimate on your… well, your car. If I remember right, it was around…. (No, not the Corvette. It wasn't a Vette! You think I'd be calling on a $140 bill for a Vette?) Anyway, Mr. Halogen, please give me a call about your, well…. It was a car, wasn't it? Yes, so I recall. Well, thank you, Mr…. What's that?… Hooligan."

One point to remember: James had expected the dealership to call with the repair cost estimate – and thus get his approval – *before* they fixed his car. But no one did. This message suggests why. And now, the second message, left not long after that first one: *"Hello, Mr. Harrybear. This is Milo Steward, a customer service rep at Leo Heavy Chevy Geo. I'm just calling to tell you, the estimate on replacing your mirror is… is…. (What's that? What do you mean I've already called him?) Oh. I'm sorry. I have the wrong number. Thanks."*

By Kirby Lee Davis

The novel made a running joke of people messing up Harrigan's name. That gag originated from how often people struggled with spelling or pronouncing my first name. As I grew older, I realized many girls and women did this on purpose. That introduced me to flirting… and yes, I was slow on the uptake, which most readers already knew.

From Hades to the Monkees

Chapter 40 shares how protagonist/newspaper reporter James Harrigan deletes phone messages. It leads readers into one of my favorite jokes in *The Road to Renewal*. I'll quote that passage here:

Snapping his index finger into the "3" and "#" keys, James sent Carol's message to Davy Jones's phone locker.

"I wonder if Micky, Peter, or Mike have lockers," he thought aloud – never questioning what personality quirk would send his rattled thoughts tripping from Hades to the Monkees.

Like many jokes, good or not, this draws from multiple sources.

Davy Jones's locker refers to the last resting place for someone (usually pirates or sailors) who drowned or died at sea, the body never recovered. First mentioned in the 1700s, this metaphor evolved into a nautical term for underwater graveyards. The namesake for this legendary pirate "locker" was never firmly identified – which may explain why my mind associated it with the pop group the Monkees.

That TV sitcom "band" started as fictional characters played by Micky Dolenz, Michael Nesmith, Peter Tork, and Davy Jones. When the NBC show *The Monkees* hit the USA airwaves in 1966, two of these actors were skilled musicians, and all four had vocal experience. Studio players filled in the band's musical gaps. But as the madcap series progressed, all four actors adapted to their screen parts and instruments, allowing them to start offering live concerts in '67.

With a stable of skilled writers providing a portfolio of great tunes, the band released nine studio albums in four years. Powered by several hit singles, including classics like *I'm a Believer, Last Train to Clarksville, Pleasant Valley Sunday,* and *Daydream Believer,* the first four albums topped the charts in the USA and several other nations. But once the television show ended in 1968, few songs charted and album sales soured. The band broke up in 1970, even though other networks ran reruns of *The Monkees* on Saturday mornings from 1969 to '73. But the sitcom's nostalgic appeal grew as syndication, home video, and cable markets groomed new audiences. After a 1986 MTV marathon drew strong ratings, different incarnations of the Monkees came together for reunion tours and albums over the next four decades. The band's last concert run came in 2021. Jones had died in 2012 and Tork in 2019, leaving Dolenz and Nesmith to thrill fans. Nesmith passed away shortly after that tour.

Radio personalities

Although *The Road to Renewal* mentions flirty radio disc jockey Carolyn Danvers early on, her on-air banter doesn't factor into the plot until Chapter 34. It flows through that council meeting to take center stage in Chapter 41 with a revelation that prepares readers for the novel's open conclusion.

While such sexy talk was not common on Oklahoma airwaves at that time, stations often encouraged DJs to develop active, edgy personalities. A few looked to "shock jock" Howard Stern, then a decade into his industry-changing career. Others emulated the "morning zoo" format antics popular in large markets. While independents like KLOD could not afford such programming, they proved adept at hiring talented upstarts ready to build on-air reputations. I based Carolyn Danvers on a few such women.

Some station managers feared these rising stars would draw unwanted Federal Communications Commission attention (and demand larger salaries). But the real threat to their business came from an unexpected source – the Telecommunications Act of 1996. Intended to help boost local content on radio markets, this new law opened the door for big businesses to buy large numbers of stations, including market competitors. In the 20 years after that law took effect, conglomerates acquired over a third of all US stations. This encouraged cost-cutting steps like centralized network station programming, slashing local content and jobs.

"Before 1996, a mid-size city might have between 10-20 radio stations with jobs for programmers, producers, on-air talent, etc.," according to a 2022 article at 35000watts.com. "Afterwards, those same stations might now be owned by 3 or 4 corporations, who stretch resources across multiple stations (or more often than not, just pull content from the corporate office via satellite). The effect was alarmingly swift: within a few years, cities what once had 100 jobs for radio professionals now had maybe 20."

Goodbye Yellow Brick Road

Chapter 41 finds our protagonist, James Harrigan, trying to work through guilt he feels over the suicide of someone he barely knew. As James meets with Sandy Travis, a friend who often provides him spiritual advice, he hears Elton John's classic single *Goodbye Yellow Brick Road* playing in the background. The cryptic lyrics mix with his sorrow, even though Harrigan doesn't really understand them.

The song's title draws from the golden road in the novel *The Wonderful Wizard of Oz* by L. Frank Baum, published in 1900. That road appeared in several sequels, the classic 1939 film *The Wizard of Oz*, and other derivative works. Through these appearances, the Oxford Advanced Learner's Dictionary said the Yellow Brick Road became a metaphor for taking a course or action expected to have beneficial results.

The song's lyrics, written by Bernie Taupin in 1973, adapt and twist that metaphor in a lifestyle choice – i.e., giving up pursuit of a life of luxury (the golden road) for a simpler existence. The website songfacts.com suggests Taupin wrote this while comparing himself to Elton, who seemed devoted to opulence at the time.

"There was a period when I was going through that whole 'got to get back to my roots' thing, which spawned a lot of like-minded songs in the early days, this being one of them," the website quotes Taupin. "I don't believe I was ever turning my back on success or saying I didn't want it. I just don't believe I was ever that naïve. I think I was just hoping that maybe there was a happy medium way to exist successfully in a more tranquil setting. My only naiveté, I guess, was believing I could do it so early on. I had to travel a long road and visit the school of hard knocks before I could come even close to achieving that goal. So, thank God I can say quite categorically that I am home."

Songfacts.com called the song's canine imagery "a sly poke" at two small pets owned by Elton's girlfriend.

An article at americansongwriter.com takes a harder line, suggesting Taupin's lyrics see the Yellow Brick Road as the path to artifice and deceit: "He purposely overplays the bumpkin act as a way of zinging a controlling romantic partner who wanted to prop him up in her penthouse *where the dogs of society howl*. Some of Taupin's putdowns, on paper anyway, read like Dylan's nastiest diatribes (*There's plenty like me to be found / Mongrels who ain't got a penny / Sniffing for tidbits like you on the ground*). Yet when sung by John, his voice arching from a resigned croon into a skyscraping falsetto, those lines seem like nothing more than a gentle farewell. If anything, Elton turns the song into a declaration of hard-won personal freedom: *Oh I've finally decided my future lies / Beyond the yellow brick road.*"

Christian witnessing

Chapter 41 spins into a spiritual debate between protagonist James Harrigan and his confidante Sandy Travis. James suffers guilt over Terrance Jackson's suicide. Harrigan feels that if he had only shared more of his faith with the young man, Jackson might have found hope to carry on.

Such fears underscore concerns many Christians bear. The Bible calls believers to witness of their faith through words and example. In Matthew 5:16, Christ says, "Let your light so shine before men, that they may see your good works and glorify your Father in heaven." This is doubly important as Christ is "the light of the world," as John 8:12 reminds us. In Mark 16:15, Jesus tells His followers to "Go into all the world and preach the gospel." The apostles set strong examples of this following Christ's ascension, as the Book of Acts reveals. 1 Peter 3:15 tells believers to do likewise: "Sanctify The Lord God in your hearts, and always be ready to give a defense to everyone who asks you a reason for the hope that is in you."

But no matter how strong their faith is, Christians often struggle to tell others about their beliefs. Some people fear public speaking, battle insecurities, or doubt they know enough to discuss the subject with today's skeptical audiences. In this politically correct age, some believers worry such talk may offend others or break the law. Some Christ followers dare not risk ridicule, debate, or attack. Some resist discussing spiritual truths they're still learning.

Having balanced many such concerns, I try to start my efforts with a prayer asking God for the right words to use. I say "try" because sometimes I get caught up in the emotions of the moment and just leap in – of I stifle myself, fearing no one really wants to hear what I have to say, or that I might say something stupid. When conflicted or confused, I often focus my testimony on how Christ impacted my life. I find these hands-on tales help build personal connections, though my insecurities often linger.

Peter expected such unrest. In 1 Peter 3:15-17, the apostle told Christ followers to speak of their faith "with meekness and fear; having a good conscience, that when they defame you as evildoers, those who revile your good conduct in Christ may be ashamed."

Sandy – a character based on several women I knew in the 1980s and '90s – reminds James that Terrance bears the responsibility for choosing to commit suicide. She also points out how James sets a good example others have noticed. When he balks, she adopts perhaps the best route and invites him to pray, taking the matter to God. That's when James changes the subject – a common tactic by those too caught up in their own will or emotions to consider other options.

In his distress, James forgets he talked to Jackson about Christ during the break-in. But that tense situation allowed little interaction, and both men had their minds on other things. Harrigan also overlooks a key scriptural truth. While believers may try to introduce people to Christ through their testimony, logic, or example, such efforts often require action by God to enable unbelievers to hear and understand this faith testimony.

Our Lord takes these first steps early on, as Paul wrote in Romans 1:20 – "For since the creation of the world His invisible attributes are clearly seen, being understood by the things that are made, even His eternal power and Godhead, so that they are without excuse."

Thus, even children born to unbelievers in the world's most remote areas are still witnesses to God's divinity.

But our Lord allows each person to choose his/her direction in life – and in a world plagued by sinful natures and distractions, this freedom leads many souls to embrace worldly logic and ways. These unbelievers often fail to recognize God or see His signs, as 1 Corinthians 2:14 explains: "the natural man does not receive the things of the Spirit of God, for they are foolishness to him; nor can he know them, because they are spiritually discerned."

In Matthew 13:13, Christ tells how this impacted His ministry: "Therefore I speak to them in parables, because seeing they do not see, and hearing they do not hear, nor do they understand."

In His love for humanity, God often reaches out to unlock unbelieving hearts. This does not violate His gift of free will any more than does His occasional hardening of hearts, for these acts still leave the recipient with a choice to make (to digest some fascinating essays about this, read Dennis Prager's excellent analysis of the Book of Exodus in The Rational Bible series).

Ezekiel 36:26 shares a time God promised to open hardened minds: "I will give you a new heart and put a new spirit within you; I will take the heart of stone out of your flesh and give you a heart of flesh." Acts 16:14 provides an example of God doing exactly that: "Now a certain woman named Lydia heard us. She was a seller of purple from the city of Thyatira, who worshiped God. The Lord opened her heart to heed the things spoken by Paul." Paul's own conversion experience demonstrates an even stronger example of Christ's intervention. Read about that in Acts 9.

Superstar

In baring his wounded soul to friend Sandy Travis, James Harrigan shares guilt he feels for a young man's suicide. When Sandy questions this, James admits an irony: how much he can relate to choosing death. Rattling off some of his own sour life decisions leads Harrigan to his divorce – which has haunted James throughout the novel. He calls that marriage another example of his taking the easy way out. Sandy contests that, noting how much he loved his ex. Harrigan agrees, which brings even more pain... just as the radio begins playing *Superstar* by the Carpenters.

Many artists chose to cover that beautiful tune since its 1969 completion. The Carpenters rocked the charts with their 1971 take. Luther Vandross scored a hit with *Superstar* 12 years later.

The lyrics reveal memories of a brief fling with a musical icon. The way Karen Carpenter sings that chorus – *Don't you remember you told me you loved me, baby?* – chills everyone who has endured such heartache. "The lyrics poetically observe the pain that comes with realizing that love is not reciprocated," an oldtimemusic.com article notes. "She clings to the hope that the rock star she loves will come back to her, despite her knowing the likelihood of that happening."

Easy To Be Hard

As protagonist James Harrigan bares his soul in Chapter 41, condemning himself over and over for life choices gone wrong, friend and confidante Sandy Travis asks why he beats himself up so much. She reminds Harrigan that even Christ endured hard times. As James ponders this, KLOD radio disc jockey Carolyn Danvers plays *Easy to Be Hard*. That classic tune from the 1967 Broadway play *Hair* fits well in a psychedelic musical attacking many elements of American society. Sung by the character Sheila, the straightforward lyrics ask *How can people be so heartless? | How can people be so cruel? | Easy to be hard | Easy to be cold...*

In 1969, the pop band Three Dog Night made the song a top 10 hit in America. Its social commentary spurred great introspection in a year of dynamic highs and lows. A societyofrock.com article pins much of that chart success on lead singer Chuck Negron. "He delivers a stunning vocal performance in *Easy to Be Hard* that's indicative of a man desperate to understand why the haves are so content to abuse the have-nots…. Three Dog Night's *Easy to Be Hard* is far and away one of music's most powerful statements on a world gone mad."

A healing story

Let's open with a religious argument intended to comfort a bleeding soul. Quoting Chapter 41:

"James, you remember that man Peter healed outside the Temple? The cripple in Acts? The Bible says he'd laid outside the Temple for years, so Christ surely had seen him – and yet Jesus let him go on with his painful life."

James leaned back as far as he could go. "So?"

"So, we are bound to run across people, hurting people, who we can't help. I mean, if you read about all the multitudes that gathered around Christ, that must have happened all the time. There had to have been hundreds who sought help and didn't get it."

Sandy Travis raises these points in hopes of derailing James Harrigan's despair. The reporter blames herself for a young man's suicide; she seeks to remind him how even Christ faced hard times in life. She draws her argument from the third and fourth chapters of the New Testament Book of Acts. They tell of a 40+ year-old man, born crippled, whose friends carried him daily to Jerusalem's Beautiful Gate to seek money from those going to the Temple. One day that lame beggar met the apostles Peter and John. "Silver and gold I do not have," Peter told the cripple, "but what I have, I will give you: In the name of Jesus Christ of Nazareth, rise up and walk." And that's what happened! As Peter lifted the handicapped man by his right hand, the beggar felt his ankles and feet strengthen. He leaped to his feet and entered the Temple with the apostles, walking and praising God!

Let's compare this to Sandy's quote – which dives into biblical mysteries.

First, the Bible is unclear about how many years Jesus spent on the earth. Most theologians estimate His human lifespan ranged between 33 to 39 years. Comparing this to Acts chapters 3 and 4 supports Sandy, for it suggests the lame man could easily have been at the Beautiful Gate if/when Christ passed by, assuming his friends were faithful in getting the stricken man there.

As a devoted Hebrew, Jesus may have traveled to the Temple up to three times each year. We're unsure how often He made this journey, for the Bible focuses primarily on His ministry. Of those few years, the four Gospels contain some differences. The Book of John says Jesus made four trips to the Temple during His ministry – two at Passover, one during an unnamed festival, and one at Hannukah. The Book of Luke mentions His infant presentation at the Temple, the family visit at 12 years of age, and the Temple events leading to His crucifixion. The books of Matthew and Mark discuss only those trips during the week before His death. Still, many theologians see no conflict between the Gospels. Many accept that Christ cleansed the Temple twice – once early in His ministry, as John writes, and again just before His crucifixion. Some scholars also note places where the four Gospels may align with Temple references in other Scriptures.

To help us mark His path, the Gospels suggest Christ taught multiple times at four different Temple locations:
- The Women's Court.
- The Court of Israel.
- Solomon's porch.
- The Court of the Gentiles.

Many projected Temple layouts suggest these four areas were within easy reach of the Beautiful Gate mentioned in Acts. But other historical and archeological evidence makes this hard to iron down.

Jerusalem's walls during Jesus's life had multiple gates and more than one path to the Temple. Most of this was destroyed during the Roman conquest of the Holy City in 70 AD. According to jewishvirtuallibrary.org, the location of most of these Jerusalem gates – including the Beautiful Gate – remains conjecture drawn from ancient descriptions.

Some scholars believe the gate mentioned in Acts 3 was also known as the Eastern Gate or the Golden Gate – a prime entry point to the main Temple complex. Other archeologists believe the Beautiful Gate may have been what's often called the Nicanor (or Nicanor's) Gate or the Corinthian Gate, which Josephus said was on the east side of the Court of Israel.

Many theories suggest the Beautiful Gate aligned with the Mount of Olives and the Temple Mount. This strikes home because Christ visited the Mount of Olives often to pray. The Bible records three stops there in the week leading up to His crucifixion – including Palm Sunday, when He descended from the Mount of Olives to enter Jerusalem on a donkey. The Messiah also ascended to heaven from the Mount of Olives.

According to holylandsite.com, someone standing atop the Mount of Olives could have seen the Temple sanctuary through the Nicanor Gate. That clear line of sight to these vital areas promises easy access – which might appeal to a revolutionary visiting teacher.

So, Sandy had some ground to stand on with her biblical projections.

Stories of faith

Let's tackle a bit more of Sandy's religious argument with protagonist James Harrigan. Picking up from last time…

"So, we are bound to run across people, hurting people, who we can't help. I mean, if you read about all the multitudes that gathered around Christ, that must have happened all the time. There had to have been hundreds who sought help and didn't get it. The difficulties that some people went to just to reach Him are sometimes why we even remember their healing. The man lowered through the roof, or the lady who had the faith to touch His robe. I mean, He made a point of letting Lazarus die, just to make his healing more dramatic."

These Bible stories revolve around acts of faith.

All four Gospels tell of Christ healing a paralyzed man. Mark 2:2-11 and Luke 5:17-26 explain how the crowd around

Jesus was so large, the four men helping this paralytic could not reach His side. So the men went to the roof and lowered their friend through a hole to Christ. Moved by their faith, Jesus healed this paralyzed man and publicly forgave his sins – which alarmed some of the scribes sitting around them.

Matthew 9:20-22, Mark 5:25-34, and Luke 8:43-48 tell how a woman suffering from a "discharge of blood" was healed by touching the edge of Jesus's garment. Christ then brought everything to a standstill by asking who touched Him – a confusing question, considering how they stood in the middle of a dense crowd seeking His attention! But when the lady admitted her act, our Lord (who knew all along what had happened) praised her courage. "Daughter, your faith has made you well," Christ told her. "Go in peace."

A biblemesh.com article explains how this fulfilled a messianic prophecy in Malachi 4:2.

John 11 tells of Lazarus's dramatic resurrection. Learning of His close friend's illness, Christ waited four days before traveling to see Lazarus. By the time He arrived, his friend was dead and buried – which fit our Lord's plan. Thanking God for His loving support, Jesus called Lazarus back to life, which amazed friends Mary and Martha, along with almost everyone else. "Jesus delayed precisely because he loved Martha and Mary and Lazarus," notes an article at desiringgod.org. "He knew that Lazarus's death and resurrection would give maximum glory to God and his friends would all experience maximum joy in that glory. It would make all their suffering seem light and momentary."

2 Corinthians 4:17 affirms this logic: "For our light affliction, which is but for a moment, is working for us a far more exceeding and eternal weight of glory."

This takes us back to Sandy's point:

"Sometimes we go through hard times. Life's a test, after all. We learn from it. How we handle it defines our character. And yes, you might have been able to help this young man, but it was his choice to kill himself, James, not yours. I don't know what shaped his life, but I know how hard yours has been, and you've not given up. He didn't have to, either. So don't beat yourself up over it."

Many Scriptures support Sandy's "life's a test" assessment.

As James wrote in the second verse of his New Testament book, "My brethren, count it all joy when you fall into various trials, knowing that the testing of your faith produces patience." This underscores how suffering helps discipline believers. "My son, do not despise the chastening of the Lord, nor detest His correction," says Proverbs 3:11-12, "for whom the Lord loves He corrects, just as a father the son in whom he delights."

Christ spoke of such "pruning" in John 15:1-4, saying, "I am the true vine, and My Father is the vinedresser. Every branch in Me that does not bear fruit He takes away; and every branch that bears fruit He prunes, that it may bear more fruit. You are already clean because of the word which I have spoken to you. Abide in Me, and I in you. As the branch cannot bear fruit of itself, unless it abides in the vine, neither can you, unless you abide in Me."

It's good to remember that this process may hurt.

"Now no chastening seems to be joyful for the present, but painful," notes Hebrews 12:14, "nevertheless, afterward it yields the peaceable fruit of righteousness to those who have been trained by it." David embraced such instruction in Psalm 25:5. "Lead me in Your truth and teach me," the shepherd king wrote, "for You are the God of my salvation; on You I wait all the day."

Joy in difficulties

Let's tackle a highlight of Sandy's religious argument with protagonist James Harrigan. When he continues to wallow in bitterness, she asks: *"Where's the joy in your life? Not that fake satire you put in your columns. Where's your happiness?"*

Joy often marks the first and longest lasting result of devoting your life to The Lord. The Bible frequently discusses this. Fifteen Hebrew words convey different meanings of joy in the Old Testament, notes wordsoffaithhopelove.com. While some of these words touch upon social or cultural actions, most refer to faith and worship.

The Book of Psalms offers a good sampling with numerous calls for believers to rejoice and be glad in The Lord – check out Psalm 14:7, 32:11, 67:4, 96:11, 97:12, 100:2, 149:2.

The New Testament taps eight Greek words to discuss joy, with one used more than 60 times. These words tell how believers savor the peace of Christ and blessed assurances of love, grace, and salvation. This joy also may reflect recognizing His love and will at work in the world.

This doesn't mean believers are shielded from sadness or hardship. The Bible warns just the opposite, for this draws from God's decision to give humans free will. That allowed sin to enter the world – which often leads to our difficulties.

Physical and emotional trials may overwhelm human hearts, which is why the apostles urged believers to comfort and support each other. Paul linked this to Christ's grace in 2 Corinthians 1:3-4: "Blessed be the God and Father of our Lord Jesus Christ, the Father of mercies and God of all comfort, who comforts us in all our tribulation, that we may be able to comfort those who are in any trouble, with the comfort with which we ourselves are comforted by God."

But sometimes, in seeking to soothe suffering souls, believers downplay or forget how deep pain strikes. In such instances, asking *"Where's the joy in your life?"* may spur dismay, anger, even hatred.

This is one reason why many Bible verses *remind* people to rejoice, for that may not be their first reaction. A rational mind may find God's hope in the darkness, but many people in the grip of anguish struggle to obtain clear thoughts. This, too, the Bible acknowledges. Take Psalm 30:4, where David praises God for answered prayer. "Weeping may stay for the night," David wrote, "but rejoicing comes in the morning."

Unfortunately, many people only gain such sensitivity and understanding after enduring pain. Believers may shiver when reading of Christ's suffering on the cross, or cringe when watching depictions like *The Passion of the Christ*, and yet their sheltered lives fail to prepare them for the promise of Philippians 1:29 – "For to you it has been granted on behalf of Christ, not only to believe in Him, but also to suffer for His sake."

Recognizing this gulf, Sandy changes tactics with Harrigan and cites the letters written by Peter and James. These New

Testament books focus on how believers may cope with suffering. Peter touched on this again and again in his first letter, hoping to strengthen persecuted Christ followers. James dives into this right after his opening greeting: "My brethren, count it all joy when you fall into various trials, knowing that the testing of your faith produces patience." Paul echoed this in Romans 5:3-4 – "We also glory in tribulations, knowing that tribulation produces perseverance; and perseverance, character; and character, hope."

Many New Testament verses urge the sick and broken to take refuge in Christ, for their needs lie at the heart of our loving God. Six of the nine Beatitudes address meek and burdened souls. To quote the last of these, Matthew 5:11-12, "Blessed are you when they revile and persecute you, and say all kinds of evil against you falsely for My sake. Rejoice and be exceedingly glad, for great is your reward in heaven, for so they persecuted the prophets who were before you."

That takes us back to Christ, whose resurrection offers hope to all. "These things I have spoken to you, that in Me you may have peace," Jesus told His disciples, as recorded in John 16:33. "In the world you will have tribulation; but be of good cheer, I have overcome the world."

This is the end…

Chapter 41's spiritual debate brings the entire novel into focus – which is a good thing, since the end draws near. While discussing joy with friend Sandy Travis, protagonist James Harrigan bemoans how worldly his beliefs turn…

"We go around thinking God wants us to be happy – and I truly believe that – but I'm only now understanding how His concept of happiness is so different than mine – or at least, from what mine was. How simply living a life in Christ, by itself, should provide all the happiness we ever need – whether we go through a divorce or a car wash that thrusts you into a federal investigation."

And there it is – James, in his sadness, falls back on his sense of humor to summarize his anguish (and most of this book). Sandy laughs at his comment but doesn't get it, so James clarifies, unloading his heart.

"Well, I mean, my old views of a happy life were so worldly. So wrong. Cars, house and home, fine clothes, all that worthless stuff. That's not what life's about. I know that, and yet, it's so hard to give up. And it's so easy to forget what God would have us do when our world's collapsing around us… or for that matter, when everything's golden and we're prospering. Sandy, I've failed so many things."

Sift that closely and you will find the roots of his next column… our last chapter.

Having already listened to Harrigan's list of shortcomings, Sandy turns their talk back to Christ:

"Through all of our lives, we have only one important decision to make. Do we believe in Christ, or don't we? If we do, we live and die for Him, as the Bible instructs us, and the Spirit leads us. And if we don't accept Him, then we just live and die. Right? Can we both agree on that?"

Her argument parallels many debates I've read about the existence of God. Those exchanges go something like this:

If God does not exist and all we know is a result of evolution, environment, or accidents, then all our concepts of purpose and morality are nothing more than opinions, changing from viewpoint to viewpoint. There are no theological absolutes, life is what you make of it, and when you die, you die. But if God does exist, as the Bible states, and He created and rules over all there is, then life has a divine purpose, spiritual realities and moral absolutes do exist for all people, whether we accept them or not, and everyone has a role to play in that grand design.

Some people may ask just whose grand design – i.e., what god – such logic leads to. This is an honest and natural question, for as Romans 1:20 notes, everyone sees The Lord's invisible attributes at work in this world – and yet, as 1 Corinthians 2:14 reminds us, most people do not understand these signs of God. And thus, sensing something worthy of faith, they spend their lives seeking what that is. That's where Christ's light and the Holy Spirit's touch competes for their attention with Satan's tempting distractions and deceptions.

Many souls choose prideful, self-pleasing options over news of our Lord. Others dismiss or ignore metaphysical questions to embrace this age of science, skepticism, and apathy. Paul warned of this in 2 Timothy 3:2-5 – "For men will be lovers of themselves, lovers of money, boasters, proud, blasphemers, disobedient to parents, unthankful, unholy, unloving, unforgiving, slanderers, without self-control, brutal, despisers of good, traitors, headstrong, haughty, lovers of pleasure rather than lovers of God, having a form of godliness but denying its power."

Sandy, a Christian, reminds James that God gives everyone – believers and unbelievers alike – the freedom to choose whether to join in His vision. Their debate – and Carolyn's decisions – set up Chapter 42. *The Road to Renewal* ends as it began, with a newspaper column. Chapter 1 shares one of Harrigan's humorous escapades, a fun tale of little importance and no resolution. Chapter 42 abandons that entertainment role to focus on life's spiritual realities. Its call to action answers Sandy's debate questions (with a fascinating twist on their joy perspectives) while potentially heightening Harrigan's running dispute with his editor.

The Road to Renewal doesn't tell us if Harrigan's newspaper published that spiritual plea. I always assumed it did, for I based Reynolds on an editor who would argue practically everything with everyone, but believed in freedom of expression in print if the commentary upheld his libel and obscenity rules. I sometimes submitted editorials in place of my humor columns; my bosses didn't mind.

Our novel also leaves up in the air:

• Whether the Easy Come, Easy Go chain paid for the damages to Harrigan's car. I assume it did, for I was refunded the cost of my real-life repairs.

• What Carolyn ended up doing. I haven't a clue where her choices would take the flirty DJ. Characters often develop lives of their own, which demonstrates another way decisions may have unforeseen consequences not just on us, but others.

• How this comic tragedy impacted Harrigan's life and career. I suspect his future somewhat mirrored mine, which I shared under my "Writing tactics" notes, page 295. But Carolyn's actions might change that.

This book's open ending disappointed some readers

wanting a more definitive resolution, but I like the book's reflective focus. After all, that is the whole point of *The Road to Renewal*. Hopefully the Afterward and these "Behind the Scenes" entries aid this, providing enough background information to sustain curious minds until they may delve deeper into subjects of interest.

Let's close with a very personal look at God's grand design. Like James, I am a follower of Jesus Christ. I accepted Him as my Savior in 1969, when evangelist Bill Glass led a crusade at the Smith Center, KS, High School gym. Though not quite 10 years old, I went forward during the invitation to commit my life to Jesus. I will never forget how my father came down to retrieve me when all was done, and Bill stepped up to shake his hand. I had always thought my father was a big guy – and he was larger than life in many ways, including an impressive physique – but Dad was a foot shorter and many pounds lighter than Bill, a former Cleveland Browns defensive end who followed Christ most of his life. That meeting forever shaped my concepts of God, reminding me how our Lord eclipses any boundaries my experiences and expectations may conceive.

Why did I take this path? Because I have long studied Christianity and believe the Bible is true. I know God the Father, Son, and Holy Spirit are as real as anything I can see, feel, and hear, for I have experienced their influence and touch. And I treasure Christ's redemption. Indeed, I love everything about Jesus – His wisdom, character, witness, and example. I can't imagine living without Christ in my life. His grace and mercy saved my soul from countless stupid decisions. He guides my steps to this day.

How did I reach this conclusion? From choices and actions that started well before I heard Bill.

I was born in late 1959, the third of four children brought into this world by two wonderful parents. They raised us in a Christian home but allowed my siblings and I to learn at our own pace and make our own decisions. As I matured mentally and emotionally – which took a long time, for I was an energetic, emotional, rambunctious punk! – I began to recognize God's invisible attributes in the sky and trees, flowers and birds… throughout life in general. These revelations led me to study my Bible and pray when I wasn't goofing around. In-between bountiful moments of selfish joy and maddening recklessness, God's word taught me how to watch Him at work in this world.

That's when The Lord reached out to me.

This started in gentle ways many people might overlook, as I did for a long time. But as my faith began to shape my character and I struggled to adopt His will over my hungry, possessive drives, God responded with nods, prods, and probably some shocks, plus assurances, leanings, slaps, imagery, and finally, words.

Things began to make sense to me, for listening to and following such holy communication brings awareness, peace, and joy in Christ, even when traveling along difficult paths. Our walks and talks help me focus on goodness and love, a beneficial gift when so many things in this world stimulate my hyperactive, stubborn, self-absorbed sides.

Some people may scoff at this testimony, which I can understand. For while God seeks such relationships with everyone, faith and worship do not free believers of their human weaknesses. I try to do good each and every day, and I'm sure my Lord's guiding touch saves me from many poor choices I might otherwise make. On the flip side, I have suffered many troubles when I didn't follow the Spirit's lead. This happens far too often, for I remain a headstrong, obstinate, selfish sinner, fully responsible for all my missteps. And I have suffered, enduring divorce and separation from loved ones, job and home loss, bankruptcy, depression, and deaths among family and friends. I often see my life as a failure, but for my choice to follow Christ.

Self-deception and redemption

By fictionalizing events from 20+ years of my life, *The Road to Renewal* weaves together many of my mistakes. We revisited several in these "Behind the Scenes" entries, but one heartbreaker remains untold. It shows my human fallibilities and throws light on God's grand design. A hint of this rises in

314

Chapter 41, as James admits some very personal regrets:

"Some of the things I've guided my life by… sometimes I can't help but question everything I've done. You know, these last days, I've caught myself telling little lies, just to ease out of certain problems. It was so easy, you know? And I'm so lonely. I actually bought a Playboy *book the other day. I was intrigued by the histories it promised –"*

"And the pictures?" Sandy interjected.

James squirmed. "Well, there was that, but to be honest – honest, Sandy – I mean, haven't you always wondered how people who pursued lifestyles we frown upon could claim to be so happy?"

"No."

"Well, I did. Do. And this book had histories of every playmate the magazine's run – and what they've done since they posed. Several told of turning to Christ since appearing in the magazine, and some even condemned the Playboy *lifestyle. Others had some tragic turns. But it amazed me how many took great joy in what they did, twenty, thirty, even forty years after appearing."*

"Keep in mind most of those women haven't lived that long. They don't really know what impact it'll have."

"I think just the opposite. Their lives are so immersed in that culture, they learn rather quickly what impact it'll have. I mean, Playboy's *fifty years old. There's at least one woman in there, Sandy, who claims to have been a Christian when she posed – and another who'd taught Sunday school before she posed. And they embraced that life."*

This draws from something I did after my divorce, for the reasons James shares. That said, Sandy correctly noted my appreciation of those photos. As a Christian, I shunned such publications throughout my life – but that didn't erase their temptations, especially after my divorce. For to my eye, women are the most beautiful beings God made. *Playboy* captured this using some of the best photographers in the world, their obvious skills appealing to my photojournalist side. With its top-quality printers and cutting-edge investigative news, interviews, and fiction, *Playboy* also earned my respect as a writer. These points played a role in how the magazine gained market acceptance and national distribution rights – which helped *Playboy* attract some of the world's most gorgeous women as models.

Sandy also predicted how many of these ladies did not recognize (or admit) the true impact of their lifestyle choices. In the quarter-century since publication of *The Playmate Book: Five Decades of Centerfolds*, several women shared disturbing stories of life within that culture. We've also heard of men led astray by editor/publisher Hugh Hefner's sexist beliefs, which built on customs wedged deep into Western society.

I wish I could say that 1996 hardcover started my exposure to pornography, but like many kids, I fell under its influence at a young age. That started in the 1960s as I grew up in a society that cherished and promoted the feminine form. In that revolutionary period of civil rights, women's liberation, sexual freedoms, rock and roll, and Vietnam, increasingly alluring fashions and philosophies popped up in magazines, movies, books, songs, ads, comics, toys… the list goes on and on. I didn't blink an eye at the revealing outfits in *The Beverly Hillbillies, The Dick Van Dyke Show, Star Trek, Hee Haw, One Billion Years B.C*…. By today's standards those images and messages may seem rather tame, but it's hard to deny their intent "to elicit sexual arousal," a key element in the Dictionary.com definition of pornography. I didn't grasp then how such messages could infiltrate thoughts and compromise standards, but Hefner did, as seen in the magazine's increasingly explicit photos and articles through the '60s and '70s. Other entertainment sectors followed his lead.

These manipulations started working their way to my surface as a high school friend led me to see a *Playboy* collection – a true eye-opener for someone who'd never viewed such things before. Another friend gave me the legendary Farrah poster, betting I wouldn't have the nerve to hang it up. Touched by her smile, I tacked that colorful Christmas present onto a bedroom wall and waited to see what would happen. That amused my father, who enjoyed showing Farrah to visiting relatives. I laughed with him, determined not to let her charms corrupt my Christian heart. I didn't recognize how such things fit one of Satan's primary tactics: use repeated exposures over time to gain tolerance, acceptance, and participation. But questions over that poster, and memories of those magazines, did make me examine how I thought of women. And I pondered why people would pursue hopes and dreams apart from Christ. Indeed, I once read Xaviera Hollander's *The Happy Hooker* for just that reason.

The turning point came as I started work at a movie theater serving the University of Oklahoma neighborhood. I loved that job – splicing together Hollywood features on huge reels for bright lanterns to project onto silver screens. I can't remember how many times I reclined in those two dark auditoriums to savor *Star Wars*, *Raiders of the Lost Ark*, and other cinematic treasures. That job helped this 1982 OU graduate land my first reporting position, for it enabled me to catch countless free movies under agreements with other theaters. From those viewings I wrote and syndicated film reviews to several newspapers, which validated my skills to editors still hiring under Oklahoma's 1980s recession.

Managing the Satellite Twin Theater was a dream job… one that encouraged me to look the other way as our owner played a midnight X-rated film each Friday and Saturday (opposite *The Rocky Horror Picture Show*). My skill in handling 35-mm prints soon earned me the manager's post, making me responsible for assembling all films. This heightened my porn exposure, since those explicit reels often needed repairs. When concerns arose that his hardcore choices might offend local officials, the owner asked me to screen each X and cut out certain frames. I then restored the footage before we sent the prints back.

All this caught up with me during an editing session. While deciding what to take out, I realized how far I had stretched my Christian sensibilities. I had accepted that job confident in my integrity, telling myself these exposures could never harm my soul. Then I found myself reliving porn scenes in my mind. I recognized how I had allowed myself to be seduced. Indeed, I had led others into these transgressions. I had sold strangers tickets to sin.

This helps explain why protagonist James Harrigan feared being alone with women, for I did. I had allowed sexual thoughts and images into my brain that I could not control. I didn't want such memories to impact how I viewed or treated others. While God soon freed me of this problem – through a seemingly happy marriage – divorce gave this specter new vitality and taught me humility.

That advances my tale fifteen years through the births of my daughters, joining a church choir, winning countless Associated Press awards, and jumpstarting my novel pursuits. As divorce wrecked many aspects of my life, several friends asked why I didn't use my reporting skills to tackle issues of faith. I surprised them with a few working ideas.

• Troubled by how some Christian congregations struggled to serve divorced adults, I contemplated writing a nonfiction book called *Why Can't My Church Be Like My Bar?* I had limited experience in this, since Oklahoma law changed at this time to let restaurants serve liquor.

• I started a devotional collection on faith lessons in popular films. I abandoned that after pastor Craig Groeschel launched his first "At the Movies" sermon series at Oklahoma City's Life Covenant Church (now Life.Church). I didn't mind, for another film idea had entered my mind.

Having experienced some of its "golden age" through my theater work, I marveled at pornography's loosening restrictions in the '90s. Spreading legalization legitimized the business in some minds, and the largely unregulated World Wide Web promised new fields to exploit. This gave some telecommunications, cable, and production companies vested interests in spreading porn's resources and opportunities.

This reminded me of 1973's *Miller v. California*, the U.S. Supreme Court ruling community standards would define local obscenity laws. Expecting lenient metro regulations to boost porn's exposure and wear down national resistance, some conservatives predicted nudity and foul language would hit public airwaves within 50 years. It ended up taking just two decades, as *NYPD Blue* demonstrated in 1993.

I felt these issues demanded a Christian-focused expose – one my experiences somewhat qualified me to write. Buying that *Playboy* book was part of that research, or so I told myself. But fearing my vulnerability to this topic, I soon threw that book away and worked instead to finish two novels on divorce (one being *The Road to Renewal*) and the allegory that became *God's Furry Angels*. I then took up the guitar (with slim success) before my employer chose me to launch a news bureau.

With all that in play, I might never have restarted the porn project without the 2008 recession. That's when I noticed several estate sales shedding dusty *Playboy* collections at pennies a copy. It amused me, recalling those who once pegged such issues as solid investments. Then I remembered Hefner's old monthly column. As a standard-bearer for the sexual revolution, his words offered solid background material for my proposed book. So I snapped up some deals and studied what I found, setting parameters to manage the data and protect my heart.

As that research exposed Hefner's ideas at work in our world, I also saw how his business struggled to fit changing mainstream moralities. Simply put, porn had moved beyond *Playboy*. As subscription prices tumbled, I signed up to see how that once-proud media giant fought to survive. This identified new issues to probe, for the "golden age" films I knew seemed mild compared to today's athletic sessions. Defenders claimed increased ownership and leadership by women had erased porn's exploitative aspects. Opponents scoffed as content entered more sensitive areas. And both sides feared the spread of lawless web pirates.

All this spurred me to dig deeper, for these trends paralleled movements within Christian communities to liberalize Bible standards, rewrite or eliminate sexual sin definitions, and undermine Scripture's authority. Those steps ripped apart denominations, churches, families, and faiths.

It was then, as I contemplated background interviews, that my many rationalizations collapsed. Although I cloaked my work as honest research – leading to some fascinating, if divisive results – it uncovered weakness in my lonely, wounded heart. Under my self-deceptions, porn's corrosive content had seduced me once again. I had set aside what I held most dear: Christ and His word. I failed myself and God.

Some of today's liberal Christian factions, not to mention unbelievers, would dismiss my condemnations. Despite my porn dabbling, I abstained from sex before my wedding, never broke those vows, and resumed a celibate life with my divorce. This, some advisors told me, showed how these sexual temptations did not rule my heart. As for my polluted mind, some spiritual revisionists mocked my concerns. How can anyone lust or sin over imaginary stories played by actors or dolled-up models little resembling reality? Who is harmed by such fantasies? And what's wrong with nudity, anyway? We're born nude! What's the big deal?

Ever the practical one, Paul offered a direct, no-nonsense answer for such debates. "Flee sexual immorality," he wrote in 1 Corinthians 6:18-20. "Every sin that a man does is outside the body, but he who commits sexual immorality sins against his own body. Or do you not know that your body is the temple of the Holy Spirit who is in you, whom you have from God, and you are not your own? For you were bought at a price" – Christ's sacrifice on the cross – "therefore glorify God in your body and in your spirit, which are God's."

How do troubled souls accomplish this? Paul tackled that in Colossians 3:5 – "Put to death your members which are on the earth: fornication, uncleanness, passion, evil desire, and covetousness, which is idolatry." Seven verses later, Paul added: "As the elect of God, holy and beloved, put on tender mercies, kindness, humility, meekness, longsuffering; bearing with one another, and forgiving one another, if anyone has a complaint against another; even as Christ forgave you, so you also must do. But above all these things put on love, which is the bond of perfection."

Such words fuel some Christian debates over sex, science, and sin. Progressives may argue that most if not all sexual drives and acts are natural – and what is natural cannot be sin, for as Genesis 1:27 says, we are made in God's image. Linking this to love gives these proponents an even stronger sense of standing. Since Scripture states God is love, whatever spreads love is good… or so their theories hold.

All such philosophies forget that God defines sin – not science, human feelings, or worldly logic. But seeing the Bible as a living document, some believers in our politically correct age seek to please everyone by interpreting Bible verses, cultures, translations, and applications through a modern, adaptive, mature lens.

Paul warns of such self-deception in 2 Timothy 4:3-4 – "For the time will come when they will not endure sound doctrine, but according to their own desires, because they have itching ears, they will heap up for themselves teachers; and they will turn their ears away from the truth, and be turned aside to fables." Christ spoke of this in Matthew 7:21-23 – "Not everyone who says to Me, 'Lord, Lord,' shall enter the kingdom of heaven, but he who does the will of My Father in heaven. Many will say to Me in that day, 'Lord, Lord, have we not prophesied in Your name, cast out demons in Your name, and done many wonders in Your name?' And then I will declare to them, 'I never knew you; depart from Me, you who practice lawlessness!'"

That quote uncovers the ultimate answer. When we dismiss earthly distractions and rely upon Scripture as our authority – as God, Christ, and His disciples instructed – believers may whittle all spiritual debates down to one point: God's will. In Romans 12:2, Paul told Christ followers to make God's will their aim. "Do not be conformed to this world," he wrote, "but be transformed by the renewing of your mind, that you may prove what is that good and acceptable and perfect will of God." Paul sums this up in 1 Corinthians 10:31 – "whatever you do, do all to the glory of God."

These verses give believers moral yardsticks to judge any ethical quandary. Simply ask yourself, how does (fill in the blank) glorify God? How does it fulfill His will?

This may remind you of another biblical yardstick – asking "What would Jesus do?" in any given difficulty. That's because Jesus used His life and death to fulfill God's will, as Matthew 6:10, Mark 14:36, Luke 2:49, John 6:38-40, Hebrews 10:5-10, and many other verses note. Christ placed God's will at the heart of our faith, as 1 Peter 2 explains.

How did I apply all this in my life crisis?

Ashamed by my failures, I acknowledged my guilt and threw away countless photos, films, and files. It was hard, discovering just how deep sin's claws lay in my aging, betraying flesh. And it remains hard, with these memories and longings still in my mind. But I did these things to renew my ties to my Lord and Savior. Confessing my sins, I dedicated my life once more to His path. I fortified my biblical studies, prayers, and diligence. And I experienced once again Christ's forgiveness and mercy.

Take hope in this, for no matter your sins, Jesus offers this same grace along your road to renewal. I am not unique in this, as Scripture reveals:

• Proverbs 28:13 – He who covers his sins will not prosper, but whoever confesses and forsakes them will have mercy.

• 1 John 1:9 – If we confess our sins, He is faithful and just to forgive us our sins and to cleanse us from all unrighteousness.

• Romans 6:23 – For the wages of sin is death, but the gift of God is eternal life in Christ Jesus our Lord.

• Romans 5:8 – God demonstrates His own love toward us, in that while we were still sinners, Christ died for us.

• 2 Corinthians 5:17 – Therefore, if anyone is in Christ, he is a new creation; old things have passed away; behold, all things have become new.

• John 3:16-17 – For God so loved the world that He gave His only begotten Son, that whoever believes in Him should not perish but have everlasting life. For God did not send His Son into the world to condemn the world, but that the world through Him might be saved.

If you have more questions about this faith and God's amazing love, let me point you towards resources I treasure.

Those contesting this truth should read *The Case for Christ* by Lee Strobel. That award-winning investigative journalist/atheist once launched a newspaper expose to debunk Christianity. He ended up becoming a believer and minister. This book explains how that happened!

While Strobel explores supporting facts for God and Christ, *The Reason for God* by Timothy Keller probes the theological questions that cause many to struggle with the faith. It is a marvelous read!

The God Who Is There by D.A. Carson weaves this all together. The book introduces readers to The Lord and Christ as it walks through the Bible. The book delivers a concise, foundational message all may understand and hopefully appreciate.

Our greatest earthly resource will ever be the Bible. Those hungry to know more about our just and loving God should take a new, honest look at the Scriptures, Old and New, for they offer an incredible lifelong learning experience. The Gospels – the New Testament books of Matthew, Mark, Luke, and John – make excellent starting points, as does Romans, 1st Corinthians, or Hebrews. If you desire a more analytical recommendation, consider Dennis Prager's Rational Bible entries on the books of Genesis and Exodus. A longtime teacher of the Torah, he writes for Jewish, Christian, and doubting audiences, going through those important books verse by verse with illuminating commentary perfect for beginners or experts.

As God's word begins to intrigue and amaze you, follow it up with more Bible reading, study, and prayer. Work to guide your steps by biblical wisdom. Welcome Christ followers around you. Learn from them, as they will from you, and build worship and accountability partners to grow in the faith. Be wary of those who edit Scripture to fit their own desires – starting with yourself. Pray for His guidance in all your actions. And when you're ready, walk with those you love into some quiet, shady glade or your chosen house of God. Breathe deep, take in our Lord's amazing creation, and ask Him to enter your heart. Accept Jesus as your Savior and pledge your life to doing His will. Then go where Christ leads you. "Trust in The Lord with all your heart, and lean not on your own understanding," Proverbs 3:5-6 tells us. "In all your ways acknowledge Him, and He shall direct your paths."

Amen!

Could you help us out?

This is an independent production. As a small business, we have limited distribution and marketing resources. So if you like one or more of these books, please:

• Consider giving copies to your friends and loved ones.

• Tell others what you appreciated about these tales, what moved you, the lasting impressions.

• Post reviews on reader and retailer websites, from Facebook and Instagram to GoodReads.com and the most valuable of all, Amazon.com. Such reviews are **extremely helpful** to our marketing efforts!

• Ask for these novels at your favorite bookstore, and encourage them to stock them on their shelves.

Please help us spread the message, so that we may continue our efforts. Thank you so much! We appreciate it!

www.kirbyleedavis.com